Christopher Fowler is the acclaimed author of fifteen novels, including the Bryant & May mysteries *Full Dark House* – winner of the 2004 BFS August Derleth Award for Best Novel, *The Water Room* – nominated for the CWA People's Choice Dagger Award, and *Seventy-Seven Clocks*, each available in Bantam paperback. He lives in King's Cross, London.

His new Bryant & May novel, *White Corridor*, is now available from Doubleday.

Visit www.christopherfowler.co.uk

Praise for Christopher Fowler's
Bryant & May mysteries:

'Witty, sinuous and darkly comedic storytelling from a
Machiavellian jokester'
Guardian

'Exciting and thoughtful . . . one of our most
unorthodox and entertaining writers'
Sunday Telegraph

'Atmospheric, hugely beguiling and as filled with tricks
and sleights of hand as a magician's sleeve . . . a
combination of Ealing comedy and grand opera: witty,
charismatic, occasionally touching and with
a genuine power to thrill'
Joanne Harris

'Very cleverly plotted . . . simultaneously
scary and alluring'
Daily Telegraph **Books of the Year**

'An imaginative fun house of a world where sage minds
go to expand their vistas and sharpen their wits . . . life
always seems livelier whenever Arthur Bryant and
John May are on the case!'
New York Times Book Review

'Fowler shocks and frightens, while making
us laugh out loud . . . original, erudite
and exciting'
Good Book Guide

Also by Christopher Fowler

Novels
ROOFWORLD
RUNE
RED BRIDE
DARKEST DAY
SPANKY
PSYCHOVILLE
DISTURBIA
SOHO BLACK
CALABASH
BREATHE
FULL DARK HOUSE
THE WATER ROOM
SEVENTY-SEVEN CLOCKS
WHITE CORRIDOR

Graphic Novel
MENZ NSANA

Short Stories
CITY JITTERS
CITY JITTERS TWO
THE BUREAU OF LOST SOULS
SHARPER KNIVES
FLESH WOUNDS
PERSONAL DEMONS
UNCUT
THE DEVIL IN ME
DEMONIZED

CHRISTOPHER
FOWLER

TEN-SECOND STAIRCASE

BANTAM BOOKS

LONDON · TORONTO · SYDNEY · AUCKLAND · JOHANNESBURG

TRANSWORLD PUBLISHERS
61–63 Uxbridge Road, London W5 5SA
a division of The Random House Group Ltd
www.booksattransworld.co.uk

TEN-SECOND STAIRCASE
A BANTAM BOOK: 9780553817201

First published in Great Britain
in 2006 by Doubleday
a division of Transworld Publishers
Bantam edition published 2007

Addresses for Random House Group Ltd companies outside the UK
can be found at: www.randomhouse.co.uk
The Random House Group Ltd Reg. No. 954009

Penguin Random House is committed to a sustainable future for
our business, our readers and our planet. This book is made from
Forest Stewardship Council® certified paper.

MIX
Paper from
responsible sources
FSC® C018179

Typeset in 10½/13pt Sabon by
Kestrel Data, Exeter, Devon.
Printed and bound in Great Britain by Clays Ltd, Elcograf S.p.A.

To Peter Chapman
Hang on, Little Tomato

ACKNOWLEDGEMENTS

This is the fourth of six Bryant and May novels, and my gratitude goes out to the indispensable team who are with me on the trip. Huge thanks to my agent Mandy Little, for her limitless energy and enthusiasm, and to Meg Davis for sage advice and encouragement. At Transworld, Simon Taylor provides the kind of support writers dream about, while Louise Page and Kate Samano makes the process of publication as enjoyable as writing the book. At Bantam, Kate Miciak always manages to make my day despite the time difference, and my US agent Howard Morhaim keeps it running smoothly.

Special thanks go out to Joanne Harris, Mike Jay, Graham Joyce, Steve Jones, Mike Marshall, Maxim Jakubowski, John Bolton, Ellen Datlow and Michele Slung for providing thoughtful answers to my dumb questions. Finally, love to Jim, Andrew, Sally, Maggie, Kath, Ren, Martin and the sassy girls at the Pineapple – I owe you all drinks.

1

CRADLE TO GRAVE

MEMORANDUM
PRIVATE AND CONFIDENTIAL

Attachments Supplied: 3458SD, 19904KT

TO: Leslie Faraday, Senior Home Office Liaison Officer
FROM: Raymond Land, Acting Head, PCU,
  London NW1 3BL
DATE: Monday 17 October

Dear Mr Faraday,
Thank you for your correspondence of 26 September
requesting further details concerning my tenure at the
North London Peculiar Crimes Unit.

If I understand you correctly, you wish me to outline
the recent problems I have experienced at this unit from
a personal perspective. While I am loath to commit
myself in writing over such a delicate matter, and dislike
'telling tales' on staff members despite their extreme
lack of cooperation over the last few months, I feel the
time has come to unburden myself to someone in a
position of higher authority. In short, Mr Faraday, I can

no longer maintain my silence. I have simply reached the end of my tether.

I appreciate that, as the 'new broom' at HO Special Services Liaison, taking over from HMCO Liaison DCI Stanley Marsden, you must have a great deal of background material to study. I shall therefore attempt to save you some work by summarizing our current situation.

The Peculiar Crimes Unit was founded, along with a handful of other specialist departments, soon after the outbreak of World War II, as part of a government initiative to ease the burden on London's overstretched Metropolitan Police Force by tackling high-profile cases which had the capacity to compound social problems in urban areas. The crimes falling within its remit were often of a politically sensitive nature, or could potentially cause social panics and general public malaise. The division's civilian counterpart at that time was the Central Therapy Unit, set up to help the bereaved and the homeless cope with the psychological stress of war. This unit closed after just eleven months because bombed-out residents continued turning to their neighbours for support rather than visiting qualified specialists. There was also, if memory serves, an experimental propaganda division called the Central Information Service (later to become the COI), which provided positive, uplifting news items to national newspapers in order to combat hearsay and harmful disinformation spread about our overseas forces, and to fill the void left by the blanket news blackouts. The PCU proved more successful than either of these, and remained in operation through the war.

I am led to believe that the title 'peculiar' was originally meant in the sense of 'particular', as the government's plan was that the new unit should handle those cases deemed uniquely sensitive and a high risk to public morale. To head this division, several extremely young and inexperienced students were recruited. One must remember that this was a time of desperation, when most able-bodied men had been taken into the armed forces, and a great many experimental ideas were proposed by the Churchill government, including the employment of Dennis Wheatley, the horror-story writer, as a member of the war cabinet.

A number of successful prosecutions were brought by the Peculiar Crimes Unit in the years that followed, with the result that the unit continued its work into peacetime. The rebuilding of Britain required the suppression of those prosecutions deemed too negative for public knowledge (a fifty-year embargo being placed on sensitive war reports), and many cases handled by the PCU at this time remained *sub judice*.

In order to provide continuity, the sons and daughters of original staff members were recruited, so that the founding team was largely replaced with new employees, but two gentlemen remained in their old positions. I refer, of course, to Mr Arthur Bryant and Mr John May (see attached file 3458SD). This is where the problem starts, for both of them, despite their advanced age, are still here at the unit. They stayed on because the unit granted them a high degree of autonomy, and their specialist knowledge, plus their refusal to accept promotion and determination to continue tackling crime at street level, won them the allegiance of young incoming staff in the Metropolitan Police Force. In years to come, as their supporters moved to positions of power, these loyalties proved useful to the detectives.

I know that the PCU has lately had some success in solving crimes that have come to the attention of the general public. I am also aware that its most senior detectives are highly respected and can offer an enormous amount of experience between them, but their manner is disruptive and their behaviour – certainly in terms of efficient, modern crime management – is unorthodox and damaging to the image of the national policing network.

Cases like that of the 'Deptford Demon', and their long-running investigation into the murders of young women committed by the so-called 'Leicester Square Vampire', last sighted in 1975, brought the PCU into disrepute. Their working practices proved questionable and the case remains unsolved to this day. The unit's brief is admittedly unusual; their cases rarely provide the opportunity to follow direct leads and named suspects, but their methodology is regarded as altogether too vague, intellectual, socialist and downright arty by those who work on the 'coal face' of crime, an image the detectives have sought to foster rather than disabuse.

Heaven knows I am no intellectual, but even I can tell that these gentlemen would be better employed as academics rather than police officers. Mr May once told me that he could be loosely termed a follower of someone called Jean-Jacques Rousseau, a rational progressive who sometimes placed feeling over reason, but Mr Bryant's philosophical attitude towards criminal investigation is more complex and troubling; although enlightened and well-read, a 'cold fish' who rarely empathizes with victims of crime, he is quite prepared to resort to the kind of Counter-Enlightenment mysticism that allows some rationalists to believe in ley-lines and crystal healing when it suits them. Simply stated, Mr Bryant and Mr May are completely out of touch with the problems of today's youth. Elderly people rarely commit crimes; how can they possibly hope to understand what is happening on the streets of London any more?

The general public must be able to feel that their lives are in safe hands. As you know, not long ago Mr Bryant accidentally blew up his own unit. Subsequently he managed to get himself shut in a sewer, and nearly died. His partner has had one heart attack, and flagrantly defies doctor's orders to lead a less stressful working life. Nor does he help our image by conducting a very public affair with a married woman. The pair keep irregular hours, behave and dress oddly, and encourage everyone else in their employ to do the same. Detective Sergeant Janice Longbright seems to model herself on Diana Dors, the fifties Rank film starlet, and comes to work in the most extraordinarily provocative outfits. I sometimes wonder if we're running a police unit or an escort agency.

Neither Mr Bryant nor Mr May believe in traditional hierarchy. They speak to their colleagues as equals, and frequently ask advice from the most inexperienced members of staff. Obviously, this will not do. Mr Bryant took his exams a very long time ago, and is unwilling to entertain the idea of modern police procedure. He's always *touching* things; it's only luck that prevents half his cases from being thrown out of court due to cross-contamination of evidence. The criminal world has altered drastically since his time. Even constables are required to pass exams in criminal law, traffic law and general police duties, but Mr Bryant has somehow been granted immunity from evaluation tests. He has repeatedly refused to take his Objective Structured Performance Related Examination, and deliberately falsifies results from his continuous appraisals.

Of course, the national police force now operates under a regime of openness and transparency, but Mr Bryant prefers to keep his superiors in the dark because he says 'it is simpler for them to understand nothing'.

As you know, my own background is in forensic sciences. When I sought promotion to a more senior decision-making role, I was brought into this unit as Acting Head. As the title implies, I did not expect to remain in the position for more than three months.

That was in 1973. I am still here, still awaiting a transfer.

By the time I joined, the Peculiar Crimes Unit had become very peculiar indeed. It could be likened to a doctors' surgery that had abandoned traditional pharmaceutical treatments for alternative therapies. Over time, these therapies became more extreme, until we have reached a point where it seems quite normal for Mr Bryant to ignore empirical data in favour of hiring a clairvoyant to search for a missing person. Mr May is not much better; his investigation into pagan elementals a few months ago did result in the capture of a wanted criminal, but he still destroyed a section of the Regent's Canal in the process, and the case appears to have involved a mass break-out of illegal immigrants from King's Cross which both he and his partner aided and abetted.

The bizarre behaviour of these geriatric detectives seems to infect those working around them, so that I am made to seem the 'odd man out'. I am openly ridiculed and humiliated. Mr Bryant's experiments, conducted without any safety precautions, are both questionable and dangerous. My instructions are disobeyed, my reputation has been irreversibly damaged, and my office wallpaper has been ruined.

Both Mr Bryant and Mr May are beyond statutory retirement age and show no inclination to leave. No one seems to know quite how old they are, as their files were apparently lost in the fire that destroyed their old offices, but I am reliably informed that Mr Bryant is three years older than his counterpart. Mr May is certainly the more amenable of the pair, possessing a relatively youthful outlook. He is at least partially familiar with technological advances in the field of crime detection, but Mr Bryant is quite impossible to deal with. In the last eighteen months he has destroyed or lost seventeen mobile phones and several laptop computers. How he managed to re-program the unit's main police transmitter frequency so that it could only receive selections from *The Pirates of Penzance* is a mystery we have yet to solve.

Speaking frankly, he is offensive, awkward, argumentative and unhygienic. He flatly refuses to follow procedural guidelines, and constantly leaves the unit open to legal prosecution. He insists on employing the services of non-professionals, including disgraced experts, discredited psychics, registered felons, unstable extremists, tree-huggers, witches, children, itinerants, actors, practitioners of quasi-religions and various 'creative' types.

Mr Bryant's informants include those on the wrong side of the law, outpatients, migrants, fringe dwellers not recognized as reliable witnesses in a British court of law, and, on at least one occasion, a convicted murderer. He refuses to document his investigations in accordance with official guidelines, his office is little more than a rubbish dump, his personal habits are disgusting and, I suspect, illegal. He smokes and drinks on duty, abuses official property, requisitions police vehicles for personal use, falsifies reports, and on one occasion borrowed clothes awaiting DNA tests from the Evidence Room in order to attend a fancy-dress party. He has an infested Tibetan human skull on his desk and has been known to keep animal parts in the unit's refrigerator for experiments.

Unfortunately, these transgressions cannot be dealt with through the usual disciplinary channels because, technically speaking, the unit is no longer part of the Metropolitan Police, and now falls under your jurisdiction. However, I am informed (by Mr Bryant himself) that you have no power over staff employed before the revised Official Security Act of 1962.

My work at the unit is personally humiliating. Whenever I attempt to exert some kind of control over him, Mr Bryant plays practical jokes on me. He once convinced me that my wife had taken a French lover, which had a disastrous effect on my marriage. Heaven knows, I like a joke as much as the next man, but in this case the next man happened to be my counterpart at the Sûreté, and did not take kindly to being accused of adultery. In short, Mr Bryant acts as if the serious business of solving crime is a children's game. Lately I have begun to wonder if he has developed a strange form of senility. Mr May frequently takes his partner's side against me. I know they are laughing behind my back. They practise nepotism, favouritism, and, in Mr Bryant's case, occasional witchcraft. The mother of their detective sergeant was formerly in their employ, and now it appears that Mr May's granddaughter, a girl with a history of psychological problems, is to join the unit. Mr Bryant and Mr May are not just representatives of the law, they are old people, and it is time for them to move on.

Which is why I would like to recommend a psychiatric evaluation report on the pair of them. If their incompetence can be officially proven (as I very much suspect to be the case) then I will finally be able to replace them with younger, more technologically literate unit supervisors. Mr Bryant's and Mr May's consistent refusal of promotion is a ruse that has allowed them to operate 'hands on' as detectives through most of their cases. An evaluation could perhaps recommend they be transferred to positions of part-time consultancy, where they would not come into direct contact with criminal investigations, and would only have powers in a reduced advisory capacity. Mr Bryant refers to himself as a 'cradle-to-grave' law officer and, in short, I think it is time he headed for his grave.

For some unearthly reason, both Mr Bryant and Mr May command an almost fanatical loyalty among the rest of the PCU staff. Therefore I am sure you appreciate the need for absolute discretion in this matter.

I remain,

Yours sincerely,

Raymond Land

Acting Head of the Peculiar Crimes Unit (1973–present day)

2

SMALL PROVOCATIONS

'I hope you're not going to be rude and upset everyone again.'

Detective Sergeant Janice Longbright examined her boss for signs of disarray. She scraped some egg from his creased green tie with a crimson nail, and grudgingly granted her approval.

Arthur Bryant took a deep breath and folded his notes back into his jacket. 'I see nothing wrong with speaking my mind. After all, it is a special occasion.' He fixed his DS with a beady, unforgiving eye. 'I rarely get invited to make speeches. People always think I'm going to be insulting. I've never upset anyone before.'

'Perhaps I could remind you of the Mayor's banquet at Mansion House? You told the assembly he had herpes.'

'I said he had a hairpiece. It was a misquote.'

'Well, just remember how overwrought you can get at these events. Did you remember to take your blue pills?' Longbright suspected he had forgotten them, because the tablet box was still poking out of his top pocket. 'The doctor warned you it would be easy to muddle them up – '

'I don't need a nurse, thank you. I'll take them afterwards. I haven't quite drifted into senility yet.'

Unlike most men, Bryant did not look smarter in a suit. His outfit was several decades out of date and too long in the leg. His shirt collar was far wider than his neck, and the white nimbus of his hair floated up around his prominent ears as though he had been conducting electrical experiments. Overall, he looked like a soon-to-be-pulped Tussauds waxwork.

Peering out through a gap in the curtains at the sea of gold-trimmed navy blazers, Sergeant Longbright saw that the auditorium was now entirely filled with pupils. 'It's a very well-heeled audience, Arthur,' she reported back. 'Boys only, that can't be very healthy. All between the ages of fifteen and seventeen, I'd say. I don't imagine they'll be much interested in crime prevention. You'll have to find a way of reaching them.'

'Teenagers are suspicious of anyone over twenty,' Bryant admitted, brushing tobacco strands from his lapel, 'so how will they feel about me? I thought there were going to be more adults here. Children can smell lies, you know. Their warning flags unfurl at the slightest provocation. A hint of condescension and they bob up like meerkats. Contrary to popular belief, they're more naturally astute than so-called grown-ups. The whole of one's adult life is a gradual process of dulling the senses, Janice. Look how young we were when we started at the PCU, little more than children ourselves. But we were firing on all synapses, awake to the world.'

Longbright brushed his shoulders with maternal propriety. 'Raymond Land says the sensitive are incapable of action. He reckons we need more thick-skinned recruits.'

'Which is why our acting chief would be better employed in parking control, or some public service which you could train a moderately attentive bottle-nosed dolphin to perform.' Bryant had little patience with those who frowned on his abstract methods. Critics offered him nothing. They made the most senior detective of London's Peculiar Crimes

Unit as irritable as a wasp in a bottle and as stubborn as a doorstop.

'They are waiting to take your picture for the school magazine. They've seen you on TV, don't forget. You're a bit of a celebrity these days. Show me how you look.' Longbright jerked his tie a little straighter and pulled his sleeves to length. 'Good enough, I suppose. I need photographic evidence of you in a suit, even though it's thirty years old. Make sure you stick to Raymond's brief and talk about the specifics of crime prevention. Don't forget the CAPO initiative – we have to reach them while they're in the highest risk category.' Seventeen-year-olds were more likely to become victims of street crime than any other population segment. Their complex pattern of allegiance to different urban tribes was more confusing than French court etiquette – territorial invasion, lack of respect, the wrong clothes, the wrong ethnicity, attitudes exaggerated by hormones, chemistry, geography and simple bad timing.

'My notes are a little more abstract than Raymond might wish,' Bryant warned.

Longbright threw him a hopeless look. 'I thought he vetted your script.'

'I meant to run it by him last night, but I'd promised to drive Alma to her sister's in Tooting. She fell off her doorstep while she was red-leading it, and needed a bread poultice for her knee.'

'Surely the head of the department ranks above your landlady.'

'Not in terms of intelligence, I assure you.'

'You should have shown him what you're planning to say, Arthur. You know how concerned he is about the media attention we've been receiving.'

The unit had lately been the subject of a television documentary, and not all of the press articles following in its wake had been complimentary.

'I couldn't stick to Raymond's guidelines on the history of crimefighting because I don't want to talk down to my audience. They're supposed to be smart kids, the top five per cent of the education system. I don't want them to get fidgety.'

'Just fix them with that angry stare of yours. Go on – everyone's waiting for you.'

The elderly detective took an unsteady step forward and baulked. He could feel a cold wall of expectancy emanating from the crowded auditorium. The hum of audience conversation parried his determination, stranding him at the edge of the stage.

'What's the matter now?' asked Longbright, exasperated.

'No one in our family was good with the young,' Bryant wavered. 'When I was little, my father tried to light a cigarette while holding me and a pint of bitter, and burned the top of my head. All of our childhood problems were sorted out with a clout round the ear. It's a wonder I can name the kings of England.'

'Don't view them as youngsters, Arthur, they're at the age when they think they know everything, so talk to them as if they do. The head teacher has already introduced you. They'll start slow handclapping if you don't get out there.' It occurred to her that because Bryant had attended a lowly state school in Whitechapel, he might actually be intimidated by appearing before an exclusive group of private pupils from upper-middle-class homes.

Bryant dragged out his dog-eared notes and smoothed them nervously. 'I'd have thought John could at least come here to support me.'

'You know he had a hospital appointment, now stop making a fuss.' She placed a broad hand in the small of his back and gently propelled him on to the stage.

Bryant stepped unsteadily into the spotlight, encouraged by a line of welcoming teachers. Having recently achieved a level of public fame for his capture of the Water Room killer, he knew he should enjoy his moment of recognition, but today he felt exposed and vulnerable.

The detective wiped his watery blue eyes and surveyed the hall of pale varnished oak from the podium. Absurdly youthful faces lifted to study him, and he saw the great age gulf that lay between lectern and audience. How could he ever expect to reach them? He remembered the war; they would not remember the 1980s. The sea of blue and gold, the expensive haircuts, the low sussurance of well-educated voices, teachers standing at the end of every third row like benign prison guards. It was surprisingly intimidating.

Most of the students had broken off their conversation to acknowledge his arrival, but some were still chatting. He fired a rattling cough into the microphone, a magnified explosion that echoed into a squeal of feedback. Now they ceased talking and looked up in a single battalion, assessing him.

He could feel the surf of confidence radiating from these bored young men, and knew he would have to work for their attention. The boys of St Crispin's were not here to offer him respect; he was in their employ, and they would choose to listen, or ignore him. For one terrifying second, the power of the young was palpable. Bryant was an outsider, an interloper. He rustled his notes and began to speak.

'My name is Arthur Bryant,' he told them unsteadily, 'and together with my partner John May I run a small detective division known as the Peculiar Crimes Unit.' He settled his gaze in the centre of the audience, focussing on the most insolent and jaded faces. 'Time moves fast. When the unit was first founded, much detection work was still based on Victorian principles. Anything else was untried and experimental. We were one of several divisions created in a new spirit of innovation. Because we're mainly academics, we don't use traditional law-enforcement methods. We are not a part of the Met; they are hard-working, sensible men and women who handle the daily fall-out of poverty and

24

hardship. The PCU doesn't deal with life's failures. The criminals we hunt have already proven successful.' His attention locked on a group of four boys who seemed on the verge of tuning out from his lecture. He found himself departing from the script in order to speak directly to them. He raised his voice.

'Let's take an example. Say one of you lads in the middle there gets burgled at home. The police handle cases in order of priority, just like doctors. They send a beat constable or a mobile uniformed officer around to ask you for details of the break-in and a list of what's missing. They are not trained as investigative detectives, so you have to wait for a specialist to take fingerprints, which they'll try to match with those of a registered felon. If they don't get a match, your loss is merely noted and set against the chance of the future recovery of your goods – a possibility that shrinks with each passing day. The system only works for its best exemplars. But at the Peculiar Crimes Unit, we adopt a radically different approach.' As he still seemed to have their attention, Bryant decided to forge ahead.

'We ask ourselves a fundamental question: what is a crime? How far does its moral dimension extend? Is it simply an act that works against the common good? If you are starving and steal from a rich man's larder, should you be punished less than if you were not hungry? All crime is driven by some kind of need. Once, those needs were simple: food, shelter, warmth, the basic assurances of survival. We can predict the sad lives of many criminals as surely as if they were specimens in a Petri dish. Let's imagine a boy like any one of you, but born on a run-down estate. His family is poor, he never knows his real father and is beaten up by his stepfather, he's trouble at school, a nuisance on the streets, put into care, abused, arrested by the time he's ten, in custody at the age of fifteen. He'll be lucky if he makes it to thirty. But he's not unique. Our prisons are full of such people. But as soon as our needs are taken care of, new crimes appear within society. There were over eleven thousand cases of gun crime in Britain last year, and nearly 30 per cent of all schoolchildren have carried a knife at some time. As we become more sophisticated, so do the reasons for our misdeeds. Once we are warm and fed and properly raised, we covet something more complex: power. Spending power, power over others, the power to be noticed. And sometimes that power can be achieved by violating the accepted laws of the land. So criminal sophistication requires sophisticated methods of detection. That's where specialist units like ours come in. Think of internet fraud, and you'll find it is being matched by equally subtle methods of detection that require as much knowledge as the criminal's. I'm sure you boys know far more about the internet than your parents, but does that place you at less of a risk?'

He's off to a decent start, thought Longbright from the wings. *A bit all over the place, but no doubt he'll draw it all together and make his point.*

'Fraud, robbery, assault and murder are all cause-and-effect crimes requiring carefully targeted treatment. But all modern lawlessness carries the seeds of a strange paradox within it, for just as ancient crimes appear in cunning new versions, others appear entirely unmotivated. One thinks of vandalism. Some will have you believe it was invented in the postwar period, but not so. Acts of vandalism have been recorded in every sophisticated civilization; the defacing of statues was common in ancient Rome. Now, though, we are reaching a new peak of motiveless transgression. Criminality has once more assumed the kind of dark edge that existed in London during the eighteenth century. London was always the home of mob rule. The public voiced their opinions about whether it was right for a man to hang just as much as the judge. The joyous assembly would jeer or cheer a prisoner's final speech at Tyburn's triple tree. They would choose to condemn a wrongdoer or venerate him. Pamphlets filled with prints and poems would be produced in his honour. He would achieve lasting fame as a noble champion, his exploits retold as brave deeds, and there was nothing that governments could do to prevent it. Criminals became celebrities because they were seen to be fighting the old order, kicking back at an oppressive system.' Bryant eyed his audience like a pirate frightening cabin boys with tales of dancing skeletons. 'Often, thieves' necks would fail to break when they were dropped from the Tyburn gallows, and the crowd would cut down a half-hanged man to set him free, because they felt he had paid for his crimes. They rioted against the practice of passing bodies over to the anatomists, and pelted bungling hangmen with bricks. If a murderer conducted himself nobly as he ascended the gallows stairs, he would become more respected than his accusers. But time has robbed us of these gracious renegades. Last week, less than a quarter of a mile from here, in Smithfield, a schoolboy was stabbed through the heart for his mobile phone. An elderly man on a tube platform in Holborn was kicked to death for bumping into someone. The criminals who perpetrate these acts are not to be venerated.'

A murmur of recollection rippled through the auditorium.

'Statistics show that the nature of English crime is reverting to its oldest form. In a country where so many desire status and wealth, petty annoyances can spark disproportionately violent behaviour. We become frustrated because we feel powerless, invisible, unheard. We crave celebrity, but that's not easy to come by, so we settle for notoriety. Envy and bitterness drive a new breed of lawbreakers, replacing the old motives of poverty and the need for escape. But how do you solve crimes which no longer have traditional motives?'

He's still got their attention, thought Longbright, feeling for a chair at the side of the stage. *Let's hope he remembers to talk about Raymond's initiatives and can get all the way through without saying anything offensive.* She knew how volatile her boss could be, but now was the time for him to exercise restraint. For once, the fortunes of the Peculiar Crimes Unit were on the rise. Indeed, they had been ever since a remarkable murder in a quiet North London street had placed them all in the public eye. Arthur's partner, John May, had appeared on a late-night programme discussing the importance of the case with several bad-tempered social commentators, a number of articles in the *Guardian* and *The Times* had examined the case in detail, government funding for the coming year had miraculously appeared, and mercifully no one outside the unit knew the reality of the case's conclusion; if they did, Longbright doubted that any of them would have survived with their careers intact. Arthur Bryant's decision to break the law in order to close the investigation had been so contentious that Longbright had turned down the BBC's offer to feature her in their film, in case she accidentally let slip the truth.

Basking in the glow of publicity, Bryant had been asked to deliver a lecture to St Crispin's Boys School, the exclusive private academy founded by a devout Christian group in 1653 in St John Street, Clerkenwell, and had shyly accepted.

Longbright turned her attention back to the stage.

'What we have here is a fundamental alteration in the definition of morality,' Bryant argued. 'What does it now mean to have a moral conscience? Do we need to develop different values from those of our parents? Most of you think you can distinguish right from wrong, but morality requires information to feed it, so you build your own internal moral system from the intelligence you receive, probably the hardest thing anyone ever has to do, judging by the number of times the system fails.

'In London's rural suburbs, not far from here, middle-class Thames Valley towns like Weybridge and Henley are awash with a new kind of malicious cruelty. Here the system appears to be failing. The criminals are not suffering inner-city deprivation, nor are they gang members protecting their turf through internecine wars based on divisions in ethnicity. They are wealthy white males facing futures filled with opportunities. So why are they turning to unprovoked violence and murder? Part of a generation has somehow become unmoored from its foundations, and no one knows how to draw it back from the harmful shallows. You all face complex pressures, problems that gentlemen of my advanced age are scarcely able to imagine. From the day you were born, someone has been targeting you as a potential market. Your attention has become fragmented. You are offered no solitude, no peace, no time for reflection. You are forced to create your own methods of escape. Some choose alcohol and narcotics, others form social cliques that combat the status quo. All of you in this hall are in danger. Many people of my age would suggest that you desire to break the law not because you've had a hard time growing up, but because you haven't. You've been spoiled with everything you ever wanted, but you still want more.'

He's forgotten the script, Longbright worried, *and he's stabbing his finger at them. At this rate he'll have them throwing things at him.* Some of the pupils were fidgeting in annoyance. They were clearly uncomfortable with the hectoring tenor of Bryant's sermon. The old detective hadn't given a lecture in years, and had forgotten the importance of keeping the audience on his side. *Keep it light in tone but heavy on factual data,* Land had warned. *Be positive but don't say anything controversial. Remember, their parents are fee-paying voters with a lot of clout.*

Bryant's raised voice brought her back to attention. 'Well, I don't believe that,' he was saying. 'Children today have a far more complicated time growing up than I ever did. At the Peculiar Crimes Unit, we have the time and capability to see beyond stock answers and standard procedures. We claw our way to the roots of the crime, and by understanding its cause, we hope to provide solutions.'

As the audience half-heartedly pattered their hands,

Longbright rose and made her way to the rear of the hall, where she accepted a polystyrene cup of coffee. Only the question-and-answer session was left now. Longbright had tried to talk her superior out of holding one, bearing in mind his capacity for argument, but half a dozen teenagers had already raised their hands. There was a palpable attitude of aggression and defiance in the pupils' body language.

'You say it's a question of morals,' said a pale, elongated boy with layered blond hair.

'Stand up and give your surname,' barked the teacher at the end of the row.

The boy unfolded himself from his seat with difficulty and faced the audience. 'Sorry, Sir. Gosling.' He turned to Bryant. 'Are you saying we're the ones who commit crimes because we lack a moral code?'

'Of course not,' Bryant replied. 'I'm just saying that it's understandable you're confused. You know that trainers are made in Korea for starvation wages, so you buy a pair from a company promising to make their product locally for a fair price. Then you discover that the company you chose destroyed ancient farmland to build their factory. How do you feel about your purchase now? You've been lied to, so why shouldn't you commit a victimless crime and steal them? You're given horrible role models, your divorced parents are having sex with people you hate and have given up caring what you do, you're expected to take an interest in the lifestyles of singers who'll make more money than you will ever see. It's no wonder you start taking drugs and behaving like animals.'

The hall erupted. Longbright covered her face with her hands. Bryant had never been much of a diplomat.

A small lad with a pustular complexion rose sharply. 'Parfitt. You just don't like the fact that we're young, and still have a chance to change the world your contemporaries wrecked for us.'

A heavy set boy with shiny red cheeks, cropped black hair

and bat ears jumped angrily to attention. 'That's right, we're the ones—'

'Surname,' barked his master, leaning angrily forward.

'Jezzard – you always blame the young, but we're the ones who'll have to correct the mistakes of the older generation.'

'My dear boy, don't you see that you no longer possess the means for changing the world?' replied Bryant, adopting a tone of infuriating airiness. 'You've been disempowered, old chap. It's all over. The things you desire have become entirely unattainable, and you take revenge for that by being angry with your seniors all the time.'

Another boy, slender and dark, with deep-set eyes and narrow teeth, launched to his feet. 'You're accusing us when you know nothing about us, Mr Bryant – nothing!'

'*Name!*' squealed the teacher at the end of the row.

'Billings. It's not us who's the problem, it's you. Everyone knows the police are corrupt racists – '

Now several more pupils stood up together, all speaking at once. Their teachers continued to demand that they identify themselves, but were ignored. Sides were swiftly being taken. Bryant had managed to divide the hall into factions. He threw up his hands in protest as the pupils barracked him.

'You condescend to us because you don't have a clue – '

'You victimize those who can't protect themselves – '

'Why is it that young people never want to take responsibility for their actions?' protested Bryant, as students popped up from their chairs in every section of the hall.

'Just because you messed up your own society – '

'Why should we be blamed for your greed when – '

'We're just starting out,' shouted Parfitt, 'and you're trying to make us sound as cynical as you.'

'I am not cynical, I simply know better,' Bryant insisted, trying to be heard. 'And I can tell from experience exactly how many of you will fall by the wayside and die before you

31

progress to adulthood, because the cyclical nature of your short lives is as immutable as that of a dragonfly.'

There were so many things wrong with this last sentence that the detective sergeant could not bear to reflect on it, and could only watch the response helplessly. The lanky boy, Gosling, was the first to kick back his chair and leave. His friends quickly followed suit. The questionable authority of the teachers collapsed entirely as chairs were knocked over, causing a defiant ripple that quickly spread throughout the hall.

Longbright had been worried that Raymond Land might get to hear of the debacle. Now she was more concerned about getting Bryant out in one piece.

3

UNLOCKING DOORS

On the following Monday morning, the 24th of October, a few minutes north of the school where Arthur Bryant had turned a peaceful assembly hall into a brawling dockyard, April stood before her front door with her hand on the lock, waiting for her heart to stop hammering.

'Don't tell me all journeys start with a single step or I'll hit you,' she warned, throwing her grandfather a sour look.

'How long is it since you've been outside?' asked John May.

'Four months, three days.'

'Then today is the day.' May placed a steadying hand on her shoulder as she twisted the door knob, slowly drawing back the latch. The world outside had lately become as distant and exotic to her as a rain-valley seen from an aircraft window. Her friends assumed that agoraphobia was a way of hiding herself, but it was more than that: she feared the removal of certainty, the loss of safe parameters. To be outside was to be placed in an uncontrollable situation. If she stepped into the street, she would no longer be protected by the rain-streaked windows of her barricaded home.

She brushed translucently pale hair aside, revealing the fierce methylene blue of her irises. Her hand trembled faintly on the lintel, as though a thousand tiny muscles were correcting her balance. Everything about her was unsteady and, to May's eyes, infinitely fragile.

Opening the door a crack, she looked out and took a deep breath, which was unfortunate as there was a truck going past. The air blurred with vibrations.

'It's no use, I can't go through with this,' April told him, fanning away the fumes with a cough, but she could not resist watching the world through the door's narrow gap. On the far side of the road, sodden shoppers mooched past with supermarket bags, unaware of the miraculous ease with which they negotiated the lurking horrors of the high street.

'April, if you don't make it this time, you won't get the job. Raymond isn't prepared to hold it open any longer.'

'All right, you've made your point.'

She pushed the door wider, taking in the expanding view of the Holloway Road, one of North London's grimmest thoroughfares. Opposite, a local newspaper placard read: MANIAC 'HEARD GOD'S VOICE' BEFORE STABBING SPREE. The sheer number of *things* alarmed her: bright-orange posters and white council vans, pushchairs and bicycles, store fronts, dogs and children, too many erratic, irrational people. They halted, turned, changed direction – what was wrong with them? Their sheer lack of organization made her feel sick.

All John May saw was an ordinary London street. An African shop fortressed by a row of red plastic laundry baskets, its windows banked with fibre-optic lamps, mobile-phone covers, signs promising internet access and cheap fares to faraway townships. A dim, carpeted amusement arcade filled with pulsing bulbs, where a single elderly woman sat mechanically feeding coins into a machine as big as a telephone booth. A betting office with emerald windows depicting idealized race scenes, litter and losers framed in its dark doorway. A McDonald's truck as vast as an ocean liner, with plasticky burgers the size of paddling pools printed along its sides.

Everywhere April looked, fierce colours jumped into view: cyan, scarlet, heliotrope, garish shapes trapped in the glare of the warm morning sun. Even the grey pavements were unnaturally bright. The buildings looked old and exhausted with overuse.

'Well, here goes.' She took a deep breath and slipped her hand into his. Then she stepped out into the street.

Agoraphobia had been April's latest response to the loss of her mother. Nearly six months earlier, following glimmers of improvement and a positive doctor's report, she had been recommended as a candidate for a new law-enforcement training initiative. The Chief Association of Police Officers was inviting non-professionals to work alongside detectives, in an exercise designed to bridge the widening gulf between police and public. It had seemed an ideal way for May to protect his granddaughter while allowing her to rediscover some independence. But she had suffered a relapse, retreating further into the shadows of her bleakly pristine flat. May sometimes felt that he was cursed: although his estranged son lived half a world away, his family suffered from similar phobias.

He released her hand and watched as she walked unsteadily to the centre of the pavement. 'That's it,' he encouraged. 'Keep going, don't stop to think, you're doing fine.'

Neither of them saw the running schoolboy.

He slammed into April, spinning her down on to the pavement, and skidded around the corner before either of them had time to react. As the detective loped forward and helped April to her feet, she looked around in confusion. 'My bag, he's taken it. My credit cards – everything.'

May reached the corner knowing that it would be too late for him to catch up. The boy had dashed across the busy road, into a crowd of market-traders gathered beneath a bridge. He was home and dry.

May called in the theft almost without thinking, relaying the description of the stolen bag, keeping watch on April as her face crumpled and she doubled over.

'Please, April, you mustn't let something like this beat you,' he pleaded, holding the phone to his chest and reaching for her with his free hand. 'It could happen to anyone. Are you all right?'

Clutching a tissue to her face, she slowly rose, barely able to catch her breath.

'Just tell me what was in the bag. I'm sure we can replace—'

He was amazed to see that she was caught in the throes of helpless laughter.

'The first time I step out of the flat in months and I get bloody mugged. The little bastard.' She leaned on him, still laughing, fighting to catch her breath. 'For heaven's sake, let's get to the PCU before something else happens.'

'Are you sure?'

'After this?' She wiped laughter from her eyes. 'Where did you park? You've probably been clamped by now.'

'You mean you still want to come?' May was taken aback.

'You're joking. Think I'm going to let kids like that get away with murder? Just tell me what I have to do.'

This was the April he remembered and loved. It was as though the pain of the last few months had been folded away like an awning, revealing her old self beneath. He had no idea how long her new-found strength would remain, but was determined to make the most of it. April was far too valuable to give up on. Her mother had died when she was just nine years old, and the loss had affected her in ways which still adopted new manifestations. May's family life had been tangled and messy, marred by small tragedies, filled with arguments and estrangements, in contrast to his partner's bare, ascetic existence. He wanted April's life to be simpler, and had the notion that keeping her around Arthur Bryant might be the answer. Bryant had a way of making everything seem plausible, possible and even probable. He cut through hesitations and protestations. He would be able to help her, if anyone could.

'Is it usual to have a cat flap in a police-station door?' asked April, studying the unassuming red-painted entrance that led to the Peculiar Crimes Unit.

'We're not a police station,' May replied. 'Crippen has to use the outside world as a bathroom sometimes, which makes him a very Camden Town cat. We hide his litter tray because he's not supposed to be living here. Raymond has an allergy.'

April knew that Raymond Land was still waiting to be transferred elsewhere, anywhere that would get him away from Arthur Bryant. It wasn't that they had nothing in common so much as that they shared things they didn't like, mainly each other. Last month, Bryant had accidentally insulted Land's wife at a Police Federation charity dinner when he had mistaken her for a toilet attendant. It seemed that no week passed without some fresh affront to Land's dignity. Worst of all, it occurred to May that his partner was secretly enjoying the feud.

'It's not much, but we like to think of it as home,' said May, pushing the street door wide. 'Top of the stairs and turn right. Sorry, we've been meaning to get the hall bulb replaced. Arthur was demonstrating Wimbledon volleys with a coal shovel and blew the electrics before putting his back out.'

The headquarters of the Peculiar Crimes Unit occupied the single floor above Mornington Crescent Tube station. The detectives looked out into the grey London streets from half-moon windows set in glazed crimson tiles. The unit had almost become a local landmark; it was even being pointed out by a guide on his 'Bizarre and Dangerous London' tour, although the guide was unsure which category the unit fitted best.

April reached the landing and looked about, touching a pile of postwar *Film Fun* magazines with the toe of her shoe. A sinister ventriloquist's dummy hung on the wall, just above an original poster for Gilbert and Sullivan's *Ruddigore* and a framed account of a 'Most Dreadful and Barbarous M U R D E R Committed by Ruffians!' dated 14 April 1826. 'It's less – professional – than I thought it would be. I only ever came to the office at Bow Street.'

'I'm sorry, we don't keep a very tidy house.' May knew that his granddaughter had a compulsion for neatness; her flat reminded him of an operating theatre. 'Why don't you take the room across the corridor?'

'This must be Janice Longbright's room.' April noted the boned wasp-waist corset that hung on the back of the door, the thick face-powders and ceramic-bottle cosmetics that spilled from an old Pifco hairdryer box, circa 1955. May moved a low-cut spangled trapeze dress from a swivel chair. Lately, Sergeant Longbright's obsession with stars of the 1950s had reached epic proportions.

'Yes, but Janice is very happy to have a guest.'

'You want her to keep an eye on me.' April picked up a dusty bottle of 'Bowanga!' Jungle Red nail varnish priced 2s.11d., and set it back in place. She had forgotten just how odd everyone was here.

'To begin with. Just until you settle in.'

'How many staff do you have now?'

'There are eight of us if you count Raymond Land, but he's not often here. Spends most of his time creeping around to his officer pals at the Met. Now that we're under the jurisdiction of the Home Office, we're waiting for a visit from their new man. Apparently, he wants to reorganize the unit to make it more accountable and efficient. Arthur and I have the room opposite. Dan Banbury is our IT-slash-crime-scene manager. Rough and ready, but a decent sort. He shares with Giles Kershaw, who's rather too posh and plummy for my taste, but also good at his job. He's the forensics officer and social-science liaison—'

'What's that?'

'Not entirely sure,' May admitted. 'He came with the title and no one's got around to asking him what it means. The lovely Sergeant Longbright you know, of course. And there are two detective constables down the hall – Meera Mangeshkar, she can be a bit stroppy but she's all right once you get to know her, and Colin Bimsley, who has been medically diagnosed with DSA, that's Diminished Spatial Awareness, which explains why he falls down the stairs so often.'

'And that's it?' asked April, shocked. 'This is the crack team that solves crimes no one else can handle?'

'Not quite,' said May with a smile. 'There's you now. Our first resident non-professional. Liaison and communication. At least, that will be the official title until we find out what you're best at. Come with me,' he beckoned. 'Let's get you started.'

'I like it here.' April wiped a patch of condensation from the window and looked down into the traffic. 'It feels safe and protected, like a nest. When I look outside, I always have to fight a sense of panic. How many active cases are you working on?'

'We've been asked to take on work from other jurisdictions around the country, and there are a couple of interesting matters in hand. A British civil servant named Garrick, on assignment in Thailand, was found in a Bangkok reptile house at the city's floating market, apparently bitten to death by green mambas. When the body was shipped back, Arthur and Giles found traces of old needle tracks in the crook of his left leg. Garrick was right-handed; addicts usually cross sides when they inject, so we figured they were self-induced. There were unused syringes in Garrick's desk drawer, but no traces of injectable drugs in his system except snake venom. We suspect he was trying to build up his immunity to the snakes by injecting small amounts of poison into his bloodstream.'

'Why would he do that?'

'Our job isn't to fathom the vagaries of the human mind, just to settle the arguments about death. Not that it stopped Arthur from trying to find out. He discovered that Garrick's previous assignment was in Alabama, where he had joined a snake-handling sect. He'd decided to convert the locals in Bangkok, but needed to prove his own abilities first. Case closed. Apart from that, we've another dead biological-warfare expert on our hands. That's the twelfth since 9/11 – more fodder for conspiracy theorists.'

'I'm a great believer in conspiracies.'

'Then you'll love this one,' said May with a smile. 'Dr Peter Jukes from Salisbury, Wiltshire, found by fishermen floating off Black Head at the Lizard Peninsula, Cornwall. The local coroner reckoned it was a straightforward matter of death by drowning, but there were unexplained injuries. Plus, his boat turned up fifteen miles away, washed into a local harbour. The coastguard concluded that it was unlikely he had fallen from the boat, because local tides and currents would have taken it into shore near the spot where he was found. Jukes told some drinking pals he was going fishing with his friend Leo, but no one of that name has been found. Arthur has turned up some darker connections: Jukes formerly belonged to a Druid sect – his family says it was a hobby – but had lately drifted into Satanist circles. The police refuse to believe there's a connection between his injuries and his interest in black magic, but we're wondering if he became an embarrassment to his employers. He operated under the Official Secrets Act, after all.'

April's interest was piqued. Denied access to her cigarettes, her hands fluttered at her sides in weak agitation. 'The government doesn't kill staff members for pursuing unusual hobbies, surely.'

'I'd like to think not, but Jukes was chief scientist for

40

chemical and biological defence at the MoD's Porton Down laboratory, part of which has recently been privatized by a company now under investigation. Somehow, I doubt we'll ever get to the truth on this one, mainly because the Defence Secretary is reluctant to acknowledge that there's a case at all. There are also a couple of outstanding cold cases which act as strikes against the unit. We're no nearer to finding out the truth about the Leicester Square Vampire, and a recent trail belonging to someone the press call the Deptford Demon has also gone cold.' May paused for a moment in thought. 'You know, you'll come up against some extreme morbidity in this job, April.'

'It doesn't worry me,' said his granddaughter, offering a tentative smile. 'So long as the two of you are near by to protect me.'

May smiled back reassuringly. But he knew that their tenure here at the PCU was every bit as uncertain as April's return to the outside world.

'Uncle Arthur says that ancient evils are always waiting to resurface in London,' said April suddenly. 'Do you believe that?'

'Yes, I do,' replied May. 'None of us ever knows when we are likely to be tested. All we can be sure of is that it will be when we lower our guard the most.'

4

THE USEFULNESS OF MEMORY

After weeks of rain, the city had spent one glorious week marooned in the stale sargasso of a warm autumn. The streets had become sticky and overheated, the residents made bad-tempered by the London dirt. A belated silly season hit the newspapers, whose editors could barely be bothered to outrage their readers with amorous sporting scandals and tales of government waste, and had opted instead for food scares and travel indignations. The great engine of the city slowed. Offices were becalmed. It was as though everyone was waiting for something to happen. London residents were seeking someone new to idolize, someone new to hate.

In the final week of October, they got their wish.

On the Monday morning, the clear skies occluded, and cataracts of cloud brought soft autumnal drizzle which dampened the dusted pavements, misting the arched windows of the offices above Mornington Crescent Tube station to give them the appearance of a disreputable sauna. The light level across London dropped until the city appeared to be lit by forty-watt bulbs.

'Well, I thought my lecture last week went rather well,'

said Bryant, poking down the sides of his armchair for his pipe-stem.

'Are you mad? They were ready to hang you.' Longbright was appalled. 'You were pelted with plastic cups. Several of the parents are still threatening to lodge formal complaints.'

May shook his silver mane in wonder. 'I've never understood your ability to enrage total strangers.'

'It was a pretty spirited debate, I must say,' Bryant told his partner enthusiastically. 'The head teacher was quite overcome with emotion.'

'Those pupils thought you were having a go at them,' the detective sergeant reminded him. 'I warned you teenagers are sensitive.'

'I can't imagine why. I never was. I didn't have time to be touchy. Kids don't understand that age and guile will always triumph over youth and enthusiasm. These days the former attributes belong to corporations, the latter to individuals, so of course any attempt at independence is suppressed. And we wonder why children write on walls.'

'Your cynicism is getting worse,' May agreed with Longbright. 'You should never begin a sentence with the words "These days".'

'That's it, I'm making tea.' Sometimes the glamorous sergeant stopped behaving like a fifties starlet and became a fifties housewife, brewing tea whenever she was upset, great steaming brown china pots of it. Now, as she went to check on the kettle, she became annoyed about Bryant's humiliation at the hands of teenagers who were understandably wary of being patronized. He had mentioned the occasion a dozen times in the past week, so the event was clearly preying on his mind. Any intelligent man could appear a fool without clear communication.

'You might as well say it; I know you're dying to.' Bryant followed her into the kitchen, ready for an argument. 'I'm out of touch with the general public. They think I'm a has-been.'

Longbright chose her words with care. 'It's not that exactly, but you have to admit that John's right: you've stopped updating your mental software. You know what he always says – "Adapt or perish."'

'And you think I've perished.' Bryant tightened his ratty green scarf around his neck. 'I'm fully aware of the gap between myself and them. It's not just age. I grew up in Whitechapel and Bethnal Green – they were raised in Edwardian villas beside the Thames, or in houses over-looking Hampstead Vale. My mother cleaned cinemas and was bombed out of her home. They're the progeny of professionals. I can't imagine their lives, Janice. I've never had children of my own. To reach them, I'd have to understand them, and I'm afraid that's utterly beyond me. They're a mystery race, some new form of protoplasmic alkaloid that looks vaguely human but isn't. I see them standing in a group and assume they operate with a single sentience, like Midwich Cuckoos.' Bryant rooted in the cupboard for some ground ginger and added it to his tea mug. 'Actually, I think I'm a little scared of them. Their references are as alien as map coordinates for another solar system. I mean, what is it like to be young these days?'

'Perhaps you need a refresher course,' offered Longbright, carrying the teas back to the detectives' office. 'This sort of thing doesn't help.' She indicated the hardback books on his cluttered desk: crack-spined copies of *The Life of Thomas Chatterton*, *Great Locomotive Boiler Explosions*, *The British Catalogue of Victorian Naval Signals* and *The Fall of Jonathan Wild, Thief-Taker*. 'Your current reading matter. You should be flicking through *Heat* and *Hello!* and the *News of the World*.'

'Janice is right,' May concurred. 'You need to watch *Big Brother* and *Pop Idol* and reality TV – that's how normal people relax.'

Bryant was disgusted by the idea. 'I would hate to think of myself as normal. What's the point of working your whole life if you end up having to do what other people want?'

'You don't have to do what they do, Arthur, just try to understand them a bit more. If a television show gets a bigger audience vote than the General Election, you should know about it. It's simply a matter of reconnecting yourself.'

'What if I don't want to connect myself to things I consider to be puerile rubbish? I want to be more knowledgeable at my age, not less. I plan to go to my grave with a head full of information.' His diluted blue eyes looked up at the pair of them in a bid for sympathy. 'I'm not going to buy a television, if that's what you mean.'

'It's never too late to change your habits,' said May patiently. 'Come with me to one of the Met's "Meet the Public" sessions. You don't have to get into any arguments, just listen to what some of the street officers and their clients have to say.'

'Please don't refer to victims of crime as *clients*. And anyway, if I did that, I'd end up wanting to kill everyone in the room,' Bryant admitted. 'That's what happens when you get older, you become irritated by the views of others for the simple reason that you know better, and they're being ridiculous. If I go to a public debate, some silly man will stand up and start complaining about police brutality until I want to beat him to death with my stick.'

'You know in your heart that's not true,' replied May, wondering if it was. 'When you conduct your guided London tours, what's the feeling between you and your audience?'

'Antipathy bordering on mutual hatred,' said Bryant glumly. 'We usually can't wait to get away from each other.'

'Then it's time you started learning to empathize more.'

'You're asking me to give up my carefully nurtured ideals and start revelling in humankind's myriad imperfections.' Bryant took up the Chatterton volume and buffed its cover with his sleeve, scattering dust.

'If you want to put it like that, yes.'

'I won't remember the names of pop stars,' he warned. 'I'd prefer keep my memory filled with useful data.'

'But how useful is the data you store?' May tipped back his leather armchair and raised his highly polished Oxfords to the desk. 'You know precisely how many Thames crossings there are between Teddington Weir and the Tower of London – '

'Of course, twenty eight, everyone knows that . . .'

' – and you told me why there are metal pine cones on top of half of the railings in London – '

'The Georgians adopted the pine cone as an architectural motif because it was the Roman symbol of hospitality, that's common knowledge . . .'

'But it's not, don't you see? Yesterday you told Janice here that there are eight statues hidden underneath Vauxhall Bridge, and that they can only be seen from a boat, but most of the people we deal with don't give a monkey's about such architectural idiosyncrasies. Why should they? Such things have no relevance to their lives.'

'Rubbish – the details of everyday living enrich us all.'

'But they're not useful. The majority is more interested in finding aspirational role models amongst celebrities, which makes you the outsider. And if you're an outsider, they'll never take you into their confidence.'

'Your utilitarian attitude is very taxing,' Bryant complained. 'I don't throw away knowledge just because it ceases to be of immediate use. Crimes are more complex now, so you never know what will come in handy. Remember how it used to be? An emerald robbery in Hatton Garden, a broken window, a clanging alarm, grassing spivs on the Mile End Road, a trip round to a safe house in Southwark, 'Can we search the premises?', 'It's a fair cop, guv', on with the handcuffs and up before the beak.'

'I think you're confusing your life with an Ealing caper,' said May drily.

'Very possibly,' Bryant admitted. 'But that's how things were in my day. Or possibly not.'

'Your day is still continuing, Arthur,' Longbright felt duty-bound to point out.

'Janice is right, old fruit. You remain accountable to the public so long as you're employed, and that means keeping up with them.'

It's a conspiracy, thought the elderly detective. *They're plotting against me.* 'All right, what do I have to do?' he asked wearily.

'Get your coat on, Mr Bryant,' said Dan Banbury, looking around the edge of the door. 'A nasty murder on the Embankment, phoned through a couple of minutes ago, sounds right up our particular cul-de-sac.'

5

ETERNAL DESTINY

The riverside spot had once been a tumbledown jumble of wharves, timber yards and stonemasons, twisted rope-walks and moss-green jetties slipping into the brackish brown waters of the Thames. The politicians gathered in the Houses of Parliament opposite had complained about the eyesore in their sight, so down it had all come, to be replaced by a single splendid building typifying the Edwardian renaissance. The architect's drawings for County Hall showed a great colonnaded crescent finished in Portland stone and red Italian tiles, with pallid sculptures, steep sloping roofs and sun-flecked central courtyards.

But nothing runs smoothly in the rebuilding of London. In the middle of the clearance and excavation, they had discovered the boat.

The vessel had been carvel-built of oak, and ran to twenty metres in length. Coins found inside it dated from the reigns of Carausius and Allectus, suggesting that it had been built by Romans late in the third century. A magnificent find, though incomplete; the broken section pulled from the reeking Thames mud had disrupted the construction on the South Bank.

The monumental edifice of County Hall took over half a

century to complete and, appropriately enough, eventually housed the wrangling assembly of London. It was grimly inevitable that the council should then be abolished and replaced by a more controversial body, which decided to move to a different spot altogether, beside Tower Bridge, in a modern building finished in brown glass and shaped like a giant toe.

Poor County Hall, ignored when it should have been admired, then reviled for the plan Prime Minister Thatcher unveiled to turn it into a Japanese hotel. When this idea also disintegrated it became an aquarium, sleek grey sharks gliding through waters where earnest councillors had once fought to divide the boroughs of London between themselves.

Here also were housed in permanent exhibition Salvador Dali's melting clocks and arid landscapes; his great elephant sculpture is placed on the Embankment, teetering on attenuated giraffe legs, where it appears to stride over Parliament itself, surely a vision that would once have brought a charge of treason. In the front of the building (for the river displays its back) the former Charles Saatchi collection of modern British art, now the Burroughs Gallery, awaits visitors, who baulk at the idea of paying to see ideas made flesh, especially when there's nothing traditional on display.

A home for artistic visions, then (for perhaps we can include its cool blue panoramas of drifting iridescent angel fish), and also a suitable place for a murder; a great wood-panelled beehive of tunnels and passages. Through the shadowed oak corridors, across the sepia parquet blocks, into the main domed chamber like an immense wooden hammam, where half a dozen gargantuan artworks stand in white plaster alcoves, their purpose to stimulate and disturb: an immense angry head, its glaring silver eyes staring down accusingly; office furniture submerged in a water-filled white box; a bizarre steel machine knotted with ropes and leather straps, perhaps designed to torture some alien species; and six foetuses tethered in a twelve-foot tank, their arrangement guaranteed to horrify and infuriate those more used to gentler forms of art.

But something was wrong here: the liquid in the tank had overflowed, slopping on to the surrounding floor, and the foetuses had been joined by a larger form.

'It was only unveiled last Monday – now it's buggered.' The young guard was uniformed but uncapped. He absently touched his bristly ginger hair, wondering if he would somehow be made to take the blame. DCs Colin Bimsley and Meera Mangeshkar had cordoned off the area and were taking rudimentary notes, but could do little until the specialists arrived.

'You're not the regular police, then?' asked the guard, eyeing the slim silver panels on their black padded jackets. 'PCU – what does that stand for?'

'No, we're not – Simon.' Bimsley checked the guard's badge and ignored his question. 'How long have you been on this morning?'

'Since nine o'clock.'

'Everything was normal at that time. Otherwise you'd have noticed, wouldn't you?' Bimsley stabbed his ballpoint in the direction of the tank. 'Body floating face-down in there, water everywhere, it stands to reason.'

'Not water, mate, formaldehyde. You know, to preserve the babies. That's what the smell is.'

'I read about this artwork. It's been causing quite a fuss.' Mangeshkar approached the tank. 'Isn't the liquid supposed to be clearer than this?'

Simon the guard turned around to see. 'Something must have gone wrong. It started turning cloudy at the end of last week. The gallery chiefs are supposed to be meeting to discuss the problem.'

'It's eleven now. The call was logged in twenty minutes ago – '

'No, longer ago than that. I rang the police as soon as I saw it.'

The Met checked it out before passing the case to us, thought Bimsley. 'How many rounds do you make during a day? What times?'

Simon thought for a moment. 'It's not like a normal gallery with an attendant in each room, because some of the art needs more attention than others. The underwater room, especially – '

'Which is what?'

'It's an optical illusion, a huge mirror of mercury that horizontally divides a council chamber in half. You walk inside and it looks like you're wading through water. That one needs a full-time attendant because only one person is allowed to enter the room at a time. The mercury has to stay completely undisturbed, otherwise the illusion is broken, so we keep a careful watch on the visitors. Some of the other stuff doesn't need looking after at all, but there are no rope barriers around the exhibits – they spoil the placement of the art – so I just have to stop kids from leaving their pawprints. I don't have to do that with *Eternal Destiny.*'

'That's the title of the piece?' asked Mangeshkar. 'The top of the tank isn't sealed.'

'No, that would cause condensation, but the glass sides of the tank are seven feet high, so no one can reach up and put their hands in.'

'If nobody can even reach the top, how on earth could somebody manage to fall in?' asked Bimsley.

'I don't think she fell in, Colin, do you?' Mangeshkar shot her partner a dry look. Bimsley looked back at the diminutive Asian officer with unrequited love in his eyes. She was still refusing to go out with him. Was she completely mad?

'Ah, there you are. I've been looking all over for you.' Arthur Bryant was stumping towards them in a brown suede overcoat several sizes too big for him, his boots squealing unpleasantly on the polished floor, the nailed steel Blakies on his soles scraping neat crescents into the wood. He was licking the sides of a suppurating sardine and tomato sandwich, trying to prevent bits of fish from falling on the floor.

'Sir, your boots . . .' began the attendant.

'Sorry about this, I missed breakfast. All these corridors seem to turn back on themselves. I've never seen so many commemorative plaques. They've left the old GLC fittings up, all those councillors' names like Wiggins and Trusspot and Higginbottom. How they loved congratulating themselves on their civic duties – you can smell the self-importance.'

All the attendant could smell was sardines. 'Sir, your boots are damaging—'

'And how appropriate that it should become an art gallery, and continue enraging the public. Hello, what have we here?' Bryant waggled his sandwich at the clouded green-tinged tank, scattering pieces of tomato everywhere.

'One more body in the formaldehyde than is meant to be there, Sir.' Mangeshkar thumbed at the glass.

Bryant's face fairly lit up. When the creases vanished, his features revealed the delight of a naughty child. '*Eternal Destiny* – so this is what all the fuss is about. Got a couple of horrified leaders in the *Daily Express* last week, didn't it? 'WHY THIS SICK ART MUST BE BANNED', the usual outraged rentaquotes from the porcine adenoidal baconheads who act as our moral guardians.'

'They're human foetuses, Sir, it's hardly surprising people are upset,' Bimsley pointed out.

'Oh, pish-tush,' said the detective through a mouthful of sardines. 'Some middle-class artist is trying to shock the masses and the tabloids are putting the wind up their readers as usual. So this notorious piece just became even more infamous, Well, well. Do we know who's bobbing about in there?'

'Not yet, Sir. The photographer hasn't arrived, and we're waiting for Giles Kershaw to come back. He's getting some lads with a block and tackle.' Kershaw had been promised that he could head the unit's new forensic team, before discovering that he *was* the team, apart from their ancient part-time pathologist Oswald Finch.

'I wouldn't go walking about near the—' began Meera, but it was too late. Bryant's boots were already trailing spilled formaldehyde across the floor.

'Oh, very cunning,' Bryant was muttering, studying the glass case from every angle. 'A very slick piece of showman-ship. Sadly ruined now, of course.'

'What's he saying?' asked Bimsley, mouthing the words at Meera, who shrugged back.

'I have a new battery in my hearing aid, so I advise you to be circumspect,' warned Bryant without turning around. 'Did you do everything I asked?'

'Yes, Sir,' replied Meera. 'The entrance doors have been sealed. You should have seen some officers posted there when you came through.'

Bryant grunted. 'A couple of single-cell constables from Lambeth, hardly a watertight cordon. I suppose the Met are too busy sorting out motoring fines.'

When the PCU had been separated from London's Metro-politan Police Force and placed under Home Office control, the move had ostensibly been made to provide the unit with new powers. The truth, however, was a little more complex. Home Office officials planned to keep a closer watch on the PCU's spending and prevent further antagonism between Bryant and the Met officers, who wanted him disciplined for continually breaking their rules.

'There's only one way into the gallery apart from the emergency exit, and that's now locked,' said Dan Banbury, snapping on a fresh pair of plastic gloves with unnecessary theatricality. 'The outside of the building is also being monitored.'

'You're confident that whoever did this is still inside here, then.'

'Don't see how he could have got out, Sir,' said Bimsley with inspiring conviction. 'The guard shut the doors the moment he found the body.'

'What about the visitors – where are they?'

'They're all in the café, Sir. Sergeant Longbright is taking their details. Somebody must have seen something.'

'Why do you say that?'

'Well, there were people in just about every room,' Bimsley explained.

'You there, how often do you make your rounds through the gallery rooms?' Bryant tapped the red-headed attendant on the arm with his walking stick.

'They were asking me that and I was trying to explain – '

'It's not their job to ask you, it's mine. Try not to waffle. How often?'

'It varies, but at a rough guess – '

'I don't want a rough guess, I want accuracy.'

'It's hard to say, but – '

'Is there something wrong with you that requires all answers to be preceded by a let-out clause?' Bryant turned his full attention to the attendant. 'A straightforward answer, is that too much to ask?'

'Every fifteen minutes,' replied the attendant, swallowing.

'When was the last time you came through the room and found everything fine?'

'Er, I think it might have been – ' Simon caught his inquisitor's eye and began again. 'Ten thirty a.m.'

'And you returned at ten forty-five to find the body in the tank.'

'No, Sir.'

'What then?'

'I heard a noise and started walking back. I hadn't got very far through the gallery, it must have been about five minutes after I'd left the main chamber.'

'What kind of noise was it that required you to walk but not run?'

'That was it, you see. Just a sort of shout, but then a crash, like someone hitting glass but not breaking it.'

'What did it sound like to you?'

'Like someone messing with an exhibit. There'd been a bit of commotion in here since we opened, because of the press conference.'

'You had a press conference this morning?'

'Yes, Sir. A chance for three of the most controversial artists to answer their critics. We had most of the national press here.'

'No television crews?' Bryant looked for a place to deposit the rest of his sandwich and momentarily considered adding it to a bronze sculpture of *objets trouvés*.

'No, Sir. Mr Burroughs wouldn't allow them in.'

'Mr Burroughs is the new gallery owner, I take it.'

'That's right. He didn't want television crews because of the documentary.'

'Ah, yes – I can understand his point.' A week earlier, Channel 4 had broadcast an inflammatory programme about the new owner of the former Saatchi gallery, implying that he was merely a showman and self-publicist attempting to ape his predecessor by commissioning outrageous works of art at inflated fees.

'The press conference finished at ten, but a few guests were still inside when we opened the doors to the public at that time, and—'

'I'm sure you'll give the others a full report,' said Bryant dismissively, heading back towards the tank. He cupped his hands over the glass and peered through the eerie green fluid, where six curled pink babies hung on wires, suspended like seahorses beneath the murky sun-shafted verdure of a pond. The corpse floating face-down above them was clearly that of a female, her hands splayed beneath her slim torso, her long brown hair spread wide and held in still suspension by the viscosity of the liquid, magnified by thick glass as in an aquarium – a modern Ophelia, distracted and driven into harsh chemical waters. Her eyes were wide, her lips slightly parted in an attitude of surprising calm. If it hadn't been for the fact that she disrupted the symmetry of the installation, she might almost have been a part of the piece. A slender brown strand of blood curled around her head and chest like drifting pipe smoke. Distorted by the green tank and surrounded by infant corpses, her body had taken on the timeless density of a painting; a damned soul fallen from the raft of the Medusa, left to drift in Gericault's icy green ocean . . .

'He's getting his prints all over the evidence.' Meera rubbed a hand across her face. 'He must know he's contaminating the site. Why does he always have to do that?'

'He's getting a feel for it,' replied Bimsley from the side of his mouth. 'He's using his instincts.'

'Couldn't he use gloves as well?'

'The press conference – was Saralla White one of the three artists interviewed? Was she articulate? Angry? Rude? Distracted? Did she seem upset about anything?' Bryant fired questions as if they were medicine balls; you had to damn well make sure you could catch them. Nobody thought to ask how Bryant had determined the identity of the corpse.

'Yes, she was interviewed,' answered the attendant. 'I watched the whole performance. She sounded very confident, her usual self. If she was upset, she didn't show it. She had smart answers to every question they asked. There was a lot of interest in her.'

'And there'll be a lot more,' Bryant promised. 'Now that she's become a part of her own sculpture.'

6

ORCHESTRATING OUTRAGE

The new owner of the County Hall Gallery, Calvin Burroughs, was producing a prodigious amount of sweat; it broke into rivulets on his broad forehead, dripped from beneath his limpid Turnbull & Asser cuffs, and bloomed darkly across his blue striped shirt-front, lending him the air of a tropical pilot. His floppy, boyish hair and expense-account gut suggested an earlier career in the wine trade, or possibly an auction house.

'How did you know it was her?' he asked, exasperated and distracted by the police officers precariously suspended above the *Eternal Destiny* tank.

'I watched the top half of the documentary on my landlady's television,' replied Bryant. 'Her tube is going. The brown fluid in front of Miss White's face obscured her features and confused me for a minute. I don't know how vitriolic that stuff is, but it probably gave her a nosebleed.'

John May emerged from the gallery's cafeteria, where he had been helping Longbright set up a system to take witness statements. Everyone in the unit was used to helping out with each other's workloads. Only April had been refused permission to leave the Mornington Crescent base, as May

57

feared that the scene would prove too distressing for her. 'You know who it is in the tank?' he asked, surprised. 'They haven't fished her out yet.'

'I remembered seeing Saralla White's distinctive red and blue tattoo. She has a Russian gang symbol just below her navel; they're currently fashionable in a disreputable way, appropriate for a Hoxton artist like Miss White. I could distinguish the markings on her exposed midriff.' Bryant's knowledge of popular criminal tattoos was the kind of cultural awareness May generally chided him for ignoring. He had always been interested in tribal scarification, and owned a number of disturbing books on the subject.

'We're ready to raise her out now, Sir,' called one of the officers.

'Put something under her,' Bryant called back, 'and take it slowly. Giles hasn't finished measuring the tank splashes.'

'Thank you, Mr Bryant.' Giles looked up from his prone position on the gallery floor, where he was finishing his grid calculations. 'Taking into account the high room temperature, which has thinned the viscosity of the liquid compound – it's not pure formaldehyde, by the way, which is a health hazard – the spread of the fluid outside the tank would be consistent with the body falling in from above. She weighs about 63.5 kilos. At a guess I'd say she fell in from half a metre above the surface of the tank.'

'I do wish you'd use pounds and feet,' complained Bryant, sticking his finger into the pool of green liquid and sniffing it.

'That's impossible,' Meera pointed out. 'How could she have got up so high? There's no ladder, no furniture to climb on.'

'We don't like to keep anything else in the gallery chambers other than the exhibits themselves,' Burroughs explained, dabbing a paper tissue around his soaked neck. 'It would detract from the art, and I don't want to leave

potential weapons lying around in the general public's way –
we'd never get insured.'

'Yet you've gone out of your way to orchestrate public
outrage.' Watching Burroughs leaking sweat made Bryant
feel cold. He found his eye straying to the body being raised
from the tank behind them, and tugged his moth-eaten scarf
tighter around his neck.

'I'm not going to get into an argument with you about the
legitimacy of modern art,' snapped Burroughs impatiently.
'You're a public servant, you're meant to be finding out
what the hell happened here.'

'Fine,' Bryant snapped back. 'At this point I would normally ask you if the victim had any enemies, but in this case
the question is redundant. Who were the other two artists
Miss White appeared with this morning, and where are they
now?'

'We had Sharinda Van Souten here, and McZee.'

'He has no other name?'

'His life is his art, Mr Bryant. I assume they both left after
reading out their statements to the press.'

'So there was no Q&A?'

'Sharinda and McZee chose to declare their manifestos
without facing press questions. Saralla White was a more
accomplished speaker, and wanted to confront her critics.
The event had been arranged in answer to charges levelled in
the documentary. I assume you saw the picket line of
anti-abortionists when you entered the building. They've
been here for almost a week, ever since the programme
aired. Orchestrating public outrage, as you put it, might
raise our profile in the art world, but in this case it's been
detrimental to ticket sales. Sensationalism is becoming old
hat; the public taste is turning back to more conservative
fare.'

It was tempting for Bryant to embroil himself in an
argument about the value of art, but he resisted for once,
restraining himself in order to concentrate on the immediate

problem. 'Rather appropriate, though,' he couldn't resist remarking. 'Someone recently described as "The Most Hated Woman in England" is found drowned in her own installation. Just think of the headlines you'll get. There should be queues around the block after this.'

'I don't care for your implication,' snapped Burroughs. 'This is a gallery, not a circus. I'm not interested in providing cheap thrills.'

Behind them, the folded, dripping body of Saralla White was winched from her own tank, and six foetuses turned slowly in the swirling fluid, as if silently signalling farewell to their creator.

'We have a witness.' Bimsley hiked a thumb back at the figure squatting on a bench in the corner of the café. 'I think he saw what happened, but he ain't saying much. Too shaken up.'

'Leave him to me,' suggested Longbright. Coaxing accounts from distraught members of the public was her speciality. Anyone disturbed by the sudden upsets of crime could find comfort in the maternal sexiness of her tightly buttoned bosom. 'What's the breakdown of this group?' She looked around the gallery café, mentally counting the hushed, fidgeting bystanders.

'Thirteen off-the-street visitors, seven more pre-booked. The place had only just opened to the public. Plus a class of fourteen children and their teacher. Six attendants. The woman standing by the coffee counter is the gallery's PR officer; she arranged the press event for Burroughs. Two admission staff, a barista in here, one cleaner clearing up after the press. That's it.'

'Who's the witness?'

'He's just a kid. Only looks about twelve years old, part of the class drawing in the gallery.'

'OK. Let's do the teacher first.' Longbright made her way over to a young man in jeans and white shirt patrolling around the seated boys. 'Mr Elliot Mason? You're in charge of these boys?'

Mason rose. With his knitted Kangol cap, soul patch and low-slung jeans, he appeared little older than his charges. He gave the sergeant a limp handshake. 'I handle the outings for this group – the Science Museum, the V & A, the British Library, stuff like that. Their regular master, Mr Kingsmere, was going to take today's class but he's off with food poisoning. A faulty prawn, apparently, though I remain unconvinced. I could have done without any trouble today.'

'Isn't this exhibition a bit too adult for children?' wondered Longbright.

'It's a progressive school. It favours the creative arts over competitive sports, but I think that's because they don't have their own playing field. And they're city kids – there's very little they haven't been exposed to. They get taken to most of the important plays and films. They're pretty adept at handling sophisticated themes.'

'Some of these boys look very young.'

'I think the youngest is thirteen, but he's exceptionally mature. Most are fifteen and sixteen. What happened in here? It's nothing to do with us, is it?' Mason's eyes held the faraway look of a dreamer whose ideals had yet to be compromised.

'There's been an incident, and we need to find out if anyone saw it happen. So, your class – it's a mix of different years. Isn't that unusual?'

'The field trips are graded according to the children's capacity for appreciation, not by their form levels.'

'Perhaps you could run me through your movements this morning, starting from your arrival?'

Mason looked around, checking the whereabouts of his charges. 'We got here at ten o'clock. The entry had been prearranged by the school, but it took a few minutes to sort out the groups because there was a press conference ending at the same time. I did a head-count and made them turn their mobiles off, and we took a walk through the gallery. I let the kids choose the installations they liked most, then set them drawing. They're keen artists. Sit them on the floor with a box of pencils and you usually have to drag them away.'

'So they were spread throughout the gallery in different rooms? How could you watch over them?'

'They're easier to keep an eye on when they're engrossed in an activity.'

'You spend the same amount of time with each group?'

'I try to, but you inevitably spend more with some than others.'

'I'm told one of the boys saw something.'

'Yes – Luke Tripp, over there. He was one of four or five kids in the main chamber. They were actually sketching the giant head, but he'd gone across to the tank and had started drawing that instead.'

'Do you mind if I talk to the group?'

'No, but try not to upset them. I could lose my job.'

'Don't worry, Mr Mason, I'm not going to provide them with any more information than I have to.' Longbright walked over and introduced herself to the row of boys dressed in blue and gold blazers. 'I'm Detective Sergeant Longbright, but call me Janice. What are your names?'

A thin, moody-looking sixteen-year-old raised a tentative hand. 'I'm Nicholas Gosling.'

'Daniel Parfitt,' said the small-boned boy with the bad complexion next to him. 'What happened? Somebody's died, haven't they?'

'Who are you two?' she asked the pair seated beside them, one slim and dark, with deep-set eyes, the other red-blotched and still carrying puppy fat.

'Jezzard and Billings, Miss.'

'When did you first know something unusual was going on?'

'We heard a splash and got up to see.'

They would have had to come around the corner to view the tank clearly.

'So all of you were in the alcove drawing the giant head?'

'Yes, Miss. Except Luke, who was drawing the tank.' Jezzard pointed down at one she had missed.

Janice knelt beside the youngest boy, bringing herself into his sightline. 'Hey there.' She checked Bimsley's notes. 'Luke Tripp, that's you?'

The child nodded faintly. He was small for his age, a pale bulbous head balanced on a pipe-thin neck, eyes staring intently at the drawing in his lap.

Longbright turned the page around and examined it. 'That's pretty good. Do you like art?'

Another mute nod.

'How come you decided to draw the big green tank instead of the giant head?'

'The babies looked easier to draw.' His voice was barely more than a whisper.

'It's a pretty big tank. Hard to get it all into one picture. I used to like drawing, but if something moved I could never catch it on paper. While you were drawing, did something move?'

Luke looked up at her with an innocence that would have been termed theatrical in anyone older. 'The lady came and talked to me,' he explained. 'She asked me what I thought of the babies. She said she designed them.'

'You mean she was the artist?'

'She got someone else to build them, but it was her idea. Conceptual artists never build their own installations, everyone knows that.'

'Oh.' Longbright felt as though she had just been put in her place. 'Then what happened?'

'She said people were annoyed with her because they didn't understand what she was trying to say. Then the man came up to her.'

'Which man?'

'I don't know.' The boy closed his sketch pad, but continued to stare at it.

'Luke, I need to get this right so I can picture it in my head. The other boys were on the far side of the chamber – you couldn't see them from where you were?'

'No, the tank is around the corner.'

'We were over there, Miss,' said Gosling, indicating the space below the giant head.

'OK. You were drawing alone, Luke. The lady came up and talked to you – did the man come in with her?'

'No, he came in afterwards, from behind the tank.'

'What did he look like?'

Luke smoothed the cover of the sketch pad. 'He was very big, like a painting. He lifted up the lady very gently and put her in the tank.'

That's ridiculous, thought Longbright. *He would have to have been eight feet tall.*

'You mean he just lifted her off the ground and lowered her in?'

'Yes.'

'Did she make a splash? Did she try to get out?' Longbright knew that the liquid in the tank had only spilled on two sides, suggesting she had barely struggled.

'No.'

'Which direction did the man come from?'

'The door, I suppose.'

Longbright glanced back. Anyone coming in through the door would have been spotted by everyone in the chamber, if they'd been facing the right way. But the boys had been lying on the floor, concentrating on their drawings, on the far side of the large sculpture.

'Do you think you could sketch this man for me? Exactly as you saw him?'

'I already did, Miss.'

'Can I see?'

Luke Tripp raised the cover of his pad and twisted the portrait towards her.

He had drawn a cape-clad highwayman in a tricorn hat, crimson ruff-collar, leather tunic and thigh boots, riding a great black stallion.

7

THE PRICE OF NOTORIETY

'Whenever the English build something enormous, the first thing they always do is have dinner inside it,' said Arthur Bryant. 'Throughout history, our councillors have dined in unlikely places like Constitution Arch and the Thames Tunnel, even inside the mastodon at the Crystal Palace prehistoric park, so you can imagine how many celebratory meals they must have had in here. I fancy it still smells of institutional cooking.' He sniffed disapprovingly. 'There's definitely an undertone of cabbage.'

Standing beside one another in the cool shadowed corridors of County Hall, silhouetted by the tall, dusty courtyard windows, the detectives could have been mistaken for elderly councillors themselves, stopping to confer about arcane LCC rulings. Few would have taken them for policemen, but from their earliest years they had dedicated their lives to the rebalancing of inequalities.

Their official biographer, who was still at work on a volume he feared would never be finished, had felt that Arthur Bryant was driven by a sense of distilled outrage, perhaps over the loss of his wife during the war, and by a temperament that prevented him from ever finding peace with anyone else. *Cherchez la femme* had been the biographer's maxim, but in this case nothing was quite that simple.

Bryant was an anomaly: a working-class academic who had positioned himself on the fringes of humanity, beyond a moral viewpoint. The fact that he studied people as if they were insects or igneous rocks was cited as a fault, but it was also his secret strength. While the men and women of the Metropolitan Police mopped spilt blood and wiped away tears, comforted and calmed the fearful, and locked up those who were a danger to themselves, Bryant never truly became involved; he lacked the basic emotional mechanism to do so. But he was no mere machine; distrusting scientific proof, he preferred to follow humankind's more overgrown paths, those instinctual routes he felt had been buried by modern reliance on technology. Criminals and victims were linked to the land, to history and to their own irrepressible natures; it was an unfashionable view, particularly in a country that was fast becoming disconnected from its past, but it proved ideal for the work of the Peculiar Crimes Unit.

John May, on the other hand, had successfully remained in contact with both his feelings and the tumbling mess of humanity surrounding him. In a sense, he was his partner's only link with the outside world. In return, Bryant gave him something May had never had: a sense of his place in the invisible world that lay beyond facts and statistics, a connection to the vanishing past.

'What do you think about this business?' John May asked quietly. 'The case is clearly within our jurisdiction. If the public start thinking they're not safe in museums and art exhibitions, the damage to other public institutions could be immeasurable.'

'Saralla White was hardly an ordinary member of the public, John. It will be important to stress that she was an employee of the gallery, and, from what I've heard, somewhat under the control of her ringmaster, Mr Burroughs. There's no question that we should take it on. This is either murder or the most public suicide I've ever come across. One is apt to suspect that drugs will be present in her system. How else could she die so calmly? We can certainly rule out an accident, unless she had decided to hang from the light fittings in order to change a bulb.'

'We can't afford another unsolved case at this point, Arthur. Any way you look at it, the scenario seems wildly unfeasible.'

'You always say that, but everything becomes unlikely when you analyse it. It's unlikely the planet still survives without having blown itself to bits. It's unlikely that society will reach a balance without murdering itself first, or that any of us will get through our lives without going mad. Open any newspaper on any day and you're confronted with unlikely crimes. What about the seventeen illegal Chinese cockle-pickers who drowned in Morecambe Bay? Or that fellow in Norfolk who suffocated his workmates in chicken slurry? What about that doctor who managed to kill over two thousand patients undetected, how likely is that?'

'All right, point taken,' agreed May, if only to head his partner off from a lengthy diatribe about the world's ills.

'A tenner a ticket, that's what the public are paying to be shocked at this exhibition, and now they've got something to be shocked about,' said Bryant. 'We need to wrap this up quickly, before any details slip out. I want Oswald Finch to get the body opened as soon as possible. What do you know about any of these artists?'

'Just what I gleaned from the TV documentary and the article in the *Guardian*. Calvin Burroughs seems to be more than just their mentor. He has complete control over his protégés, because he's invested a lot of time and money in his big three. They were all unknowns before he began grooming them for this new venture. His first discovery was also the oldest, Sharinda Van Souten. She's half-American, born in India, probably the most traditional member of the group. She built the giant entwined ceramic bodies at the far end of the gallery. She's been re-creating classical Indian statuary in the context of modern Indian society for some years now. It was Burroughs who encouraged her to place her figures in adventurous sexual poses, something that has brought censure from the present Indian government. They're pretty strong stuff for the uninitiated; the art pupils were allowed to see the figures but not to make sketches. Apparently the teacher was less worried about upsetting his kids than getting complaints from their parents. Van Souten also produced the *Burning Bride* statue that drew attention to attacks on Indian women by their husbands. She's fighting for new legislation dealing with the problem.'

They turned and began to head down the twisting corridor, moving deeper into the great wooden honeycomb.

'Burroughs' second find was McZee,' May continued, 'a former Glaswegian hip-hop artist who switched to multi-media art after studying psychologically repressive regimes. He couldn't get any more financial support in his native Scotland – some kind of long-running feud with his funding body – and came South. He's exploring the links between fear and power in the torture of political prisoners. Good stuff, solid and committed to human rights, but shocking all the same, and the right-wing press don't like some of the links he makes with members of the British Cabinet. He also created a piece modelled on Picasso's *Guernica* about trial without representation and entitled it *Guantanamo*, which has upset the American ambassador.

'Saralla White has the highest profile. Since she started sculpting, she's been living out her private life in the public eye, using various elements in her art – boyfriends, miscarriages, sexual traumas. She's a mouthy East-Ender with a couple of drug busts behind her, turned up drunk on TV, that sort of thing. Apparently, her mother was an illegal abortionist who was incarcerated in Holloway for a time in the sixties. The babies in the tank are intended to represent six abortions undergone by her friends, other artists whose lives would have been altered if they had become mothers. Saralla White is a liberal and is naturally pro-abortion, which opens her to attacks by the religious right and pro-family hardliners.'

'You're a mine of information, I'm glad you were paying attention,' smiled Bryant. 'I tend to fall asleep within minutes of Alma putting her TV on, but then she only watches shows about antiques and Welsh choirs. Think it was murder?'

'The fact that the PCU got the call suggests that somebody thought it was. Still, they delayed passing it over. It should have come through within minutes of the general emergency code going out, instead of sitting on a desk while the plods checked its validity.' The detectives made their way back along the passageways towards the main chamber. 'But I also think we might be looking at some crazed form of suicide. Anyone who purchases illegal abortions and places them inside an art installation might be considered unstable.'

Bryant's wry smile caught him by surprise. 'I don't think Saralla White was unstable. She's been a very clever young woman. She manipulated this controversy about the artwork herself.'

'You only saw the top half of the documentary, Arthur. How could you assume that?'

'Simple. The foetuses aren't real. They're painted plastic facsimiles, convincing enough but definitely sculpted. Anyone taking a few minutes to study the contents of the tank should be able to see that the same creases and folds of the limbs are repeated in several of the babies. They were all struck from the same basic mould. White was feeding the press a story they wanted to believe so badly that they rushed it into print without any detailed fact-checking. They're making sure that their readers are more interested in the lives of the artists than the artwork. No doubt Burroughs colluded by controlling access to photographers. The only other time most reviewers would have seen the piece is at the press show.'

'Suppose she went out of her way to find identical babies?'

'They're fake, John. I think she painted over polyurethane, which would require a petroleum-based coating. Chemistry caught her out. She hadn't counted on the reaction of the formalin compound on their painted surfaces. That's why the tank has turned cloudy. Burroughs might be a patron of the arts but he's also an opportunist. I'm betting he's in on her story. He'd already called a meeting with her to deal with the tank's contents. It's the price she had to pay for notoriety, a compromising deal with her patron.'

May stopped before the chamber and placed a restraining hand on his partner's shoulder. 'We don't know that yet. Let's talk to him again, and find these other two artists. Perhaps there was some professional jealousy between them. With someone like Saralla White, how do you separate her personal and public lives? Or her enemies from her friends?'

'It wouldn't be the first time someone had killed for the sake of art. What about the Water Room murders? Look how deeply artistic passions ran there.' Bryant checked his watch. 'How much longer can we keep everyone here for?'

'The children will need to be released soon. The rest should be good for another hour or so, if we get Janice to be nice to them. I'm sure you must be very excited. On a purely investigative level this one's right up your street. Impossible death, single point of entry, no motive, no suspects and a single witness who reckons the culprit was a man on a horse.'

'Oh, I don't get enthused about such things any more,' said Bryant, barely able to suppress the gleam of excitement in his eye. 'Locked-room mysteries are the inventions of dreadful novelists, more's the pity. Besides, there'll be a motive. You know how many homicides there were last year?'

'Eight hundred and seventy-two,' May replied without hesitation.

If Bryant was impressed, he didn't show it. 'Home Office figures show that 63 per cent of female victims and 40 per cent of male victims knew the main suspect in the case. Furthermore, around 60 per cent of those women and 12 per cent of the men were killed by a lover, partner or ex-partner, which proves how much more vulnerable women are from assault by a male attacker. We'll find a former lover with a grudge against White, and we'll be interviewing him in the next twenty-four hours, you wait and see.'

'I read the same Home Office document,' May countered. 'Those figures still leave a hefty percentage of motiveless murders. And stranger-homicides tend only to get column inches if the victim is a pretty girl, which leaves a lot of cases unnoticed and unsolved.'

'Come on, John, you know that stranger-crime is usually the result of coincidence. All it takes is a tiny fluctuation in the laws of chance, a decision to take one route home rather than another, and you get a random murder. How can we be expected to solve those?'

'Scotland Yard is always banging on about its 90 per cent murder-detection rate, but that means a lot of killers who might strike again are still wandering the city streets.'

Both detectives had a propensity to become evangelical about fighting crime, but in different ways. May's righteous anger was borne of a vocational desire to protect the innocent. Bryant was more concerned with understanding the moralities and beliefs of urban society. He feared that one day they would become incomprehensible to him, and had vowed to retire upon the realization.

'By the way, how did you manage to get here before me?' asked May suddenly.

'I was giving Victor a run, if you must know,' said Bryant, referring to the rusting yellow Mini Cooper that still sported a chain of vermilion daisies painted around its roof during the first Summer of Love.

'You told me the exhaust had fallen off.'

'It has.' Bryant looked at him blankly. 'What of it?'

'You can't drive it like that. It must sound like a Lancaster bomber.'

'That's right, I have to turn my hearing aid off while I'm driving, but at least people know I'm coming. I made a vicar jump into a hedge this morning. I was in Vauxhall visiting my psychochiropodist. She reads feet,' he explained. 'Apparently I'm about to have an unexpected brush with death. Either that or I've got a bunion. Let's go and see if Kershaw's discovered anything.'

8

LOCK AND KEY

They found Giles Kershaw stretched prone on the floor, taking digital shots of the green-tinged fluid samples splashed from the installation tank. 'The body will be nicely pickled in preservative, although contamination will throw off my tests,' he remarked, tearing off his plastic gloves and flipping them into a zip-bag. Scientifically trained officers tended to see crime victims as specimens, but the PCU staff cared to an unusual degree, despite how they sounded.

'What do you think is in the solution?' asked Bryant, thumping his stick against the tank.

'I'm a forensic pathologist, not an embalmer, but I can tell it's a pretty lethal chemical concoction. She wouldn't have lasted more than a few seconds after ingesting it, and the instinct to draw breath upon falling in would have paced up the poisoning process. The gallery should never have been allowed to leave so many litres lying around in an unsealed tank. It's like dumping an open barrel of toxic waste in a public place. If it got warm in here, the stuff could start evaporating into the atmosphere.'

'Good, that gives us something to hold Burroughs on,' said Bryant with relish. 'I didn't like the cut of his jib.

Matching silk tie and handkerchief, far too spivvy for my taste. What else have you got?'

'A couple of bootprints, black rubber soles, here and here.' Kershaw pointed to some thick streaks and crescents on the parquet. 'They tend to leave marks on this kind of wood flooring when someone's treading on the side of the shoe, or slipping, say in a scuffle.'

'That's not much to go on,' May complained. 'Could be anyone.'

'Not quite, old sausage.' Kershaw flicked a lick of blond hair from his eyes and pointed to the faint black print. 'These are motorcycle boots, a large size, possibly 45, 47. The striations at the edges, see here? The soles are designed for grip. I've come across this distinctive pattern before, River Road Men's Twin Buckle Engineer Boots, pricey and well-made. Feet spaced far apart but not running or jumping – the prints are too consistently light – so it's a pretty wide stride. Gives us a height of, oh, something between six one and six three. Big guy. Height's no real indication of strength, of course – a lot of tall people are rather weedy and hunched – but it's suggestive all the same. The corpse is heavy-set but quite short.'

'You're not telling me he could have thrown her into the tank like a shot-putter?' Bryant was incredulous.

'You're right, it doesn't seem very likely,' Kershaw admitted, tossing back his hair in an affected manner that annoyed Bryant intensely. 'She would have to have been rendered inert for him to achieve it, which begs the question: if White was unconscious, why would he bother to drown her, why not polish her off outside the tank?'

'Because the killer was making a point,' Bryant explained testily. 'He wanted her to be found floating inside her own artwork. A sense of drama, a bit of poetic justice. Surely that's obvious.'

'In which case you're talking about a pretty advanced

level of premeditation,' warned May. 'Let's not jump to conclusions until the post-mortem.'

They headed for the cafeteria, where Sergeant Longbright met them, handing over a chaotic stack of forms and leaflets. A siege mentality had settled across the gallery. The schoolchildren were being dismissed, while the remaining visitors slumped on uncomfortable steel chairs, complaining about being kept behind. 'Here are the basic statements,' said Longbright;. 'I had to do it longhand because my batteries have gone.'

'Serves you right. Notepads shouldn't be electronic,' Bryant sniffed. 'You never heard of a pencil going wrong.'

'I wrote everything on the backs of gallery guides, sorry about that. You can add your own notes at the bottom of each page. I'll type them up later.' Janice Longbright was no ordinary DS, but had an assortment of oddly developed talents, all focussed on the idea of pruning Bryant's chaotic scraps of investigative information into some cohesive form. She'd been doing it for years and getting no thanks, as her mother had before her. 'The visitors are getting pretty restless,' she warned. 'I've let them make calls to warn their families that they've been delayed, but no one's been allowed to leave the gallery. Colin has made up a simple floorplan. It should give you a rough idea of where everyone was when the body was discovered.'

Bryant squinted from the drawing to the gallery. 'You haven't got much sense of scale, have you?' he complained.

'I wasn't planning to submit it for the Royal Academy summer exhibition,' Longbright bridled.

'There's no need to get shirty.' He riffled through the witness statements. 'Anyone outside the main chamber hear a scream or a splash? It's pretty quiet in here.'

'That's because there's an ambient noise-cancellation system in operation.' Calvin Burroughs pointed up at a pair of small black speakers bolted into the corners of the room. 'It damps down background sounds and allows better

76

concentration. It also means that there's very little bleed-through from one room to the next.'

'Even so, two of the kids in the main chamber say they heard a shout.' Longbright checked through the statements and found the appropriate pages. 'Gosling and Parfitt. I interviewed them separately, they both said the same thing. A high-pitched cry, presumably a woman, short and sharp, nothing else.'

'And they didn't do anything?'

'They're teenagers, Mr Bryant. Eventually they decided to go and have a look, but it wasn't a very organized response.'

Bryant nodded at the crowd as he unwrapped a boiled sweet. 'Any men over six foot amongst that lot?'

'The teacher, Elliot Mason, I'd say he's about six one.'

Bryant peered over the coffee counter and checked out the teacher's shoes. 'Suede slip-ons, they're no good. Turn the place over, every cupboard and crawlspace, see if you can find any discarded clothes or footwear. You'll have to use the Met boys, I can't spare unit staff. I don't suppose there's anyone in here actually wearing motorcycle boots?'

Longbright shook her head. 'No, and no equestrians, either.' In reply to Bryant's quizzical look, she explained. 'I think our only witness has an overactive imagination. A boy called Luke Tripp, reckons some kind of horseman rode into the gallery, grabbed White and threw her into the tank. I told him he'd have to talk to you.'

Bryant looked over at the schoolchildren and blanched when he spotted their distinctive navy and gold blazers. 'Oh no,' he groaned. 'Not them. It's the school where I gave the lecture last week, St Crispin's. I can't talk to them. They'll be prejudiced against me.'

'These are the kids who barracked you?' grinned May. 'Don't tell me you're scared of them.'

Bryant unfolded a pair of filthy spectacles and squinted through them. 'I don't know if these are the exact ones, although that jug-eared homunculus over there looks familiar. But they're from the same school. They're bound to have heard what happened. John, couldn't I leave you to talk to them?' he wheedled. 'It's cold in here, I need to go somewhere and warm up.'

May and Longbright watched in amazement as Bryant tucked in his unravelling scarf and shuffled slowly from the cafeteria. 'Well, I've never seen him like this before,' said May, worried.

'I think they really got to him,' Longbright shrugged. 'He's convinced he's lost his touch. It's not a generation gap, it's a solid brick wall; he won't listen to the young, and they won't listen to him. You're the only person he'll take advice from, John. Can't you have a word, show him how it's done? If he cuts himself off like this, he'll become even more isolated.'

'Arthur always says he's too old to change. But he'll have to learn a few new tricks if we're going to get Leslie Faraday off our backs. The new minister is gunning for us. Take a look at this.' May unfolded a sheet of paper and passed it over.

Longbright read the memo. 'Where did you get this?'

'From Rufus.' May employed the young hacker to keep an eye on emails running between the Home Office's hopelessly insecure central server and the unit. 'Faraday's planning to make a name for himself by "clearing out the dead wood", as he calls it. The file corrupted as I downloaded it, so I lost the date and recipient, but I suspect Raymond Land has had a go at him about us. The last thing we need right now is Arthur providing them with more ammunition.'

Before Longbright could voice an opinion, Giles Kershaw came over to join them. 'Mr May, there's something you should see.' He held up a plastic bag and shook a flat metal key into the palm of his glove. 'Machine-cut brushed aluminium alloy, nicely stencilled and finished. No obvious fingerprints, but I'll run it under a spectroscope.'

'What is this?' asked May, squinting at the stencilled sections.

Kershaw took the key back, as if suspecting that May could not be trusted with it. 'A pictogram of some kind. Now watch.' He tilted the metal and angled his pocket torch over it. 'Set the light source to one side and it reveals a picture.'

They found themselves staring at a V-shaped outline of a mask topped with a tricorn hat.

'Where did you find it?' asked Bryant, intrigued.

'Placed right against the side of the tank, where I think it was intended to be found. He's left us a calling card. But look at the serrated edges. This isn't a standard configuration. It wouldn't fit any cylinder or mortise lock that I know of, so why cut it in the shape of a key at all? Besides, it would bend if you tried to twist it. And there's another thing. Check out the back.'

He turned over the card to reveal a row of numbers. '21. 9. 17. 05. He's set us a puzzle.'

May caught Longbright's eye and knew they were thinking the same thing. 'If there's one thing that will restore my partner's enthusiasm, it will be this,' he said. May remembered the first time he met Bryant, at the age of nineteen. The young trainee detective had asked him to decipher a message hidden in butterfly wings. 'Arthur may not know much about the young, but he knows an awful lot about breaking codes.'

9

PHANTOM IN THE NOOSE

Janice Longbright knelt on the wooden flooring and swept broken glass into a dustpan. Someone had kicked in the front door, popping the latch from the strike-plate, splintering the jamb from the brickwork. The lounge was trashed; the television and CD player were now just dusty dented boxes spilling bare wires. They had urinated in the bedroom, and split a sofa with a breadknife; pointless, random acts reeking of bitterness. A neighbour – young, single, nursing a sick daughter – had seen them, but had been too frightened to respond. The cheery constable sent over by Haringey nick had joked with his print-man as if enjoying a beer with him. The occasion was too ordinary to care about. Nurses were the same, chattering around terminal patients.

Longbright was sanguine about such thefts. No matter how many times the Mayor told residents that crime was his priority, she knew that it was the real price of living in London, paid by almost everyone during their tenure here. Insurance would cover the loss, but it could not replace the torn-up photographs of Gladys, her mother. When she spotted them in pieces on the floor, then, and only then, did she allow a brief tear to fall.

*   *   *

All police units are under-funded, but the PCU had been so broke for so long that the sudden budget increase they had experienced after the successful resolution of their last case had merely confused the staff. John May had upgraded the computers, Sergeant Longbright had bought a coffee machine and Arthur Bryant had purchased a set of highly inappropriate Aubrey Beardsley prints. Still, the improvement in the Morning Crescent offices was noticeable. There was decent computer software. There was a reception area. There was a sofa. There was a nasty smell in the bathroom, but as it stemmed from Bryant's abortive experiment to determine the burning point of horse hair, nobody knew how to get rid of it.

Janice Longbright caught up with her boss on Monday afternoon, as he was about to enter the unit's interview room.

'Where have you been?' asked May. 'I've been phoning you for the last half-hour.'

'Sorry, Chief, my flat was burgled at lunchtime. Some little sod kicked the door in and stole my telly. I was waiting for the K-Town cop shop to send someone around.'

'Can you not refer to Kentish Town by its gangster name? And why on earth didn't you get Banbury to come over?' asked May, amazed.

'Wouldn't like to pull rank. Not fair on other people.' Longbright tucked a lacquered curl back into place and thrust out her formidable chest. 'Hope I'm not too late.'

'No, they just arrived. Come in.'

May and Longbright seated themselves beside Luke Tripp and his immaculately tailored mother. It was intended that the sergeant would gently coax the boy into providing a more detailed description, but one look at Mrs Tripp's face forced them to change tactics. May ran through the legal ramifications of the statement, then let Longbright placate the unhappy parent.

'Your son is the only witness to this crime,' she explained.

'Nobody else saw the man he described anywhere in the vicinity of the building. That's why we need him to provide exact details of the event.'

'You're suggesting he's a liar.' Mrs Tripp turned to her son. 'Luke, darling, you don't have to tell them anything if you don't want to. They're not real policemen.'

'It's true we're not bound by the rules of the Metropolitan Police Force, Mrs Tripp, but we have other powers granted by the Home Office that you may find quite draconian if we choose to enforce them. I think it's easier for everyone if Luke just tells us, in his own words, exactly what he saw.'

'Is that a threat?' asked Mrs Tripp. 'My husband's in a senior management position at Sotheby's. He'd have something to say about this.'

'That's fine, Mrs Tripp. We'll be happy to accept his advice if we need a Ming vase valued, but as far as your son is concerned, we'd like to get to the truth.'

'I don't care for sarcasm.' Mrs Tripp smoothed her son's hair. 'Luke is an only child. He's highly sensitive. When he was little, all his friends wanted to be pilots and firefighters. Not my boy. His big dream is to star in his own play at the Royal Court Theatre. He paints, he sings, he loves listening to Donizetti. Although he looks young, he's nearly fourteen. An experience like this could seriously affect his school performance. The man he saw was a murderer.'

'That's why Sergeant Longbright is here,' May explained. 'She's trained to deal with precisely this kind of delicate situation.'

'Then the sergeant alone should talk to my son.'

This was precisely what May had wanted. 'Fine, I'll be outside if you need me,' he said quietly, rising to leave.

Longbright left a respectful pause until after the door had closed. 'Perhaps we could go back to the moment when your class first arrived at the gallery, Luke,' she suggested.

*   *   *

Arthur Bryant's office was starting to look like a collision between a greenhouse, a secondhand bookshop and a cryptozoological museum. Shoving aside the dead cactus Raymond Land had angrily returned (Bryant had placed it in the Acting Head's office as a gift, but it had germinated poisonous seeds that left purple stains everywhere; finally, in desperation, Land had sprayed it with lighter fluid), he adjusted his spectacles and studied the numbers on the aluminium key again.

'Well, obviously it's a date,' he said finally. '21. 9. 17. 05. The twenty-first of September, 1705. I have a book of historical dates somewhere.' Seated at his green-leather desk beneath a pool of amber light, he appeared to have regained some of his former confidence. He rattled an aniseed ball against his false teeth as he took down a gilt-edged volume of British history and began leafing through it.

'Hmm, work began on Blenheim Palace, War of the Spanish Succession, the Queen of Prussia died, nothing very relevant there. Queen Anne would have been on the throne, but we need something more localized, something . . .' A smile crept across his face. 'I think we need to schedule a staff meeting,' he told Kershaw.

At four p.m., all members of the PCU staff were summoned to its freshly painted briefing room. April sat nervously at the rear, until coaxed to a front seat by her grandfather. She had no idea what to expect from her new job, except that its daily operations would prove unorthodox. The senior detectives preferred to conduct discussion groups before assigning work to their colleagues. According to Bryant, creativity was the key to criminal investigation, not data control. Most Met officers found his theories ludicrous, and argued that his effectiveness was the result of blind luck.

April looked expectantly around the room, wondering what would be demanded of her. Crippen threaded his way between her legs, looking for affection. The moulting feline belonged to Maggie Armitage, the unit's affiliated information source for all crimes involving elements of witchcraft or psychic analysis, but she had loaned Crippen to Bryant indefinitely because he had given her accordionist fleas.

'Our first officially recorded briefing session,' Bryant began, dragging a polychromatic scarf from the rack and knotting it around his throat. 'It marks the start of a new level of efficiency and professionalism here at the PCU. Would anyone like a sherbet lemon? There are flying saucers and Liquorice Allsorts as well.' He shook the box of childhood confectionery and dumped it out on the table before him. While Longbright was serving tea, Bimsley tipped his chair too far back and fell off it. Meera tapped her pen impatiently and shot him a filthy look.

'I hope you've all had a chance to look at the initial report?' May's question cued paper-rustling and murmurs. 'I've just been talking to Raymond Land, and he informs me that the White murder has been given Signal Crime status.' Signal crimes were criminal acts that garnered a disproportionate amount of publicity, sending out disturbing signals to the public about the unsafe state of society. They were required to be dealt with quickly and quietly, before faith in the national policing system sustained damage. 'Given its high profile, we'll need to clear the decks here for at least forty-eight hours, so Janice will help reprioritize your outstanding casework. White's death has already made the news, and there'll be plenty more to come, especially if we fail to find leads. I've appointed Dan Banbury to act as press liaison officer.'

The stocky, crop-headed crime-scene manager turned to the rest of the group. 'Before we start running through witnesses and suspects, a bit of media news. As you know, the unit can't afford bad publicity after receiving increased funding. We'll have Shadow Cabinet MPs screaming like stuck pigs. We've not scheduled an official press conference yet, but they'll be doorstepping White's family and friends for opinions as I speak.

'The tabloids are all planning to take the same tack: crazy artist used state funding to fling a pot of paint in the public's face, made enemies wherever she went, basically deserved what she got. The *Guardian*, *The Times* and the *Independent* want to ask the bigger questions about safety and security in public places. They'll run interviews with abortion opponents, and speculate on internecine troubles within the art world. There's been a suggestion that Saralla White may have had a stalker. Ever since she got plastered on national television, she's been painted as a bad girl in the press. She also appeared in a notorious nude photo-shoot for *Loaded* magazine, and released internet footage of herself having sex with a male friend in the toilets at Claridges, no less. She was good at deflecting criticism, and apparently referred to the last act as "guerrilla art" and "a political statement". She's had trouble in the past, and there's also the question of her own medical history.'

'What do we know about that?' asked May.

'She was sectioned twice in her early twenties, and has a history of substance abuse, mostly alcohol and amphetamines,' said Longbright, checking her notes. 'Her body's being released to Oswald for examination later today.' Oswald Finch, the unit's pathologist, was an ancient professional doomsayer who took delight in refusing to retire. Goading Bryant into a state of apoplexy was one of the things that kept him alive. 'Arthur, perhaps you'd like to look in on Finch?'

'Nothing would give me less pleasure.' Bryant peered in annoyance over the top of his reading glasses.

'Dan has half a dozen more interviews tabled for this afternoon,' continued Longbright. 'John, you mentioned meeting with an anti-abortion group?'

'That's right.' May rose to his feet and drew on the white wipe-clean board behind him. 'Murders carried out by anti-abortionists are more prevalent in North America than here – they've had thousands of criminal acts committed at abortion clinics since Roe *v.* Wade.'

Mangeshkar raised a hand. 'What's that?'

'The 1973 legalized-abortion ruling, Meera. At the extreme end of violent incidents visited on pro-abortionists we get high-profile bombings, anthrax threats, knife attacks and shootings. The links here are interesting, because such acts are often organized by websites, and strongly tied into the religious right.'

'Which explains the lower incidence in England,' interrupted Bryant. 'We have far fewer active Christian fundamentalists here. These sites, like the Army of God network, also incite racist and homophobic attacks, and are known to target Islamic groups. They talk about the slaughter of God's children. This, I suspect, is the main reason why Raymond wants us to give the case highest priority. I can't help wondering if he's had some kind of tip-off from the Home Office. George W. Bush is coming to London next month, and his administration banned a number of abortion procedures, as well as reducing federal funding to organizations that perform abortions. Faraday may well be concerned about political leaders drawing links with the murder.'

'We don't know that, Arthur.' May disliked his partner's habit of forming speculative connections, but was usually powerless to stop him. 'Let's stick to the basic facts for now.'

Bryant dug about for his pipe, saw numerous pairs of eyes facing him and thought better of it. 'Fine by me,' he told them. 'Here are some facts you might like to consider. One, the Burroughs Gallery has a single entrance through which every visitor must pass. They can't be admitted to the artworks without a barcoded, timed ticket. Without the ticket, the main glass doors can't be opened.

'Two, the register has been tallied and matches the exact

number of visitors County Hall received yesterday morning. The employees have their own passes, all of which are accounted for. If any of them had arranged to slip someone else into the gallery, the counter clerks seated on either side of the narrow entrance hall would have seen them, and besides, they wouldn't have been able to access the main gallery.

'Three, there are two emergency fire exits, neither of which, according to Mr Banbury here, has been opened in several days. There are no keys missing, and no signs of forced entry. All the windows are designed to open no more than three inches, due to health-and-safety regulations.

'Four, in order to enter the octagonal central chamber and kill Saralla White, the murderer would have had to pass through at least two other rooms. All of the rooms were occupied by several visitors, but nobody passed them. There were even some occupants in the main chamber, schoolkids drawing at the far end of the room – but they didn't see anything. Which just leaves sensitive little Luke Tripp sitting near the tank when it happened, and he has maintained a consistent story – despite some probing trick questions from Janice here – that he saw a horseman in funny old clothes ride up on a glossy phantom stallion and make off with the nice lady.

'Finally, we have this.' He held up the bag containing the aluminium key. 'The attendants swear it wasn't there when they opened up. A stencilled pictogram of a man's masked face, and he's wearing a tricorn hat, just as Luke said he was.' Bryant tried to sound annoyed, but everyone could see the excitement in his eyes. 'On the other side of it is a date, the twenty-first of September, 1705. It's this date that convinces me young Luke Tripp isn't lying, or even mistaken in what he saw. On this day, an Essex butcher's wife gave birth to a legendary criminal, one Richard Turpin. So now we have a physical description of the man for whom we are meant to be searching.' Bryant conveniently ignored the fact that the highwayman had died over two hundred and sixty years earlier. 'Etchings of Dick Turpin depict him at around twenty-six years of age, in a wig and tricorn, fresh-coloured features scarred with smallpox, broad cheekbones, narrow chin, at least five feet nine inches tall, broad-shouldered, powerfully built. He was arrested for horse-stealing and executed at York on the seventh of April, 1739. So what do we have? A politically sensitive situation, an impossible crime, a murky motive, no obvious leads and a suspect who's been dead for nearly three centuries. Although of course we might simply be searching for a phantom who models himself on a hanged highwayman. I think you can see why the call came through to us.'

'This means that we've been given another chance to screw up in front of our peers,' warned May. 'No one is to make a move without clearance from Mr Bryant or myself. Any questions at this juncture?'

'You don't think this is some kind of set-up?' asked Bimsley. 'I mean, to make the unit look bad.'

'I can think of a dozen easier ways to do that,' said May.

April raised a tentative hand. 'Are you speaking to Ms White's former lovers? There's been quite a lot of acrimonious stuff printed about them in the papers lately, because of her abortions.'

'If you have any useful news items, I'd like to read them.'

'Calvin Burroughs was having an affair with her, that's why she . . .' April looked around and shrank back into her seat. 'Sorry.'

'Please, if you've heard anything, April, you must share it with us. And that goes for all of you. We'll be interviewing her fellow artists, her work colleagues and anyone who was close to her. Janice has task-lists to distribute. Let's get started.'

As the meeting broke up, Bryant lit a surreptitious pipe

at the window, and allowed his thoughts to wander to nooses and duelling pistols. Most of all, he wondered why anyone would link themselves to an almost forgotten breed of British criminal, and what they might gain by doing so.

10

VULNERABILITY

He stood above London and surveyed his rainswept domain.
The black cape cracked about his boots, and the wind
tried to tear the tricorn from his head. The brief heatwave
had quickly broken and the city had begun a slow slide into
winter. Flat-bottomed clouds the colour of charcoal scraped
the peaks of the city's financial towers. Great planes of
shadow darkened the postwar concrete of the blocks behind
Smithfield, endless grey buildings medievally arranged. From
here, the city looked like an arrangement of giant filing
cabinets finished in the colours of the office: silver, paper
and steel. It was oddly homogenous in the face of indifferent
planning, as though its spirit was deliberately seeking to
impose order on chaos.

He stood astride the parapet but could not yet be seen, for
he did not exist.

'I say, do we have any money?' asked Giles Kershaw,
flicking a flop of blond hair out of his eyes as he peered
around the door.

'I wish you'd go to a barber. You look like a footballer.
What do you want money for?' asked Bryant, crinkling his
eyes suspiciously.

'I want to run some more thorough tests on the aluminium key, which will necessitate an omnibus trip to the delightful borough of Peckham and an exorbitant invoice for the use of their equipment.'

'Give it here. I'll show you how we used to do it in the old days.' Bryant pulled his antelope-horn magnifying glass from a drawer and twisted an anglepoise lamp into position.

'Really, Mr Bryant, I hardly think—'

'I know, that's your problem, old sock, coupled with an over-reliance on technology. What is it you're looking for?'

'That's precisely the point, Mr Bryant. I don't have to go in with a prepared agenda, electronic examination will tell me what there is to see.' Kershaw snatched back the bag. 'A magnifying glass might have been good enough in the olden days, but it's not now. All I need you to do is sign the evidence out and wait until I deliver my report.'

There was a time when Bryant would have argued the point until dusk, but the humiliating circumstances of his recent lecture continued to crimp his confidence. Perhaps Kershaw was right. May had long insisted on the importance of modern technology in criminal investigations. What point was there in clinging to past habits? 'Fine,' he sighed. 'Run it through your spectromolo-thingie, you'll probably find out a lot more than I would. Just remember to fill out your documentation.'

Kershaw seemed taken aback, disappointed almost. 'Oh,' he said, nonplussed. 'Thanks.'

He took off quickly, before Bryant could change his mind, squeezing past John May in the hall.

'What's the matter, Arthur?' asked his partner. 'You look like you've lost a shilling and found sixpence.'

'Will you show me how to work the computer properly?' Bryant nodded curtly at his new laptop.

'Of course not. In between asking lots of fantastically annoying questions, you'd find a way to destroy the unit's intranet, and I'd end up killing you.' Bryant's talent for spreading malignant plagues through the most benign technical equipment had made him an object of terror among IT technicians. 'Besides, you don't need to know. You've got me to do it for you.'

Bryant fingered the frayed edge of his corduroy waistcoat, purchased at the Gamages summer sale of 1948. 'I thought perhaps you could show me websites, you know, about music and celebrities – the sort of things young people like.' *Young people* was in italics, like a tropical disease or a new species of fern.

'So that's what this is about.' May could not resist an inward smile. 'You have a team who are paid to research that sort of thing, so that you can stick to what you're good at.' Bryant was usually convinced he was right in the face of unshakeable odds. This new doubting demeanour was unsettling. 'Delegation,' May concluded feebly. 'Let someone else do it for a change. You've devoted your life to this place. You've paid your dues.' But he could tell that Bryant thought he was being put out to pasture, and had no way to convince him otherwise.

'Cool gaff,' said Colin Bimley, admiring the red-brick exterior of the double-fronted house while they awaited an answer. 'She's got a bob or two. When I get promotion, I'm going to get on the property ladder.'

Meera Mangeshkar snorted derisively. 'Yeah, right. From a rented bedsit in Stoke Newington to a two-million-pound townhouse in Holland Park.'

'Sneer all you like, mate. You'll be sorry you turned me down one day. I'm not going to be slapping the sidewalk in a padded parka for the rest of my life.'

'No, you'll be sitting at a cheap desk filing reports and dropping bits of burger into the keyboard of a seven-year-old computer, before going down the local for eight pints of bitter and a curry with the lads.'

Colin subjected his colleague to intense scrutiny. 'I don't

know what makes you so sarcastic, but it's incredibly unattractive.'

Mangeshkar sniffed. 'So now I'm ugly.'

'What do you care what I think? You've already told me I'm not good enough for you.'

'I never said that.'

'So will you go on a date with me?' Colin asked, sensing a gap in her defence.

Before Meera could answer, the front door opened.

'I don't know where she got this new identity from,' said Eleanor White. 'Certainly not from us.'

'What do you mean, new identity?' asked Meera, setting aside her notepad.

Mrs White fell silent, distracted by something fluttering past in the garden. The lawn was an absurd shade of countryside emerald that could still be seen in expensive parts of the city. 'This working-class thing,' she said finally, sniffing drily and turning from the windows. 'Her name was Sarah, you know. Perhaps she thought "Saralla" sounded more exotic. She dropped out of Oxford. She was training to be a biochemist. We didn't hear from her for two years. Can you imagine how that made us feel?'

Meera was in danger of sinking in the immense floral sofa. She felt suffocated by the arrangements of dried flowers, the emetic purples and greens, the gathered flounces of material around the tables and curtains. A woman like Mrs White cut little ice with her, even if she had just lost a daughter. She belonged to a breed of county women who dwelt in bay-windowed Edwardian villas and never showed emotion to those they perceived as social inferiors. Meera had grown up in a battery of pebbledashed Peckham council flats where the sound of police sirens bounced nightly off the balcony walls.

'She reappeared when she had run out of money, of course.' Eleanor White tapped out a cigarette and lit it.

'Living in an East End squat with some other so-called artists, including the one who made her pregnant. Casually announced that she was a sculptor, if you please, not that she'd had any formal training. Didn't look like she'd had a bath or a hot meal in months. My husband Patrick refused to give her a penny, but I couldn't let her leave the house without something. She was our only child. The next time we saw her was on the television, drunk, swearing at a man who had once interviewed President Nixon. Then that disgusting magazine photo-spread, her sex life revealed, the abortion, and the rest I don't even want to think about. Patrick won't have the subject mentioned in the house. Soon afterwards we started hearing that her – installations, is that what you call them? – were fetching record prices with private collectors.'

'You must have taken some pride,' Meera wondered, 'at least, in her success.'

'Pride?' Mrs White was horrified by the idea. 'To have our name dragged through the mud? To see such muck being sold to the public? There are plenty of other ways to be successful. An animal can be seen rutting in a farmyard, but that doesn't make it talented. She became famous for exposing details about her private life that no decent wife would share with her husband, it was nothing to do with having artistic talent. We were deeply ashamed of her.'

And you're more ashamed than ever now, thought Meera. *She died before you could find a way to call a truce.* 'Can you think of anyone who might have wanted to harm her? A former boyfriend? Someone who hated her work? Perhaps even someone who felt jealous of her fame?'

'There were plenty of boyfriends. The artist, and her supposed mentor. She left the first one when she started to make sales.'

'Do you remember his name?'

'Oh, it was something strange and made up, the way they do.' Mrs White stopped. 'Don't give me that disapproving look, young lady. You think I'm just one of those un-demonstrative Englishwomen who never showed her daughter love. But it wasn't like that. We only ever wanted her to be happy. Of course we hoped she would share our values, even if she considered them old-fashioned. We believe in dignity, honesty and Christian kindness – there's nothing so unusual in that, is there? Some emotions require privacy. Why would she want to throw it all back in our faces? I don't understand.' Her fingers traced the outline of a photograph on the side table. 'I still can't believe our sweet little girl changed into such a monstrous person. This is a terribly poisonous time to be young.'

Meera realized that Mrs White was ashamed to be seen crying, and watched with a softening heart. 'We'll talk to everyone who knew her,' she promised. 'We have every hope that her killer will be found. We'll try to give you back your little girl.'

But she wondered if such comforting words were true. It was the lonely who left themselves open to attack. Eleanor White's daughter had been insulated by a public life and a large circle of friends. It made her death all the more unlikely, and the chance of discovering its cause almost impossible.

They left Eleanor White sitting in her floral lounge, bewildered and diminished, surrounded by the silver-framed memories of a daughter she now realized she had never tried to understand.

11

DEPARTING SOUL

'Ah, there you are,' said Arthur Bryant, strolling into the damp converted school gymnasium in Bayham Street that passed for an autopsy room. To combat the falling temperature, he had swiped a shapeless brown rollneck sweater from the unit's evidence room that made him look even more like a de-shelled tortoise.

'Where else would I be, seeing as my rehousing request has been declined?' Oswald Finch, the unit's pathologist and the only man on the force older than Bryant, straightened his bony back with a series of audible clicks, scowling at the covered body in his aluminium trough. His permanent look of disdain had left him with a face like a sepia photograph that had been crumpled up and flattened out again.

'Yes, I heard about the refusal. I'm afraid it's the new Home Office chap, Leslie Faraday. He's been appointed to oversee the operation of all specialist units, and isn't happy about our meagre budget rise. The usual story, he's never been too ambitious, but now he fancies making a name for himself. I daresay he thinks he can do so by getting us closed down in the ruthless drive for efficiency. It's the unsolved cases; we've too many on our books. It makes him look bad.'

'Of course it does,' Finch barked. 'Good God, look at your resources, they're embarrassing. You've no crime lab of your own, you're forever cadging equipment downtime from the Met. We live in an era of DNA matches, environmental signature indices and psychological profiling, and you're still sullying crime scenes with your sausage fingers and poking about in filthy old books on Wiccan mythology. You're a living anachronism, Bryant. The only grant you're likely to get will be from the National Trust: Upkeep of Ancient Monuments.'

Coming from a man who swore he was present at the first demonstration of television, this was a bit rich. Finch fluttered his long, delicate fingers at the walls. 'Look at this place. I could go to the police about the ventilation, except we *are* the police. The extractors are the same ones they used when it was still a prep school. The cover fell off the one overhead and nearly brained me, and it still hasn't been fixed. If it got too hot the teachers simply opened the windows, but we can't do that with decomposing bodies around. Human fat sticks to everything, you know, and the smell lingers for ever. No woman will come near me.'

'You're wrong there, Oswald. Nobody at all will come near you.'

'That's it, laugh at my expense while you still can. My job is about accumulating facts. One inaccurate detail compounds itself until the entire case collapses. It's not possible to be accurate about anything in here. And without factual evidence, everything else is just conjecture. It's all right for you to play arcane guessing games, but my reputation is on the line. I've tendered my resignation to Raymond Land. I've had enough. I'm buying a smallholding in Hastings and will see out my days there alone, an embittered untouchable.'

'If you have to pick a leper colony, I suppose Hastings is as good as any.' Bryant stuck an exploratory finger in his ear and wiggled it, thinking. 'Will you have a leaving party?'

'What's the point? I hate chocolate cake, and I don't suppose there's anyone left to even buy me a card. All my friends are either dead or not feeling very well.' He stared gloomily into his dissecting tray.

Bryant checked his finger, then dug in his pocket for a sherbet lemon. The smell of the room was starting to get to him. 'What can I do to perk you up?'

'Find me an assistant. I'm not supposed to leave an unpacked body unattended. My bladder's a colander. What if I need to go for a wee?'

'I didn't realize you'd become incontinent as well. Every minute we're getting older. Flesh fails, hairs turn grey, we crumble to pieces as the world regenerates, so why not be happy in the knowledge that we'll all inevitably fall to bits? Why do you always see the gloomy side of everything?'

'Oh, I don't know, it's probably a side effect of spending the last half-century surrounded by dead people.'

Bryant squeezed his eyebrows together in concentration, racking his brain for something cheerful to say. 'I know. I've been meaning to mention this for ages. You remember Nugent?'

'Your ostracod?' Finch's eyes strayed to the corner of his workspace, where for four years a tall glass of water had stood untouched. One day, Bryant had turned up with an object that looked like a hairy yellow oyster sitting in a tumbler of liquid. He had explained that it was a rare bivalve, a primitive form of mollusc taken from the Thames, and that they needed to keep it alive for an experiment the unit was conducting. Finch had named it, and assiduously fed the creature from an eyedropper containing a nutrient solution every day for four years, until one morning he had come in to find the glass empty, whereupon he was informed by Bryant that he had overdosed it and ruined the experiment. Finch had carried the guilt with him ever since.

'What about it?' he asked.

'Nugent didn't die,' said Bryant airily. 'It wasn't an ostracod. It was a mango seed.'

'You are *utterly impossible*,' sputtered the pathologist.

'Oh, don't be such a spoilsport. I've done worse things. I switched Raymond Land's verucca cream for superglue last month; it took him several hours to get his shoes off. There you are, you're more like your old self already.'

'I suppose it was you who unscrewed the handle of my brain knife as well. I was taking the lid off an Archway Bridge jumper and the damned thing nearly took my eye out.'

'Not my suicide from last week? Why were you examining his skull?'

'One of your lads discovered that he'd stopped in the street to complain of a headache just before he made the leap. I wondered what sort of pain would drive a man to jump from a bridge, and looked for a tumour. He had a morbid fear of hospitals and hadn't been near one in years. There was a growth on his brain the size of a duck egg, large enough to re-open a suture in his skull. It had been caused by a rare parasite, cystercosis, caught on a business trip to Mexico.'

Finch's great strength, even at his advanced age, was an enquiring, restless mind. He liked tidy endings and sought resolutions to everything, which was why Bryant's un-fathomable moods annoyed him so much. 'You play these ridiculously childish tricks on me without any sense of risk or responsibility,' he complained.

'You shouldn't take life so seriously,' said Bryant. 'Think of it like pipe tobacco. It's dark, bitter and finally destroys you, but provides a few moments of heaven on the tongue.'

'And it can make you ill,' snapped Finch. 'There's a woman on my table who died in her late twenties for no good reason I can think of. If I don't take her seriously, who will?' Finch did not appreciate that the detectives took death very seriously indeed.

'All right,' conceded Bryant. 'Let's see what you've got.'

Finch unwrapped the corpse from a foil bag that gave it the unfortunate appearance of a giant Marks and Spencer ready meal. 'Well, it wasn't technically drowning,' he told Bryant, 'although there's liquid in her air passages and the lungs are swollen. She was poisoned by the liquid in the tank. It sent her into laryngeal spasms the moment she swallowed it. I couldn't wait around for the preliminary composite breakdown to come back, so I knocked up a couple of my own tests. It's a mixture of synthetic preservative, water, vegetable dye and some form of antibacterial weedkiller that was meant to keep the tank clean but reacted with the objects in it, causing the clouding and increasing the potency of the poison. It's also flammable.'

Finch stepped back from the body-tray with his head on one side. 'Getting her into the tank, though, that's the thing, isn't it? No defence marks on her hands, arms or shins, and your man Kershaw tells me there were no scuffs on the glass, so she went over cleanly and without a fuss. I don't have to tell you that this is very unlikely in any circumstances. I understand there were no ladders or chairs, nothing for the killer to stand on.'

Bryant scratched the end of his bulbous nose, thinking. 'Therefore we have three options. One, she went willingly into the liquid, which we have to rule out for the simple reason that she knew its potentially lethal composition. Two, she was hurled into the tank during some kind of argument, which at least a dozen visitors to the gallery would have overheard. Three, she was knocked unconscious or sedated first. So what have you checked for?' Bryant always knew when Finch was holding something back.

'Puncture marks. I agree that sedation has to be the answer, something fast-acting. It would have made her a dead weight, of course, harder for someone to lift and throw, but at least she wouldn't have been fighting. I was hoping to find evidence that she was injected prior to immersion, but there's nothing.'

'What do you mean, nothing?' Bryant was appalled. There was always something to discover. That's what pathologists were for.

'You're expecting me to find a grain of sand stuck in her earhole and match it up to one on the killer's boot. I'm afraid it doesn't happen like that. I'm sorry, this isn't some Hollywood police show, you know.'

Bryant cast his eyes around at the dated equipment and water-stained walls. 'I'm painfully aware of that.'

'I know it's boring for you, but there's nothing of interest here. I checked for wrist bruising, something to show she'd been hoisted by her extremities, but there's nothing at all.'

'Are you absolutely sure?' asked Bryant. 'She doesn't look right.'

'Of course she doesn't look right, she's brown bread. Dead people rarely look like themselves. What they look like is what they've been lying on; thanks to hypostasis I can give you the death position and the contact surface, providing the body is Caucasian and hasn't been moved for a while, but this one's a floater, so I can't even do that.'

'You think she was lifted kicking and screaming, then chucked bodily into the tank? The killer must have had at least one hand over her mouth, otherwise the whole gallery would have heard her, even with the electronic sound-dampers.'

'I suppose she could have been chloroformed, but if she had time to draw breath you'd have to be strong, in order to hold her until she was forced to breathe. I've known struggling time to last anything up to four minutes.'

'What about the physical strength required? What are we looking for? A Russian shot-putter?'

'I heard you're after a man on a horse.' Finch's disconcerting smirk reminded Bryant of Lon Chaney trying out a new look in his make-up mirror.

'We have a small child who's an unreliable witness. Like most imaginative children, he probably has a history of telling fabulous lies.'

'All I know is that she became immersed in the tank, drew a breath, swallowed and died. How your man did it is a mystery I've no interest in solving. What more can I do? I'll need to send away liver and lung samples, as well as ingestion residue for toxicology analysis. They can run some immunoassay and chromatography tests. There might have been an allergic reaction, I suppose. Obviously, it's not something I can handle in this dump. I hate to admit it, but I'm as out of my depth as she was.'

'Perhaps we both are,' agreed Bryant. He was usually forming some kind of opinion by now, no matter how ridiculous or bizarre it seemed, but today he felt utterly lost.

'One other thing I should mention,' said Finch. 'It doesn't impinge on the circumstances of her death, but you should know she was pregnant.'

'You're joking.'

'I'm not the kind of man who jokes,' Finch reminded him.

'She was dead set against having children at this time, campaigning in favour of abortion. How far gone?'

'I'd say about fourteen weeks.'

'The abortion laws are pretty restrictive.' Bryant knew that women required signatures from two doctors before they could access abortion services. 'I'll see if she made any enquiries.'

'She'd been there before,' said Finch, snapping off his gloves and binning them.

Bryant uncovered Saralla White's face. Usually, he did not care to see features from which life had fled, but he was hoping to find some clue in any remaining shred of spirit. 'In the notes on her artwork, Saralla White was pushing for abortion on demand with a single doctor's signature. It was a subject she felt strongly about. Suppose she fought over the termination with her boyfriend? That would give us a suspect.'

'There's the difference between us,' said Finch. 'You think about suspects. I think about the victim. There's more to life than finding who's to blame.'

'This isn't about life, Oswald,' Bryant reminded him.

Finch did not take kindly to being challenged. 'You might have a word with your man Banbury,' he said, changing the subject. 'I do bodies, not clothes.'

'What do you mean?'

'He delivered her corpse fully dressed. I thought we'd agreed that it's not my job to undress them.'

'Why did he do that?'

'Oh, something about her outfit. She was wearing a sort of bandsman's tunic, silver buttons all the way down the front. Banbury thought if the killer had been forced to manhandle her over the wall of the tank, he might be able to lift partials from them.'

'I hope he took prints from everyone who was in the gallery.' Bryant covered White's face once more, disappointed by what he saw. 'There's nothing here.'

'What did you expect to find? Strands of ectoplasm wending heavenward as the soul departs?' asked Finch sarcastically.

'We once believed the eyes caught the last image seen in life,' said Bryant sadly. 'It's natural to seek answers in the face.'

'Then it was a waste of time looking.' Finch started to cover the rest of the body.

'It's never a waste of time,' said Bryant. 'Even taking into account that her facial muscles have relaxed, I would have thought there'd be some indication of stress in the features. She looks calm. She was caught by surprise and died quickly, without undue pain. That's all any of us can ask.'

'That's unusually morbid of you,' Finch sniffed. 'You were due to have your first intimation of mortality about

103

forty years ago. Don't tell me it's finally caught up with you.'

He expected the elderly detective to come back with a stinging rejoinder, and was amazed when Bryant walked quietly and thoughtfully from the room.

12

THE BARRIER OF YOUTH

John May stood on the worn steps of St Crispin's Senior School, St John Street, Clerkenwell, and studied the building's facade, a fuss of railings and crenellations, stone urns, wreaths, garlands, 'improving' mottoes and blunted statuary depicting Christian martyrs. Above the door, letters cut into a single block of white Portland stone read 'FOUNDED IN THE YEAR OF OUR LORD, 1685'. Through one of the double-height central windows, May could see a dozen pupils hunched in the pale light of their computer terminals.

'Hard to believe it's been here for so long,' said Elliot Mason, echoing May's thoughts. The teacher was still wearing his knitted beanie, and looked out of place. 'Not on this site, of course – this building's late Victorian. The coping stone was moved from the original site somewhere further east. For three centuries St Crispin's was open to all devout Christians who had the will to learn. Now it's reserved for the paying elite. There's a five-year waiting list to attend. So much for progress. Sorry, I saw you at the art gallery this morning. Your sergeant interviewed me.' Mason introduced himself with a faint handshake.

May had been educated at a good grammar school in Vauxhall, a step above his partner's experience in

Whitechapel. He had reached maturity in a world of crow-black gowns and mortar boards. Consequently, the young teacher's relaxed clothes and attitude came as a surprise to him. 'Why do you choose to teach here?' he asked, surveying the exterior.

'The pay's better than working in a state school, and there's slightly less chance of getting stabbed. Sorry, there's a limit to my altruism. In my book you can have a vocation and still meet your mortgage payments. It looks like it's going to rain. The kids will be off soon. Are you coming in?'

'I wanted to talk to the class that visited the gallery this morning,' said May. 'I know they gave statements, but I wondered if we'd missed something. We've had trouble getting hold of your head teacher, Dr Westingham.'

'He likes the school to keep a low profile. Apparently he had kittens when he saw the lunchtime news report. He's an utter slave to parental demands, lives in fear of losing his exclusive status.'

'He has no reason to worry. We're just gathering information.' They climbed the worn steps together.

'He fears guilt by association. God forbid that the big bad world should intrude into these sepulchral halls, staining the innocence of his children. They might have fee-paying parents, but they're the same as every other hormonal delinquent in the neighbourhood. They nick stuff from a better class of store, and lie more professionally, but apart from that it's business as usual: skinning up doobies in the kiln room, playing hockey with frozen mice in the biology lab, hanging around the girls' school in Rosebery Avenue, shoving each other into strip clubs – they can get into Soho during their lunch hour and still be back in time for the first module of the afternoon. Come on, I'll dig them out for you. They won't take any orders from me, of course, a lapsed socialist with a persecution complex and artistic aspirations. They smell my fear and play on it mercilessly.'

'Why were you taking the class?'

'I already explained to your sergeant. Their teacher, Mr Kingsmere, has an upset stomach and stayed home this morning, so I had to take his place.'

'You were inside the County Hall gallery while it happened – you didn't see or hear anything unusual?'

'I walked through the main chamber a few minutes before the alarm was raised, then went to the café.'

'Why didn't you stay with your class?'

'I needed to change into trainers. I was breaking in new shoes and they were killing me. Here we are. The element of surprise is the only weapon I have against them.'

Mason led the way through corridors built in the time of James II that had now been relaid for computer trunking, and stopped before a wide mahogany door, flinging it open.

The pupils within were all working at their terminals, and barely bothered to look up. May had expected them to react by becoming statues, freezing in a variety of violent postures, their internecine cruelties caught in mid-brutalization. It was what teenagers would have done in his day, but back then lessons had been focussed on blackboards and rote-learning, and any diversion had been welcomed.

'Would all of those boys in Mr Kingsmere's art class please make themselves known?' asked Mason. A number of hands were desultorily raised. 'Come on, Gosling, Parfitt, I know you were both there. You too, Jezzard, Tarkington, Billings and the rest of you.' Further hands crept up like unfurling ferns. Nobody was pleased about being drawn away from their screens. Adults – especially ones involved in law enforcement – would only ask pedantic, irrelevant questions, and would take ages doing so. 'Outside, please. The remainder get on with your work.'

The boys might have been moving underwater. Their pantomimic exertions as they left the room suggested that they held little respect for the relief teacher.

'These are all Kingsmere's lads,' explained Mason. 'He's the only teacher in the school who gets to pick his own pupils, and he takes the brightest ones for a single year for extracurricular activities. Puts them through hell and they love him for it. Funny how some teachers can't put a foot wrong. Of course, private all-male schools tend to become a trifle Hellenic when you're dealing with this age group, too many hormones flying about, although these days the subject is avoided in case the parents come after us with burning torches.'

'So it's just hero worship?'

'Oh, absolutely, there's nothing in it. He's a very charismatic man. Kingsmere takes art, gym, comparative beliefs, media, social studies and IT. The loyalty of his class bothers Westingham, who always suspects teachers of trying to undermine his authority. But I'm sure you don't want to hear about our petty intrigues. OK, they're all yours.'

May found himself facing fourteen teenaged boys, assembled in a ragged line around the main hall. 'Where's Luke Tripp?' he asked.

'Here, Sir.' The tiny Luke stepped forward from behind the others.

'How old are you?'

'Nearly fourteen, Sir. Small for my age. What I lack in height I make up in genius.' The others snorted. 'That's why the King – Mr Kingsmere – takes me.'

'You're the one who saw the horseman.'

'That's right, Sir.'

'Don't you think it's a bit of a long shot, trying to convince police officers that you saw someone gallop into the gallery and sweep Miss White off her feet?'

'Your sergeant asked for the truth, Sir. I had the impression of a man on a horse. I wouldn't say for certain that it was one.'

'I'm not sure I understand what you mean.'

'Neither am I, but it's all I can tell you. He looked like a highwayman, straight out of the Alfred Noyes poem, you know, "He'd a French cocked-hat on his forehead, a bunch of lace at his chin," except he didn't.'

'You're so gay, Tripp,' muttered someone.

'Get back in your own gene pool, Tripp,' said someone else.

'I drew a picture – ' the boy offered, ignoring his class-mates.

'I know, I saw it,' May told him. 'Nobody else can shed any light on this, I suppose.'

The pupils looked at each other blankly. Eventually, the pustular Parfitt raised his hand. 'Maybe he was in fancy dress, or performing some piece of terrorist art.'

'We didn't see the horse, but we think we know who Tripp saw,' said the chubby, bat-eared Jezzard.

'How could you, if you didn't see anyone in the chamber?'

'We all took a look at his drawing, Sir. The sergeant showed it to us.'

'Well, who was it?'

Gosling glared at Jezzard, but finally spoke up. 'We talked about it between ourselves, and we'd rather not say, Sir, in case we're wrong.' Silence settled on the group. *This is going to be a long day*, thought May.

Elliot Mason walked with May across the school quadrangle as rain blackened the playground. 'I know why they won't talk to you,' he said. 'It's a private matter between the boys, and it's a can of worms you don't want to open. They can be very tight-lipped when it suits them.'

'I just want to get at the truth,' May told him. 'If they're holding something back, I'll just keep returning until I find out what it is – unless you want to tell me.'

Mason gave the school a guilty backward glance, as if the masters had stopped to listen. 'This has always been a pretty mixed area. The Roland Plumbe Community Estate is nearby. It's better than it was, but it's still pretty rough. The school doesn't have its own playing fields, so it hires them, and the quickest way to get there is by cutting across the corner of the estate. The estate kids don't take kindly to an invasion of their turf by posh boys. They're members of a local gang that's conducting a bit of a class war with St Crispin's. It's possible the attacker might be among them. I get the feeling the boys have a particular nemesis there, but they won't be prepared to tell you who it is, simply because it would mean an escalation on both sides. We had a fatal stabbing some while back, and it took a lot of work to bring everyone back under control. Nobody wants to lose that.'

'Then it's in everyone's interests for them to provide the unit with a name. This is a murder investigation, Mr Mason.'

The relief teacher stuck his hands in his pockets. He looked uncomfortable. 'If they start naming suspects on the estate, and your team heads over there to take interviews, there's going to be trouble. The boys will be blamed, and somebody here will end up getting hurt.'

'We'll provide them with protection,' offered May, but Mason was already shaking his head vigorously.

'You don't understand. These lads go through quite enough without facing an additional daily threat of violence, and you won't be there when you're needed. The police are never around when it really matters. Kids these days are far craftier than you or I can imagine. The last thing we need around here is a war.'

I've been telling Arthur I know how to handle the younger generations, May thought. *Now it looks like I'm being put to the test.*

13

SMOKE AND LIGHT

The stones of the city still held autumn's dying warmth, but as the detectives reached the centre of Waterloo Bridge, the biting river wind numbed their fingers and reddened their ears. The Thames was high, dark and wide, the crepuscular evening pinpricked with the crimson lights of police boats. The skyline seemed to be updating itself daily. Blade-edged blocks of black glass and rows of amber fountains shone from Tooley Street to the waterside. The concrete sides of London Bridge had been illuminated a friendly vermilion. New apartment buildings sported strips of azure neon. The metropolis had finally shaken off the decades of dirt and darkness imposed on it by the war.

'Pray don't talk to me about impossible crimes,' warned Bryant, rattling his walking stick along the balusters of the bridge like a truanting schoolboy. The musty odour of mildew and estuary mud was discernible in his nostrils. It was the time of year he liked best, when most of the tourists left and the city grew more intimate. 'I've seen them all. We had a gassing in a locked room in a Deptford boarding house in 1957. All the doors and windows were sealed with tape. The killer had used a duplicate key and sucked the tape into place with a vacuum-cleaner nozzle. There was that

111

schoolmistress from Putney in 1964, stabbed in her own bedroom, no murder weapon, the door locked from inside, a roaring fire in the hearth, do you remember? Her husband had murdered her, taken the knife and climbed up the chimney, dropping petrol and matches into the grate from above. What about the KGB? They were masters of the impossible. We've had cases in London of an air rifle wired into a piano, a dagger dropped from a night-club balcony during a shower of confetti, a poisoned umbrella and a trained monkey armed with a hypodermic syringe. I don't see why this is presenting such a problem.'

'Times have changed,' said May. 'Those sort of crimes disappeared in the twentieth century. These days it's about drugs and territory and grudges and saving face.'

'Then why does Saralla White's death have all the hallmarks of a John Dickson Carr novel?' wondered Bryant. 'A populated gallery, a noisy, messy murder that nobody sees or hears, a killer who appears and vanishes at will, an artist killed by her own work, and an animated poem in riding boots and a tricorn hat who comes galloping through a building before leaving a calling card. Doesn't it sound to you like someone's been reading old detective stories?'

'When you say it like that, it does sound ridiculous,' May admitted. 'But put it another way. Think of a pregnant pro-abortionist undergoing a humiliating death in a public place, and ask yourself who we're looking for.'

'A paradox,' Bryant nodded. 'She's in the middle of going public with a powerful pro-abortion statement when she finds she's carrying a child. Suppose she wants to keep it? Where does that leave her beliefs? We must find the father.'

'White's so-called boyfriends are proving a let-down so far. Both have alibis and neither have seen her for weeks. Calvin Burroughs is a more interesting case because he admits to having been obsessed with her, but seems vague about when the affair ended. I've warned him we'll run DNA tests to sort out the paternity if we have to. Perhaps the answer lies in an area we haven't considered. Our killer is anxious to draw attention to himself. They don't normally go to such extreme lengths as this. One of the boys I met at St Crispin's said that the act feels like a piece of performance art, and he's absolutely right, but in that case why not have more witnesses? Why rely on a child to describe what he saw?'

'It's the calling card that bothers me, John. It carries the suggestion that he'll do it again. If there are no leads among her lovers or her immediate family, where are we supposed to start looking – in the artistic community, among anti-abortionists? This could be a random, unique act of violence. It takes two events to make a pattern.'

'There's probably a simple explanation. We'll find out what that is when we talk to our chief suspect.'

'I'm sorry, did I miss something? Suspect?'

'That's right. We're seeing McZee tonight. There were two other artists at the press launch, remember? We can rule out Sharinda Van Souten – she was accompanied by her agent the whole morning, and had only met White once before. McZee is on record saying he hates White and everything she stands for. He was arrested for assaulting a police officer in Manchester two years ago.'

'What's that got to do with it?'

'He was fingerprinted. The partials on White's silver buttons aren't fully attributable, but Banbury reckons they contain an oil residue on the thumb, linseed. That suggested a painter, so we ran a match against every artist who had exhibited in the gallery, and AFIS came up with a shortlist with his name on it. The spread-out configuration of both hands is consistent with someone pushing on her chest.'

'Artistic adversaries, eh? It could be Turner and Whistler all over again.' Bryant could barely conceal his excitement. 'Well, what are we waiting for?' His impatience overtook him, as did a bus, which nearly ran him down as he stepped into the road.

May helped his partner back on to the kerb. 'I think we'd better use my car, don't you?'

'Don't be ridiculous,' barked Bryant, snatching back his arm. 'It's hardly a ten-minute walk along the Embankment.' So saying, he set off toward the bridge's steps at a terrific pace, just to prove the point.

'I hate him already,' said Bryant in a voice somewhat louder than a stage whisper. 'Eminently slappable.'

McZee, the twenty-three-year-old artist formerly known as Josh Ketchley of Sidcup, Kent, stood before them in ripped jeans, Timberland boots and a stained white T-shirt. He was also wearing what appeared to be an elderly lady's dress, floral, pleated and baggy. Calvin Burroughs, the gallery owner, had warned them that his young star had a habit of making public protests about age, race and gender.

'Yeah, we had an argument,' he told them, tentatively touching his number-one crop and checking to see if anyone else was within listening distance. 'So what? She was being a hypercritical pain in the arse as usual.' The artist was supervising the crating of his work in the gallery's cavernous delivery bay.

'What time was this?' asked May.

'Just after the launch officially ended – about five to ten. I didn't want to stay around and suck up to the press. She thought we should work the room together, said I was betraying Calvin's trust by not networking and hyping the art. I told her that's not what it's about. She liked to milk the stories about her private life. I said the public doesn't need to know who the artist is shagging to understand their work.'

'Did you touch her when you argued?'

'Actually, I think I pushed her away from me. She does this little-girl act when she wants something, prodding you in the chest. I wasn't in the mood for it.' McZee sighed wearily. 'I suppose this is about the pictures.'

114

'What pictures?'

'The pictures of us she put out on the internet. The private ones taken in the Sanderson Hotel.'

'You don't mean Claridge's, do you?'

'No, mate, that was someone else – *Temptation in Toffs' Toilet*. I was *Sex Secrets of Shamed Love Rat*.'

Longbright brought tabloids into the unit every day, and several had exploited the scandal of the volatile artist who had discovered her partner was cheating on her.

'We'd been seeing each other non-exclusively for two months when she put those shots out. She filmed us on her digital camera and dropped the footage on to her website while I was in the shower. Thought it was funny. So I said "Laugh at this," and finished with her.'

'How do you feel about her installation?'

'The *Eternal Destiny* thing? I thought it was a cheap shot, labouring the obvious. I mean, how many new British artists do you know who are pro-life? She had the foetuses manufactured in China. That's how much she cared about human rights.'

'So you have no personal issue with a woman's right to choose.'

McZee gave him a strange look. 'Of course not.'

'Did you know she was pregnant?' May had caught the artist by surprise. 'When did you break up with her?'

'This was, like, over a month ago.' For someone who was happy to share his partner with a number of lovers, McZee looked surprisingly shaken.

'So she might have been carrying your child,' May pressed. He wanted to catch the young man before he had time to absorb the news. 'You don't seem very upset about her death.'

'It hasn't sunk in yet.'

'Tell me more about the argument you had.'

'It got pretty heated.'

'How heated?'

115

'A shoving match. Handbags at dawn, pretty embarrassing when I think about it. Let's put it this way: it would have given fuel to anyone who thinks artists are a bunch of self-centred wankers.'

'Did anyone else witness this?'

'No, we were in the next room to the press conference, beside my installation. The smoke detector is broken in there. You can have a fag without setting off the alarm.'

'Would you care to show us?' asked May.

McZee led the way to a chamber containing a slender glass box filled with blue smoke and wire filaments. The piece was thirteen feet high.

'Oh, give me strength,' muttered Bryant.

'Hang about, it's not on yet. It has to be turned off every fifteen minutes. There's an overheating problem, but we're working on it.' McZee flicked a wall switch and the filaments within started to glow. The swirling smoke coalesced about the fine wires, momentarily forming slender moving figures. Soft atonal music played from synchronized speakers.

'Good Lord.' Bryant caught his breath, staring with wide blue eyes at the shifting ethereal forms.

'Not your kind of thing, eh?' said McZee.

'On the contrary,' replied Bryant, 'I think it's absolutely beautiful.'

The detectives left the gallery and headed back to the Embankment. 'He obviously had a real fight with her,' said May as the panorama of the river opened out before them. 'Did you see the scratches on the side of his neck? A pity there were no witnesses. I have to vote him to the top of our suspect list. He could be lying when he says he didn't know about White's pregnancy.'

'I wonder how it works?' asked Bryant dreamily. 'The shaped filaments clearly heat the atmosphere, but how does he get them to dance like that? How can he conjure up something so wonderful from bits of old rubbish?'

'Are you listening, Arthur? We have a suspect. It's what you want.'

'But not *who* I want,' Bryant admitted. 'I've still got my eye on Calvin Burroughs. His star was about to change her much-publicized attitude towards children. If he's the father, he has the motive.'

'He nurtured her and lost her, Arthur.'

'Yes, and the work of dead controversial artists skyrockets in value.'

'You've a point there. Look at Haring and Basquiat.'

'That boy McZee is interested in organic forms, natural beauty, humanity. What could be more natural than a baby? Someone like that could become very passionate about the idea of termination.'

'So he chooses to kill them both? It wouldn't make any sense.'

Bryant was still misty-eyed by the time their taxi reached Tottenham Court Road. 'I'd written myself off as a Rossetti fan,' he told his partner. 'Whoever would have thought modern art could be so extraordinary?'

'Can we concentrate on the matter at hand?' May asked with irritation.

'That's precisely what I'm doing. I was just thinking, perhaps there is an argument against McZee. If an artist can create moving three-dimensional figures from a few light-bulb filaments and some gas, what other illusions could he create? A highwayman on a horse, perhaps? You'd have to admire his ingenuity.'

'You were just as ingenious. I remember some of the scams you had for getting around rationing quotas after the war – raising crows in your attic so you could eat them in vinaigrette sauce, and that scheme for creating artificial bacon you nearly had us thrown in jail over.' Bryant made no reply. 'You wanted to change the laws of the land and reinvent the wheel in the process. You really don't see any connection between yourself and the young as they are today?'

'None at all,' said Bryant sadly. 'The more I see talent in others, the more I feel like I'm bumbling off into some obsolete corner, where all the broken washing machines and fridges end up.'

May was determined not to allow any excess of sentiment into the vehicle. 'Shall we keep an eye on Josh Ketchley's movements?' he asked.

'Call him McZee,' Bryant replied. 'The boy has earned it. But put a tag on him, all the same.'

14

PROTECTOR OF THE LAND

The staff of the Mornington Crescent unit would never win awards for office organization, but on Tuesday morning they were more chaotic than ever.

Whenever a major investigation commenced, boxes were dumped where they could be fallen over, and precipitously stacked files could be guaranteed to cascade like decks of cards. Banbury had removed and bagged a number of items from the crime scene, but had lost the key to the evidence room, so they sat at the top of the stairs waiting to break someone's ankle. Crippen the cat had spent most of Monday hiding under May's desk after getting his tail caught in the photocopier, leaving his post only to drop off a surprise in the upturned crash helmet that Meera Mangeshkar had foolishly left on the floor beside her locker. The dying cactus had fallen over, impaling Bryant's Wendigo spirit doll on its spikes and possibly damning him to an afterlife in limbo.

Everywhere she looked, April found evidence of Bryant's surreptitious pipe usage. Even when he wasn't at the unit, it still looked as if he was: there was a piece of toast stuck on the wall above his chair, and several of his fished-out teabags had been impaled on his desk with darts. His carpet slippers, cardigans and half-eaten sandwiches were strewn over the furniture like votive offerings.

This was only her second day working at the unit, but April had already given up trying to keep the place tidy. As she unzipped her backpack and prepared to offer a hand to anyone who asked her, she wondered what she was doing here at all.

'My grandfather thinks he's helping me,' she told Longbright, 'but I feel like I'm just in the way.' It was true, she had got under everyone's feet the previous day.

Sergeant Longbright looked up from her screen and thought for a moment. 'Well, what are you good at?' she asked. 'John says you have a gift for spotting the things other people miss. He says you make fresh connections. That's a very useful talent.'

'I spend a lot of time alone. I guess you become more observant. It's like always being outside, looking in.'

'So you see the bigger picture – that's good. How about helping me collate the remaining interviews? You can go through them and see if there are any common factors we've overlooked. They're already divided into High, Medium and Low Interest – it's Arthur's system, not mine. He subdivides documents into a lot of arbitrary levels no one really understands, including personal philosophy, favourite book and shoe types, but the basic idea is sound enough. He's got eight potentials listed as suspects, including Saralla White's own mother, her rival artists, the gallery owner and the 'Other Unknown Suitor', although where he got that from is a mystery that he doesn't seem keen on divulging.' Longbright shook her immaculate coiffure in wonder. 'Who uses a word like *suitor*, anyway? You'd think by now I'd have an inkling of how his mind works, but it's a sealed labyrinth.' She slid over a stack of paper. 'Hard copies. I load all the reports electronically, but he prints them out.'

'I know, he's such a Luddite.'

'It's not the Luddism, it's the toner. We're on a budget.

You know it's his birthday tomorrow? We're having a whip-round. John's buying him a new mobile. Guess who'll have to read the manual aloud half a dozen times.'

'Everybody has to do that, Janice. Here, this will cheer you up. Last night's paper.' April unfolded a copy of the *Evening Standard*. '"The Highwayman", computer rendition. They latched on to the name pretty quickly.'

Longbright examined the picture. 'They must have got hold of a copy of the kid's drawing. How the hell did they source it so fast?'

'I don't know, but the article reads pretty much the same as the ones on the net and the afternoon cable reports. Very little information, no direct attribution. The story's all coming from one source.'

'How can you be sure?' Longbright sat back in her chair.

'The same handful of facts is spread thinly through all the tabloids this morning. They haven't got much more than the witness's description, a photograph of Meera accompanying Luke home, and the usual frank descriptions of White's past lovers, although the *Sun* rates White's sexual partners in terms of performance. I noticed that the *Daily Mail* had got Calvin Burroughs' age wrong, so I checked the other reports and found the error repeated. My guess is it's a single tabloid stringer, someone who's sold non-exclusive rights to the story. The broadsheets aren't trusting any of it until they get more direct sources. It's too bizarre for them; I think they smell a publicity stunt of some kind.'

'Saralla White is dead, April. That's not a stunt.'

'How do they know that for sure? She reinvented herself, and pulled all kinds of bizarre hoaxes to gain notoriety. She once described herself as a "reality hacker". And she's revealed an incredible amount of detail about her sexual life. I did some internet research last night. The unofficial websites fill in some of the blanks she left: in her early unknown days she self-published a biography called *Macroslut*, but no one paid any attention. It's now changing hands on eBay because it's filled with hand-coloured photographs that she later destroyed. There's one particular section Uncle Arthur should find interesting. It turns out Saralla White had a husband, although she always denied the marriage. She took some incredibly nasty photographs of him, naked and aroused, including one where it appears he's been drugged and tied to a toilet cistern. He works somewhere in the City, and he's probably still furious with her.'

'How did you find out all this?'

April shrugged. 'Tracking sites and podcasts is another thing you do when you can't go out. Any time a computer is touched it leaves a trail. The only way to destroy evidence like that is to unplug the thing, dig a hole in the ground and cover it with dirt. Besides, I like making connections. Maybe I take after my grandfather after all.'

'Well, it's a talent we can certainly use around here.' Longbright handed her the rest of the interviews. 'Don't even think about leaving again.'

Dan Banbury placed a magnetic disc on the blurred screen-grab at the top of his suspect board, moving the photograph of McZee down.

'So we're agreed,' said May. 'Until we receive any further information, McZee drops to second place behind this unknown husband.' He squinted at the head shot, trying to make it out. 'Is that the best you can get? Can't you enhance it?'

'What with?' asked Banbury. 'We haven't got the right on-site equipment. I can send it off to WEC, see if they'll stick it on to one of their jobs.' The unit had been promised its own crime lab, but someone – May suspected Leslie Faraday – had refused to sign off the new agreed budget.

'Then get some better shots. Her sex life's been spread all over the web. You must be able to get something more than a vaguely male shape caught leaving a restaurant with her. Meera, do you want the bad news?'

122

'Let me guess, I'm doing surveillance on the artist formerly known as Josh Ketchley,' said the young Indian officer without looking up.

'Right, and take Bimsley with you.'

'Can't, Sir. We've no spare vehicles, so I've been given permission to use my bike.'

'You're not watching someone from a pushbike,' said May.

'No, Sir, a reconditioned 1000cc Kawasaki. I stripped it down myself. No room for an uncoordinated pillion rider. No offence, Colin.' She flicked a smile at PC Bimsley, whose heart skipped a beat. Something about small, strong women opened his soul to the sky.

'Very well, but stay in the warm somewhere, I'm not having you catch pneumonia,' May sighed. 'Did anyone see Arthur leave the building this morning?'

'He said something about following up a lead from one of the teachers you interviewed,' said Kershaw.

'He has no right to go off by himself,' May complained, throwing down his pen in annoyance. 'What does he think he's doing?'

The Roland Plumbe Community Estate had been built on one of London's less visible sites, above the brown concrete towers of the Barbican, below the drab grey bricks of Finsbury, sandwiched between Bunhill Fields and St Bartholomew's Hospital, a negative place where bombs had wiped out history and planners had exercised so little imagination that it could only become the province of the poor.

The apartments had been prefabricated from imperfect concrete slabs containing air pockets that soaked up rain and trapped it in the walls. The triangle of land on which the estate survived had been cleared of wartime rubble and used for asbestos-lined bungalows until 1962, when the great block had risen under new plans for working

Londoners enthusiastically approved by Prime Minister Harold Macmillan.

The main building had seven long balconies, and had once had parks at either end, but these green spaces had been lost when two wings were added. The resulting alteration to the original plans left the estate claustrophobic and lightless. Successive councils had tried to alleviate the gloom with bright colours, but in the early 1980s the first graffiti arrived, and it had never been successfully removed without wrecking the paintwork. The stilts upon which the central block stood proved impossible to light adequately, and provided an ideal home for lurking street gangs.

This is what happens when well-meaning architects decide how the working classes should live, thought Bryant as he tightened his moulting green scarf around his throat and stepped on through tumbling plane leaves. *The professional classes should be made to live here for a while before they start pronouncing on the causes of antisocial behaviour.* Looking ahead at the bleak grey wind-tunnels that daily greeted residents beneath the building, he could not imagine how the human spirit survived intact in such a place.

Fundamental flaws were obvious, even from ground level. The steel lifts opened on to the street side of the building, providing a haven for anyone looking for a place to inject or relieve themselves. The bedrooms had been intended to look out on to parkland, but now the tenants were overlooked by other apartments, which destroyed their privacy. The architects weren't entirely to blame, he supposed. Who could have foreseen how much society would change? In wartime, who could have imagined the end of the traditional urban family unit? He passed a bleak playground consisting of a scarred green roundabout and broken swings, beyond peeling prefabricated garages that had been hastily erected on the only remaining free ground, and headed into the darkness beneath the block's concrete stilts.

Walking between pools of oily water into the threatening

124

shadows, Bryant reflected that one of the benefits of old age was finding how few things scared him. He had survived a war, seen friends die before his eyes, witnessed the ebb and flow of various fads and panics that had briefly gripped the country. He had watched politicians pronounce on the end of civilization, and had listened to grieving, desperate families as they coped with the loss of their loved ones. Dark alleys had no power to harm him now.

'You shouldn't be here alone, Mr Bryant.' Lorraine Bonner stepped from the shadows to greet him. She was a heavy-beamed black woman in her mid-forties, with a broad face predisposed to smiling. Dressed in a bright-red patchwork overcoat, she brought a cheerful touch to the surrounding gloom. 'I came to get you 'cause the main lift is buggered.'

'How did you know me?' asked Bryant, shaking her hand.

'I saw you on television. They seem keen to bill you as an English eccentric.' As they walked, she linked her arm in his. Bryant liked the gesture of warmth in such a chill environment. She reminded him of his Antiguan landlady.

'Television is only interested in freaks,' he told her. 'I'm afraid that's probably how they see me. Celebrity is fleeting.'

'Well, you look normal to me, love. We'd better get off the street. The school will be starting sports practice soon. The kids have to pass through here, and their enemies lie in wait for them. It's not a good idea to get caught in the middle, know what I mean?'

She led the way to a goods lift at the rear of the building and ushered him in. 'You're lucky, this one's working today. The first time in three weeks. It's wicked on your legs.'

Mrs Bonner was the head of the Roland Plumbe Residents' Association, and liaised with housing officers when she wasn't working at the Middlesex Hospital. She had called the police to point out that the man she kept seeing on the rolling news had been sighted by residents on the estate. Meanwhile, Bryant had just finished reading his partner's notes on his meeting with Elliot Mason, and the teacher's mention of trouble in the area suggested that the call was worth checking out.

'We'll go to the community office,' she said. 'My kids are at home with colds, and I wouldn't inflict them on you today. They're hyperactive and can take some getting used to.'

'I'm not good with children,' Bryant understated, entering the glass-walled office. It was typical of so many community rooms occupied by people in states of emotional distress. No technical innovations here, just Post-It notes, brown folders, papers, Kleenex boxes, children's drawings, cheap orange plastic chairs and stained carpet tiles, nothing that could be stolen or used as a weapon.

'Everyone comes here with their problems,' Mrs Bonner told him, flicking on the fierce strip-lighting. 'They can scream and shout, it don't make any difference to me. I wait for them to calm down, then explain what we can do. It's probably like your job.'

No, thought Bryant guiltily. *My job's not as tough as this.* 'You can see the whole estate from up here,' he said.

'Yes, I can keep an eye on the troublemakers. We employed some guardians to patrol and separate the gangs, but we had to get rid of them after they started taking sides. This job has a dangerous habit of getting personal on you. The main trouble is the gangs, but they're not really drawn along ethnic lines, it's mostly territorial and circumstantial.'

'What do you mean?' asked Bryant, who knew little about everyday urban life.

'It's circumstantial because they've got no money, Mr Bryant, so they've got nowhere to go, which means they stand around in groups, and that makes it territorial. Doesn't help that the rich kids have to cut across their turf three times a week.'

'Who gives them guidance?' Bryant asked. 'Are there still

such things as youth clubs? We had all sorts of activities available when we were young.'

'No disrespect, Mr Bryant, but youth clubs went out with Teddy Boys. These kids should spend less time with their mates and more with their folks. They need role models, but now they're beyond the age where they'll trust any adult to give them guidance. They've no shame. They'll terrorize the older tenants, then lie straight-faced to the police. They know their rights. It's all "Lay a finger on me and I'll call Claims Direct."' She checked a large appointments book on her desk. 'Don't get me wrong, we've never had no gun crime here – that's for the drug-problem estates – but most of the kids routinely carry knives, and in flashpoint situations they do get used. This is the estate diary. We enter all incidents, no matter how small. The idea is to catch the rising problem, not its aftermath. See here, just this morning a couple of kids told their parents they saw this highwayman of yours. He was running through The Street – that's what they call the ground-floor passage under the stilts, it runs the entire length of the three blocks. Nobody uses it unless they have to.'

'Do you have CCTV?'

'Yes, but the camera lenses are so scratched and fogged that they don't show anything. The council was supposed to replace them last year. Besides, the kids all wear hoodies. We rely on other residents to keep watch.'

'This sighting, do you know if it was before the story broke in today's papers?'

'I couldn't say, Mr Bryant. Don't imagine they read the papers.'

'Well, do you have an accurate description of what they saw? They might have noticed some detail we've missed.'

'Here, I typed it out for you. Black leather suit, riding boots, eye-mask, hat. Looks like a comic-book character, they said, tall and broad. They reckon they've seen this man on the estate before, dressed exactly the same way each time. He always appears just as it's getting dark.'

'Always?' asked Bryant, alarmed. 'When did they first see him?'

Lorraine crossed to a filing cabinet and checked her notes. Bryant noticed that she had the lolloping gait of a woman with hip trouble. 'Six months ago, maybe longer. A couple of kids say he's always been around the estate, as long as they can remember, even when they was little babies.'

'Does he scare them?'

'No, apparently they think of him as a kind of guardian. Sort of a protector of the estate. Because of the badge, see.'

She tapped the Roland Plumbe Community Estate's logo on the Residents' Association letterhead, an artisanal fifties symbol that owed its influence to the Festival of Britain's design ethic. At its centre was the outline of a horseman in a black cape and tricorn hat. The date on the logo was 1954.

My God, thought Bryant. *Don't tell me he's been around for over fifty years.*

15

WINTER LIGHTNING

Danny Martell was in trouble again. His natural atavism usually left him with nothing more than a hangover. He jokingly dismissed these lapses of character to friends as Out-of-Pocket Experiences, but the latest occasion had proved altogether more serious.

Marc Morrison, his agent, had called him this morning with a warning to watch out for tomorrow's press. The agent did not admonish; what point was there in telling his clients to stay away from call-girls and cocaine? *In for a penny, in for a pound,* Morrison figured. Some clients were always going to screw up their careers, so they might as well crash and burn now to leave room for the ones with more self-discipline.

Morrison had learned the hard way. He had once taken on a well-behaved children's TV presenter who, out for a drink one evening, had been drawn into a night-club act by a fire-eater, who had pulled open the boy's shirt and teased his chest with a flaming brand – no big deal, just part of the act. Except that the act was on stage in a club that hosted weekly gay nights, and the show had been taped by the management, and the tape had found its way to the *News of the World*, who ran an outraged feature suggesting that the boy was unfit to be allowed near children. They included a photograph of the bare-chested presenter grimacing as the flame neared him, surrounded by copy that somehow managed to suggest the club was a haven for paedophiles, heterosexual orgies, gay sex and Satanism. Nobody in the industry believed the story except the BBC, who fired the presenter, who took a barbiturate overdose and was found dead in his Maida Vale flat, which at least solved his image problem. So it was best not to get Morrison started on the subject of tarnished images.

But Martell was a bigger challenge. He wasn't likely to kill himself, and he wasn't likely to get another high-profile job after this, either. It wasn't his first slip from grace; this particular romp was the third in an ongoing relay of dropped hurdles. Freelance paparazzi spoke disparagingly of his weakness for Brazilian supermodels, so clichéd, so *vanilla*, but they were happy to exploit it.

For the past two years, Martell had been hosting Britain's most popular Saturday teenage-lifestyle show on ITV. Now he could see himself having to present lunchtime cookery quizzes on zero-audience channels like ChefTV. He was going through a bad patch: his wife had left him, which would have gained him sympathy except that he sold his side of the story to the *Sunday People*, and it wasn't very sympathetic, or even feasible.

No one understood the pressure he was under. Danny was a perfectionist. He had turned a lousy show into a smash hit, work ate up every hour of his day – how could he hold down a relationship, or have any stability in his life? Who could he trust?

Even when you're a success, he thought, *it becomes a matter of degree. You're not as successful as a hit show on another channel; you're successful in England but not the USA; you're successful for a season but not on a yearly aggregate.* These days even his leisure time was pressurized. *Celebrity is about access,* he remembered. *It's your only weapon. Someone pisses you off, you deny them access.* But he could no longer afford to do that.

One lousy Monday evening in a Clerkenwell lapdancing bar – a couple of short lines, a few cocktails and home to bed. He hadn't exactly behaved like Caligula. He hadn't seen anyone he'd recognized, either, hadn't had his picture taken, so where were the shots coming from?

His agent told him to expect a headline in the national tabloids, and at least four pages of revelations, maybe more, in the Sundays. In just a few hours his career would be downgraded, and there was nothing he could do about it.

As he pushed open the door to the gym, he wondered if the channel would carry out their threat to terminate his contract. He was due to start a new season of shows, but was still in pay negotiations. At the very least, they'd negotiate a cut in salary.

For a second he thought he heard something, a sound he hadn't heard in years – but it disappeared before he could properly register it.

As he headed for the changing room, he told himself there was no point in stressing about the future. Worrying would only spoil his workout. He insisted on having the entire gym to himself; it had caused a fuss at the time, especially as it meant evicting the women's group that met here on Tuesday evenings, but he had stuck to his guns and asked his agent to strike a deal with the owner, booking out the final hour for his exclusive use twice a week. Actually, it hadn't been that tough to arrange as the gym was badly in need of renovation, and most of its users had moved to a more fashionable fitness centre in High Holborn.

He had put on twelve pounds in the last few months, and his doctor had warned him about the consequences of neglecting his regime while working in such a high-pressure job. Stepping into the weights room in coordinated blue and white Lycra gym gear and rubber sports sandals, he caught sight of his belly in the mirror and felt a twinge of embarrassment. *Thank God there are no photographers to get a shot of me like this*, he thought.

He puffed for ten minutes on the rowing machine, watching the rain as fat grey droplets started to spatter the first-floor windows of the renovated Smithfield apartment building opposite. There was a storm coming, and he'd just had the Jaguar washed.

He wished he'd never made the fitness video; it had been intended as a bit of fun, but now every crew he worked with expected him to give them dietary guidelines. Didn't they realize he had simply been given a script and told where to stand? Didn't they have any idea how many times he'd been swabbed with towels and fresh make-up between takes? Fitness wasn't necessary when you had good lighting.

Needles of pain flittered between his shoulder blades. *Pain is good*, he told himself. *This is helping. I could shed a stone, lay off the chems and stop having to pay for sex, really turn my life around.*

On the wall opposite was a luscious poster of an impossibly slender Brazilian girl in a tiny white string bikini, her skin the rich umbrous colour of dates. She was probably eighteen, no more than twenty, high buttocks, flat stomach, large breasts. He pulled at the oars, stretched his legs, felt a warm lolling in his shorts. *Girls like that can have anything. The rest of us have to work at it.* Sweat was dripping into his eyes, so he slowed his pace and groped about for a towel.

How many weeks would it take, he wondered, how many hours spent on this damned Californian torture rack to burn the extravagances of the last few years from his body? The effort of climbing out of the rowing machine nearly sent him reeling back to the changing room.

I shouldn't feel this bad at forty-eight, he told himself. *People forget all the years I worked the clubs before I got a break. Now all they can do is shout at me in the street, 'I won't try that again!'* Why did he ever come up with such a stupid catchphrase? He should have known it would shadow him to the grave, probably be carved on his tombstone. He moved to the pectoral press, adjusted the seat and lowered the weights. Fifteen reps on this, if he was lucky, then some abdominal crunches and off for a shower.

A low rumble of thunder vibrated the windows. The approaching storm outside made the empty gym a melancholy place. Its brightly painted walls required music and a foreground of pumping athletes to bring the room to life. He was about to raise his hands to the rubber grips and begin his set when he heard the noise again. This time it was clearer, louder, more defined. A horse's galloping hooves, a rush of wind, a whinny, as tailored and distinct as a BBC sound effect.

It sounded as if it was in the next room. The gymnasium had been constructed across the first floor of a converted warehouse. There were apartments above, behind and below – somebody had their television up too loud.

He began to work out, feeling the now-recognizable streak of pain flash along the line of his buried musculature, and wondered if he had set the weight too high. Beginners always did that, the trainer had warned him. Perhaps it hadn't been such a bright idea, firing her, but it would have been too distracting trying to exercise while catching glimpses of her moist tanned cleavage.

Forked lightning forms a zigzag; it takes the path of least resistance through the air. He saw it but didn't believe what he was witnessing, because it was here, inside the room with him, a crisp white line tinged blue at the edges, passing before his eyes.

He felt the arrythmic pulse deep within the cage of his chest, like soldiers breaking step, or a band squeezing an unfamiliar chord into a well-known song. Something bad was happening. His heart hadn't skipped a beat; it was beating too often, and could not regain its rightful balance.

Extreme heat in his flesh – the palms of his hands – a searing pain that reached to the insteps of his feet. A plunge into icy bitterness – a hollow forming deep inside, as though something had just jammed and collapsed. A tangle of seared nerves, and a sensation of falling, dropping away.

He had been pushing the elbow pads of the Nautilus machine forward, but now they whipped back, releasing him. As he fell, he knew that the terrifying silence in his chest was caused by the sudden stopping of his heart.

He was almost relieved to know that he would not have to suffer the indignity of seeing tomorrow's headlines.

16

VOLUPTUOUS HARM

'I'm sorry to pull you out in such disgusting weather,' Dan Banbury apologized. 'Nobody saw the storm coming in.' The young cockney crime-scene manager had been playing squash at Islington's Sobell Centre when he received the summons, and was still sweating so much that he had trouble fitting his disposable gloves. 'I rang your mobile for ages but there was no answer.'

The pair were standing outside the first-floor door of the Fitter Body Centre. Arthur Bryant undid the buttons of another shapeless raincoat he had purchased from Caledonian Road Market. He had taken his partner's advice and treated himself to some more clothes. Unfortunately, the ones he had chosen were every bit as horrible as the items in his existing wardrobe.

'No, it doesn't ring any more. I only realized someone was calling when I saw it vibrate across the table into my landlady's Ruby Murray. We had a date in Brick Lane with a biriani. I'll be tasting it all evening now.' He picked a piece of curried prawn from his jumper and flicked it over the stairwell.

'You'll be glad you came, though. I think you're going to like this.' Banbury spoke without a trace of irony. 'Ostensibly, we're looking at a heart attack on an exercise machine. No one's been into the gymnasium apart from Mr Martell himself.'

'How can you be sure?' asked Bryant.

'The owner is a German gentleman who apparently loves Martell's TV show. He cleared the gym at eight fifteen p.m., ready for Martell to come and do his workout at eight thirty. There's a bit of resentment from the City boys over the fact that Mr Schneider closes the gym for private sessions several times a week, but his name is on the lease, and there are no by-laws preventing him from doing what he likes with the place. Presumably he gets paid well for the service.'

Banbury tapped a grey metal box beside the entrance door. 'Standard smart-card system. One swipe gets you in and out. Each card is registered to its member, so the staff know exactly who's in the place at any given time. It's also a security measure – they have a few minor celebrities using the place and don't want photographers grabbing shots of people in the showers. The point is, all the cards are accounted for. Everyone came out, the room, showers and toilet stalls were all checked, then fifteen minutes later Martell arrived and swiped himself in. He never checked out. The box hasn't been tampered with, so it looks as if he was the only one inside.'

'Who found his body?'

'The cleaner came in to turn off the running machines and wipe down the wash basins. She called the owner, who called Clerkenwell nick, who called us. I took a quick look and closed up again, because I wanted you to see exactly what I saw.'

'Let's cut through some of the mystery, shall we?' Bryant shoved at the door, but couldn't open it. Looking around, he lifted the entry card from Banbury and swiped himself inside.

'Hang on, Sir, we haven't—'

'Don't worry, I'm not going to touch anything.'

136

'I was going to say we haven't checked that it's safe.'

'Why would it need a safety check?' called Bryant, searching for lights. 'I thought you said he died of a heart attack.'

'It looks that way,' replied Banbury, moving ahead to where the body still lay. 'There are – anomalies.'

'You're being cryptic, Banbury. Kindly stop being so.'

'It's just that we have two witnesses, two old birds in the apartment opposite. They called the police. I think you'll be rather interested in what they have to say.'

Bryant halted and raised a finger. 'Wait, when you say "interested", you mean "irritated and frustrated", don't you? Kershaw's oddly euphemistic speech patterns are starting to rub off on you.'

Banbury looked sheepish. 'What I mean is, they're a bit of a handful. I think it will be a late night at the unit. The Highwayman's back.'

Bryant's watery blue eyes widened. 'You're calling him that as well?'

'Everyone's picking up on the nickname, Sir.'

'Did he leave another calling card?'

'Not that we can see. He did better than that this time.'

'Let's have a quick shufti at the crime scene first, eh? Where's John?'

'I believe he's on his way. He was—'

'Out with Monica Greenwood, his married lady friend, yes, I know. While her husband is still lying comatose in hospital. The man has no scruples when it comes to attractive women. He behaves like a racing driver around them, always leaves them windswept and out of breath. Either it's the effect of his overbearing charm or he only dates asthmatics. I don't know where he finds the energy.'

'Actually, Sir, you seem to have more energy than any of us,' Banbury admitted. 'You're a positive inspiration.'

'Don't be obsequious, Banbury, nobody likes a creep. And I don't have excess energy, I'm just on these new tablets. Two sets of gel capsules for different times of the day. The blue ones fire my engines and the red ones leave me utterly disoriented. Pray I don't get them muddled up. Now, where's the body?'

The gymnasium ran in an L-shape around the apartment building, its exterior wall cut with tall gothic windows overlooking a quiet side road leading away from the cavernous meat market. St John Street could be glimpsed in the distance, a broad curve of Victorian turrets and sharp glass boxes. The building was a former furniture repository for Gamages, the long-vanished department store in Holborn. The wide, bright space and high ceilings had made it ideal for conversion, although to Bryant's thinking it seemed perverse to fill the place with running machines when there were perfectly good footpaths alongside the Thames.

They found the lights and flicked them back on. One side of the L was dedicated to cardiovascular equipment, the other to controlled weight systems. At the far end of the latter, Danny Martell had fallen on to his knees and lay face-down on the blue carpet tiles, a portly supplicant worshipping in the temple of Narcissus. Motes of dust filled the still air, lending the fitness room a hazy, dream-like aura.

'Do you feel it?' asked Bryant, taking stock of the scene. 'Something strange, an odd presence.'

'The air is ionized, but I think I know what you mean. And I'm not normally sensitive to bad feelings.' Banbury looked about uncomfortably as the skin on his arms prickled.

'Do you believe in the physical manifestation of evil?' Bryant was staring at him oddly.

'I'm a scientist, Sir. But as a Christian I believe . . .' He chose his words carefully. 'In the absence of good.'

'Hm. It's just that some death sites – ' Bryant thought for a moment, and decided not to share his philosophy. 'Why isn't Kershaw here?' He looked around for the unit's crime-scene manager. But for the photographer and the two Met officers guarding the gym entrance, they were alone.

'He had to go to Orpington tonight, Sir. His sister's getting married at the weekend. She's having a hen night and asked him to look after the kids.'

'Her second marriage?'

'No, Sir, first.'

'She's not supposed to already have progeny if she's only just getting to the altar, it's like ordering dessert before your main course. Next you'll be telling me they're from different fathers.'

Banbury could never be sure when his boss was joking, although he knew that the old man was not as conservative as he sounded. Indeed, Longbright had warned him to treat the detective's outbursts with caution; Bryant's sense of humour at crime scenes was hard to fathom, as if he deflected his feelings about death with provocative changes of topic.

The old detective used his hated walking stick to lower himself beside Martell. Without Kershaw to examine the body, he would have to rely on his own observations. 'Very florid in the face. The burst blood vessels are suggestive. Should he have been using these ridiculous things without supervision?' He peered into the dead man's eyes, staring from different angles like an optician checking for glaucoma. Martell's pupils beamed down into the floor unnervingly.

'Good question. He'd only started here last month. The owner tells me he hired a personal trainer, but she quit after he touched her up. Martell fancied himself as a bit of a ladies' man.'

'I can't imagine a lady finding him anything but skin-crawlingly repellent.' Bryant wrinkled his nose in distaste. 'He was some kind of celebrity, I understand?'

'If you count TV game shows, *Saturday Night Laughter*, stuff like that. Rather on the smarmy side for my taste.'

'Not a reason to purchase a television, then.' It was bad enough that Bryant could hear Alma's set through the wall of his lounge, without having to buy one of his own.

'It's funny, he starred in the biggest-selling health and fitness DVD in Britain, but look at the state of him. He must have worn a corset for the cameras.'

'How do you know it was a heart attack?'

Banbury knelt beside the body. 'Without Giles, it's a bit of a guess. The high sclerosis, the fact that he's quite a few kilos overweight and was exerting himself. There's booze on his breath. There's also blood in the eyes. Heart-attack victims feel a pressure, a squeezing sensation in the centre of the chest that stays for a few minutes. They tend to sit down and wait for the symptoms to go away, but the pain spreads to the shoulders, neck and arms. They get light-headed and feel nauseous, sweat or get short of breath, so Martell might have figured it was the effect of the workout. But then there's this.' He carefully lifted Martell's right hand to reveal a small triangular mark on his forearm. 'There's another on his left arm, and one in the middle of his chest.'

'They look like burns.'

Banbury pushed back the left sleeve of Martell's top and turned the cuff inside out. 'I think they were made by the heads of the zips on his workout gear, one on each sleeve, one running up the middle. They're all welded shut. Extreme heat.' He pulled down the neck of the top to reveal a livid crimson scar across Martell's throat. 'He was wearing a medallion on a chain. That's left burn marks too. In the light of these, I'd have to say we're looking at signs consistent with electrocution.'

'So he was sitting on the seat – how do you operate this thing?' Bryant peered around the back of the machine. 'What on earth does it do?'

'Builds the pectoral muscles, Sir, like this.' He held his arm with the radius bone at right angles to the humerus. 'You raise your hands and hold the grips above your head on either side, pushing the pads forward with your forearms until they meet in the middle, then slowly releasing them.'

'What on earth for?'

'It's good for the chest.'

'Not in his case. Looks as if he was seated here and fell forward after over-exerting himself.'

'That's what I thought, Sir. In which case the burns make no sense. I don't seen how he superheated so suddenly.'

'There have been numerous documented cases of spontaneous combustion,' suggested Bryant. 'Nothing left of people but their shoes.'

'Beg to disagree, Sir. None ever properly substantiated, bit of a folk myth.'

'But I've seen photographs of the process occurring,' Bryant insisted.

'With all due respect, you've seen pictures of the aftermath, charred remains. It's an old wives' tale stemming from a single photograph of a woman who fell into a fire, taken in the 1920s, although it's true that the body can change its temperature very quickly. We're extremely adaptable machines.'

Bryant wasn't happy about being corrected, but was willing to concede the argument. 'Do you have a workable theory about this?' he asked.

'Think we should talk to the witnesses now, Sir. They can shed some more light.'

Channing Gifford and her partner, whose name Bryant failed to catch, lived in a first-floor apartment of such minimalist design that he thought they must have been recently burgled. The thieves had made off with most of the furniture, leaving bare floors of black slate and tall, clear vases of Calla lilies perched starkly against hard white surfaces. In a thin blue tank running the length of one wall, a single angel fish hovered listlessly.

Bryant and Banbury were ushered in, but there appeared to be nowhere to sit. Channing wore a white leotard with a sweater on top of a black shift so that she looked as if she had got dressed twice. She was as elegant as an ostrich, minus the exuberance of plumage, and clearly adored her partner, who was giraffe-tall, and moved with the same loping gait.

'We teach modern dance, you understand,' Channing explained. 'We were warming up at the window, doing some gentle stretches – '

' – very gentle stretches – ' confirmed the partner unnecessarily.

' – and watching the storm break. There were quite a few flashes of lightning, but far away, in the direction of – '

' – Lambeth. Then we saw the flash inside,' said her partner, whipping her long head in the direction of the gym opposite. 'A lightning flash, and we – '

'We saw him.'

'You saw Danny Martell?' asked Bryant.

'We know he lives there because fans sometimes wait – '

'They wait outside the door of the gym. They call his catchphrase up at the windows.'

'We've had to get your officers out on numerous occasions, but you never do anything.'

' – do anything at all.'

Bryant didn't notice their sudden accusatory tone. He was too busy wondering how anyone could live in a lounge without seats. 'And you saw him in the room, working out?'

'We weren't watching,' said Channing hastily, 'but a man that size is hard to miss. He blew up after his wife left him.'

' – blew right up,' her partner agreed. 'Poor diet.'

'We saw the lightning flash inside the room. It looked as if it came from the ceiling, a thin blue streak.'

'Or perhaps through the window,' added her partner. 'But it hit him.'

'You're sure of that?'

'Most definitely,' said Channing. 'He screamed and fell forward. That's when I called the police.'

'You didn't think of going over to see what had happened?'

142

'No, we have a history with that gym – '

' – an unpleasant history.'

'It would be a great help if only one of you spoke at a time,' snapped Bryant, who hated couples completing each other's sentences.

Channing looked at her partner and silently acknowledged an agreement to take over the story. 'We went to the window, to see what was happening, and – '

Channing's partner opened her mouth. Everyone held their breath. Bryant shot her a filthy look. She shut it again.

Channing continued, ' – and we saw this man leaving the building. He was closing the main door behind him.'

'Why did you notice him particularly?' asked Banbury.

'He was a tall man. But it was the way he was dressed, you couldn't help noticing. At first I thought he was a motorcycle courier. You know, a black leather suit, tight- fitting, big black boots. But he was wearing a black half-mask that stopped at his cheekbones, and above that he was wearing a black hat, but quite small, like a futuristic version of a traditional highwayman. We once did a modern-dress production of *The Beggar's Opera,* with McHeath wearing something similar. And he had a little pigtail, like they used to, at the back. It put me in mind of that dreadful poem.'

'Have you seen any pictures of him in the press?' asked Bryant.

'No, we don't buy newspapers, they're full of lies. Why?'

'Did you see where he went?'

'He looked around, then ran off in the direction of Farringdon Road.'

One of the busiest thoroughfares in central London, thought Bryant. *Somebody else must have seen him.*

'If you think of anything else – ' Banbury began, closing his notepad.

'Well, of course we did, because of being dance teachers.'

Channing's partner could not resist speaking out. 'It was the way he moved. Great strides, unnatural and awkward, as if walking hurt him. You see it in dancers all the time when their muscles are healing.'

Bryant moved to the window and looked down into the shining yellow puddles below. In his mind's eye, he saw the Highwayman turn from the deep-grey shadows of the building's archway and lope away towards the lights. Almost as if he wanted to draw attention to himself.

'Good job they were looking out of the window, Sir,' Banbury consoled as they walked back towards Bryant's Mini Cooper.

'They had no choice. There was nothing to look at in the flat.'

'There was a fish. I've always wanted a pet.'

'Fish aren't pets, Banbury, they're ornaments. Why didn't he leave a calling card this time, that's what I want to know.'

'If he did, we haven't found it,' Banbury agreed.

'Why not? He wants us to acknowledge him. Why not make sure by leaving the card again?'

'You don't think it was some kind of freak side effect of the storm?'

'Lightning has some unusual properties, Banbury, but I'm fairly sure it doesn't come through windows and strike people indoors,' Bryant snapped back. 'Although my mother used to make us cover the mirrors and lay our cutlery flat during thunderstorms. I want that gym taken apart brick by brick. The Highwayman must have gained admittance to the room somehow, in which case he'll have left entry or exit marks. You of all people should know that.'

Banbury was already shaking his head. 'I only had time for a quick look, but unless I'm missing some kind of secret passage, I really don't see how he could have effected an entry. Apart from anything else, Danny Martell would have seen him; he had an unobstructed view of the door from his seat on the machine. If he'd felt threatened, he would have got up, and we know he didn't do that.'

'What are you suggesting?' asked Bryant. 'That we're dealing with some kind of supernatural agent who walks through walls, the living embodiment of a lousy half-remembered poem who's come down to earth for the sole purpose of exacting bloody vengeance on minor celebrities?'

'I didn't say that, Sir,' Banbury pointed out. 'You did.'

Outside the apartment building, Bryant lit his pipe and leaned against the cool glazed bricks, looking across the street to the gymnasium. If the Highwayman was so determined to make it appear that no killer had been at the scene, why was he prepared to show himself to witnesses? Bryant's fascination with crimes of paradox was well documented, but even by the peculiar cases of his own past, this was outstanding.

Something else was here, though; the death sites were public areas associated with wealth and security, not squalid back alleys. There was a sense of voluptuous harm being visited upon random strangers by a dispassionate, cruel mentality. The feeling was shocking because it was so alien. Long ago, Bryant had developed a psychic sensitivity to London's buildings and landscapes, but rarely had he experienced the impression of such a malevolent personality. It tainted the atmosphere and left behind a darkly spreading stain . . .

The grey dome of St Paul's rose beyond the low office buildings. The screeching of seagulls reminded him of the river's nearness. Something tugged at his memory, the faint impression of an earlier case, its detail fading now like a footprint in soft sand. Puzzled by this half-recollection, he crossed the street and walked to the building's doorway.

There, at the base of the steps, was a scratched V in the stonework, with another, inverted, on top of it. With a little imagination, the symbol could be interpreted as a tricorn hat atop a raised collar. The markings were fresh.

The Highwayman had left another calling card.

17

RENEGADE MINDS

They met in the middle of the bridge.

What had once been undertaken as an evening constitutional had now assumed talismanic value, a requirement of their continued survival. Throughout the passing decades, the pair had walked beside the surging sepia waters of the Thames to the bridge's centre, and now the habit was unbreakable. They reserved their secret histories for this moment, their private doubts, their hidden knowledge. It was one of the few places where Bryant was still legitimately allowed to smoke his pipe, and where May could steal a few puffs on a forbidden cigar. Although they usually walked at sunset, early on Wednesday morning the bridge proved to be a convenient meeting place before their return to the unit. A thin dawn mist spiralled from the river, its tendrils clinging to the stanchions of the bridge, sharpening the air with the brackish tang of mud and mildew.

'God, what a business,' said May, passing over a cardboard coffee cup. 'We have to keep a united front on this, Arthur. It will sink us otherwise.'

'You pessimist,' said Bryant, sniffing his coffee. 'Has this got sugar in?' He leaned on the cold stone balustrade and marvelled at the rising dark outlines of the city. 'Look how it's changing.'

'You always say that,' May countered. 'You love St Paul's, the Gherkin, County Hall, the Royal Festival Hall and the London Eye. You hate the Mayor's building and Charing Cross Station. I know exactly what you're about to say because you always say the same thing.'

Bryant was affronted. 'I'm sorry to be so predictable. Habit and familiarity provide me with comfort. What's wrong with that?'

'You're going to get out those strange boiled sweets now, aren't you? The ones nobody sells any more. What will it be today – Cola Cubes, Rhubarb and Custard, Chocolate Logs, Flying Saucers?' He turned to face his astonished partner. 'Come on, what have you got?'

Bryant looked sheepish as he opened a crumpled paper bag, revealing strings of red liquorice. 'Fireman's Hose,' he said apologetically. 'Do you want one?'

'No, I bloody don't.'

'What's wrong with you?' Bryant's trilby had folded down his ears, and his scarf was pulled up to his nose. He looked like a superannuated schoolboy who'd been held back for half a century. Nobody would take him seriously looking like this.

May sighed, turning back to the balustrade. Before them, a pair of police launches were fighting the tide, heading towards Greenwich. 'Look at us. How absurd we are. All these years spent bullying bureaucrats for budgets, working ridiculous hours, losing friends, having no social life, leaving no trace of our efforts. All the stress, all the pain, and we're no further forward than the day we met each other.'

'That's not fair.' Bryant dunked a rubbery length of hose in his coffee and sucked on it ruminatively. 'Think of the destinies we've altered. The lives we've saved. The weight of knowledge we've accumulated.'

'You understand less now about the criminal mind than

when you started,' said May. 'You're always complaining that life is speeding up around you, yet you make absolutely no effort to change.'

'What is this about?' asked Bryant suspiciously.

'Nothing – I'm just frustrated, that's all.'

'We're still investigating. We haven't been beaten yet. You don't fool me. Something's happened.'

'It's our ambitious new Home Office liaison officer,' replied May. 'Leslie Faraday has ordered psychiatric evaluation reports on us. He's gathering background material as ammunition.'

'When did you hear that?'

'I found an email waiting for me from Rufus when I got in last night.'

'Faraday won't find anything of interest. Why are you so worried?'

'Perhaps you don't understand the gravity of our situation. He's looking for a way to shut us down, and he wants it done as quickly as possible.'

'You don't know that for a fact.'

'You have no friends in the Met, Arthur. I do, and they keep me informed. You forget some of the things Faraday could uncover. We freed thirty illegal immigrants last month. We hid their trail and falsified the case's documentation. Do I need to remind you that you also placed a minor in a position of danger, allowing him to be lowered into a sewer with a registered sex offender?'

'When you put it like that it sounds bad,' Bryant admitted.

'That's how Faraday will put it. Wait until he discovers how many cold cases we have on our files.'

'That's part of our remit, John. Half of those investigations were already cold when they came to us.'

'If he re-opens any of them, he's going to find more than just procedural anomalies. We've broken rules. We've faked reports. We've buried evidence.'

'Only for the benefit of the victims, John, and to ensure

149

that justice is done. Truth and fairness are more important than procedure. "A foolish consistency is the hobgoblin of little minds" – Ralph Waldo Emerson.'

'But when a policeman disobeys the law he becomes the worst kind of criminal in its eyes. We won't just lose the unit. We could both go to jail. We've been behaving like renegades for too long.'

Arthur selected another strand of liquorice and chewed it. 'This morbidity doesn't become you, John. I'm usually the negative one. Put it out of your mind. You know how the system works – if we get this right, everything else will be swept under the carpet. We never make mistakes; when we break the law, it's absolutely deliberate.' He beamed hopefully, his bleached false teeth expanding what he'd intended as a life-affirming smile into something both innocent and creepy.

'There's something else you should know. The rumours are starting up again. April has only just joined the unit. I don't want her to hear them. I can't have that conversation with her right now.'

'She'll be fine. You always said we were a family, didn't you? We'll look out for each other and ride it out. Come on, concentrate on the case. I can't do it without you.'

May shook his head. 'I'm not sure I can walk into the briefing room and face everyone this morning.'

'You have to see it as a challenge. Two very public deaths, linked by sightings of a horseman.' His scary smile grew wider.

'They're linked by more than that,' said May.

Bryant could see that he was holding something back. 'Have you found anything out?' he asked.

'There's another link. I couldn't sleep after reading the email, so I started looking for Saralla White's ex-husband, the executive whose sex life she first exposed. It only took a few minutes to locate him – he'd left a trail through dozens of websites. His name is Leo Carey. He was working at Bell

& Lockhead in the City, handling public relations for their corporate clients, but was fired because his wife's exposure of their private life destroyed his credibility. Guess what he does for a living now?'

'I've no idea.'

'He's Danny Martell's publicist. I got hold of his mobile number and rang him. He told me he'd met up with Martell on the night of his death. Even better – they had a fight.' He raised his fist. 'A proper punch-up.'

Bryant's smile grew so broad that his teeth nearly slipped out. 'You're joking.'

'It set me thinking. PR agents jealously guard their contacts, but their circles overlap. I'm pretty sure both victims have a number of colleagues in common. We just haven't uncovered them yet.'

'What did they fight about?'

'You can ask him that yourself,' said May, checking his watch. 'What time to do you make it?'

Bryant squinted at his ancient Timex. 'Twenty past.'

'Twenty past seven?'

'Not entirely sure, old bean. My hour hand appears to have fallen off.'

'They're holding him for us at Albany Street. I said we'd get there as soon as we could. Did you remember to pay your Congestion Charge this morning?'

'Don't be ridiculous, I wouldn't know how to. I've never paid for Victor.' His rust-bucket hippie era Mini Cooper was hardly worth more than a month's congestion fees. 'I keep a length of reflective tape in the glove box, pop it over the number plate this side of the cameras and take it off on the other side. I don't feel guilty about it – the unit should be exempt. We've one staff car between eight, and I'm certainly not going to wait at a bus-stop to get to a crime scene.'

May broke into a smile, digging a package from the jacket of his smart suit. 'I thought you might like to pay it today.' He handed his partner the box. 'Happy Birthday.'

'It's my birthday? Are you absolutely sure?' He thought for a minute. 'Good heavens, October 26th, you're right. I wondered why Alma served my eggs with her earrings on this morning.' He tore open the paper and examined his gift. 'This is really most kind of you, John,' he grinned. 'What on earth is it?'

'It's the very latest in mobile technology. You can access the internet from it and find your position from satellites, and do all sorts of things.'

Bryant was touched. He ran his fingers over the sleek brushed metal of the telephone as if handling a piece of Meissen. 'You mean you're actually trusting me with a gadget?'

May shrugged. 'I have to take a leap of faith some time. It might as well be now.'

Leo Carey was more accustomed to conducting consultations in the calm woody gloom of Claridge's or the immaculate ethereality of the Sanderson Hotel. He glanced up at the moulting distempered walls of the Albany Street nick with as much discomfort on his face as a film star posing for a police mug-shot. His sleek Bond Street-tailored suit and Cambridge tie did little to erase the photocopied image of him tied naked to a toilet that was currently making its way around the police station. Every few minutes, one of the Met constables peered in through the meshed-glass of the interview room and smirked knowingly.

'Popular opinion is formed by small groups of highly influential people,' Carey told the detectives. 'Everyone else is unimportant. It's my job to ensure that the key opinion-formers attend our events.' The grinning officers at the window were distracting him.

'Take no notice of them,' May advised. 'Tell us about Saralla White.'

'I'd been working for British Petroleum as an image consultant,' Carey explained. 'I met Sarah at a launch party,

152

while she was still repping graphic artists around town. She told me she was being kicked out of her Bermondsey flat, and had nowhere to stay. I took her for a bite to eat, and she suggested sleeping on my sofa. We'd only known each other for about an hour! I'd never met anyone like her before. She was so angry and passionate. I had just broken up with Olivia, my girlfriend. I had no experience of girls like Sarah before. She was exciting to be around.'

'And before you knew it, you'd become involved,' May prompted.

'She wasn't easy to be with, mind you, too volatile for comfort, but a lot of fun. Life was never boring. Then I found out why she'd lost her apartment.'

'We know about the drugs. She was dealing cocaine from the premises. We have her arrest details.'

'It was nothing to do with me. And nothing was ever proven. The case got thrown out of court because someone had messed with the evidence. At that point Sarah decided to stop representing artists and become one herself. She came up with an angle, changed her name to Saralla and asked me to help her get media attention.'

'Are you saying that her artistic status was just a pose, that she didn't believe in the causes she supported?'

'No, she believed in them, but I taught her how to use her own personality to create controversy. Belief isn't enough; you have to go out and stir up trouble in the public arena. I taught her everything I knew, and did my job a little too well. She was keeping a weblog of our life together, complete with photographs and filmed footage, and was publishing it behind my back. We fought and I threw her out, but by that time she no longer needed me. Her career had taken off. That should have been the end of it, but she wouldn't keep her mouth shut. The more the press goaded her, the more she told them. She embellished the truth, then completely reinvented her past. Suddenly I was no longer her mentor, but the man who made her pregnant and forced her to have an abortion. She needed a villain in the story, and had enough photographic evidence to flesh out her fantasy.'

'When did you last see her?'

'I didn't. I mean, I broke all contact after hearing about the photographs.'

'Why didn't you take any legal action?'

'Damage limitation. The more you defend yourself, the guiltier you look. My clients started cancelling contracts, so I got out before the company folded on me. I came from an entertainment PR background, and needed to build a client base.'

'So you started low by picking someone with an image problem,' Bryant surmised.

'Martell came with such a bad reputation that nobody else wanted to touch him. I figured if I could make this a success, other offers would come. I thought that after Sarah I could handle anyone, but Martell was a nightmare. Insecurity is a tough trait to deal with. There were rumours about his private life. The tabloids were suspicious, and went fishing for stories about how he spent his evenings, but he was dumb and vain enough to keep taking the bait. This latest escapade has broken within hours of his death, so everyone will think he killed himself. Martell was convinced he'd lose his TV deal. He'd used up all of his friends. He was still popular with the public, but his ratings were starting to slip. He caused offence on ITV 1's breakfast show last week – he was caught on camera making sarcastic comments about his fans – and was getting hate mail as a consequence. If you're going to start manipulating public opinion, you need a clever game plan, and Martell wasn't exactly the brightest bulb in the billboard.'

'Tell us about your argument with him,' May suggested.

'Martell rang me at four yesterday afternoon and asked to meet me at the café in Russell Square in an hour's time. He admitted that he'd gone to a lapdancing club on Monday night, where he'd met a couple of girls who took him back to the Great Russell Hotel for champagne, drugs and a little fooling around – the usual tired old story. Except that the girls told him they were Russian fifteen-year-olds who had come here illegally on a vegetable lorry through the Channel Tunnel. You'd think he would have smelled a rat by now, but instead he went with them. So they're back in the hotel room, and every time the girls break off to take calls on their mobiles, they're actually shooting digital footage of Martell and sending it over the internet to *Hard News*. Turns out they were a couple of twenty-something journalists working for the Blue Dragon herself.'

'Who's that?' asked Bryant.

'Janet Ramsey is a smart Tory bitch who's obsessed with illegal immigrants, and happens to be the new editor of *Hard News*. I couldn't believe he'd been so stupid. It was the kind of story the red tops fantasize about in bed at night. I was just getting somewhere with him, and he had ruined our deal. Martell had a family audience. I told him I had no magic formula to rehabilitate him in the public's eyes, especially with the current social panic about paedophilia still raging. Things got pretty heated between us. I was annoyed that his agent hadn't informed me immediately. It didn't help that Martell had been drinking. I told him I wasn't prepared to represent him any longer, he told me I was useless. He tried to hit me, but fell over a chair. Finally he stormed out.'

'What time was this?'

'About a quarter to six. You can check with the staff in the café. They're bound to remember – we made enough noise.'

'What did you do then?'

'I paid the bill and walked off towards Kingsway, trying to clear my head. I had something to eat at a French place near Lincoln's Inn Fields – I can't remember the name, but it would be easy to find. Then I caught a taxi home.'

'Do you believe him?' asked Bryant as the detectives drove back towards Mornington Crescent.

'He had a fight in a public place, he couldn't lie about that,' said May. 'But do I believe him? I think so. He had a reason to take revenge on Saralla White, and Martell was about to ruin his new career, but it's hardly enough to make you dress up as a highwayman and construct something so insanely baroque – and that's what we're talking about here, a form of insanity. Carey doesn't seem mentally troubled. Everyone in business operates with a kind of personal agenda that might look odd to an outsider. It doesn't make them a killer. If the only suspects we have are perfectly rational men and women, I don't see how we'll find someone who's insane. We can't employ any kind of deductive reasoning.'

'Then we must apply the science of irrationality,' Bryant replied. 'You know what I think we need? Some experts in the field of orchestrated mayhem. I'll draw up a list. I may be required to meet with – unusual people.'

May knew what that meant: his partner would be phoning everyone from chaos theorists to necromancers. 'No, Arthur,' he warned his partner. 'I don't want any of your fringe-dwellers involved. Not this time.'

Bryant was shocked. 'But I've found a new spirit medium who produces electronic ectoplasm that can be charted on a computer – '

'No, Arthur, not the Camden Town Coven or the Southwark Supernaturals or that creepy biochemist who impersonates his dead wife, or anyone else who could be mistaken for a mental patient. Our every move is being watched, and now is not the time to start behaving strangely. We do this my way, or not at all, do you understand?'

Bryant's pout of disapproval said it all. 'You just admitted that we can't follow the usual routes of deductive reasoning. What are we supposed to do?'

May sighed, turning away from the ebbing river. 'I don't know, but we have to think of something fast, before we find ourselves locked out of our own investigation.'

'We can't do it by ourselves,' Bryant admitted. 'We need other talents.'

'Then let's use the PCU staff. There may not be much budget, but we have access to renegade minds.'

'I like your thinking. That's the Battle of Hastings spirit.'

'We lost the Battle of Hastings, Arthur.'

'So we did.' Bryant bit off the last of his Fireman's Hose. 'But this time we'll win.'

The detectives returned to work in a mood of doubtful optimism.

18

SOMETHING OF THE NIGHT

Raymond Land was utterly exhausted.

The years of chasing after devils and phantoms had taken their toll. He couldn't believe he was still stranded here at the unit, like a Japanese soldier guarding a forgotten Pacific atoll decades after the war had ended.

Because the war *had* ended. The kind of crimes the PCU had been set up to investigate no longer existed. If anything, it was easier to recognize the kind of cases the unit didn't get. They didn't get ones with identifiable characteristics, criminal associations, reliable witnesses, usual suspects or even much actual evidence, whether in the form of CCTV footage, DNA or fingerprints. Those under investigation rarely had previous convictions. The PCU prided itself on tackling original, unrepeatable crimes, but such tragedies were in decline. Despite its recent high-profile successes, the unit was an anachronism. Strong young men and women were needed to combat social disorder and the pervasive influence of drugs across the capital. Scarface-quality cocaine was selling in Florida at thirty-five dollars a gram, and was heading towards London in the form of addictive new compounds. The Met had five areas each the size of a complete force elsewhere in the country, and it still couldn't cope. No matter what the massaged Home Office statistics said, as far as public perception was concerned, prostitution, murder, burglary and vandalism were all on the increase – right now a team of Ukranian gangsters were running around North London attacking people with blowtorches – and here he was, playing nursemaid to a group of addled academics who read science-fiction comics and attended poetry readings in their spare time.

His opposite equals were laughing behind his back. The unit staff ignored him. His superiors could barely remember his name. His wife was in the process of leaving him for a younger man, and wanted to take their children. His only friend was Sergeant Renfield, the astonishingly un-pleasant desk officer at Albany Street nick, and Renfield only bothered calling up to arrange a drink because he knew he could thrash Land at billiards. Stanley Marsden, the former DCS HMSO liaison officer, had been allowed to escape with his pension, so why had he been left behind?

Land had stopped hoping for a transfer or a promotion years ago. All he wanted now was a little appreciation. He would settle for a grudging acknowledgement that he had managed to wrangle his wayward detectives out of lambastings, lawsuits and lynchings. Surely he deserved the smallest nod of respect? Truth was, nobody liked the facilitators, but they were necessary, like men who un-blocked drains.

Strangling his tie into a tiny knot and flattening his straggly greying hair in the mirror, he set off for the formal meeting with Leslie Faraday in the minister's Whitehall office. He had been warned not to mention anything to his detectives, who had just arrived and were compiling information in Mornington Crescent's conference room, oblivious to the axe hanging over their heads. He felt guilty, but something had to be done in order to preserve his own sanity.

*   *   *

'Before we go any further today, let's review,' said May, drawing on the whiteboard behind him. 'Saralla White and Danny Martell, both low-grade celebrities, both killed in highly unlikely circumstances. And in both cases, we have sightings of this gentleman.' He taped up an artist's impression of the Highwayman. The morning's newspapers carried new renditions of their supposed nemesis, one computer-generated from a description provided by a pedestrian on Farringdon Road.

May slapped the board, startling PC Colin Bimsley, who was still recovering from his dog's birthday party – an excuse to visit the local pub for a lock-in the night before. 'No fingerprints at either crime scene, no fibres, nothing except a couple of incomplete bootprints in the gallery. Dan – do the honours on those, would you?'

Banbury rose and pulled up a sheet of paper covered with lifted prints. 'Perpetrators always leave footprints at a crime scene; my problem was locating them, and I found none outside the gallery itself. I shot monochrome film to punch up the contrast on the ones raised from inside. These pictures were taken with a dioptric lens and oblique lighting, and it's fairly apparent from the scale bars that this is a rubber-soled motorcycle boot of an unusually large size. I underestimated just how big they were. I'd say we're looking for someone around two metres tall – that's six feet six inches, Sir. Electrostatic lifting got me a couple of flecks of metal in the tread, minuscule traces of aluminium, but they could have been picked up anywhere. Nobody in the gallery was wearing boots, unless somebody changed their footwear, in which case we should have found the original pair. We ran the prints through SICAR – '

'I'm sorry, what's that?' asked Mangeshkar.

'Shoeprint Image Capture and Retrieval software. We now have a confirmed brand, but it's common and available from just about any motorcycle shop in the country. More-over, the tread is worn, so it's no use looking through recent

160

pairs sold. I'm concentrating on Martell now. Giles and I are going to the gym to see if we get anything more in natural light, and I hope to have something to report by the end of the day.'

'Meanwhile,' said May, 'in the absence of any other physical evidence, what conclusions can we draw about the circumstances surrounding these two deaths?'

'Don't worry about speaking out of turn or sounding stupid,' Bryant added. 'You know how John and I operate. Nothing you say has to go outside this room. We're not minuting the session.'

Meera Mangeshkar was the first to raise her hand. 'Both victims had enemies they'd never met,' she pointed out.

'How do you know that?'

'It stands to reason. They'd both expressed controversial opinions in the public arena. White was picketed by pro-lifers because of her statements on abortion. Martell was getting hate-mail from family groups because of his remarks on TV. They could have attracted a stalker with strong right-wing views.'

'That would fit with the traditional profile,' said Giles Kershaw. 'White male, mid-twenties to mid-thirties, interrupted education, unemployed, few friends, embittered. Classic serial-killer stuff, in fact.'

'Dear God, let's not jump to conclusions about a bloody serial killer,' warned May. 'The press will be running photos of Anthony Hopkins in a flash – *what serial killer may look like* – we'll end up starting the kind of social panic this unit was originally set up to defuse.'

'Besides,' added Bryant, 'I'd say the use of the highwayman costume has a profound resonance that goes beyond the knowledge of most uneducated men.' He sat back, refusing to elaborate.

'Both of the victims had fights just before they were murdered,' Bimsley pointed out. 'And they both had estranged ex-partners who were upset with them. White's mentor and the possible father of her child, Calvin Burroughs, and her former boyfriend, Leo Carey. And there's Martell's ex-wife.'

Emboldened by the others, April half-raised a hand. 'Anyone could find out where the victims were,' she offered timidly.

'What do you mean, April?'

'Well, their movements are published on websites and in celebrity lifestyle magazines. Their favourite restaurants, even their home addresses are easy to discover. Anyone could have figured out the times of their appearances at the gallery and the gym.'

'Very good point,' said May. 'Anything else?'

'The physical impossibility of the murders,' suggested Banbury. 'We've been over the figures a hundred times. Not a single person unaccounted for in the gallery. Thirty-two adults and fourteen children surrounding the room in which she was killed. No other way in or out except via the electronic turnstiles. The same situation with Martell: no one else in the gym, which was locked from the inside. White was dropped into a tank over eight feet high, as if she really had been thrown by someone on the back of a horse. Martell was hit by lightning in a room that has no electrical appliances apart from the recessed neon-lighting panels overhead, none of which had been tampered with, by the way.'

'What about the paradox of the Highwayman himself?' asked Bryant. 'You don't attend a fancy-dress party if you don't want to be noticed. So why go to the trouble of leaving no trace at the murder site if you're then planning to parade around in period costume? He wanted someone to spot him. Why else would he wear the outfit?'

'He could belong to one of those historical societies,' said Longbright. 'You know, Cavaliers, Roundheads, guys who dress up and re-enact the Battle of Culloden. I can run a check on memberships.'

'You don't have much of a physical description to go on,' warned May.

'We know he's tall, about six-six, broad-chested, black-haired – '

'The hair sounds like a part of the disguise.'

Longbright tapped at her notepad. 'The witness reports suggest he might have five o'clock shadow, which would probably make him dark-haired. No fingerprints because he's wearing leather gloves.'

'We can't go to Land with this,' said May. 'None of it hangs together.'

'That's what bothers me most,' Bryant admitted, tipping back his chair dangerously. 'He leaves an elaborate calling card at the first crime scene, then leaves a very different one at the second. He dresses conspicuously and chooses to attack in public places, but nobody sees him in the act of taking lives. And – ' Bryant's watery blue eyes dilated, refocussing across the room at a point halfway up the wall, like a cat. Everybody waited.

'And what?' prompted May.

Bryant was thinking of the symbolic head on the logo of the Roland Plumbe Community Estate. But as he looked at the anxious faces surrounding him, he found himself unable to elucidate his half-formed thoughts. Kershaw had placed the Highwayman's age between twenty-five and thirty-five, the statistical range for a serial killer, but Bryant was sure these were no crimes of passion; they were calculated for some other purpose entirely. He wanted to explain that they were not looking for a stalker or a madman, but for a very moral human being, someone filled with a righteous sensitivity and the invisibility of ordinariness. In the eyes of the killer the victims were immoral and deserved to suffer. It was why the Highwayman wanted to be seen. He desired acknowledgement, recognition for his services, perhaps even hero worship. The choice of clothes, grand and elegant, the deliberate appearances in crowded spaces.

Bryant wanted to say all this but something stopped him, because he felt he would lead them all to a strange and dangerous place. It would confirm Faraday's worst suspicions and jeopardize the unit's existence. *There is another, far more sinister force at work here,* he thought, *and I daren't trust myself to voice my darkest feelings.*

The Right Honourable Leslie Faraday MP was seated behind the most imposing desk Raymond Land had ever seen, an acre of green glass that made him appear to be sitting upright in a stagnant pond. The pudgy, wide-eyed young man with slicked sandy hair whom the detectives had first met in the 1970s was now a bloated, bald and bad-tempered time-server who had never managed to shake off his image as the government's most pedantic minister.

In a long and almost entirely unmeritworthy career he had been shunted all over Whitehall. When civil servants are bad at their jobs, they are never cast out and prevented from pursuing their chosen career; they are merely moved elsewhere until they find a department that will have them. As Minister of State for the Arts, Faraday's remark about Andy Warhol's work consisting of 'boring old photos painted in the kind of colours black people like' had resulted in the outraged cancellation of a major exhibition. As Minister for Rural Affairs and Local Environmental Quality, he had managed to bring the nation's low-waged road-gritters out on strike during the worst blizzards in a century after calling them 'a bunch of work-shy Irish layabouts'. As Minister of State for Sport, he had sparked off a race row by inviting a white South African paramilitary leader to a Brixton Jail cricket match. After spending two years as a Minister Without Portfolio (where, by definition, he was unable to find anyone to offend), he was rehabilitated in the Home Office with a new brief: to make specialized police units pay, or shut them down.

Incompetent men exist in every profession, but they are

easily dealt with. Faraday remained in Whitehall because of his single great talent, also his curse, which was that he never forgot anything.

'Mr Land,' he announced. 'We met on August the seventh, 1971, did we not? It rained all afternoon. Then I met you with Mr Bryant, and again with Mr May two years later, under more clement circumstances. How are you?'

Shaking his hand, thought Land, was like dipping your fingers into warm Swarfega – clammy and clinging. As Faraday reseated himself, his brown suit constricted his stomach and his shirt collar seemed to throttled him almost to the point of asphyxiation. He tapped at an old-fashioned intercom. 'Deirdre, could we have two teas? Brooke Bond, very weak for me. And see if we have any of those ginger biscuits, the oblong ones with the little bits of peel in.' When he suddenly tipped his chair back, Land thought for a moment that he had submerged, but he bounced up again in a move that had been practised across an eternity of dull Whitehall afternoons. 'I must confess I'm at a bit of a loss to know what to do about your two detectives,' Faraday admitted. 'I mean, they've been at the unit a jolly long time, so they must be doing something right.'

'I was hoping you'd give me some advice, Sir,' said Land. He waited for a response. A clocked ticked distantly. Dust settled.

Faraday sighed like a leaking, tired balloon. 'From your memorandum, it's clear that you'd like to transfer to a more – professional – unit. I've given the problem some thought, and have decided that, because I know Mr Bryant and Mr May personally, I'm probably not the right chap for the job, so I'm going to hand the matter over to my new assistant. He has the kind of specialist knowledge that might be required for a more covert operation.' Faraday pressed a buzzer on his desk. 'Deirdre, would you send in Mr Kasavian?'

Although Land had only met Faraday a handful of times, their wives had once been crown green bowling together, and he thought he had the mark of the man. Now, though, he sensed that he might be getting out of his depth.

As Mr Kasavian entered, the sun passed behind a cloud outside Faraday's office and the room was plunged into shadow. Kasavian looked as if he was used to this. Tall, dark and, well, *saturnine* was really the only word, there was more than a touch of Mephistopheles about him, and he would probably have enjoyed the comparison. His slicked-back hair and jet-black suit lent him the air of an Edwardian funeral director.

'I'll take over now, Sir,' Kasavian warned Faraday, effectively dismissing him from the conversation. He towered darkly between them, folding his hands behind his back with an unsettling crick of the knuckles.

'I read your memo with interest, Mr Land, and found that it suits our current need to cut spending by a third across the specialized units. The simple fact is that murder is becoming far too expensive. As I'm sure you know, the cost of a single investigation can take up a tenth of an area's annual budget. The Serious Organized Crime Agency is planning to use the National Intelligence model to coordinate cross-agency operations for now, but their long-term plan is to consolidate all specialist units with the minimum of disruption. I hardly need outline the benefits: an end to so-called "blue on blue" clashes, and a huge financial saving for the government. It is imperative, therefore, that we arrange for the PCU to be closed down. And to do that, we must remove its senior detectives. The problem is that they command a certain amount of respect among older law-enforcement officials, so they must be quickly discredited.'

'Mr Bryant and Mr May are entirely decent men,' said Land. 'Their intentions are honest, if a little misguided.'

'Come on, Mr Land, you can't have it both ways.' When Kasavian's hooded eyes turned on the subject of his attention, it was as though steel shutters had slammed down, screening off the weaknesses of the human heart. 'You described specific instances of their incompetence to Mr Faraday *in writing*. I've begun checking into Home Office records on our dealings with your unit, and there seem to be an astonishing number of irregularities, including – if we can lay our hands on the original documents – some of an extremely serious nature involving a number of illegal immigrants. Clearly, we've only uncovered the tip of the iceberg. If these detectives have been allowed to twist the system to their own ends, there will be others who are just as guilty. All those who support and admire them must be made to see the truth. Who knows how deeply this corruption runs through the unit? For all *I* know, even you may be involved.' Mr Kasavian's black eyes glittered with malice. 'Later today, I have a meeting with representatives of the Fraud Squad to begin auditing your casework. You may consider this the start of the PCU's first internal investigation, and hopefully their last. I suggest that if you personally wish to remain untainted, you had better make sure that your own dealings are in order.'

Now that he was finally getting what he had wished for, Raymond Land started to have doubts. If Kasavian could so quickly agree to dismissing two senior members of the force, he would easily turn his attention to others. But it was too late; the wheels of Whitehall were slow to grind forwards, but once started, they would not be stopped.

19

ARRHYTHMIA

It was cold enough to condense breath in the converted school gymnasium, and that was how Oswald Finch liked it. Some nights he worked until his fingers and nose turned blue. The lower half of the room was below street level, and remained cool until the two sticky months of the English summer, when everything, including Oswald, started to smell bad. Where climbing frames had once stood against the narrow windows, there were now four body lockers. The sprung wooden basketball floor had been covered with carpet tiles that retained the acrid reek of spray bleach.

'Are you still here?' asked Bryant, leaning in the doorway. 'I thought you'd have gone by now.'

'How can I, when you keep sending me bodies?' Finch complained. 'Raymond Land refuses to accept my resignation, says it will have to wait for a few weeks while he's sorting something out. It's unfair, keeping me at my post like this. Do you have any idea how long it takes me to get up in the morning? If I'd have known it would get so difficult to tie my laces, I'd have bulk-bought elastic-sided shoes back in the fifties.'

'Come on, I know there's nothing you'd rather be doing than opening up a cadaver. It's unnatural, but nothing to be ashamed of. I see you've got Danny Martell on the slab. What have you found for me?'

'Someone should run statistics on how many television comedians suffer untimely deaths.' Finch prised open a fatty yellow flap of chest flesh and peered inside, wrinkling his long nose. 'They seem to peg out at an earlier age than the rest of us, and in more unusual ways.'

'Not strictly true,' said Bryant. 'Look at Bruce Forsyth. He'll live for ever, or at least his wig will. For most celebrities, the trick is surviving the scrutiny of the gutter press.'

'If you make a deal with the devil you must expect to be damned,' said Finch gloomily. 'This man Martell – his body was not in good shape. Take a look.' He unfurled another section of the black micromesh mylar sheet from his dissection tray and revealed the bloated corpse of the entertainer in full. 'This is what years of fast food, high stress and sitting in cars shouting at the traffic do to you. That's not a liver, it's low-grade foie gras. To be honest, I only opened him up out of nosiness; a first-week intern could look at his face and say what caused his death.' Finch tapped the chest with the car antenna he used as an indicator. 'Dicky pump. His valves are leaky, his pipes are furred, his blood's virtually all fat. He's suffering from arteriosclerosis, so I'm looking at ventricular fibrillation that went into a fatal heart attack. But then I have to add the witness reports about this so-called lightning flash. Did they really see some kind of electrical pulse strike Martell?'

'I wondered if it might have been the reflection of a distant lightning strike on the window of the apartment,' said Bryant. 'That would have been an easy mistake to make. The storm looked close.'

'But if it *was* an electrocution, that gives us a cause for the VF. An electric shock will cause the heart's ventricles to twitch – it will if applied to any of the body's muscles – but the electrical cycle is so fast and erratic that it can interfere with the normal contractions of the heart. The muscles quiver without pumping, and a fatal arrhythmia occurs. It happens with low-voltage appliances like hair-dryers and toasters. The current needs a single point of entry.' He turned over Martell's hands and pointed to a pair of faint red blotches on his palms. 'We've got something here: marks indicating that a shock passed from one limb to the other, right across the chest, deregulating the heart.'

'We considered that,' said Bryant, 'but Banbury failed to find anything on his initial examination of the room. None of the equipment is operated electrically. The weight-lifting equipment is based on mechanical leverage. There are a couple of wall plugs for vacuum cleaners, but they have safety caps that haven't been touched in a couple of days.'

'I can only tell you what killed him, Arthur, not how it was done.' Finch folded the fatty flaps of Martell's chest shut like the curtains of a toy theatre. 'It wouldn't take a very powerful electrical device, just one with an alternating current. You can survive a low DC, it's AC you have to watch out for.'

'There was nothing in the room, Oswald,' Bryant insisted.

'Then I'm afraid there's something you've missed,' replied the pathologist. 'How are you getting on with White?'

'It seems increasingly likely that Calvin Burroughs was the father of her child, but it's too early to say for sure.' Bryant sniffed the air. 'If you let me smoke my pipe in here, it would get rid of the ghastly smell.'

'This is meant to be a sealed sterile area. You are not allowed to smoke your disgusting Old Navy Rough Cut Sailors' Shag in here. I found fag ash in my body tray last week and knew it was you.'

'I mix it with eucalyptus leaves. It's medicinal.' Bryant picked up a pair of steel rib-cutters. 'Can I borrow these? I'm thinking of having a barbecue at the weekend.'

'Just leave things alone.' Finch snatched the instrument

from him. 'If you really want to help, get me Giles Kershaw as an assistant.'

Bryant smiled slyly. 'Will you stay if I do?'

The ancient pathologist went to wash his hands at the sink. 'I'll think about it,' he said, making bear-catching-salmon motions that told Bryant the water was scalding. 'But things will have to improve around here,' he added, shaking off water.

'Then I'll have a word with Raymond.' Bryant tipped his head back at Martell's corpse. 'The zips on his tracksuit top were welded shut, by the way.'

'They were?' Finch looked up, amazed. 'Why didn't any-one tell me this?'

'You complained about bodies arriving with their clothes on.'

'You remember those two Japanese ladies who sheltered under a tree in Hyde Park during a thunderstorm? They were struck by lightning, and their zip fasteners melted. Judging from the marks on Martell's wrists, it sounds like the same thing. That changes everything. All you have to do now is find out how it was done.'

'On the case, old sausage,' said Bryant, slipping the rib-cutters into his overcoat pocket and sauntering from the room.

20

ANCIENT BLOOD

Dan Banbury and Giles Kershaw had so little in common that they were ideally suited to working together.

There were some similarities: both were in their late twenties, both had been high scorers at university, neither had much field experience. Despite their intelligence and enthusiasm, the unit was able to buy them cheaply, because each possessed a flaw. Banbury had spent his entire childhood in his bedroom in Hackney operating increasingly sophisticated computer networks while his parents explored new methods of destroying each other's happiness downstairs, and the period had taken its toll by leaving him with no social skills. He assumed everyone was interested in crime-scene technology, and bored civilians into submission at the slightest provocation. Years of junk food and immobility had left him with the unprepossessing air of a root vegetable, a turnip in shape, a parsnip in colouring. Women made a special effort to avoid him. Lately he had dieted, exercised and taken advice on a haircut, so that he now approximated a normal human being, but he still fell short in the area of normal conversation, and women still avoided him.

Giles Kershaw came from a posh, impoverished family

whose country home had been sold to the government in 1976 and turned into the National Museum of Farming Implements. His speech was so strangled that his tongue fell over in conversation, and hardly anyone in London could understand him. The police force is no place for the upper classes. He was the first person in his family ever to have a job or buy his own furniture. As a consequence, he had suffered snubs from his friends and ridicule from his colleagues. At least he had social skills – rather too many, in fact – and was prepared to teach Banbury the basics. It was no secret that Bryant and May saw the duo as potential successors who might one day come to inherit the unit, should it miraculously survive that long.

Still, Banbury and Kershaw had never worked closely on a case together before, and bets were being taken in the unit staffroom as to whether they would prove a successful combination or end up conducting a class war. The PCU's new independence meant that its component parts had to fit as well as members of a football squad. That meant no stars, no upstaging, no missed passes. Their first test came the following morning, in the sealed-off gym behind Farringdon Road, as the pair unpacked their equipment: bags, pots, sacks, swab kits, water-bottles, tape, labels, print powders, flat-packed boxes, cameras and a mobile Smartwater Index tracer that Banbury was dying to try out.

'Perspiration stains,' Giles Kershaw indicated, walking around the exercise equipment. 'Looks like there are plenty of them on the machine Martell was using.'

'A man of that size should have been leaving pools of sweat,' said Banbury. 'Never see the point of exercise myself, so long as you get the odd walk in. The patches must have dried fast, but we can still get a residue match. Maybe it wasn't all his.'

'Don't get into the glands, old sausage, they're too un-reliable.' Sweat contained amino acids, fats, chlorides, urea and sugar in varying amounts, but its construction varied in the body from one day to the next. 'I take it you're assuming his attacker managed to slip under the door with his portable lightning conductor, then leave the same way.'

'I don't know, maybe he killed Martell by remote control.'

'Perverse but possible, I suppose.'

Banbury dropped to his knees, then shimmied under the seat of the exercise machine, examining its base. 'He certainly didn't come in through the main door.'

'You can't be sure of that.'

'Martell left pristine prints on both inner and outer handles. You can't open a door without touching the handle. The prints should be smudged, otherwise we must assume no one else came in via the entrance. Forget the windows, they're barred and dead-bolted.' Banbury wriggled back out and rose to inspect the grip-bars. 'There's no other access, so there has to be something here you've missed.'

'Something *I've* missed? You're the crime-scene manager, lovey. I don't know why you're examining those – Martell never touched bare metal. Both the grips have rubber slip-covers.'

Banbury pulled at the foot-long grips, but they fitted tightly over the steel arms of the machine. 'You're right, he shouldn't have come into contact with metal. There's no way to get these off. Give me a hand.' Between them, they managed to move the machine out and check beneath it. 'If you were going to electrocute someone here, you'd have to assume your victim would be wearing rubber-soled trainers, so I guess the current would need to pass through his hands. Martell wasn't wearing workout gloves.'

They tore up four carpet tiles and exposed a red rubberized layer coating the concrete floor. Banbury climbed behind the machine and examined the white ceramic wall tiles. 'Hang on a minute, take a look at this.' He shone a penlight into a centimetre-wide hole between the tiles.

'Clutching at straws,' said Kershaw, disappointed. 'It's just an air bubble in the grout. What's behind there?'

174

'A private apartment, I don't know who it belongs to. The hole looks like it might go all the way, though.'

'Not big enough to pass anything through.'

'Yes, it is. Let's get the keys.'

They found the caretaker and had themselves admitted to a narrow flat thickly perfumed and decorated in claustrophobic seventies paisley patterns of green, yellow and brown.

'Mme Briquet divides her time between here and her villa in Menton,' explained the caretaker. 'She wouldn't like me letting strange men into her flat.'

'We're not strange,' said Kershaw. 'We're from the Peculiar Crimes Unit.'

'All right.' The caretaker regarded him uncertainly. 'Just don't disturb anything.'

'That depends on what we find, mate,' Banbury bridled. 'We might have to tear the place to bits.'

Kershaw silenced his partner with a look. 'We'll be terribly careful,' he promised. 'This will only take a moment.'

They located the connecting wall to the gymnasium. Banbury tapped on it experimentally. 'Kitchen,' he said. 'Look at the cooker. Interesting.'

Kershaw couldn't see what was interesting about an ancient upright electric Canon, but held his tongue. Banbury knelt and felt around in the gloom. 'Blimey, there's some muck behind here,' he complained.

After a few minutes he heaved himself to his feet, dragging a coil of fine copper wire from behind the stove. 'He's a clever sod, but we've got him.' He waved the roll in a chubby fist. 'Did you ever have a home physics kit when you were a kid?'

'Certainly not.'

'So what did you do for fun?'

'I went shooting on our estate.'

'Yeah, there were a few shootings on our estate, too. Better warn the caretaker this apartment's part of a crime scene now. His tenant's going to have a fit.' Banbury scratched himself thoughtfully while studying the wire. 'I won't get prints off this, but I might be able to lift a palm heel from the cooker front. He had to push it back into place.' He produced a Zephyr brush from his kit and twirled it experimentally. 'You know, the Met have put more technology on the street than any other force in Europe. They're outside my flat monitoring radio waves from fake ice-cream vans, and still couldn't stop my car from being nicked. They'd be useless at something like this. This is the kind of crime I joined the unit for. It requires belief in the absurd. Even in death, you can be given proof of the desperate ingenuity of human nature.'

'I'm pleased you approve of the killers we attract,' said Kershaw, nonplussed. 'Go and get the rest of your kit. It's time we scored one for the unit.'

Arthur Bryant found himself back at the Street, the dingy, litter-strewn concrete corridor running beneath the central block of the Roland Plumbe Community Estate. His route took him through a flooded concrete stairwell where a sodden mattress slumped beside stacks of broken kitchen furniture. He shook his head in wonder, unable to imagine why anyone would deliberately despoil their home territory.

Bryant's parents had conformed to the wartime London cliché about East End pride and poverty. In Bethnal Green it was common for a wife to embarrass her old man by taking his Sunday lunch down to the pub. His mother aired the family's bed linen, but never her emotions. Whenever she was angry she cleaned the house, and the house was always spotless. Women of whom she didn't approve were accused of keeping a dirty home. He wondered what she would have made of the estate.

Lorraine Bonner was waiting for him again. She had called the unit an hour earlier to tell him that the Highwayman had been sighted once more. 'Mr Bryant, this is getting to be a habit,' she smiled, passing him a plastic cup. Word of

176

Bryant's heroin-like addiction to strong tea had obviously got about. 'The girls are over here.'

She led the way beneath an arch to a mesh-glassed stairwell door. Inside, two teenagers sat on the steps. Bryant recognized the look they shared: pale, scraped-back hair tied into a short ponytail in a style derogatively referred to as a Croydon facelift, hoop earrings, puffa jackets, studded jeans, charm bracelets, baby-pink shoes over white socks. One was smoking, both were chewing gum. They appeared to be soured, sullen and battle-hardened at thirteen, and perhaps they were, but Lorraine reckoned she could scratch the brittle surface and discover ordinary teenage hopes and insecurities. Such youngsters had been referred to as Chavs for decades, but this mysterious term had only recently passed into universal use.

'Danielle, Sheree, this is Mr Bryant. I want you to tell him what you told me.'

'I'm not a policeman, strictly speaking,' he quickly explained. 'I'm trying to find out if the man you saw is—'

'We seen him on the telly,' said Danielle suddenly. 'The Highwayman. It's the same bloke. We all know who he is 'cause he's in, like, a gang and that. We seen you and all. What you going to give us if we tell you?'

Bryant had been hoping they had not seen him before. The testimony of his witnesses would now be tainted by previous exposure. 'Where did you see the Highwayman?' he asked.

'Third-floor bridge.' Danielle looked at her friend for confirmation.

'You mean the balcony that runs along the front of the block?' asked Bryant.

'The bridges connect the two newer wings to the central block,' Lorraine explained. 'There's one on the third floor, and one on the sixth.'

'He was standing there like, "Come on, then, come and get me," like he was disrespecting and fronting out being so hard,' said Sheree in a sudden rush.

'Can you describe him to me?'

'He was wearing these raw leathers, you know, like a biker, only a black mask over his eyes and this cap thing and boots and whatever.'

Bryant knew it would be a struggle getting the girls to articulate clearly enough for a witness statement; they had rarely been challenged to describe anything in detail. How much of what they said was culled from artists' impressions on TV and in newspapers? Perhaps they simply wanted attention, and had invented the sighting.

Sheree launched another assault on the English language. 'St C is blatantly taxin' us saying it's someone on this estate just 'cause we got the Saladins and they're Yahs and they diss us and saying we're slack and that, so when they come here sharkin' us we're gonna bust 'em up.'

'I'm not at all sure I understood a word of that.' Bryant turned to Lorraine for help. His recent reading matter had taught him that most London teen slang was Jamaican, but that it changed from one borough to the next. He tried to imagine how it would be to grow up in a permanent atmosphere of threat.

'The Saladins are a gang of boys who hang around here causing trouble,' the community officer explained. 'A couple of them have ASBOs, so we've been able to curfew them, but they still turn up on the estate after dark.'

'Is there anything else?' Bryant asked the girls doubtfully.

Danielle pulled her mobile from her jacket and flicked it open. 'I took a picture,' she said, turning the image to him. 'He was there for ages, so I zoomed in and got some really mint close-ups. Sell it to ya.'

Bryant stared at the mobile in amazement. It was like being shown a photograph of the Loch Ness Monster, except that these children were unlikely to have tampered with the image. More importantly, it was their first piece of real proof that the Highwayman really existed.

'I'll need to borrow the phone,' he told the girls.

'That is, like, so no chance on that!' squealed Danielle, with her friend in support.

'I'm afraid you don't have a choice. This is police evidence.'

'You ain't having it.' Danielle thrust out a defiant chin.

They could erase the shot if you handle this badly, he suddenly thought. *Learn from your mistakes at St Crispin's.*

'Tell you what, I'll trade you this.' He produced the beautiful chrome-trimmed state-of-the-art mobile May had bought him for his birthday.

Danielle examined it carefully, then handed over her phone.

John's going to kill me, thought Bryant as he walked away with the evidence in his pocket, but another thought excited him. The Roland Plumbe Estate gang, the Saladins. He could scarcely believe they existed.

The area of Clerkenwell, and specifically the gothic arch of St John's Gate, was the dwelling place of London's most venerable traditions and legends, the home of old religions and ancient mysteries. For half a millennium, the Knights Hospitallers had flourished in there. The charitable hospital of St John of Jerusalem had been filled with wounded crusaders, and its priory church was inextricably bound with the Knights Templars. In 1187, when Saladin retook Jerusalem, he had allowed the Hospitallers to flourish. On 3 October 1247, the Knights Templars presented King Henry III with a thick crystalline vase containing the blood of Christ. The authenticity of the relic had been attested by the seals of the Patriarch of Jerusalem, and by all the prelates of the Holy Land. The fateful location of Christ's blood supposedly lay lost in the ruins of Clerkenwell.

And the Saladins still survived.

Lorraine had shown him the gang markings of the Saladins painted along the walls of the Street, a red and white cross-hilt, the symbol of the knights themselves. The wiping of a crusader's sword represented an undefiled life. He had seen other gang markings: a spray-painted chevron between three combs, a modern version of the arms of Prior Botyler, the design taken from the original priory window of St John's. The prior of St John had ranked as the first baron of England. In the 850-year-old diagonally buttressed crypt, caskets had been stood upright and ghosts had supposedly shuffled through the silent nights.

Bryant wondered now if Clerkenwell, the home and heart of the crusades, an area forever linked to the city of Jerusalem and to the blood of Christ himself, had spawned new acolytes every bit as dangerous as their Christian ancestors.

21

LOYALTIES

Dan Banbury flicked on his desk lamp and ushered Bryant into his office at the PCU. He tried not to appear excited, but this was his first chance to shine before his superior, and his mask of calm rationality was slipping.

He opened his file on Danny Martell's murder, clicking on a scaled photograph of the copper coil. 'I think we've an extremely demented individual on our hands,' he said, pointing to the image on screen. 'I asked myself: Why didn't he kill White and Martell in unprotected private spots? Why wait until it was virtually impossible to get at them?'

'Because the impossibility is what makes it appealing,' said Bryant.

'Exactly. Martell kept to a regular schedule, so first of all our perpetrator needed to make a floor plan of the building, and he found what he needed next door, in an apartment kept empty for half the year. This was a lot easier to gain access to than the gym. Of course, the idea was to make us think he'd been in the gym when Martell was killed – a little bit of magician's misdirection there. Giles and I talked to the caretaker, who has no idea how many keys his tenant kept to her apartment. Great security on the gym, lousy system for the flats. We're trying to find the tenant to see if she had

181

direct contact with the Highwayman, but I think we'll draw a negative to that.'

He opened another image, the floor plan of the apartment. 'Inside, the kitchen gives him what he needs, a party wall to the gym. Next, he requires something with an alternating current, and finds an added bonus: there's an old-fashioned, free-standing electric cooker. He drills a tiny hole through the wall. This is the weakest part of his plan, as he could damage the wall on the other side and give himself away. If he'd known it was tiled rather than painted, he'd probably have rethought the move, but he's lucky. The drill-bit exits through the grout.

'Now, he unplugs the cooker and swaps the thirty-amp plug for a pair of insulated copper wires, which he feeds into the hole. He probably gains access to the gym early one morning, a day or two before Martell comes for his work-out, and pulls the ends of the wires through. This last bit is tricky, as he needs to use a needle and thread to sew the uninsulated ends of the wires through the rubber grips on the pectoral fly machine. I tried it myself; it took a good five minutes, but I did it without having to remove the handle-cover. He threads them in a single line that can't be seen against the black rubber. When Martell arrives for his workout, the killer lets himself into the apartment and switches on the current. Martell's hands and chest are covered in sweat, making him the perfect conductor. The circuit is completed, and the current interrupts the rhythm of the victim's heart. At which point, our Highwayman pulls firmly on the wire coil, unthreading it from the grips and reeling it back through the hole. I tried this as well, and it was dead easy to do.'

'There's one thing wrong with your theory,' said Bryant. 'He'd have to be mad as a bag of snakes to go to so much trouble.'

'Maybe he was excited by the sheer absurdity of the act,' Banbury suggested.

'You're forgetting that he doesn't even get to see it. Arsonists usually stick around to witness the results of their work. Due to the spontaneity of their actions, murderers are generally present during the act itself. Where is the pleasure in this glorified piece of Heath Robinson tomfoolery? Where is the profit?'

'As you said, maybe he's barking. I'm just telling you how it was done.' Banbury was disappointed with the effect of his news.

'For which I thank you, but it gets us nowhere. How are you getting on with the photos on the mobile?'

'It's a cheap Nokia. The picture quality's not great, but she took several shots, so I was able to replace the blurred sections from one frame with sharper ones from another, creating a composite. The resolution is a little clunky, but take a look.' He opened the graphics file and expanded the reworked image.

'So now we have our man,' said Bryant, adjusting his bifocals and craning forward. 'There's something very familiar about this picture.'

The photograph showed a broad-chested figure in black leggings and a leather jacket, standing on the bridge of the Roland Plumbe apartment block looking down into the quadrangle, his hands on his hips in an ironically heroic pose. He wore a slender black mask that covered the area around his eyes. A lock of thick black hair protruded from his cap, which was a smaller version of the traditional highwayman's tricorn.

'What's that at his waist?' asked Bryant, thumping the screen with a wrinkled finger.

'I can enlarge the image and lighten it a little, but we'll lose some sharpness.' Banbury went to the graphics menu and blew up a square section. He tried a second time, but the detail was lost.

'That's all right, I can see what it is,' said Bryant, satisfied. 'He's wearing a flintlock pistol. He really is a highwayman.

Ah, Janice, how did you get on with the historical societies?'

Longbright had entered with her notes. 'Plenty of English Civil War buffs, mostly Cavalier and Roundhead uniforms, although someone usually comes along dressed as Cromwell. A few Crimean War fans – crimson outfits with epaulettes and gold buttons, hardly our man's cup of tea. And some First World War nuts, but I'm reliably informed that it's only the German and Prussian officers' uniforms that attract a certain type of obsessive. Nobody wants to be a British Tommy. Nothing about highwaymen, though. I tried the theatrical costumiers in Shaftesbury Avenue. They have one highwayman outfit made for a film called, let me see, *Plunkett and Macleane*, for film and television use only, and it's not been rented out in months.'

'What's he doing hanging around a block of council flats?' Bryant wondered. 'Does this mean he lives there? Was he returning home?'

'According to the time register on the mobile, the shots were taken several hours after Martell's murder,' Banbury pointed out. 'That means he's dressing up for the sheer hell of it.'

'Or he has a purpose we've yet to discern.' Bryant rose and walked to the window, looking down into the wet streets of Mornington Crescent. 'If it turns out that he lives on the estate and he's a member of the Saladins, does that mean he has a darker intention, something that connects with the location of the blood of Christ?'

'I'm sorry, you've lost me there,' said Banbury, perplexed.

'Oh, nothing.' Bryant had decided to keep his more contentious opinions about the case secret, although he had mentioned his suspicions to May, who had headed back to Clerkenwell to run a different kind of check.

John May climbed the steps to the entrance of St Crispin's and removed the list of names from his pocket. He felt like interrogating the pupils who had humiliated Bryant, just to

184

put a dent in their confidence, but knew that acts of retaliation had a way of sticking to the conscience. Instead, he went to visit the relief teacher, Elliot Mason.

May found him in a sweat-stained tracksuit, bent double in the ground-floor corridor, trying to claw back some breath. Mason looked so puny and bookish, it came as a surprise to see him involved in physical education.

'If you're here to talk to the kids again, I can't help you,' the teacher warned him. 'Mr Kingsmere is back, so they're not under my jurisdiction any more. I've just taken the second years for a sprint, and it nearly killed me. The Head knows how much I hate competitive sport. We've got a sports master called Gossage who spends his entire life in the open air and shouts all the time. He looks like a shaved sheep, very red and meaty. The boys call him Sausage. You'd think he'd be fit but he's always off having operations, so I've copped his roster. I'm supposed to supervise post-run ablutions, but once you've experienced the smell of thirty gym-kits in a locker room, you'll do anything to get out of it. Care to walk very slowly with me?'

'I don't want to upset the applecart by getting the boys out of their class again,' said May. 'Actually, you can probably help me.'

'Fire away,' wheezed Mason, who looked as if he might collapse at any moment.

'The Saladins, a gang that hangs around the Roland Plumbe Community Estate. I've never heard of them, and we've nothing on file under that name. Are they new? Some of the boys here suggested they knew something about the man we're seeking. I wonder if the gang might even be harbouring him. Some of the kids on the estate reckon that the Highwayman's identity is common knowledge.'

'Dear God, don't start believing children,' sighed Mason. 'Let's go back outside so I can sneak a Rothmans. There used to be a time when it was the kids who had to hang around the bike sheds smoking, not the teachers.' They returned to the school steps, and Mason guiltily lit up. 'Remember Matilda, who told such dreadful lies?'

May recalled the Hilaire Belloc poem. 'You're saying they all lie?'

'Not intentionally, perhaps, but even the simplest truths can become fabulously distorted. As far as I'm concerned, teenagers are incapable of recounting the simplest fact without embellishment. Their capacity for self-deception is astounding. They seek authorship, they want to be the one who creates the interest. It's the oddest phenomenon. I don't remember being like that.'

'So what is the truth, then?'

'There's certainly a gang on the estate, if you can call it that. A loose group united in apathy would be a more accurate description. Two years ago, one of the seniors here was stabbed in the stomach after tangling with them. He made a remarkable recovery, but his parents withdrew him from the school. Big hoo-hah, I'm surprised you don't remember it.'

'We're no longer part of the Met,' May explained. 'We don't have access to the notes on cases that fall under their jurisdiction. Did they make an arrest?'

'Nothing was ever proven, but the enmity still runs deep. There's a racial element, too. The boys here are mostly lapsed Church of England or Muslim. Some of the Saladins are committed hard-line Christian. They believe in the fiery sword of God's vengeance – probably the result of playing too many computer games. The gang's ringleaders are white skinheads, but they're not like the ones I remember from my teenage years. The territorial boundaries between teens shift so fast these days, you never know where new allegiances lie.'

'How do you know so much about them?' asked May.

'The school's athletics pitch falls inside their boundary. I see them hanging about all the time. Picking up on their conversation is a teacher's habit, I'm afraid. Still, I wouldn't take too much notice of your informants.'

'Oh, why not?'

'Kids join gangs because they crave a sense of belonging. They're looking for respect outside of the parental unit. Your man is a loner, isn't he? Why would he be hanging around with a bunch of kids?' Mason took a drag on his cigarette while he considered his own question. 'Ah, I see, the grim spectre of paedophilia rears its head. You think he's preying on them.'

'That would give us an entirely different profile,' said May.

'Then I'd suggest you dismiss your information as idle gossip. The estate kids have no money, no power and nowhere to go. Talking is the cheapest thing they can do. I grew up on such an estate myself,' Mason explained. 'I spent my entire childhood being mercilessly bullied by the grammar-school kids up the road from our flat. Now I'm teaching them. It's not an irony I care to dwell on.'

'I wonder if you'd like to add espionage to your skills, and report back to me if you hear this gang mentioned by any of your boys, particularly in connection with the Highwayman?'

'With pleasure,' Mason agreed. 'Sometimes I fantasize about teaching in one of those new glass open-plan schools, being free to concentrate on the intricate beauty of sonnets or the heavenly grace of a Tiepolo in the safety of a controlled, airy environment. Instead, we're wedged into these dark Victorian corridors, where every room seals its secrets behind a thick oak door. Children are phenomenally susceptible to their surroundings. The gloom breeds odd loyalties in them.'

'What do you mean?'

Mason paused for a moment, thinking. 'If your man is somehow associated with the Saladins, it might be because he's anxious to gain their approval.'

'Why would he need the approval of a bunch of disenfranchised children?' asked May.

'That's rather the question, isn't it?' Mason agreed. 'Idolatry is a powerful weapon in the right hands.'

'You're not suggesting he has a political agenda?'

'It must have occurred to you. Insurrection requires partisanship. You could ask yourself what this guy is trying to achieve rather than what he's already done. Every crime requires a motive, doesn't it? Perhaps the Highwayman is trying to inspire a grassroots revolution against capitalism.'

'I hardly think he'd pick off B-list celebrities to do so,' said May.

'The point is that to your average muzzy-headed schoolboy he's rather an alluring figure.'

'But he's a murderer.'

'There's a period before teenagers fully develop when they can become very amoral. I look at their blank little eyes and often get a chill. We like to think we can instil them with a value system, but they largely develop it independently of us. Trust me, the Highwayman appeals to them. Teachers have first-hand experience of the power of charisma. We're either reviled, tolerated, or worshipped unconditionally, like our illustrious Mr Kingsmere.'

Mason peered through the window, then suddenly dropped his cigarette and ground it out on the step. 'Ah, speaking of whom, it appears you might meet him after all,' he told May. 'Here he comes now.'

22

RESONANT GROUND

The damp autumn winds met around the weather vane on the roof of St Crispin's, twisting the protesting copperwork figure of the school's most celebrated pupil back and forth. On the walkway below, a tall strong-featured man in his mid-forties ambled towards the detective with a troop of noisy boys in tow.

'You must be the other one – Mr May, isn't it?'

Mr Kingsmere appeared to be too well-groomed for someone involved in scholarly pursuits, from his designer stubble to his fashionable shirt and casually expensive shoes. He stopped before them and smiled with practised charm.

'The school had experience of your esteemed partner recently – not an entirely successful event, I understand. Unfortunately, I was unable to attend. Parfitt, Jezzard, Billings – some of my top pupils. These wretches here tell me there was some misunderstanding between them and your poor old Mr Bryant. Perhaps we can set matters right between us all.' People always seemed to stress Bryant's maturity when mentioning him.

'I imagine you're busy, but perhaps we could talk when you have a moment,' May requested.

'If you've finished with Mr Mason, why not come to

my study now? It'll be quieter away from these gawkers. Jezzard and Parfitt, that means you too. Home room, the lot of you.'

His hand hovered above May's shoulder. 'The brightest two per cent in one of the most academic schools in the country, and all it takes to stun them into silence is the presence of someone outside their immediate peer group. Too much time spent in their bedrooms chatting on the internet to girls they'll never touch. All that stuff one hears about schoolkids having rampant experimental sex doesn't apply here. These are a timid lot, but they're troublesome enough on the surface. That's why I attempt to teach them how to behave in public, to little effect – you were going to ask about that, weren't you?'

'I had heard you were popular with the pupils,' May admitted.

'There's no real trick to loyalty, John – may I call you John? You barter with them, that's all. Teenagers are materialistic little buggers. The ownership of many shiny little items seems to reduce their sense of living under threat. I give them stuff. Of course, the trouble is that this school has a remit to preach traditional Christian values, empirically accepted history and the English literary canon as if deconstruction and post-modern historical relativism didn't exist. I expect intelligent children to question the received wisdom of their elders, and make no bones about treating them differently. The kids in my extra-currics have trouble conforming, because they make connections other kids don't make. They're quick to see through the illusions of the external world, but it encourages them to acknowledge the legitimacy of value-judgements. A good thing in my book – most pupils don't go deeper than what we term "seals and Nazis".'

'What do you mean?'

'Oh, you know.' Kingsmere flagged his hand at the posters lining the walls. 'Received ideas and lazy opinions. Seals are

190

nice, Nazis are evil; everything else falls into one camp or the other.'

'Surely some truths are constant and universal,' said May. 'The earth is round not because we currently *think* that to be the case, but because science has proved it not to be flat.'

Kingsmere gave a knowing smile. 'The objectivity of science is easily exploded, Mr May. We live in a reflective age which recognizes that most personalities, institutions and beliefs no longer fit into neat logical categories.'

'But without a certain degree of generalization and simplification there can be no understanding,' May argued.

'An understandable attitude from a policeman, but a rather naïve stance, I fear. We need to step beyond the tyrannical pedantry of facts to arrive at a more sophisticated level of theoretical interpretation,' Kingsmere explained, not expecting his guest to understand.

'I can assure you that if we ran the police force on Derridan deconstructivist ideologies, we'd never arrest anyone because the degree of their guilt would depend on the fluctuation of individual opinion.'

If Kingsmere was surprised by May's conclusion, he was careful not to show it. 'A good argument for replacing constables with academics,' he said instead. 'The school's top two per cent should be allowed to free itself from the straitjacket of a dogmatic education and explore modern liberal relativism. Most private pupils aren't any brighter just because their parents pay for their education. Actually, they downplay their intelligence because they have a choice of being smart or popular. My job is to single out the smart ones and keep them here long enough to find practical applications. The pressures on them are enormous. Since the dotcom goldrush, private schools have been treated like banks – parents put their kids in when they're flush, draw them out again when they're broke. If you think divorcing parents are bad for a child, try removing him from his peers and dumping him in some budget-strapped state school. Here we are.'

They were now deep within the venerable building. Kingsmere used a swipecard on his study door, which surprised May. The reason quickly became apparent, for the room was a technological revelation: flat-screen computers, underlit glass tables, transparent circuitry and touch panels, the graceful white plastic of Apple Macintosh, the pristine organization of an operating theatre. 'This is where I take my extracurricular classes. The best way to encourage learning is to trick them into doing it for themselves. After twenty minutes surrounded by this equipment, they have to be torn away from it.'

'A far cry from the book-lined studies of earlier times,' said May, looking around with approval.

'It's a modern version, that's all. The school was left an endowment for technology. Thank God for rich St Crispin's old boys. Look, I'm sorry if my lads embarrassed your partner. I've taught them to question authority, but they can sometimes take things too literally. It wouldn't have happened if I had been here, I can assure you.'

'Don't worry, Mr Bryant prefers a spirited exchange of views. It happens a lot.'

'Perhaps I should allow you to explain the purpose of your visit now.'

May felt he was being led through the conversation like a pupil, but put it down to the teacher's habitual manner of dealing with his young charges. 'I understand you were off sick earlier this week, so I don't know whether you've heard much about our investigation.'

'I read about it in the newspapers, of course. The police seem to be going out of their way to avoid the suggestion that London might have a serial killer on the loose.'

'The term usually denotes someone driven to commit murder by aberrant, uncontrollable passions. That hardly seems appropriate in this case. The victims fall into the common geographic profile – both murders were committed in the same area – but they were not the focus of violent desires. I've heard that some of the pupils here have been getting into fights with a gang on the nearby estate.'

Kingsmere appeared disappointed by the mundanity of the enquiry. 'So I understand,' he said. 'The seniors, mostly. It's a territorial matter of little interest. The sixth form use the back of the estate to reach the rugby pitch and the athletics ground. It's a very old dispute.'

'I thought the Saladins were new. We have around thirty-seven registered – that is, official – gangs currently operating in central London, so it can be hard keeping track of them.'

The teacher cocked his head, intrigued. 'How does a gang become official?'

'It gets registered if one of its members tries to shoot you, Mr Kingsmere.'

'What I meant was that the territorial dispute goes back a long way before gangs. Our school has been on the same site for centuries, and the estate was built during the postwar slum clearance. The boys argue, with some justification, that we were here first. Tensions have existed here for many generations. I set a local-area research project last year, and we found that as early as the eighteenth century the poorer residents of the neighbourhood had appointed someone to champion their rights. Hang on, let me see if I can find the document.'

A new light of enthusiasm fired him as he powered up his laptop and began searching through project files. The square whiteboard above his chair filled with data.

'This one, in particular, may strike a chord.' He briskly tapped the screen as if drawing the attention of an unruly class. 'In 1929, a guy called Albert Whitney led a revolt by the tenants of Three Bells Street against exorbitant rents charged by their landlords – to wit, the owners of this school. Three Bells Street was destroyed during the war, and now lies beneath the rear grounds of the Roland Plumbe

Community Estate.' Kingsmere flicked off the light, as if keen to keep any further information to himself. 'If ever there was a case for psychogeography, this is it.'

'Psychogeography is a process based on empirical data,' said May with a certain amount of malicious relish. He had used this argument before with his partner.

'Data that comprises the temporal value judgements of the superstitious, uneducated masses,' snapped Kingsmere.

'Either way, it's the kind of hostile territory that attracts the attention of vigilantes,' May told him. 'It will warrant further investigation.'

As he left the school, a nagging doubt about Kingsmere wedged itself in May's mind. Connections were slow to form, synapses failing. He felt sure there was something he had forgotten, as though a harmful half-remembered dream was even now fading from his memory.

'I'm over here,' said the hole, as a fistful of toothbrushes came flying out of it.

John May walked to the edge of the earth mound and looked down. His partner was on all fours in the muddy pit, scrabbling at sheaves of half-buried Bakelite handles.

'What on earth do you think you are doing?'

'I told you it was a toothbrush factory,' Bryant panted. 'The estate agent insisted it was dentures.'

'I'm sorry?'

'My new apartment – it's converted from the only remaining part of a toothbrush factory that survived the wartime bombing. This whole area was riddled with small workshops.'

'After all this time I still don't understand you,' complained May, giving him a hand out of the quagmire. 'You go missing from the unit without telling anyone where you're heading, and now I find you at home. And why do you have to know the history of the ground you live on? Why can't you just leave things alone?'

'Well, yes, that would be the easiest thing to do,' Bryant admitted. 'But so many questions would remain unanswered. Did you not wonder how I managed to buy this place so cheaply?' Bryant had made his new home on the unfashionable side of Chalk Farm, which bordered the expensive, celebrity-riddled Primrose Hill.

'Let me guess. It was cheap because it has a peculiar shape, uneven floors, damp patches, a leaky flat roof that appears to be made of tin, and is built on a piece of overgrown, triangular wasteground barely ten yards from a heavily used railway line?'

'It has character.'

'It has mice.'

'And it has no foundations. That's why it was cheap.' Bryant stamped mud from his wellingtons and entered the yellow-brick apartment through an old-fashioned green stable door.

'So it's liable to fall down as well. You know it was never designed to be lived in. I wouldn't be surprised if it was illegal to do so. Poor Alma, how she must miss her cosy apartment in Battersea. Have you got any heating?'

'Not as such,' Bryant admitted. 'Now that you mention it, Alma has been glancing covetously at brochures on Antigua lately. The toothbrush-making machinery probably kept the whole place warm in winter. Never mind, there's a stack of broken trestle tables at the end of the garden. I could burn them if it gets really cold.'

'Look, I'll bring you a portable radiator. And throw out all those filthy toothbrushes.' May's St John's Wood flat was as clean and bare as an operating theatre. Even April had warned her grandfather that he was exhibiting signs of an obsessive-compulsive disorder. May reacted to the chaos of the world around him by creating a hygienic haven where he could work and think far into the night. Bryant, on the other hand, seemed to be living with the ants.

195

'I rather thought I'd create an artwork with the tooth-brushes, although I'm not sure how easy it is to carve Bakelite. I suppose my fleeting interests are a bit of a curse. To whom will I pass on all my arcane knowledge? I do admire your ability to draw a line underneath the past and leave it alone.'

'It's the best thing to do,' said May, searching for some-where clean to sit. He was worried that his partner was digging in the garden when he should have been con-centrating on the case. Every few months, fresh fears assailed him about Bryant's advancing age affecting his abilities. Everyone had doubts as they grew older, but when wrong decisions were made in the course of crime detection, lives were at stake. He hoped he would once again be proved wrong, but could not shake the feeling that they were now living on borrowed time.

'Exactly, you see. England has the most contemporary theological landscape in Europe. Why not make the most of it? Continuity has been fractured, leaving a spiritual vacuum. The meaningful aesthetics of family and religion have fallen by the wayside. We have tribalism but no belief system against which we can measure ourselves. And just when we're free to reinvent ourselves on this wonderful blank canvas, to finally prove responsible for our own destinies, international corporations are busy trying to fill the void. What could be more grotesque than companies behaving like vengeful deities by copyrighting the genetic code, or stopping seeds from reproducing? So someone must remain behind to remember the past, and I've appointed myself for the task. Do you want tea?'

'I'll make it,' May insisted. 'You get cleaned up.'

Bryant's landlady had been hard at work in the jumble of cavernous, damp rooms that now constituted their home. Touched by her decision to give up her Battersea apartment for him, Bryant had placed the new property in her name, in order that she could continue to call herself his landlady. In return, she had transformed the inhospitable chambers, dividing areas off for dining and relaxing, but making sure not to touch the room designated as Bryant's study.

Here were stored the surviving texts and artifacts that shaped and informed his life: Beethoven sonatas and Socratic dialogues, Greek mythologies, treatises on the Essex Witches and the dinner parties of Attila the Hun, accounts of Walpole, Cibber, Keats and Pepys, the poems of Philip Larkin and the concerts of Sir Malcolm Sargent, eyewitness accounts of the Conquistadors entering Mexico City, the discovery of Virginia and the great Knightsbridge safe-deposit raid of 1987, the kings of England and fights historical (from Marathon to Waterloo in order categorical), books on insects, dowsers, the art of skittles, great sea disasters, sand dancers, Japanese ferns, sausage-making, code-breaking, the films of Launder and Gilliat, underground rivers, bus routes of the 1920s, the lost lion statues of London, the whereabouts of Lord Lucan and the private diary of Laurence Shirley, the only British earl to be hanged for murder, folders filled with clippings of forgotten crimes, photographs of dead admirals and the décor of Victorian brothels. On top of this nightmarish mélange was a brand-new stack of youth-oriented lifestyle magazines. May was touched by the thought that his partner was at least trying to adjust to the modern world, although he had no doubt that the attempt was doomed.

'You recall we were having a conversation about the English concept of home,' called May, searching for cups. 'You said the convoluted shapes of London streets trapped residents in coils from which they never truly escaped.'

'You only have to look at the figures, dear chap. We're bombarded by adverts for faraway places, but many of us barely manage to stray more than a few miles from where we started.'

'Something came up earlier. I went to see the teacher of the pupils who barracked you. He's a postmodern relativist with a chip on his shoulder about elite education, but he managed to suggest something interesting about the Highwayman. According to him, the area on which the estate is built has always had a champion, a kind of vigilante. What do you know about distance decay?'

Bryant thoughtfully poured out some sepia tea and passed over a tray of misshapen biscuits. 'Oh, I read an article about this. People subconsciously make an energy analysis before they go anywhere. Consequently they make lots of short trips but few long ones.'

'That's right. Criminals carry out mundane crimes close to home, and travel further afield to commit violent acts. They keep a buffer zone around their immediate area of residence in order to avoid recognition. Villains escape to the safety of home, but still often return to the scenes of their crimes. Are these raisins?' May pointed to something in a lumpen biscuit of dubious provenance.

'I don't know. Alma's eyesight isn't what it was, so they could be dried peas.' Bryant scrunched his features as a biscuit fought back against his dentures. 'Ever hear of Governor Joseph Wall? He had a man flogged to death in Gorée, an island off the coast of the Gambia, in 1782. After guiltily hiding out in France and Italy, he returned to England and wrote to the Secretary of State offering to meet the charges against him. Twenty years had passed, and he didn't realize that the matter had been completely forgotten. Naturally, we thanked him for returning, then executed him. My point being,' Bryant paused for breath as he brought out fresh biscuits and, more mysteriously, a plate of dried figs, 'that the man felt he was unable to go home without giving himself up, and chose to take that risk, which suggests that the territorial instinct maintains a very powerful hold on us. Now, if that territory consistently attracts a certain class or type, they'll always return. So if we assume that our Highwayman's possible home base is on the estate, it would explain why he has travelled within a certain radius to commit his attacks. He might be choosing his victims not by their celebrity status, but by the fact that they venture into his field of operation.'

'You'll be pleased to know there's a piece of geographic profiling software available that can calculate this,' said May, risking a biscuit. 'We need to place the Highwayman at this home site, and find at least three locations where he's been known to commit violent acts. For each location we plot out a different likely area in which the offender lives, and see where the areas overlap to form a hot spot. Then we conduct door-to-door interviews. If it turns out that one of our existing suspects lives within the radius, we conduct DNA testing.'

'Very impressive,' Bryant conceded. 'Where might this software be?'

'At the moment it's only leased to the Houston FBI, but we could—'

'Faraday is holding the purse-strings, remember?'

'But when lives may be at stake – '

' – we'll need to fall back on human ingenuity.'

'We could at least ask Raymond Land tomorrow. He wants us both to meet with him first thing, says it's urgent. That's what I came to tell you. I tried calling, but your mobile's not responding.'

'Ah, er – I don't have it at the moment.'

'The one I bought for you? What do you mean?'

'I'll explain tomorrow. For now, I'm using my old mobile. At least I would be, but it fell into the hole while I was digging out the toothbrushes.' He pointed to something May had taken for a tinned chocolate sponge on the draining board, but now realized was a mud-coated phone. 'Let's see what Land wants,' he sighed. 'I'm in the mood for a fight.'

The Highwayman was poised on the apex of the roof, looking down at the city, his black tricorn hat tipping a thin stream of rain over the edge of the building. He felt a dark energy coursing through his nervous system, a sense of power over the residents of the streets below. His boots gripped the slates as he breasted the wind, keeping his balance. He turned to face the rising air currents, his cape lifting in the chill night, a creature conjured from a mythical past, a killer for a harsh new era.

23

INCRIMINATION

Raymond Land looked out through the great tiled crescent front-window of the PCU on to Koko's nightclub, housed in the century-old Camden Theatre, three kebab and pizza takeaways, a Sainsbury's Local hidden behind a fortification of steel delivery trolleys, a makeshift internet café filled with students, a pockmarked statue of Richard Cobden, the repealer of the Corn Laws in 1846, and a red-brick terrace where, until just a week ago, a blackened pawnbroker sign had read OLD PAINTINGS & VIOLINS EXCHANGED, this last piece of street furniture having survived above a shop for more than 160 years until mysteriously vanishing into some property developer's auction. It was a typical London scene, the old and new wedged untidily together in easy symbiosis.

But Land wasn't thinking of the view. He nervously pushed his strands of grey hair across his head as he seated himself behind the protective width of his desk. As much as he hated his job, he was far more disturbed by confrontations. He lined up his pens and studied his guests: May, smartly suited and seated patiently with his hands in his lap; Bryant, wiggling a pipe cleaner about in the bowl of his briar, unconcerned.

'I shouldn't worry about it if I were you, Raymondo,' said Bryant now, squinting into the pipe-stem and blowing bits of burned tobacco everywhere. 'Faraday is merely a mild laxative; he eases things through the system. There's little he can do about us.' If he was worried, he hid it well.

'I keep telling you, it's not Faraday,' Land pointed out. 'He has a new hatchet man called Oskar Kasavian. That's who you need to look out for.'

'I don't understand how you've put us in this situation,' said May with some exasperation. 'You went to Faraday to complain about us, didn't you? Surely you must have seen where such an action might lead.'

'I was frustrated and angry,' Land admitted. 'You know how I get, John. I thought it might gee you up a bit.'

'It's going to do more than that. By the sound of it, we have a survival battle on our hands.'

'And it's all your fault,' added Bryant unnecessarily. 'Do I need to remind you how many times we've covered up your mistakes? "The sinking ship drowns all the rats" – Confucius.'

'Now look here, Arthur, you can't deny that the number of cold cases on your files has been creeping up, and there's little chance of them ever being closed. They must be brought to some sort of resolution, or you'll be used as an example of outdated detection techniques, and will forfeit your careers. Kasavian has spent this week going through all the records. He's noticed that the unit has one particularly problematic case outstanding – one that goes back a very long way.'

'You're talking about the Leicester Square Vampire,' said Bryant. 'You know that's not solvable.' His nemesis had been carrying out random attacks on the streets of London for decades. The acts themselves always took the same form, although descriptions of the attacker varied, and there were no links between any of the victims. 'A case is cold from the point when its official investigation ends until the day its secrets are finally exposed. Good God, look at Napoleon and the wallpaper.'

'I'm sorry?' said Land, confused.

Bryant sighed, as if he was talking to a recalcitrant child. 'Historians long suspected that Napoleon was poisoned, so they put a sample of his hair in a nuclear reactor to find out if it was true, irradiating the strands and passing them through a spectrometer. Wallpaper was made with arsenic back in the 1820s. The idea was to prove that he had somehow come into contact with the—'

'Enough!' Land slapped the table, surprising himself. 'You simply don't appreciate the gravity of the situation, Bryant.' He knew that this particular cold case was the Home Office's trump card. Kasavian needed a single documented instance of malpractice within the unit, and had picked up on rumours that neither of the detectives would wish to be confirmed. 'The outcome of this will affect us all.'

'Oh, come on, Raymond, everyone knows you're looking to get transferred. You'd be happy guarding a model village on the Isle of Wight, but we've still got a future here.'

'A future?' Land was incandescent. 'What are you talking about? *What* future? All you have left is a past, and look at the trouble *that* always causes. Look at the trouble your screw-ups will cause now, at the worst possible time for all of us.'

'I say, there's no need to be rude.' Bryant felt affronted. He glanced uncomfortably at his partner. This was the last thing either of them needed. 'Do we have to go into the Leicester Square business?' he asked sheepishly.

'It's too late, the investigation is already in motion. It's all going to come out into the open. You need to put your house in order fast.'

'We're making progress with the Highwayman,' pleaded Bryant. 'Don't force us to defend our position on a case that's been rumbling on for over thirty years.'

'The debunking of phantoms and bogeymen is what you

do best,' said Land. 'You had a clear remit: to stop the general public from panicking, to protect the vulnerable, to remove danger from the streets. Admit it, you lost sight of your duties.'

'We had to look at the bigger picture. Our job is to help keep the city in equilibrium between myth and reality.'

'I don't hold with all that spiritual holy-water-sprinkling demon-summoning nonsense, Bryant. You're a policeman, you can't afford to hold eccentric views. Some kind of closure must be reached over the Leicester Square Vampire. I'm not prepared to leave this job under a cloud. Take a fresh look at the case. A nutter in a costume attacking total strangers – he might have more in common with the Highwayman than you realize. Who knows, perhaps one case will help inform the other.'

Bryant examined the idea. A pensive pout crippled his face, shifting his ears and hiding his eyes in pockets of wrinkled flesh. It wasn't an attractive sight. 'You know, Raymond, sometimes you actually come up with a useful suggestion,' he said, brightening. 'Admittedly it's not very often, and usually accidental when it does happen, but on behalf of the unit I accept your challenge.'

May felt like dropping his head in his hands. If there was one thing more dangerous than seeing his partner demoralized, it was seeing him fired with enthusiasm.

DS Janice Longbright could hear everything that was going on in Raymond Land's office simply by listening to the grate. The Edwardian offices were still fitted with fireplaces, although the chimneys had long ago been bricked up, and Land's pleading wheedle droned down through the iron bars of the draught trap beneath the chimney breast, revealing his most secret plans to her.

She remembered hearing how her mother had also eavesdropped on her superiors, although in wartime the task had been a little easier as the wall between their offices had been blown down. Still, it paid to take heed of the prevailing mood in the PCU, especially when the detectives were facing fresh censure.

Now, as she sat reapplying Jungle Fever Glamour Stick to her lips (one of several cosmetic lines favoured by Longbright despite being discontinued in the UK in 1968, but mercifully still on sale in Botswana owing to their exotic brand-names), she could hear the Acting Head's voice rise to a tremulous quaver as he sought to pass the blame for his actions.

There had been plenty of scares before, but she knew this time it was serious, not just because the Leicester Square Vampire had never been caught, but because Bryant's over-confidence had led to the most damaging moment of his career – one which had almost wrecked his friendship with John May.

Kneeling beside the fireplace, she recognized the gravity of the threats which Bryant so lightly dismissed, and knew that the Vampire's case was a Pandora's box of trouble just waiting to be opened. They were all bound to be implicated in the blaming process. After all, it was she who had recently destroyed the original documentation, burning the incriminating paper trail in the very grate where she now sat hunched in horror, listening to Bryant's enthusiastic words.

Her mind flashed back to the moment she had helped to hide the evidence – was there anything she had missed? With any luck, all remaining files had been reduced to embers in the unit's fire.

But what if something still survived? What if it had already fallen into Kasavian's hands? The damage could only be undone if the detectives acknowledged the problem. And they would never do that, because at the very least it would involve destroying John May's tentatively renewed friendship with his granddaughter.

Longbright had warned them about mixing their personal

lives with business. This time, she felt sure, the habit would ruin them all. She retreated to the evidence room at the rear of the building and quietly unlocked the door.

The only box that had survived the unit's fire contained a single damning document about the case dating from 1992. Standing on a chair and rummaging on the top of a cupboard, she pulled a manila folder free and slipped the loose page inside her jacket. Raymond Land had never seen the sheet because it contained a drunken confession from the one person qualified to know the truth of the matter: John May himself. It had not been destroyed because there were two additional signatures at the bottom of the page belonging to the officers who had witnessed its writing. A subpoena would draw the truth from them, and unless they could be traced and coerced into refuting its contents, there was nothing to be gained by obliterating the original. May had clearly forgotten his admittance of guilt in the shadow of the tragedy that had unfolded that night, and Bryant's memory was notoriously unreliable.

Longbright had never faced a situation like this; her loyalties were suddenly divided between performing her duty and honouring her mentors. Her mother had raised her to believe that no one was above the law, especially not those who administered it. But who could vouch for the mitigating circumstances that had resulted in the escape of a murderer, and the tragic death of an innocent civilian?

The Detective Sergeant locked the door and returned to her office, made miserable by the dilemma that called her own moral code into question.

24

SHADOW CITY

As Meera Mangeshkar arrived for her shift, she heard the detectives arguing with Longbright in their room opposite. She had become used to the seesaw sound of their bickering, but went over to listen anyway.

'You may as well come in, Mangeshkar, we have no secrets here.' May rolled a chair over to her. 'Ever hear of the Leicester Square Vampire?'

'Before my time, Sir.'

'Accidents of birth do not excuse your ignorance,' snapped Bryant. 'Caligula reigned before you were born but you've heard of him, haven't you? We were asking ourselves what the Highwayman has in common with the Leicester Square Vampire, and the answer is that they both started social panics. Look at the hysterical press reaction, and remember what Lord Macaulay said: "We know no spectacle so ridiculous as the British public in one of its periodical fits of morality."'

'You mean like the video-nasties scare of the eighties?'

'Exactly. Panics occur when individuals feel threatened and mobilize themselves into vigilante groups. Mods and Rockers, paedophiles, even UFO sightings have all sparked waves of hysteria. Saralla White and Danny Martell are being tarred and feathered because they represent the failures of a generation. Martell ran a show that was popular with teenagers but hated by their parents, until he lost his remaining audience. White advocated multiple partners, abortion and drugs, but was a hypocrite. As people age, they form habits and take sides. The Highwayman is a godsend. According to the right-wing press, he's only doing what people across the country don't have the guts to do. The general consensus is that his victims had it coming. Journalists are so busy tracking down dubious witnesses that they've not stopped to consider the effect of their actions.'

'You mean they're writing a bunch of toss about him.'

'Succinctly put, Mangeshkar. This editor at *Hard News*, what's her name?'

'Janet Ramsey,' Longbright pointed out.

'She's intent on turning the Highwayman into some kind of hero. And to think she started out writing in the *New Musical Express*. Well, you scratch a liberal and find a conservative. Look at her editorial.' He rattled the magazine angrily. '"So-called 'artist' Saralla White had the morals of a tramp and a string of terminations to her credit. The man who financed her career, the owner of London's notorious Burroughs Gallery, was himself the father of her unborn illegitimate child." My God, where are they getting their information?'

'As you said, Sir, no shortage of enemies ready to put the boot in.'

'Wait, it goes on: "Self-styled 'Teen Lifestyle Guru' Danny Martell's own secret sleazy life involved hookers and drugs. Both died in a manner appropriate to their wasted existence. Can we honestly say that either of them will be missed?" Longbright, get me a meeting with this woman, would you? What she's printing is irresponsible and dangerous. We don't want a repeat of what happened with the Vampire.'

'Why?' asked Meera. 'What happened?'

'His victims were accused of bringing their fate upon

themselves, just because they were women out alone at night, some postwar notion about unaccompanied females being of loose character. Crime reporters turned the whole thing into a moral issue and a political point-scorer. Janice, where are the Vampire's files?'

Longbright caught her breath. She had managed to hide the essential page in the back of her desk. 'I think they were all burned,' she replied. 'Your fault, I'm afraid. I'll see if there's anything left, but don't expect much.' She got up and clumped off, returning a few minutes later with the singed cardboard container, denuded of its single incriminating document.

'Is that all we have to show for three decades of sightings?' Bryant settled his spectacles on his nose and peered into the carton, where a handful of damp clippings lay stuck to the bottom.

'We'd have more if you hadn't blown the place up,' Longbright reminded him, tipping the pitiful contents across his desk. The best form of defence against Bryant, she knew, was distraction.

'Don't worry, I remember most of the details.' May spread the jaundiced newspaper clippings out. 'First recorded assault was 26 March 1973, in an alleyway connecting Leicester Square to Charing Cross Road. It's bricked in now as part of the Odeon complex – another smelly, piss-stained piece of old London gone, and good riddance. A nineteen-year-old female on her way home from a nightclub was beaten and bitten around the chin and neck. The same MO occurred six times that summer, enough for us to link the cases and for the press to coin a nickname. The early victims were all women between the ages of seventeen and twenty-three, all on their way home from nights on the town. Two of them were known to us because they'd been arrested on immorality charges. Two were of mixed race. The press then implied that the victims had led their attacker on because they were provocatively dressed in mini-skirts, and because

209

they weren't white. A message there to anyone who thinks the seventies were enlightened.

'The Vampire returned in 1974 after a quiet winter, the attacks continuing intermittently until a boy – Malcolm somebody, his name isn't here – died of his wounds. He was the first of two fatalities that year. We didn't have computers to help us identify bite marks then, and at first we missed the link, but he was the son of an Austrian diplomat, and suddenly there were funds available to pursue a full investigation. The problem was that, like the alleyways where the Vampire carried out his attacks, every lead turned into a dead end. We ended up with numerous witness reports – there are a couple of brief descriptions here. Tall, athletic, dressed in a black cape, spotted running into a cul-de-sac, thought to have scaled a sheer wall and escaped somehow. The "Vampire" tag stuck not because of his clothes, but because nearly all of the victims had been bitten, the severity depending on how long the Vampire had been left alone with them. We didn't know then that biting was so common in sexual assaults. Databases were still difficult to cross-reference in those days. And you have to realize that in the seventies his outfit wasn't so strange.'

'That's right,' Bryant took up the story. 'Victorian capes for men had enjoyed a revival. Christopher Lee had just starred in a modern Dracula film which saw him running along the King's Road in a billowing cape. The image had already been planted in the minds of the young. The press played up the danger, and pretty soon we had drunken vigilante groups roaming the West End as the pubs turned out, searching for this phantom figure who drained his victims' blood and walked through walls. The whole thing became a ridiculous urban legend. People supposedly sighted him stalking across the rooftops. The Vampire operated in a tight area that, thanks to geographic profiling, we now know wasn't where he lived. We made mistakes. The unit had been brought in to try and stem the escalating anxiety in the capital. The mythology became self-perpetuating as the Vampire started to act on his own press reports; if they said he'd been seen wearing a top hat, then he wore one the next time he ventured out. If they said he could escape through solid brick, he staged a stunt to suggest that was exactly what he'd done. He played up to his public, and started taking risks. We nearly caught him.'

'What do you mean, "nearly"?' asked Meera.

An awkward glance passed between the detectives, and they fell uncharacteristically silent. 'The operation went wrong,' said Bryant, gathering up the clippings and tidying them away.

'Did the attacks continue?' asked Mangeshkar.

'For a while, yes.'

The room went quiet. The constable shot the others an enquiring look, but was ignored.

Longbright finally broke the stillness. 'Could we get back to the case in hand? Perhaps we should take another look at possible suspects.'

'All right,' May agreed. 'Let's start with the boy, Luke Tripp. We know his testimony is over-imaginative – there's no way he could have seen a man on a horse in that gallery, so we have to assume that fear made him exaggerate what he saw.'

'Therein lies another paradox,' said Bryant, who so loved paradoxes. 'The pose Luke drew is exactly the same as the one described by Channing Gifford, the dancer living opposite the Smithfield gym who spotted the Highwayman from her window. It's the same as the pose struck in the digital shots taken by the estate girls. The head also matches the official logo of the Roland Plumbe Community Estate. But the schoolboy saw the Highwayman up close and in the flesh before anyone else did, therefore he can't have copied someone else's description, because he had nothing to base it on. What, then, are we to make of his testimony?'

May rose and strode impatiently to the crescent window.

'We can't be sure of that. We have to check for further sightings.'

'I circulated the Highwayman's shot to every motorcycle courier company in Greater London, as you asked,' said Longbright. 'I thought his outfit might be similar to one of the distinctive leather suits bike messengers wear, but so far no one has come back with a positive match.'

'We'll have to do all the follow-up work ourselves,' said May. 'Faraday won't recommend putting more officers on the street because he's corner-cutting to prove he can meet his end-of-year budget. So long as we're always pulled in after the event, we can't be expected to prevent further tragedies. Not unless we're somehow granted the gift of second sight.'

'But that's exactly what we need to develop,' said Bryant, 'and I know how to go about it. We need someone who understands why such mythical bogeymen recur in the city. Recognize the cause and you locate the solution.' He tapped his partner on the shoulder. 'Come with me.'

'Oh no, I'm not heading down this route,' May warned. 'You heard Raymond, no table-tappers and ghost-watchers, just solid data-gathering.'

'You're absolutely right, and I'm sticking to my promise. She's just a white witch. I don't suppose you have a problem with that, given this area's rich connections with witchcraft.'

'You might just as well say the area's connected with carrots because there's a vegetable stall outside the Tube station,' said May hotly.

'Come on, John, have you forgotten the lecture I dragged you to about the Mother Damnable of Kentish Town, Jinney the Mother Red Cap, who frequently lodged the notorious highwaywoman of Oliver Cromwell's days, Moll Cutpurse? She was a fortune-teller, healer and practitioner of the black arts, and her life was filled with cruelty and insanity. Mother Red Cap's partner incinerated himself in her oven, and later, when she was close to death, crowds saw the devil enter her house and take her soul. The witch's hair dropped out in two hours, and the undertaker had to snap her stiff limbs to fit her into a coffin. She, Mother Black Cap and Mother Shipton, all three notorious witches, lived within half a mile of one another. Coincidence? I think not.'

May looked at his partner and his heart sank. It was true that the city threw shadows filled with mystifying figures from its past, whose grip on the present could still be felt on certain strange days, when the streets were dark with rain and harmful ideas. John May knew this, because Bryant had once introduced him to the witches' alarming descendants, who continued to live – and die violently – in the immediate neighbourhood of their ancestors. But now his task was to prevent his partner from favouring the pursuit of his hobbies over practical investigation.

'I'm not coming with you, Arthur,' he warned.

'I need to get you out of the office, John. We have to talk about the Leicester Square attacks. Please.'

Bryant buried himself inside his voluminous threadbare overcoat and looked for somewhere to stick his smouldering pipe. For a moment, with his head all but vanished and smoke coming out of his sleeves, he looked rather like a witch himself, melting after being drenched by a bucket of water. 'It's early. I'll have you back here in no time.'

May reluctantly rose, but stopped at the unit entrance. 'Can't you see what they're trying to do? They're dissipating our strength, dividing us between two investigations in order to make us fail at both. The Vampire is an irrelevance not worth wasting time and money on. We need to concentrate on the matter at hand. One success is better than none.'

'We can't ignore this, John,' said Bryant softly. 'Not when you know it involves the death of your daughter.'

25

ATTRACTING EVIL

'How could I have told them the truth, with April in hearing distance?' pleaded May.

'You'll have to talk to her at some point.' Bryant bundled himself against the cool morning air and set off across wet pavements for the unit car park, a quadrangle of bricks cracked with drain-fed weeds, where horses were once stabled for the gentry of Camden Town. 'You can't leave these things hidden for ever. It's not fair on the poor girl.' He produced a bent pickled-onion fork and prised open the broken door lock of Victor, his Mini Cooper.

'How can I ever broach the subject? She'll hate me for all the years I've lied.'

'You know my views on that. You should have made a clean breast of it years ago, instead of letting the problem compound itself.'

'You've always been brutally honest with people because you don't care what they think, but I can't lose April now, just when I'm getting her back.'

'Get in, for heaven's sake.' Bryant peered at his partner through the rain-stained windscreen, but May had not moved.

He was remembering the day with terrible clarity.

The sticky heat rising from London streets at dusk. A cloud of starlings tumbling above the plane trees. Tourists ambling towards the cinemas of Leicester Square, where *The Silence of the Lambs* and *Terminator 2: Judgment Day* were showing. The detectives, tired and fractious, waiting in the shadowed doorway of an amusement arcade. Longbright radio-linked in a hot patrol car below Leicester Fields, in Panton Street. So much waiting, with nothing to do but argue.

The press had grown bored with the unsolved assaults. Leicester Square had been redeveloped as a pedestrian zone, and it was assumed that the Vampire had ceased operation in the area, despite the occasional unconfirmed sighting. During the summer of 1991, the brutal murder of a woman in her late twenties in an alley off Cranbourn Street prompted fresh attention, and the case was reopened. This time the victim was blonde, well-educated, attractive, and therefore more likely to extract outraged cries for justice. The hunt for the killer of young Amanda Wakefield began in earnest.

Three nights before the detectives' vigil, a fight had broken out in another Leicester Square backstreet, during which a homeless man was half beaten to death by a murderous gang of youths supposedly looking for the Vampire. The Police Commissioner had been pressurized to take action, and the unit had grown too desperate for a break.

Arthur Bryant had been the first to notice the physical similarity between Amanda Wakefield and May's own daughter, Elizabeth, but it had been John's idea to plant a decoy matching the description of the victim. The pair had been blinded by their need to resolve the investigation.

Elizabeth offered to help draw the Vampire out into the light.

Only Detective Sergeant Longbright had felt uneasy as she dressed her up for the part. Elizabeth had been armed with a police radio and a pepper spray, in case of trouble, and although she was small in stature, her strength and determination made her a formidable opponent. Everyone was confident. Bryant had employed a psychic to teach her about sending the right signals to her potential attacker, but he had also noted a practical detail that no one else had remarked upon: most of the victims had worn baseball caps. Hardly anything surprising there, of course, the whole of London was wearing caps that summer – but Bryant wondered if the Vampire avoided the bareheaded because they could look up and identify him more easily.

He spent the afternoon watching Elizabeth as she trod the same route as those who had died. By nine p.m. it seemed unlikely that the Vampire would appear. He had never operated at night. The dusty sun was low behind buildings glowing with soft citrine colours. Shadows stretched and cooled. And Elizabeth had decided to depart from her pre-arranged route, slipping between the narrow walls of Bear Street, picking her way through stacks of restaurant refuse in her search for a killer.

Her call for help went unanswered. She had not realized that the high buildings would block her radio signal. May was puzzled by her disappearance; she should have been back at the end of Irving Street by now. Craning his neck to search the gathering crowds, he grew apprehensive. The detectives warned Longbright that they had lost contact with their decoy, and ran into the streets.

Bear Street had an alley running from it where bars and cafés stored their waste-food ready for night collection. It was closed at one end, and presented such a forbidding appearance that no pedestrians used it. Drums of ghee made the ground slick, and there was a sense of lurking rodent life.

May was the first on the scene, slowing from a run to a walk as the feeling of something terrible prickled at his throat. The restaurant backs were deep in shadow now, and the noise of the crowd in the square had died away. He studied the filthy brick alleyway, the steel rubbish containers and plastic sacks of leaking leftovers, the cook in a first-floor window smoking a cigarette on his break, the backs of buildings resembling some ancient part of London because they had no need to make themselves attractive. He called up, 'Did you see a young woman run in here?' but the cook spoke no English and merely stared back.

As soon as he saw her jean-clad legs on the ground, he knew his daughter was dead. She had been struck down from behind, and lay on a patch of oil between a pair of plastic wastebins. His first thought was that she had slipped over on the oil. Then he saw the bloody knot of hair, the arm twisted beneath her torso with its palm up. Her head pressed up against the base of a drainpipe at an impossible angle.

He remembered nothing more of that dreadful night.

A pair of Met officers forced a bottle of brandy on to him to numb the shock, not caring that they were breaking the law by doing so. May drank deeply. He was to blame, he told them, for ignoring the rules, for not trusting his senses.

Back at the unit, he insisted on signing a document to that effect, with the officers as witnesses.

Nobody had spotted the Vampire re-emerge from the grey dead-ended alley. An open door led to the kitchen of a Chinese restaurant, but the cook insisted that no one had entered or left. He had, however, seen a tall man in a cloak halfway up the end wall of Bear Street – the idea was preposterous, the details unforthcoming, so the sighting only made matters worse. But the drainpipes made perfect ladders here, and it was clear that he had climbed them. The phantasm's panicky mythology had hidden obvious truths.

May had taken a brief leave of absence, returning to work too quickly, assuring them all that he was coping well.

Elizabeth's daughter was just nine years old when she became motherless. Her father had moved out from the family apartment five years earlier, and had now remarried in New Zealand. April's worst childhood fear, that she would one day find herself alone, was suddenly realized. She found herself unable to talk to the man who had discovered her mother's body, and was sent to live with his sister Gwen. Her psychological problems began soon after.

May knew he should never have involved his daughter in a hunt for a killer. The detectives were too adept at attracting evil. As forensic experts combed the walls and roofs searching for evidence of the Vampire's escape, May damned himself. Bryant, too, cursed his own arrogance, but no amount of blame could bring Elizabeth back.

And April changed. The girl with smiling eyes was replaced by a sombre, fearful child who found terrors in every building's shadow. In the absence of factual evidence, legends took hold. The Vampire became a bogeyman, an elusive phantom that existed only in tortured dreams.

Trails grow cold, and need evidence if they are to be revived. Elizabeth's death had marked the Vampire's last appearance. What, wondered May, could now be gained by reopening the wounds of a tragic past?

26

SHARED TRAGEDIES

John May sat up in the passenger seat and looked around. 'Why are we on Prince of Wales Road?' he asked.

Bryant had stopped the Mini Cooper before a familiar Victorian red-brick building. 'I've been talking to you for the last ten minutes,' he said. 'Weren't you listening?' Whacking a disabled sticker on to his windscreen, he clambered out to tap his walking stick on the wooden sign that had been affixed to the tiny church's gate: COVEN OF ST JAMES THE ELDER - NORTH LONDON BRANCH. The crimson neon above the door still read 'Chapel of Hope', a leftover from the previous tenant.

'I know you detest the idea, but we need to talk to Maggie Armitage,' Bryant explained. 'The Vampire files may have been destroyed, but she's been keeping diaries for years. If you remember, she acted as my occult consultant throughout the case. I'm hoping she still has records of every sighting.'

'Yes, but they'll be useless because she's mad.'

'You say that about every woman over forty who holds strong convictions.'

'I know all about her convictions, Arthur, I've seen her arrest file.'

'Our cases don't have traditional signifying elements, so I have to rely on people like Maggie. You never warmed to her, did you?'

'I know she means well, but when the two of you get together, she fills your head with these ridiculous ideas, like the time she convinced you that she could trap the Black Widow of Blackheath inside the Woolwich Odeon by spraying the balcony with luminous paint.'

'We caught her, didn't we?'

'Only because you blinded her halfway through *South Pacific* and she fell down the stairs trying to get to the toilet.'

'I'll admit it sounds odd when you put it like that. What are you trying to say?'

'Just that there's no point in looking for things that don't exist.'

'You think things don't exist just because you can't see them,' Bryant scoffed.

'Well, yes, strictly speaking, invisibility is a fair indication of non-existence.'

'Rubbish. What about gases, sub-atomic particles, magnetism, religious faith, the unfathomable mysteries of romantic attraction?'

'Don't drag biology into this. The Leicester Square Vampire and the Highwayman have nothing in common beyond the fact that they've both caught the public imagination. I just don't see how going through some barmy old white witch's rambling diaries is going to help reopen – '

The woman standing in the doorway listening to him was small, plump and resplendent with sparkling appendages. Shells, amulets, chains, bracelets, semi-precious gemstones and what appeared to be pieces of broken china tied in string dangled from her unnerving bosom. Chiming and jangling, she threw her arms wide to hug Bryant, leaving him smothered in cat hairs and cake crumbs. 'Darling, monstrous man!' she laughed. 'You only ever call when you want something, but do come in.'

'You look very well,' said Bryant cheerfully. 'You seem to be ageing backwards.'

'Yes, I probably am,' said Maggie casually. 'We conducted Day of the Dead celebrations in Miccailhuitontli last month, and the high priest traded me some Mexican rejuvenation paste for my Vodaphone battery. It did wonders for my epidermis, although it did take the glaze off my mixing bowl. And Mr May, my favourite non-believer, we'll make a disciple of you yet, come in. Your granddaughter is here, so pretty and vulnerable that one fears for her. But so clever – she's one to watch.'

'I don't understand,' said May. 'What's April doing here?'

'Oh, we're friends of old, although I've yet to dispel the darkness from her soul, something I suspect only you can do. Do come through.'

She led the way through pools of gloom into the hall of the deconsecrated chapel, past oak pews, across the perished parquet floor treacherous with loose blocks, through a miasmic aura of lavender, ginger and sandalwood. The late-afternoon sunlight illuminated two grim stained-glass windows illustrating the suffering of Christ, and threw bloody patches across the ragged walls.

'Sorry about the Christian symbols,' Maggie apologized. 'We've been meaning to replace them with something more inclusive. If I have to look at the beatific Virgin Mary every time I cross the nave, I think we should at least have a representation of Ormazd, the Persian principal of goodness, as well. Maureen's been up Columbia Road on the lookout for a nice Buddha, but they're an arm and a leg. She found one in a salvage yard, but had no way of getting it back because she had her Lambretta stolen while she was meditating.'

May shot his partner a weary look. 'Arthur says we need to talk to you about the bogeymen of London,' he said, trying to sound benevolently indulgent. 'I suppose you know we have one on our hands.'

'I've read about it, who hasn't? Quite catching the public imagination.'

'Arthur also wants to go back to the Leicester Square Vampire.'

'And you wish to expose my diaries to the light. Very well, but in return you must help me put up our Christmas tree, we're short of strong lads.' She pointed to a bedraggled pine propped in the corner.

'Don't tell me you've forsaken your usual pagan iconology and have become infected with the pernicious spirit of Christmas,' said Bryant in surprise. 'Aren't you a few months premature?'

'We're equal-opportunity worshippers,' Maggie pointed out. 'Anyway, Christmas is incorrectly placed in the calendar, so we've moved it forward by way of recompense. The celebration is rooted in the belief that during the winter solstice, the door between our world and the one containing evil spirits is left open. When dark entities attempt to step across the gap in search of human souls, we ward them off with talismans, hence all the ornaments. And that's not a Christmas pine, it's a representation of the great snake Yggdrasil.'

'It wasn't last year, when you stuck a fairy on top of it,' Bryant reminded her. He recalled the deformed angel she had constructed from dead pigeon wings, crêpe paper and a cat skull that owed less to the spirit of St Nicholas and more to Ed Gein.

'I hope you won't try to weasel out of our canticle service again this year,' said Maggie. 'Maureen dropped beetroot salad inside the harmonium, so it sounds like it's being played by Hornblas, the patron devil of musical discord, but that's what happens when you scoff snack lunches from a jiffy bag. Come into the office.' She led the way to a small room stacked with books and newspapers, in the midst of which an ancient computer screen stuttered and rolled. April sat in one corner, almost buried behind the white witch's notebooks.

222

'Your handwriting is awful, Maggie,' she complained. 'Half of it looks back to front.'

'That's because it is, darling. Mirror-writing. Arthur taught me years ago. I'm left-handed, you see; it makes less mess to go right to left on right-hand pages. Arthur is here with your grandfather.'

'I think we've got what you asked for, Uncle Arthur,' said April, tapping her notebook.

'You've already briefed her?' asked May, surprised.

'You'd be proud of me, Grandad – I got on a Tube train this morning.' She raised a small amulet shaped like a miniature astrolabe. 'Maggie gave it to me for my agoraphobia.'

'Chased silver,' said Maggie proudly. 'A colony of druids on the Orkney Islands nearly blinded themselves making it.'

'Wait a minute. How long have you two known each other?' asked May, waggling a finger between them.

April smiled conspiratorially. 'Get in the game, Grandad. Uncle Arthur introduced me to Maggie years ago. We don't all have to stay in touch through you, you know.'

'I don't want you filling her head with strange ideas,' May admonished. 'She has quite enough to worry about.'

'Rubbish, the child is old enough to make up her own mind about the world.'

'I've been assisting Maggie online for a while now,' April explained. 'When I couldn't go out, she found me in cantations that could help.'

'There was nothing magical about them, it was just good psychology,' Maggie assured him. She stood beside April, examining the books. 'Would you care to hear what we've found?' The white witch hauled up her spectacle chain and squinted at a sheet of April's notes. 'The first publicly recorded attack of the Leicester Square Vampire was, as you rightly say, in 1973, but the first time you mentioned such an incident to me was just after the war.'

'Are you sure?' asked Bryant, rubbing his watery cobalt eyes. 'I don't remember that.'

'Because your predator had no name at that point,' Maggie reminded him. 'It was an isolated incident. He sucked blood from a Wren.'

'Show me.'

She turned the diary to him. 'Two days after that he attacked a nineteen-year-old typist from Dagenham, bit her on throat and wrist, cracked two ribs, multiple bruising.'

Bryant read the entry. 'Didn't I follow this up? John, do you remember?'

'Only vaguely,' May admitted. 'I recall that the girl was badly shaken. We had no leads, and there were more important things to worry about. We were trying to find a murderer stalking the cast of *Orpheus* in the Palace Theatre.'

'You may not have realized it, but the Leicester Square attacks continued with a fair amount of regularity,' said Maggie. 'We only found it because of the Panic Site. It's a website set up by Dr Harold Masters.'

'That strange academic who runs the Insomnia Squad?' asked Bryant. Masters' group of intellectual misfits regularly stayed up all night arguing about everything from Arthurian fellowships and Islamic mythology to the semantics of old Superman comics. It was a wonder they were still able to hold down regular jobs.

'Lately he's been cataloguing social panics and outbreaks of mass hysteria. He noted activities consistent with mob violence around the square and traced them to dozens of attacks over a period of over forty years.'

'That's rather a long time for someone to operate in such a small area without getting caught, don't you think?' said May.

Maggie ignored him. 'You wanted to know how he picked his victims, Arthur, when and where he decided to strike, so I rang an old psychic friend of mine.'

It was on the tip of May's tongue to ask if the psychic had

answered the phone before it rang, but he thought better of it.

'Unfortunately, Madam Lilith's information proved to be incorrect.'

'There's a surprise,' May said without meaning to.

Maggie fixed him with an eye that could have drawn the past from a paperweight. She returned to April's notes. 'The various witness descriptions are remarkably consistent.'

'I checked news files on the web and found myself going back even further,' said April. 'His first appearance may well have been in the 1740s.'

'You mean we're looking for some kind of ageless, mythical monster?' asked Bryant with excited incredulity.

That was enough for May. He threw his hands up in protest. 'Has everyone gone mad? We are not looking for him or any other kind of monster, thank you, we're after someone completely different, someone who has been operating for barely a fortnight.'

'Are you, though?' asked Maggie. 'Across the centuries there have been many attackers who have gained mythical status. They seek to leave behind a permanent mark on the city.'

'It's true,' Bryant agreed. 'London has a secret all-but-forgotten history of crimes and criminals that have caught the public imagination. James Whitney, William Hawke, the Earl of Pembroke, Dr Thomas Cream, Charley Peace, Thomas Savage, the Hammersmith Ghost, the Lollards, the Kennington Maniac, the Stockwell Strangler, the London Monster, Jack the Ripper. Few were ever caught, but all excited interest and grew to legendary status. The Highwayman is merely the latest in a long line of seemingly superhuman English villains.'

'How does this knowledge connect us to the present, exactly?' asked May. 'You're not going to try and convince me that they're all linked.'

'But they are, John, via the children on the Roland Plumbe

Community Estate. There has been trouble on the site for generations, owing to arguments over land access. In every village, town and city, champions are found, victims are chosen, villains emerge, and gradually the most memorable ones enter the realm of legend. These cases are rooted in fact, but acquire supernatural status because of the hysterical reaction of the public. If their deeds passed unnoticed, they would never find a place in history. Hue and Cry was a procedure that developed by which a robbery victim could insist upon passers-by giving chase to catch the criminal. It encouraged mob hysteria. Look at the Ratcliffe Highway Murders of 1811, and how the public hammered a stake through the heart of the killer's corpse before burying him under a pavement. Panic swept the capital. Families began locking their doors for the first time, and Parliament recommended the creation of a police force. Or take the case of the London Monster. April, do you have my original notes on him?'

'Here. Do you want me to read them back?'

May was about to protest, but decided against it. His granddaughter was clearly interested in helping with the case, and perhaps it was better to hear her out.

April began to read aloud. 'Between 1788 and 1790, women in Mayfair were terrorized by "The Monster", who would creep up to them, mutter indecencies and then stab their buttocks with a thin, sharp instrument.

'The Bow Street runners failed to catch him, so a wealthy Lloyd's insurance broker called John Julius Angertstein offered a reward of fifty pounds for his capture. The money encouraged false accusations and vigilante attacks as passers-by hysterically screamed "The Monster!" at anyone they didn't like the look of.

'Such a sense of panic settled over the capital that the lives of innocent men were endangered. Fashionable women were encouraged to wear copper-plated petticoats to protect themselves from attack. After over fifty females had been

226

assaulted, a young artificial-flower-maker called Rynwick Williams was arrested when one of the more unstable victims pointed him out to a vigilante. He was convicted after a couple of ridiculous show trials, despite the fact that he had a cast-iron alibi for one of the worst outrages.

'The London Monster wasn't alone; the Hammersmith Monster also scratched lonely women, and despite being caught and committed for trial, he seems to have reappeared eight years later for further attacks. By now, though, he had been branded a "ghost", appearing in a large white dress with long claws.

'This version has an interesting coda: one hundred years later, in 1955, he acquired a retroactive history via the *West London Observer*, which stated that he appeared every fifty years in St Paul's churchyard when the moon was full, walking between the tombstones with blazing eyes, wrapped in a white winding sheet. At the date of his next visitation four hundred ghost-hunters turned up in the churchyard. The police were forced to seal off the area until midnight, when the ghost was due to walk, but nothing happened. Then someone remembered that British Summer Time had made the visitation an hour late, so the crowd stayed on, and were rewarded with the sight of a ghostly floating creature in brilliant white, with no legs, rising on a strange wind and drifting from the church porch into one of the tombs. The legend was now complete. In fact he's due to walk again this very month.' She slammed the diary shut.

'So you're saying that these London myths are created by fearful populations rather than the villains themselves?' asked May, trying to understand.

'Obviously there has to be a defining action at the start,' said Maggie. 'But remember what happened when the *News of the World* released information concerning convicted paedophiles to their readers: rioting, hysteria, mob violence. It's not just an English phenomenon. Look at Nancy Reagan and the "Just Say No" campaign that had parents submitting their children to drugs tests. In Lagos, Nigerians started believing that they could be killed by answering specifically numbered calls on mobiles after midnight. In China, there was a hair-cutting panic. And in Indonesia in 2004 there was a scare involving *Kola Hijau*, the 'green demon', who committed assaults clad in bright-green underpants. Even the London Ambulance Service recently fell for the old story about gang members driving without car headlights, believing that if they flashed the oncoming cars to warn them, they would be shot dead as part of an initiation ceremony. Scaremongering panics like these surface regularly, only to be debunked as nonsense before rising again.'

'But the Highwayman has actually killed two people.'

'Look at his victims – objects of hatred, misunderstanding and public ridicule by the middle-aged middle classes. Think of vilified TV comics whose careers nosedive after scandals. The public reaction: "No smoke without fire." Worst fears are confirmed: "I always felt there was something odd about him." But if the public figure is admired, the public is prepared to overlook faults. The politicians and actors we know to be gay will be accepted if they show themselves to be honest people. Politicians with murky histories and an inability to speak plainly – one thinks of Mark Thatcher, Jeffrey Archer and that ghastly ex-politician with the publicity-mad wife – are subject to suspicion and receive no aid. Those who remove objects of public suspicion are therefore in a position to become celebrities themselves.'

'Good God, does this mean we have to start protecting every disliked celebrity and parliamentary member in the city?' asked May. 'We'd never be able to do it.'

'Exactly. The Highwayman has found himself a perfect modus operandi. He's impervious to anticipation. And no doubt he's relying on the fact that we will never be able to follow his game plan, assuming he has one.'

'So you don't think he's randomly picking victims according to his own temperamental outbursts?'

'No. The acts are far too premeditated to make me believe he has no plan. He craves popular support. He won't attack anyone the public truly admires.'

'That still doesn't help us.'

'Perhaps not, but it helps to build a profile of the person we're searching for. The case histories of the past always shed light on the present.'

'But we're not talking about hysterical outbreaks in Mayfair – these are perverse, clever cruelties.'

'I agree that the attacks differ in one crucial aspect,' said Bryant. 'They're not designed to frighten the public but to reassure them; to prove that someone is on their side, acting on their behalf. The Leicester Square Vampire inspired fear, clearing the streets at night by reminding everyone that they were vulnerable. His acts were unfathomable, possibly politically driven, but it's likely that the Vampire himself had no explanation for his actions. Our Highwayman is of a different psychological makeup. He's unemotional, an insider, a calculator of odds, above-average intelligence, multi-faceted, perhaps even a split personality. But he wants to be seen as a champion. And we haven't seen the last of him.'

'How can you be so sure?'

'There are always more than two items on any agenda.'

'So the Leicester Square Vampire had no agenda?'

'Hard to tell, but he appears to have been operating over an unusually long timescale. April, are you serious about sightings dating back to the middle of the eighteenth century?'

'There are listings with descriptions here, but you know what the internet is like; UFO sightings are given the same weight as accepted historical truths. It's as much a source of rumour of factual reference.'

'We still have to close his case before Faraday and

Kasavian can use it to shut us down,' said Bryant. 'I suppose we could re-examine the physical evidence, open the bodies of his victims and arrange for Janice to visit his survivors – although I should think their memories will prove unhelpful after all this time.'

For once, May gleaned a practical purpose in talking to the white witch. He began to see how Bryant connected people and events, across decades and districts, through history and hardship, applying their shared tragedies to the present problem. 'Fair enough,' he agreed. 'We'll divide the unit staff into two groups. You lead the cold case, I'll take over on the Highwayman. We'll share the information, and if either team hits an impasse, let's agree to swap investigations. Meanwhile, we stay out of Faraday's way as much as possible. And if anything goes wrong, you do what I tell you.'

'It's a deal,' said Bryant, eagerly shaking his partner's hand.

'I still can't believe you gave away my birthday present,' said May, shaking his head in wonderment.

27

ENGLISH CRUELTIES

His real name was Alexander Garfield Paradine, and he was related to the Earl of Devonshire, but everyone called him Garfy and thought he was the son of a taxi-driver who had been discovered in a Skegness talent competition.

You needed the common touch to succeed on television; it levelled the playing field between you and the viewer. While his fans imagined that he drank at his local and ate in chip shops, he had been dining at the Groucho Club and hooking and slicing at Sunningdale. It was part of the pact to allow them their dreams that they too might one day become like him.

He'd been lucky in the early years, becoming an alternative comedian without having to haul a one-man show around Edinburgh for several festivals. He'd become popular on the university circuit, garnering a strong student following, but he had longed for a wider audience, and as his career shifted from late-night cult shows to Saturday-evening clip-fests like *You're On Camera*, the pact with his youthful fanbase had become strained. His privacy was repeatedly invaded by viewers who felt they owned him. They clambered over the wall of his house in Henley-on-Thames, and followed his wife back from Waitrose, photographing her on their mobiles.

To reduce the pressure, he reinvented himself, but by the time he was cutting his teeth on dramatic soaps like *Manchester Emergency*, his fans had turned on him. No one, neither critics nor audience, was prepared to accept him as a serious actor. Taking a role in the BBC's prestigious two-parter *Dombey and Son*, his mannered performance was disastrously received. His Christmas single proved popular with mums and dads, but he was derided in the West End musical *Don Juan*, so he began missing performances, pleading laryngitis. As a consequence, the 2.5-million-pound show ran for just seventeen performances, making enemies of his backers.

He caught sight of his profile in the glass doors, and didn't like what he saw. At thirty-seven, his boyish looks were going; he had to face the fact that he was starting to look too used-up for romantic leads. His eyes had bagged; his jowls had sagged; he looked tired. He made the tactical error of appearing in a Conservative Party broadcast advocating the rights of fox-hunters, and lost his remaining student fans overnight. Then came the drink-driving ban, and the unsuccessful spell in rehab. He gained a reputation as the tabloids' favourite drunk.

Now he hated his former fanbase, never more than when they shouted 'Oi, Garfy!' across busy streets, or bellowed his catchphrases as he alighted from cabs. With the grim predictability of a star on the slide, he punched a photographer outside Stringfellows, and was filmed intoxicated and crying in the Met Bar. Knowing that it was a small step from here to playing villains in seaside pantomimes, he reinvented himself again. He became a born-again Christian, went to Capetown for a facelift and hosted a morning cable show that picked up a surprisingly loyal following. His ghost-written book *Loving Someone Other Than Yourself* became a top-ten bestseller. But his fickle TV fans had moved on.

The younger generation, whose attention he sought and craved, now loathed him as a representative of everything their parents respected.

As he pressed the entry buzzer beside the glassed doorway in St John Street, Clerkenwell, he considered the wisdom of another makeover. He needed to choose a charity, one with a high profile, preferably involving children. His agent could do all the sourcing. He'd agree to sign over a percentage of the royalties, attend some photo-ops, perhaps even adopt a Romanian orphan so that teenagers could see he was sincere. They were the audience that counted; they had the buying power that excited sponsors. Hell, at least it was a game-plan.

At his back, the swollen pale-green sky prepared to release expectorations of rain. He cupped his hands over the glass and tried to see inside, then checked the address on his printout. The offer of the radio voiceover had been sent directly to his home, bypassing his agent, the message merely specifying the time and place. He would have binned the request, but it was for a teen magazine and he couldn't afford to pass up the chance.

He cupped his hands again – no one in the foyer, all lights out; it felt like the wrong address, except that the number was stencilled above the door in chrome. He tried the handle, and was surprised to find the door unlocked. As he entered, hard neon fuzzed on overhead. He noted the sign pinned on the deserted steel reception desk – SOUND STUDIO 4TH FLOOR – and summoned the lift.

Anthony Sarne swam with the same languor he possessed out of the water, his tanned arms lifting and falling through the warm blue shadows. He was most contented like this, on his own in the calm evening gloom. Rolling on to his back, he studied the glass roof as he lazily drifted beneath it. He had swum thirty lengths of the tiled Victorian pool; now he could relax in the last few minutes before dressing and going to dinner.

The tight-fitting plastic goggles dyed his cool green world. Chlorine affected his vision adversely. More than ever he found himself wearing shaded lenses of some kind; his eyes were increasingly sensitive to light. He was forty-eight and in good shape, happy with his body, vain about his ability to maintain a flat stomach. He still had his pick of the girls, and his current mistress, an astonishingly athletic nineteen-year-old from Korea, watched him with a possessiveness that made his enemies hate him even more. His wife pretended everything was fine, of course, and rarely came up to town any more.

At this time of night there were usually a few lane-ploughing high-flyers left at the Oasis swimming pool in Holborn, but tonight they had showered, dressed and dispersed to hone their aggressive business techniques on their loved ones. One other swimmer remained, a boy with cropped black hair and defined musculature, seated motionless on the edge of the deep end. He leaned back, staring into the sharp mesh of light that filtered from an arabesque of glass bricks set in the side wall. Above the diving board, buttresses of bright light from the overhead neon splintered the refracting depths.

His feet reached down and touched the sloping floor of the pool. Standing very still, he allowed the water to settle. The boy rose from the poolside and padded away to the changing rooms.

Now there was nothing to keep him in the water. Lately, to his consternation, he had begun swimming almost every other evening. It had taken him a few months to understand that he was not drawn here by the determination to get fit, but by the thought of boys in their swimming trunks. This sea-change in his sexuality was unexpected and unwelcome. He was revolted by the surfacing of this secret objective, but found himself helplessly returning to the baths.

The boy had gone. The water stilled and fell silent. It was time for him to exit the pool and dress. The sense of excitement he had briefly shared with his swimming companion faded away as he rose from the chlorinated water.

The shower was capricious. He had learned by now to hammer the temperature dial with the heel of his hand. The baths had individual booths, but only low tiled walls separated them. He had covetously watched young men soaping themselves from here, prepared to take the risk of someone spotting his sidelong glances. Ashamed by his desires, he knew he deserved to be caught. He thumped the dial and water began to flow. Overhead, rain started to course down the glass panels of the roof. The nearby laser-lights in Oxford Street designed to fanfare London's Olympic status traced Mobius patterns across low yellow cloud. The sensuality of warm shower-water unlaced his thoughts, and his mind drifted.

It snapped back into focus when he saw a cloaked figure in a tricorn hat outlined against the roof glass, illuminated by the reflecting water.

Alex Paradine alighted at the fourth floor and found himself in a nondescript corridor, dimly lit and decorated in the grey gloss paint and smoked-pink pastels of buildings constructed in the late eighties. He wondered if the whiskies he had consumed half an hour earlier would reveal themselves in his voice. Following the printout signs to the studio, he struggled to imagine who would use such a place – a local radio station, perhaps? Columns of mortar-crusted bricks leaned against the wall to his right. Bare wires hung down from a pair of missing ceiling panels like the roots of forced plants. As he followed the paper arrows, Paradine grew more suspicious.

His suspicion turned to amazement when he saw the leather-clad figure – was he a motorcycle courier? – leaning in the shadows at the end of the corridor, motionlessly watching him.

*   *   *

Absurd. He had to be imagining things. Could his alcoholism have advanced to the stage of hallucination so quickly? Before Anthony Sarne had a chance to think through the answer, the cloak above swept open to reveal a blood-scarlet lining, and a steel-shod boot heel stamped on the glass above the swimming pool, sending sharpness through the still air. Some kind of ridiculous film stunt, Sarne thought vaguely, wondering if hidden cameras were capturing the event. Or a reveller in fancy dress, a drunken fugitive from an office party about to make the kind of mistake that would get him arrested. But the figure was already pounding away across the skylight, and the shower water was turning cold – colder still and reeking. Sarne glanced up at the battered steel nozzle to be blinded by something that seared his eyes, and he recognized the smell even as its greasy viscosity caused him to slip and land on the tiled floor of the shower stall with a bony crack.

It seemed as absurd as the vision overhead, but the shower nozzle was spraying him with petrol.

The courier raised a gloved hand and beckoned as Alex Paradine kept walking forward. He was almost a welcome sight, an indication that someone else here was prepared to risk making a fool of themselves. A smile showed beneath his eye-mask – a Mardi Gras carnival character, got up as a nightrider, but for what purpose? His beckoning right hand slowed and raised itself, so that the black palm showed – the universal symbol to halt – and Paradine found himself responding. Now the index finger alone was raised, and the rider twisted his fist, pointing down to the floor. Paradine followed the courier's indication with his eyes, and felt the carpet tiles shift beneath his feet.

Sarne tried to rise but petrol was flooding across the floor of the booth, and his bare legs were slipping as the reeking liquid pooled about him. He realized he was sitting on the drain, preventing it from emptying, but was unable to get up. The fumes fuddled his brain even as they made him nauseous. The most important thing, he knew, was to stand, but it seemed so difficult to negotiate a way clear from the path of the spattering spirit.

Pushing hard against the tiles at his back, he woozily shoved himself upright and lurched to a standing position, concentrating on stepping out of the poisonous cascade. He was about to throw himself forward, when he glanced up and saw the tiny descending light in the gloom of the cubicle. There was just enough time for him to register the dropping match before its flame combusted.

It seemed impossible, but the floor was bowing beneath Paradine's feet. He began moving forward, but the shifting of his weight caused the pale-green tiles to sag still further, until he realized that he was actually dropping through the corridor floor.

For a moment, nothing more happened – he fought to maintain his balance while absurdly sinking into the ground. The motorcyclist remained motionless, watching impassively, as though he had been expecting this to happen all the while. The carpet tiles were parting fast, splinters of wood beneath them piercing his trousers and striating his legs. Then, sickeningly, there was nothing below him but dead air.

Paradine plunged down into darkness. The fall seemed to last for ever. It occurred to him that this acceleration towards a painful and abrupt oblivion was merely the last stage of an effect that had been occurring for some time now. The final unforgiving rupture of flesh into concrete, when it came, offered agonized purification.

The shower was transformed into a tiled oven as it filled with molten fire. Flame bellowed and belched, ceramic cracked, and above the noise rose Sarne's scream. The fire formed a scorching red whirlwind around him. He saw the flesh of his bare arms blackening, and over the roiling blaze in the booth, the mask and tricorn and the implacable eyes, peering down at him from a safe vantage point above the inferno.

Two men dead, blackened and shattered, one figure watching before striding away in black leather boots and a crackling cape – a new London legend on the rise to everlasting infamy.

28

DUAL IMPOSSIBILITIES

'We'll need a burns man, old fruit.'

Giles Kershaw dropped like a collapsing deckchair and crouched at the base of the shattered shower booth. He shone a slender torchbeam across the black body, its flesh crusted like barbecued chicken skin. Over an hour had passed since the fire had burned out, but the atmosphere in the changing room was thickened with an acridity that still stung the eyes.

'We don't have a burns specialist,' snapped Bryant. 'You're supposed to have covered this sort of trauma in your training.'

'I have, Mr Bryant. I've just not come across anything like this in the field before.' Kershaw viewed the twisted corpse with ill-disguised incredulity.

'I'm sorry the unit can't provide you with more traditional methods of death, Mr Kershaw.' He studied the charred mess of limbs and broken tiles, and softened a little. 'Just take a few deep breaths and do the best you can. How was your sister's hen night, by the way?'

Kershaw was pulled up short. If there was one thing everyone knew about Arthur Bryant, it was that he never showed the slightest interest in the personal lives of his employees. His concern was neither natural nor appropriately timed – when it came to handling pleasantries, he had the air of a hotel guest picking the wrong moment to tip a porter – but he was clearly making an effort to be sociable, and Kershaw accepted the gesture in good grace.

'Very good, Sir, thank you.' He examined the shower stall. 'Well, this isn't a job for FIT, because the fire was deliberate, not accidental.' The Fire Investigation Team was a specialist service intended to aid police investigations by mapping the source, growth and demise of fires. 'The triangle stayed intact long enough to kill him. There are three points on the triangle after ignition: heat, fuel and oxygen. Fires have to stay alive by moving, and they do that by conduction, convection or radiation, but there were no pipes or other objects in the cubicle to aid the transfer of heat, and the ceiling above is too high for it to have spread easily.'

'There's a faint V pattern of scorching on the rear wall,' Bryant pointed out. 'What's that?'

'It means combustion started low, and a pool burn here on the floor, see?' He indicated a dark halo-shape on the cracked tiles. 'An accelerant, petrol obviously.' Kershaw lifted some scraps of burned matter and dropped them into a nylon sack. 'Chromatography can break down the chemical structure of the vapour in the bag. God, it smells like a burger bar in here. My tummy's rumbling.' He stepped back from the cubicle and took some air.

'Can you tell whether he was dead or alive when the fire started?' asked Bryant.

Kershaw swallowed gamely and concentrated. 'That's straightforward enough. A positive reaction for carbon monoxide in his blood will prove he was still breathing, and we'll check for soot in the air passages. Hyperaemia – inflammation caused by the healing process of leucocytes, the white blood cells – will be present around blisters. Look at this.' Kershaw indicated what appeared to be knife marks across the top of Sarne's skull. 'Heat ruptures caused by the splitting of the soft tissue where the bone is closest to the skin.'

He rose once more and stretched, pushing blond hair from his eyes with his wrist. 'Usually it's not a very practical way to kill someone, but he was standing in a narrow glazed box and basted with petrol – he might as well have stepped into an Aga. We know he was showering when he went up. That's burned bare flesh, no fibres that I can see, apart from the remains of his trunks. A polyamide of some kind, they melted on to him. It's telling that the shoulders are the most heavily burned part.'

'Oh, why?' Bryant leaned closed to examine the roasted body with a handkerchief attached to his nose.

Kershaw unwittingly pulled Bryant's old trick of not answering the question. 'I was thinking perhaps he'd struck some kind of flame like a lighter, but why would anyone smoke in a shower? And besides, that would have left him with his arms bent, at about mid-height, and the scarring's not right. We know this was petrol, not a gas explosion, and there are several odd things about that. First, the boiler is down in the basement, so it couldn't be faulty pipework; too many metres away to cause an explosion up here. If the petroleum was thrown into the shower unit, it would have to be lit pretty damned quickly before the victim could jump out of the booth. And there are no splash burns on the surrounding floor tiles in front, which you'd have had if someone was tossing the contents of a can. The deeply charred upper body suggests it was tipped from above, except that our perpetrator didn't climb up from the adjoining booth, because the walls are still wet from a previous shower, and there are no scuff marks breaking the water patterns.'

'What about over the back wall?' Bryant asked.

'You'd have to be about seven feet tall to do that. Don't tell me we're looking for Spring-Heeled Jack.'

241

'Then there's only one other answer. The petrol was sent through the pipework itself into the showerhead.'

'You'd have to saw into the existing pipe and manually pour the stuff in, but gravity would do the trick from that height. Why would anyone go to such effort? It's the kind of deranged thing—'

'That the Highwayman would do. Yes, isn't it?' Bryant raised a knowing eyebrow and walked away.

'You're right, Sir, more Highwayman sightings,' said Mangeshkar, grabbing him at the entrance to the changing room. 'Up on the rooftop about ninety minutes ago. Plenty of people in the flats opposite – this time we've got more witnesses than we can wave a stick at. He ran across the flat roof, stopped at the skylight, climbed down the far side – full regalia, tricorn, cape, black-leather bodice, boots. Colin is up there now having a look around.'

'He wants to be placed at each site,' muttered Bryant. 'It doesn't make sense. Keep a lookout for a calling card – it could be a symbol just a few inches across, scratched into the brickwork.'

On several occasions, the Leicester Square Vampire had left behind a sign of his presence, probably made while he was waiting in the alley for a victim, although the police had never publicized the fact. Signs and signals in the ancient streets – Maggie Armitage's theory about the capital's mythical attackers leaving their mark.

'Got anything on the victim yet?' Bryant asked Sergeant Longbright, who was working on her laptop in the changing room. She had bleached her hair a fierce shade of blonde and cut it in a style that reminded him of Ruth Ellis, the last British woman to be hanged. *What a wonderfully strange creature she is*, he thought admiringly, studying her for a moment. *So like her mother.*

'His identity's easy. We got that from the wallet he left in his clothes locker. Anthony Sarne, another demi-celebrity. Lane-changing politico. There are dozens of web pages on him – seems he inspired animosity in an awful lot of people.' She turned the screen to face him. 'There's a career synopsis here if you want it: early success as a Labour candidate, disillusionment, a switch of sides to the Liberal Democrats, a court case involving payments to a Mayfair prostitute that seems memorable only for the predictability of the press headlines – wife and children stood by him, blah, blah. Disgrace, eighteen months in jail for lying under oath, re-emergence as a hard-line Tory, reinvention on a TV reality show, now a *Daily Express* columnist. He prided himself on the fact that he never apologized for his actions, but this determination seems to have driven his wife away, resulting in divorce proceedings and some ugly public mud-slinging. Cue more punning headlines in the tabloids.'

'Show me,' said Bryant, bending to examine the screen. 'I remember him. Well, at least he remained entertaining in adversity. One of those characters people refer to as "larger than life", when they actually mean he was an opinionated, obnoxious womanizer. He came out with the most frightful spurious rubbish in court, no wonder they sent him down. People with no sense of shame always make good copy. At least we have a clear pattern now.'

'I don't see one,' said Longbright, flicking through the screen pages.

'That's because we've been searching for someone with an emotional attachment to the victim, but these are all celebrities, whether we like the idea or not. They live in the public arena, and are expected to pay their dues to the people who made them famous. They're publicly account-able. When they fail themselves, they fail their fans. We're not looking for jilted lovers, betrayed rivals or deceived wives. It's someone who feels personally let down by the actions of these people. White admits to abortions, Martell wrecks his career, and Sarne upset just about every-one.'

'It doesn't exactly narrow down the suspects, Sir.'

'Quite the reverse,' Bryant replied, sighing. 'We'd be hard pushed to find someone who didn't hate him.'

He stood outside the Oasis with his smouldering pipe, watching the rain-spattered taxis rounding the curve of High Holborn towards St Giles Circus, and considered the predatory tactics of murderers. But instead of the Highwayman, he found himself thinking about the Leicester Square Vampire.

Although Bram Stoker had set Dracula loose in a Northern coastal town, the modern vampire suited an urban setting. *Cities attract predators*, he thought, *and vampires are the most predatory creatures of all. They leech from their hosts, and as the good-hearted grow weaker, they gain strength. To do this, they must first gain a position of intimacy. Physical contact is required, and to gain such proximity requires an element of sexual attraction. Their victims, therefore, are willing to different degrees, and continue to remain in sexual thrall until the object of their desire is no longer able to influence them, and the spell is broken.*

Cities attracted lonely people who were vulnerable and ready to believe. Vampires came in all shapes and sizes. Their attraction masked moral and physical decay. *Beware the creatures of the night, for they prey on those who trust . . .*

John warned me about this, he thought suddenly. *They're dividing our concentration. I won't let them win.*

John May stepped closer to the ragged hole and looked down. 'A hell of a fall,' he remarked. 'Four floors back to ground level, plus the basement. How was the body?'

'He hit his chin on the way down, leaving most of it behind on the second floor. The impact spun him around, so by the time he passed ground level he was twirling like a Catherine wheel. It did a lot of damage, and that's before the landing broke both his legs and his right arm. It also pushed a rib clear through his heart. It was over quickly, if nothing else.'

Dan Banbury joined May at the edge. 'This was a very neat trap,' he added with a hint of admiration. 'People can be bloody ingenious when they put their minds to it. Although the killer probably imagined his victim would fall straight down the centre of the hole and break his neck. This is for you.' He passed over a plastic bag containing the dead man's wallet.

'Alex Paradine,' May read from the ID card inside. 'I would never have recognized him.'

'You know him?'

'Only because he's on television. They call him Garfy. He's a comedian, TV presenter, actor, whatever. He thought he was coming to a recording session.'

'How do you know that?'

May lifted a slip of paper from the wallet by his fingertips. 'He had this address written down. There's an hour booked out on it. Look around. There are at least three sheets of A4 paper directing him to a non-existent studio.' He pointed at the page still taped at the end of the corridor. 'Someone goes to the trouble of luring him here and preparing an elaborate, not to mention risky, method of death – and then leaves the handwritten signs behind. Why would he do that? Why pull off this kind of remote-control trick successfully, only to leave behind something that helps to reveal the method?' He looked around, thinking. 'He was in a rush and forgot them. But no one else knew his victim was here, so why hurry?'

'I think the murderer was on site when it happened,' Banbury pointed out. 'Let me show you.' He led the way to the rear fire-stairs, then down to the floor below, keeping his eye on the ragged hole in the ceiling.

'The building's been empty for nearly two years,' said May. 'The developer hasn't had any luck finding a tenant; there's a banner out front offering reduced rent. I remember passing it at least eighteen months ago. There's probably too much available office space around here. You can tell the holding company ran out of money; half the floors aren't finished. This ceiling was left open so that electricians could get at the trunking, and the panels were never put back.'

'Maybe our man works on the site and knows about the unfinished floor, or perhaps it was a passing opportunist.' Banbury picked up a cracked sheet of board and showed it to May. 'Either way, he sees the hole and paves it over with a thin sheet of hardboard, then lays carpet tiles taken from the stack left on the floor above.'

Banbury considered the hardboard for a moment. 'But I'm guessing that it bowed, or just didn't look right. So he searches around for something else, and wedges a pair of wood beams across the gap from the underside, for added strength. He must have shoved them in pretty tight.'

'Why do you say that?'

'If you step on something that feels like it might give way, you back off immediately. The floor had to feel strong enough to walk on, otherwise the victim wouldn't have advanced. Even then, if he'd kept going, he might have made it across. Something made him stop, and in that moment he grew too heavy for the floor to support him. This is an exercise in smart carpentry. I wasn't much of an academic when I was a nipper, but I was good at woodwork. It's a very peculiar way to kill a man. Not exactly foolproof. That's why I think he was here, to make sure it worked.'

'Sir, we've got a witness,' PC Colin Bimsley announced, rushing into the hall so quickly that Banbury had to steer him away from the jagged gap in the floor. May imagined the spatially challenged officer following their victim head-first into the hole, and wondered how they had ever been landed with such a lumpen constable. 'It's definitely the Highwayman again. Boots, gloves, mask, funny hat. Italian woman who runs the Nero coffee bar across the street saw him leaving the building.'

'That's impossible,' said May. 'Janice called in a sighting

246

halfway across town just a few minutes ago. They've got a victim fried alive in a shower, for God's sake. He can't have been in two places at once.'

The distracted crime-scene officer was looking at him helplessly, waiting for advice.

'Banbury,' May said aloud, 'help me out here. Find something normal for me, tell me it was an accidental death, that he just blundered on to an unfinished floor.'

'Can't do that, sir,' Banbury apologized. 'Nothing remotely normal about this at all. We've got another decent set of boot marks, though. I need to bag the carpet tiles and run some tests, but I can already tell the prints are similar to the ones in the Burroughs Gallery. If it's the same attacker, we're getting a pretty unusual profile.' He wiped his hands on his jacket. 'He doesn't like to touch his victims. Always keeps his distance, never gets his hands dirty. No contact means no prints, no DNA, no fibres. The outfit helps, although it seems unnecessarily theatrical.' He doubled down and pulled another carpet tile free. 'There's some kind of gunk on the boot-heel. Smells like wood glue. He might have picked it up around here, but it's worth checking.'

'Look out for a symbol scratched somewhere outside the building. Arthur thinks he always leaves a mark, a pair of Vs, one inverted. He stands and watches them die,' said May, realizing the truth. 'Or he arranges it so that he's near enough to be sure of their deaths. And there's no emotional response at all, except perhaps a very controlled level of dispassion. If you need me, I'll be over the road.'

May made his way to the dark bar of the Jerusalem Tavern in Britton Street, sidling along a squeezed, warped corridor to a miniscule back room filled with stuffed animals. The pub's name was another reminder of Clerkenwell's strange connection with the Knights Templars. He ordered a marsh-green bottle of King Cnut Ale and sipped it, tasting barley, nettles and juniper.

What could I have said? he thought. *Maybe I've finally*

247

cracked up. Too many years spent dealing with abnormalities, listening to Arthur and his pals explaining why dowsers and sun spots can help catch criminals, instead of following my instincts and using more traditional procedures. I could have become a Met superintendent years ago, a nice safe earner. Instead I spend my time wandering about in the realms of the unnatural, looking for vampires and shape-shifters.

At such times, May knew there was only one course of action. His partner operated as the other side of his brain; the two halves needed to be reunited, in order to find some sense in the surreal. If Bryant really thought he could uncover the truth, now was the time for him to use any method necessary to do so.

29

DEIFICATION

In the last two months, *Hard News*, self-billed as Great Britain's first daily magazine, had become the periodical with the fastest-growing circulation in the country. Janet Ramsey, former cable newsbabe and Page Three model, was its Senior Features Editor. On Friday morning, she swooped into the Covent Garden office that had once been the headquarters of the British Cabbage Association and searched for somewhere to dump her Starbucks Double-Shot Skinny Latte on the mess of smoked-glass desks. 'Are you the new runner?' she snapped. 'Get me a fresh one of these.'

'Do you have the money?' asked the lanky young man who had been leaning outside Ramsey's office, waiting for instructions.

'I don't carry loose change on me, darling, I'm like the Queen. Sub me until I get change of a twenty.'

'Not on my wages,' the runner told her. 'Cash up front, I'll get change.'

'I don't know where we find you lads these days,' Ramsey complained, digging in her purse grudgingly to pay him. 'A century ago we'd have been putting you up chimneys and lowering you into drains with canaries.' She beckoned to Roat, her art director. 'Dump the old shot we had of the

Highwayman – the picture quality was horrible. What was it photographed through – a heavy denim veil?'

'This isn't *Vanity Fair*,' said Roat. 'It was taken by a barista through a steamed-up coffee-bar window.'

'Can't you find another shot of him, one that isn't so blurred?

'He's a murder suspect, not a catwalk model,' sighed the art director. 'We'll retouch the jaw and lips, bring out the tricorn and the mask, make his eyes more sinister.'

'That's not technically legal,' Ramsey warned.

'It was good enough for *Time* magazine and O. J. Simpson,' the designer reminded her. 'It would help if I could reduce the size of the splash.'

'Then put it on page three and come up with a symbol for the front cover, something we can use to identify the Highwayman whenever he's sighted. Don't go over the top, but make it demonic and sexy.'

'This just arrived for you, Janet,' said the runner, handing her a brown envelope.

'You're not entitled to use my first name,' Ramsey warned. 'Actually, you can open it, it might be hate mail.'

'You've been peed on by a member of Oasis, surely you can withstand a little Anthrax,' sniffed Roat, watching as the boy tore open the package.

'What do we have here?' Ramsey scanned the four photographs. 'Well, well.' She dropped the photographs on her desk with a smirk that revealed the mouth-enhancing limits of her lipstick. 'Someone appears to be on our side. The Highwayman has had some professional pictures taken. Look at them, they're like forties studio shots.' She rattled her Versace charm bracelet at the runner. 'Envelope, envelope. Where did this come from?'

The runner was examining something he had removed from his nostril. 'Dunno. Post room?'

'Show some initiative and find out.' She passed the pictures to Roat. 'See if you can do something with them.'

'Can I spend some money on artwork?'

'All right, but don't go mad. We'll run a large strap across the cover, something like HIGHWAYMAN DELIVERS DEATH VENGEANCE TWICE IN ONE NIGHT. Deliver, you see? Like "Stand and deliver"?'

'OK, but "vengeance"? He's killed two more innocent people.'

'For God's sake, nobody's innocent any more. Two very *disliked* people. All right, I take your point, give me something bland and non-committal like MASKED MAN'S DOUBLE SLAUGHTER RAMPAGE, get Francesca to work out the details, and shift POPE ADMITS THERE IS NO AFTER-LIFE to the bottom of the page, the story's unsubstantiated.'

'She's your sub, you tell her,' said Roat, stumping back to his desk.

'I have to do everything around here.' Ramsey slammed her office door behind her and examined the cuttings on her wall. To date there had been seven amateur snaps of the Highwayman taken, only four of which were verifiable. It would help if they knew where he was going to strike next. According to Simon, the tubby trustafarian who occasionally turned up to write the insider's pop page, the Highwayman's face had already made an appearance on stencils and flyers for a club night in the West End. She could take a leaf from the trend, ask Roat to tidy up the symbol a bit, get it adopted by the nation's teenagers. Publish some souvenir memorabilia, do a contra-deal with T-shirt printers and knock up some shirts bearing his image, hand them out at gigs and clubs, condemn his actions in print, of course, but run some iconic imagery on mobile phones to whet the public's appetite. It was important for the magazine to own his image. She called Francesca in.

'Couldn't we get a band to record a song about him?' she asked. 'What would it take to turn him into a cult hero?'

'A little cash,' said Francesca, who loathed her boss and coveted her job, but was forced to smile and offer help until she could think of a way of derailing her. 'You don't need to shift many downloads for a hit single. We'll be fine so long as he sticks to attacking unloved celebrities, but what if he decides to go after a national hero? Launching a campaign around him could backfire on us.'

'Never worry about things that haven't happened yet,' snapped Ramsey. 'The public has a ten-second memory. We're not condoning his actions, Francesca, we're riding on his awareness level. When six million people show an interest in a lousy paperback about finding God, it's your job to understand why they do so, it doesn't mean you have to like it. The English are irrational creatures and *ipso facto* unintentionally hypocritical. We merely reflect their failure to appreciate their reduced moral status.'

'Sometimes I think you're working on the wrong paper,' said Francesca. 'Lately you've been using long words and showing scruples.'

'Everyone blasts the tabloids, nobody condemns the readers,' replied Ramsey, swinging her white leather chair round. 'I think about the process more than you, that's why I'm in the job you want but will never have. I went to Cambridge and I showed my breasts in the tabloids. These facts aren't mutually exclusive; the stereotypes are formed in the public mind, where I can benefit from them.'

She flicked at her computer and ran a coral-coloured false nail down the screen, crackling static. 'If this report is to be trusted, the Highwayman killed twice within the same half-hour last night. The public won't know what to think, so it's our job to tell them. Either we vilify him, "this depraved monster" etcetera, which leaves our readers with no course of direct action, or we promote him – luckily, he looks bloody sexy in these stills – and they can follow his exploits. They can feel as if they have a share in him. I think our course of action is clear, don't you?' She looked out at the city streets shrouded in autumnal morning vapour. 'They're looking for new gods, and we've got one for them. Vengeful, unforgiving, filled with righteous wrath, roaring down from the sky like a fiery angel. We'll give them what they asked for.'

'I don't see what you're so angry about,' said Bryant, pulling open each of his desk drawers in turn and rummaging through them. 'Have you seen my special tobacco?'

'It's not special tobacco, Arthur, it's grass from your mutant marijuana plant, and I've thrown it away – yes, I know you're going to say it's medicinal, but Janice thinks Raymond Land is searching the offices for incriminating evidence, so it had to go.'

'I'd appreciate you dropping the sharp tone from your voice,' said Bryant, still rummaging. 'You sound so unnerved.'

May dropped wearily on to the corner of his desk. 'Is it surprising? I want to find a flesh-and-blood killer, not some mythical creature who slips through the night like a wraith. I'm giving you permission to explore alternative methods of investigation. You should be thrilled. Instead, you're telling me you'd rather use my methods. Why must you always be so perverse?'

'I'm not, I'm being open-minded, like you requested. And I don't make distinctions between reality and myth. The former often ends up becoming the latter. Look at Atlantis.'

'What are you talking about?'

'Men have been looking for Atlantis ever since Plato's dialogues, even though he probably intended the story as an analogy. Despite this, American oceanographers are using up their grant funds in attempts to place the lost continent in locations ranging from Ireland to Cyprus. Fiction affects and alters the truth, you see? If a scientist fell overboard on such a trip and drowned, we could say that he died as the result of belief in a myth.'

'Four deaths, Arthur! This is not about some ancient myth.' May looked at his bitten nails, wondering how much longer he would last without suffering another heart attack.

'In a city of almost eight million people, at least a handful must have strange and potentially harmful belief systems, and we can root them out using standard investigative methodology. Janice and April are searching the victims' backgrounds for common elements, something they've shared in the past that has marked them out from the rest of the population. Because you're right: there are no illogical murders, only irrational ones. A youth bludgeons an old lady for a handful of change. The boy has an addiction, the pensioner is vulnerable. He behaves irrationally but quite logically. One has simply to consider the moral dimension. The boy's need forces him into a situation we consider morally repugnant, but if he failed to act logically, by attacking a stronger victim living further away, we would have no way of locating him. Without logic, our working methods collapse. You're right.'

'Will you stop saying I'm bloody well right?' May was frustrated and becoming increasingly annoyed. 'How can you use logic here?' he demanded. 'The man is wearing nineteenth-century clothing, for God's sake.'

'And there is a reason; we simply haven't deduced it yet. The Lord Chancellor wears a tricorn hat during proclamations in parliament, did you know that? Perhaps there's a political link.' Something rang a distant bell in his head, but he dismissed it.

'And what about the timings on Sarne and Paradine? There's nothing logical about the Highwayman being sighted in two places at once.'

Bryant patted the papers on his desk. '"I do not mind lying but I hate inaccuracy" – Samuel Butler. The witness reports actually fall within fourteen minutes of each other. The distance between the two sites is too much to cover on foot, but perhaps he really does have a motorcycle. It would partially explain the outfit.'

'Nothing explains anything in this investigation,' cried May, exasperated. 'I'm expecting Faraday through that door any minute to demand why we haven't locked up a suspect.' He rubbed his eyes with the heel of his hand and dropped into the chair opposite. 'What I'm saying is, I've come around to your way of thinking. We need to try something new. Run me through the combined timeline Banbury and Kershaw came up with.'

'Let's see.' Bryant adjusted his bifocals and squinted at the page. 'Have you been using my watermarked Basildon Bond? I keep this for special, you know, it's not for scribbling on.'

'Give it to me. I don't know why you have to get everything printed out, it makes a mockery of the electronic age.' May snatched at the papers impatiently. 'Eight thirty p.m. – Sarne arrives at the Oasis swimming pool for his evening dip. The pool is due to shut at nine. There's supposed to be a guard on duty but he's gone off somewhere, nobody seems to know where. A couple of other swimmers have timed tickets for the previous half-hour, but they've gone to change by the time Sarne hits the water. The Highwayman is spotted on the roof above the pool at around eight forty-five by one of the class instructors, but incredibly, she doesn't consider the incident unusual enough to report.

'At exactly the same time, in Clerkenwell, Paradine checks into the empty building in St John Street looking for his recording studio. He goes up to the fourth floor, using the stairs because the lift isn't connected up. You'd think he'd twig that there was something wrong, but presumably he's merely keen to get the job done and leave. His agent has no record of the booking, so we're checking his phone messages and emails to see if someone rang him direct.

'On the fourth floor he walks along the corridor, steps on to the faked-up covering and falls through the unfinished floor. The Highwayman is seen leaving from the site at nine p.m.

'Meanwhile, Sarne is finishing his laps in the pool. He gets out of the water and heads for the showers. Turning on the hot tap, he gets dowsed in ordinary unleaded engine petrol and set on fire. Banbury traced the exposed section of water pipe into the ceiling and found it sawn through. Fitted over the end was a plastic accordion hand-pump containing petrol residue. The killer simply waited for Paradine to turn on the tap before stamping on the pump and tossing a match down through the grille. Still, it seems an absurdly complex method of death. The pipe must have been cut earlier the same evening, because the shower hadn't been reported out of action.' He tossed the paper back on to his desk. 'The combined reports of the entire unit, and they amount to virtually nothing. Four locations with no link between them, and four victims with no shared attributes beyond a public profile.'

'You want me to use my methods?' Bryant asked. 'Then we need to find out what inspired this nightmare figure to be conjured to life. How can we protect potential victims if the public believes they somehow brought retribution upon themselves?'

'We're reviewing the few unlikely suspects we do have. Janice is arranging that for later today.'

Bryant pulled the collar of his ratty jumper up to his chin, shrinking into his chair with the effort of thought. 'The most common attribute shared by the victims is their increasing level of infamy. As your granddaughter pointed out, their movements are known; it makes them easy targets. Four people have died, and one has been born: the Highwayman has already begun the process of passing into our shared mythology, just as Jack Sheppard and Jonathan Wild did before him. He is conjuring himself into existence, aiding his own birth, building the creation of his own myth. How? By dressing outlandishly, by leaving a calling card, by posing for photographs and allowing himself to be seen. He craves a different kind of notoriety from that achieved by his victims. He desires admiration and respect, and that will be the weakness that causes his downfall.'

Something in Bryant's speech struck a familiar chord. 'You're talking about setting up a potential victim for him.'

'The thought had crossed my mind.'

'You know how dangerous that is. Look what happened with the Leicester Square Vampire.'

'This time we can have total control. You don't even have to be involved, John. The unit will take all the risk. Besides, there's something else for you to do. Look back at the birth of our myth-figure. Who first gave us the image of the Highwayman?'

'The boy who was drawing in the gallery.'

'Then return to him. Even if he doesn't know it, the boy holds the key. While you do that, do I have your permission to bring in some alternative expertise?'

'You have my blessing,' May agreed. 'Just make sure there's nothing to connect us in the event of an internal investigation.'

30

SECRET LANDSCAPES

As he struggled with a recalcitrant length of bookbinding tape, Arthur Bryant thought back to the white witch's comments about legendary London monsters.

How many had left their marks behind in ancient streets, to be traced to the present day? As a tour guide, he had taken tourists around Chelsea, showing them the artists' houses where nervous talk of foreign fiends once filled the drawing rooms, then on to Vauxhall and Rotherhithe, where cut-throats and footpads had operated in the alleyways and under the arches. In London's poor areas the dangers had been more real, and the residents had found little time to fret over the presence of imagined devils, but in wealthy and penurious neighbourhoods alike, the legendary monsters of London had left few physical signs of their presence. All that could be seen were a few untended plaques, a gravestone or two, sometimes a public house where a villain had gathered with his cronies. Monsters lived on in family memories, and were turned into stories to frighten children.

Bryant patted the binding tape on to his copy of *London's Most Notorious Highwaymen* and returned it to the shelf behind his desk. So, if there were no outward signs of the city's night creatures left, why did their stories survive? Did grandfathers still terrify with tales of Sweeney Todd and Jack the Ripper, or were these legends now too tame to recount? Denis Nielsen, Fred West and Dr Harold Shipman were the British bogeymen of the twentieth century, and the infamous catalogue of their victims would lengthen in the twenty-first as the full extent of their crimes was revealed. But they had been identified, analysed and locked away. For a murderer to become a myth, something more was required, an element of the unfathomable. Could it be that as the lives of murderers were dissected and placed on public display, their power to thrill future generations was diminished?

Londoners still spoke of the Leicester Square Vampire precisely because he had never been caught. Was that the purpose of the Highwayman, to provide a nemesis for generations to come, to achieve perverse immortality through incompleteness?

Bryant sat back and untangled his pipe from the scarf he kept wrapped around him in the overheated office. The geographical factor bothered him. Two of the murders had occurred in the area surrounding Smithfield, the former execution site of London's villains for over four hundred years, before it was moved to Tyburn tree. Once the mob had gathered there to witness death by fire and roasting chair. Was it really coincidence that modern-day scoundrels should suffer similar fates in the vicinity? He kept coming back to Clerkenwell, and its connection with the blood of Christ. All London areas maintained links with the past, no matter how well hidden they were. Even the pubs surrounding Lincoln's Inn Fields had bars named after the Templars. Everything was there for a reason. The past misled and taunted him, but tightened its grip as his age advanced.

And now that he had been given permission to explore the history of the city's murderers, he sensed a recurring pattern at work, something that ran all the way from the London Monster to the Leicester Square Vampire and the Highwayman. Certainly, similar murderers seemed to have existed under a variety of names. London's bogeymen were part of the folklore that crusted the city like barnacles on a slow-sailing liner.

Bryant picked up his collapsed trilby from the chair and bashed it back into shape. It was time to consult an expert on the meanings of London's secret landscapes. Creaking up from his seat, he decided to start by paying a visit to his old friend Oliver Golifer, owner of the Newman Street Picture Library.

Oliver Golifer's broad, broken nose, badly shaved pate and ironing-board forehead gave him the appearance of an East End thug sired by Magwitch. Strangers picked Saturday-night fights with him just to prove to their girlfriends that they were hard, which was unfortunate because, although he had the heart of a kitten and the intellect of an Oxford don, he was still happy to knock someone to the floor for their arrogance. He had developed this pugilistic tendency at an early age in response to taunting about his admittedly ridiculous name. This amused Bryant greatly, because while Golifer had the reputation of a bruiser, he could also be as camp as a French operetta. He welcomed the detective with meaty hands the size of Sunday roasts before ushering him through the cramped store front.

'Nice to see you looking so well, Arthur,' he whispered. As a child, he had accidentally drunk some bleach his stepfather had saved in an orange-squash bottle, and it had corroded his vocal cords, reducing his voice to a sinister sussurance as menacing as his features. 'I see you're all over the news again. I'm assuming that's what you're here about. What's on your mind?'

'It's a question of motive. You've read about the investigation?'

260

'How could I have avoided it? The gentleman you're searching for is a self-publicist. The tabloids have been praying for someone like him to come along for years. I've already opened a picture file on him, although I'm sure they're only variations on the shots you already have.'

He led the way through the warren of rooms to racks of yellowing envelopes, filed in a complex system involving dates, locations and subjects. The proliferation of internet picture sites meant that Golifer no longer needed to keep the library open, but it appealed to his sense of continuity to do so; Newman Street had housed picture libraries as long as photographs had been taken. Its walls were lined with famous images: Emmeline Pankhurst being carried away by constables, a fascist throwing a Molotov cocktail at a police cordon, Ban the Bomb gatherings in Trafalgar Square, Poll Tax riots, vacant celebrities alighting from limousines into photographers' lightstorms.

'I'm interested in his field of operation,' Bryant explained. 'I was waylaid by Clerkenwell's historical connections for a while, but I think that may be a blind. If you connect the murder sites properly, one place seems to exist at the centre. What do you have on Smithfield?'

'Hm. Bull in a china shop,' replied Golifer enigmatically. He rooted about for a few minutes and finally held up a damaged print of one such enraged bovine creature destroying several hundred Wedgwood vases. 'In the early part of the seventeenth century, drunken herdsmen used to get their cattle to stampede on the way to the market at Smithfield, just for a laugh. The beasts used to rampage into shops and houses, hence the expression.' He studied Bryant's face thoughtfully. 'You want to go even earlier, don't you? Thinking about the old execution site?'

'The area's psychogeography is hard to ignore.'

Golifer dragged over another box and opened it. 'Is your partner still seeing that married woman behind her husband's back?'

'Monica Greenwood? I'm afraid so.'

'Dirty old sod, good for him.' Golifer's gurgling laugh sounded like someone unblocking a sink. 'What about you? I heard you were knocking about with some old bird as well.'

'Mrs Quinten and I have an understanding, that's all,' Bryant bridled. 'I enjoy her company. We play skittles together.'

'Your landlady won't be pleased. Alma always had a soft spot for you.'

'Can we get back to the subject in hand? I don't ask you about your bedroom arrangements.' Bryant reknotted his scarf, tightening it in some agitation. 'What else do you have on Smithfield?'

'I know it used to be called "Smoothfield" – a flat ten-acre grass field with a horse market on Fridays. Early twelfth century, that was. Farmers added other livestock, punters went to watch tournaments and jousts, then they came for public hangings. It was all considered entertainment. Witches and heretics were roasted alive in cages. In Mary Tudor's reign over two hundred martyrs were burned. Duels and disorder, death and drunken debauchery, that's Smithfield for you. Now it's all rowdy nightclubs. Goes to show some things hardly change.'

'Perhaps it was no accident he picked these sites,' said Bryant.

'What about the other two?'

'I thought of that. The Oasis swimming pool is very near the site of Seven Dials' notorious rookeries; they sheltered many a famous murderer. Which leaves the Burroughs Gallery on the South Bank as the odd one out. That part of the Thames was hardly more than a rural riverbank until the Festival of Britain in 1951. My theory is that he had no choice in that location, because it's where White's art piece had already been installed.'

'A bit of a dead end there, then. You must have tons of forensic information to go on, even if you're low on suspects. Surely the bizarre methods of death have left you with something?'

'Less than you'd think. We're due some more results later today.'

'So what do you need me for?'

'I thought you might – oh, I don't know, help me get a synapse jump-started or something.'

'Well, I can certainly help you with highwaymen. Come with me.' Golifer led the way to a circular iron staircase at the rear of the shop and squeezed his bulk down it. They descended into a mildewy basement filled with overloaded shelves. 'They've always been a popular subject for prints. After all, so many of them became folk heroes. Let me see what we've got.' He slid out a long box from beneath one of the counters and began drawing out envelopes. 'Take a look at these. We've got prints of around thirty highwaymen operating in England, from Captain James Hind to Jack Shrimpton and John Cottington. But of course there were hundreds of infamous highwaymen – and a few women. The trouble is that most of the illustrations are rather similar in styling.' He carefully lifted a sheet of tissue paper covering one of the prints, which bore the caption *Mrs Huntingdon is much received of dissatisfaction by robbery and an offer of marriage from Mull-Sack the Murderer.*

'These are all hand-tinted from books published between 1880 and 1925, when the subject came back into vogue. The main features are common to your photographs: flintlock pistol, tricorn hat, greatcoat – usually crimson, occasionally blue – gloves and high riding boots.'

'What's that?' asked Bryant, pulling out his reading glasses to squint at an object depicted on the bottom of the sheet.

'Ah, that's a rather more private part of the highwayman's lore,' said Golifer. 'A secret known only to London's criminal fraternity. It's the fabled Highwayman's Key.'

Bryant found himself looking at the key left behind in the Burroughs Gallery.

31

THE ASSONANCE OF MYTHS

John May pushed his way between the moping vines draped from the railway embankment as the boy passed by no more than six feet away from him.

He had intended to talk to Luke Tripp as he left the school, but something had held him back. The detective's age counted against him; the boy would not confide in someone he saw as ancient and alien. He was making his way alone from St Crispin's, and had reached the edge of the Rolande Plumbe Community Estate. If the private school pupils were wary of crossing the estate gang's territory, their caution had not infected Luke, who kept a steady, unfaltering pace as he passed into the shadow of the ground-floor columns. Aware that he was the only other figure crossing the bare open space of the estate's grounds, May dropped back.

Tripp knew exactly where he was going. Not once did he raise his head to check his route, or hesitate before altering direction. His slender form appeared and vanished between the columns as May kept pace. He thought of something Bryant had said: *Even if he doesn't know it, the boy holds the key*. What did he mean?

Luke was perhaps a hundred paces from him when he

broke into a run. *The little devil knows I'm here*, thought May. *What does he think he's doing?* The boy reached the concrete staircase at the end of the corridor and took the steps two, sometimes three, at a time. May felt his pulse rise as he tried to keep up. He smelled the acrid stench of urine. As he passed the first-floor corridor he momentarily lost sight of his quarry, but heard his shoes thumping on the steps above. Then, as if he had been lifted into the air, they simply stopped.

May halted too, listening to the faintly falling rain above the pounding of his heart. He moved cautiously upward, keeping to the dark inner core of the stairs, until he reached the point where the boy should have been. Looking down, he saw where the wet footprints ceased. Although the staircase was open on one side, there was nothing beyond the waist-high concrete barricade but rainy air beneath low cinereous clouds; they were between the first and second floors of the block.

May's nerve endings tingled with unease. He felt himself in the presence of the Highwayman. Foolishly, he had ventured here alone. To open his radio line now would be to give away his position on the stairs.

A time-switch clicked above him and the stairway was suddenly outlined in dim yellow light. Above a burned-out sofa and a drift of beer cans, he saw the hand-painted stencils that twined and crowded each other across the concrete. Familiar gang signs of fate and luck: crowns, stars, pitchforks, hearts, horns, dice, stars, pyramids. He peered more closely at the recurring stencilled motif of black Vs, and realized he was looking at the tricorn hat and collar once again. As a familiar spasm in his back kicked in, he stood upright to ease the pain and found himself faced by a dozen watchful shadows.

'We collected a key from the floor of the gallery, beside the installation that contained Saralla White's body,' Bryant explained. 'Made of aluminium, exactly like the one in this picture.'

'Well, you've been left a pun of sorts,' said Oliver Golifer. '"A thieves' key, unlocked for the good of the public", as I believe the City Marshall once called it. The key is meant to consist of three main sections: the ring, the pipe – that is the stem – and the wards, which are the cut sections that interface with the inside of the lock. There are fourteen wards in all. The key and its parts are both literal and figurative.' He unfolded a second print of a highwayman, down the side of which was printed a list of words and phrases. 'The ring is made of gold, signifying the virtuous profession of highwaymen. The pipe is made of silver and is hollow, signifying the secret art of handing out bribes. The wards – well, here you are. First, boldness. Second, neatness. Third, flattery. Fourth, treachery. Fifth, diligence. And so on through obedience, lying and cruelty – these last few words are water-stained and unreadable, but you get the idea. You'll probably find books that go into great detail about the thieves' key if you're that interested, but it seems a bit arcane. I can't imagine that your average murderer would know or care much about them.'

'He cares enough to dress himself in an exact replica of the clothes in these prints,' Bryant pointed out. 'Who knows how far his interest extends?' He pulled his moulting scarf tighter around his neck. 'Thank you for the information, Oliver. I have absolutely no idea what I shall do with it, but I'm sure I'll think of something. There is another matter to be dealt with; you don't have a file on the Leicester Square Vampire, by any chance?'

'I haven't heard anything about him in years, but I seem to recall some press shots,' said Golifer. 'Let me have a look.' He led Bryant to a back room filled with locked metal boxes. 'Most of these photographs are in the public domain, but your lot prefer us to keep them away from public gaze because, technically, they involve still-unsolved crimes and could be needed as evidence.'

'The Met is no longer "my lot", as you put it,' said Bryant, ruffled. 'We report directly to the Home Office now, and I'm not sure which is worse. Why don't they keep the pictures themselves?'

'No room, apparently. I asked them to pay for some better security down here, but they refused.' He unclipped one of the box lids and drew out a selection of large bordered monochrome photographs taken in the 1950s. 'These are the earliest ones we have. Didn't you once get a priest involved to exorcise the spot where he appeared? You reckoned he could run through walls like *Le Passe-Muraille*. I'm sure I remember a scandal.'

Bryant sighed. When it came to his investigative technique, everyone remembered the scandals. 'It was a long time ago, Oliver. I was desperate for a break in the case. Three deaths, sixteen attacks, I was prepared to try anything at that point. He ran to ground and we never found him.'

'So why the interest now?'

Bryant scratched at the grey stubble on his cheek. 'Because I'm sure now it was all trickery, jiggery-pokery designed to make us think he was superhuman. He was motivated less by the need to attack than the desire to make an impression on the world. That's what we have here. Rampant egotism. The superior being flexing his muscles. And because of that, we never managed to close the case. I don't want history to repeat itself. Do you have any earlier prints of legendary London murderers? Engravings, stuff like that?'

'The usual plates of Spring-Heeled Jack, Charley Peace, Jack Sheppard – things you'll have seen plenty of times before.'

'Let me see them. You never know.' They returned to the print files, where Golifer pulled down a vast, mildewy volume of prints.

'Who are these characters?' asked Bryant, stabbing at a

page. The print showed four black-faced men, covered in dirt and ashes, making off with several screaming children.

'Ah, they're the Flying Dustmen,' Golifer whispered. 'A good example of real-life characters who were absorbed into London's mythical history. Charles Fox was one of a group of bogus refuse-collectors known around St Mary, Islington, as the Flying Dustmen. He and his cronies stole baskets of ashes from households. Back in 1812, contractors paid £750 a year to the parish and employed several men and their carts to empty the dustbins. They hired women and children to sift cinders, which fetched half the price of coal, and provided siftings for brickmaking. The regular dustmen feared they would lose their Christmas bonuses from households, and issued written warnings to customers about the rogue collectors. The ringleader was caught and prosecuted, but for many years parents use the image of the dust-clad thieves to frighten their children into good behaviour.'

'How one misses the ability to frighten children.' Bryant turned through the pages, fascinated.

'Now, if you're looking for a man with the reputation of vanishing through walls, there's John Williams, who supposedly slaughtered a draper and his family with a chisel before striking a second time and killing a publican, his wife and maid with a crowbar.'

'You're talking about the infamous Ratcliffe Highway Murders of 1811.'

'That's right.' Golifer indicated an etching that showed a curly-headed sailor stretched out on an inclined platform. 'This is a good example of how the public colluded in manufacturing a legend. Hysteria swept Wapping and the surrounding area because the murderer seemed super-human, vanishing from the upper rooms where the deaths occurred, and there were over forty false arrests. Finally, a seaman named John Williams was taken in with virtually no evidence against him, and after he hanged himself in suspicious circumstances at Coldbath Fields Prison, he was paraded through the streets with the maul and the chisel inserted into a board beside his head. The High Constable of Middlesex and hundreds of parish officers and constables escorted the cart. Suicides were buried at crossroads in those days, and Williams is interred at the crossroads of Cannon Street and St George's Turnpike. But for years after, the area was infected with a kind of poison. Residents said they heard and saw his vengeful ghost, and even to this day the area has a strange feeling, especially when it's rainy and the wind is high, and everyone else is indoors. Murderers who operate in mysterious – that is to say, unsolved – circumstances are survived by a peculiar assonance that can last generations.'

'Exactly so.' Bryant studied the prints on the crowded walls. 'Wait a minute.' He raised up the copy of the photograph Golifer had shown him, a small blurred shot taken in Leicester Square by a tourist, and narrowed his eyes, comparing it to the lithograph on the wall. The Met had discounted it, but Bryant had long believed that the snap of the Vampire was genuine. This was the evidence no one else remembered, not even Longbright, who assumed she was official custodian of all remaining documents. He laid the curled photograph on the table. 'Bit of a coincidence, isn't it?' he asked Golifer, pointing to the wall print that showed a strangely outfitted man standing on a rock. 'The clothing of the two figures is almost identical.'

'I never noticed that before,' Golifer admitted.

'I think we were misled by the nickname conjured up in the press,' Bryant surmised. 'The cloak, the boots, the jerkin, the high collar; it appears the Leicester Square Vampire wasn't modelled on Dracula at all, but upon someone else entirely. This print you have is familiar from my childhood. You know who this is, of course.'

'Yes, he's a myth – '

'Not at all. He was very real. Born in the reign of Henry II, with a pedigree *ab origine* no higher than a shepherd. He

270

trained as a butcher, and was equally brilliant with a back-sword, a quarterstaff or a bow. He fell in with a bad lot, took to such a level of violent thievery and murder that travellers lived in terror of him and would pay him for safe passage through the woodlands. He died in a Yorkshire nunnery at the age of forty-three after a nun bled him and took too much out. Rehabilitated after his death as a righter of wrongs, a working-class champion.' Bryant lifted the print from the wall and set it down. 'We know him today as Robin Hood.'

May studied the gang before him. He rarely thought about his own frailty; he was usually too concerned about his partner, whose lack of robustness, coupled with a curiously youthful impetuosity, frequently lowered him into the freight-train path of harm. But right now, he could see the risk in his own situation. He noted the gender mix and grew warier; girls could display a shocking viciousness that bolstered boys into more violent acts.

He waited for them to make a move, but nothing happened.

They formed an unbroken barrier across the stairway, waiting in silence, unnervingly still. They wore the uniform of the disenfranchised: thin grey hoods over curve-peaked caps; sweatpants or low-slung-jeans. The girls had scraped-back hair, gold hoop earrings, pale bare midriffs with tattooed mock-celtic symbols, the usual fake brands worn in too-small sizes that made them appear thin and feral. May knew that their language would comprise a barrage of shorthand patois, street-American and incomprehensible slang. He felt an equal measure of sorrow and respect for those who had been stranded here by circumstance, but lately his faith in the redemptive power of the nation's youth had been tested to breaking point. He knew that their spectrum also included a percentage of vicious teens trapped between the twin hatreds of innocence and adulthood. The difficulty lay in divining the composition of the group.

Drawing all the confidence he could muster, he moved forward to the next flight of stairs. Almost imperceptibly, the crowd closed around him, sealing off his exit. A girl popped gum loudly. A boy spoke in a murmur too low to be perceptible. Somebody laughed.

Knives, thought May. *They'll be carrying knives, and I have no way of alerting anyone before they make their move.* Did they know who he was? It was absurd to be caught out in such a place, surrounded by families and apartments, without recourse to aid, but he knew that estates like these could be the loneliest places on earth. The Borough of Camden, which had more such estates than most, had the highest suicide rate in London, and all their tree-planting and traffic-calming efforts were undermined by the continual desire to cram in more housing.

He felt the shock of contact with a stranger, a boy's fist shoving at his back, then another, and within seconds the entire group was pushing him towards the staircase, others making way in front of him, clearing the path to the concrete steps. His centre of balance shifted as others kicked at his legs, and then he knew that nothing could stop him from plunging headlong down the stairs, because they would not allow him to catch at their arms, watching in insolent silence as he fell.

And fall he did, as the shatterproof light on the landing spun overhead, the rough brick wall grazing his hands but affording no purchase.

He glimpsed the landing below, and braced himself for the bone-cracking jolt of the concrete.

But it never came. Instead, broad hands caught him beneath the arms, raising him upright and setting him down on the landing. As he caught his breath, he found himself looking up into the faces of two police constables in yellow traffic jackets. Pushing between them came a stocky sergeant with a familiar if unpleasant face.

272

'Go on, you lot, piss off before I run you in,' he told the group, waving them away dismissively before turning his attention to the detective. 'I don't know what you think you're doing here, May, apart from trying to get yourself kicked senseless.'

Sergeant Jack Renfield's father had been Sergeant Leonard Renfield, an old enemy of Bryant's at the Met, and like his father he had been pointedly denied promotion several times, for which he blamed Bryant's damning reports. For once, though, May was pleased to see him.

'I suppose your grubby little partner is somewhere around here, too,' said Renfield, looking around with suspicion.

'No, I'm here alone.'

'Christ, May, I'd have thought you'd have more sense. You're lucky my lads didn't knock off early and were still keeping an eye out.'

'I owe you one, Jack. What are you doing here, anyway?' asked May, dusting himself down.

'Chameleon,' replied Renfield somewhat confusingly.

'I beg your pardon?'

'Operation Chameleon. A three-month initiative to disrupt gang organization on London estates. We've got men reporting back from all the major flare-up spots, and I don't need you disrupting their work. I suppose the PCU's involved. We all had a good laugh about your Highwayman pictures.'

'Why?' asked May, puzzled.

'Because they weren't taken here, were they? An idiot can see that. The sightlines don't match up. These little sods were having you on.'

'You're wrong, we have witness reports from two girls who gave Arthur the shots from their mobiles.'

'Then they were winding him up, weren't they?' said Renfield.

'What do you mean?'

'Check the rooftops of these blocks, May – each one has

273

its chimneystacks in different order, and I can tell you there ain't any like the ones in your pictures. My men should know – they spend enough bloody time up there.'

'Then why the hell didn't you tell us?' asked May angrily.

'Not our case, is it?' replied Renfield. 'We thought you big-brained desk-jockeys had the answers to everything. Let's not catch you around here again, eh? You're too old to be out in a place like this on your own, May. You're not up to it, mate. Next time we might not be able to reach you before you're kicked to death.'

32

HALL OF INFAMY

April had inherited her grandfather's fondness for organization. She catalogued her books, arranged her music alphabetically, kept lists, left notes, tidied the mess of her life away into drawers, and somewhere along the line her habits had tipped into compulsions. As much as she tried to create order, little in April's life made sense to her. There were still too many gaps and unexplained events in the past.

She sat on the floor of her new office, folding each recorded sighting of the Leicester Square Vampire into its own folder, matching the dates and locations against the scrawled notes in Maggie Armitage's transcripts. The white witch's handwriting was hopeless, but she was exact on every detail, even though she exhibited a tendency to drift from the subject whenever the mood took her.

April cross-referenced the notes with Arthur Bryant's accounts of all his cases, histories that dated back to the war. The detective's diaries ran to over thirty volumes. Luckily, they had been kept at home, and had therefore survived the blaze which had destroyed the unit, although some had been severely damaged by water. As she opened the next volume, tracing the Vampire's repeated sightings, she was surprised to find that half a dozen pages had been neatly trimmed out with a sharp knife. She checked the dates on either side of the removed sections, and unease settled within her.

They were the days marking the death of Elizabeth, her mother.

April had never blamed others for her misfortunes, and had freely admitted her own mistakes, but there were forces at work beyond her control. Some dark and windswept chaos in her family's past refused her the sustenance of a normal life. Her grandfather could have provided answers, but he had always been reluctant to discuss the events surrounding the loss of his only daughter.

April traced the edges of the cut pages, and thought back to ambiguities of her childhood, knowing that they held the key to her troubles. Like a woman wary of visiting the doctor for fear of what she might be told, she decided that the time had come to ask him for honesty. It would put an end to the hearsay that had circulated around the unit for so long.

'None of this makes any damned sense. It doesn't follow the accepted psychology of murder.'

May threw the folders back across the table to Longbright. 'Attacks take place in an atmosphere of mutual fear. Anger escalates into violence. It erupts on the spur of the moment. You try to stifle the noise and the fuss your victim is making, and you accidentally kill him. The anger drops like wind leaving a sail, much more quickly than it arose. You just want to damp everything down, but by then it's too late. It has exploded like a crack in a piece of pressured glass, and there's nothing you can do to mend it, so you cover your tracks, hide it all away, but you're not thinking straight. You won't realize your mistakes until later, when there's nothing you can do to correct them. A great rock of remorse settles in the head, like the aftermath of guilty sex. Does that sound anything like what we have here? No, because despite my partner's insistence in the absolute necessity for logic, in this case logic doesn't apply. There's some aberration . . . something we're missing . . . something very bad indeed.'

He watched the glistening traffic from the window, rubbing his sore arm. 'This isn't a whodunnit, pick the likeliest from a list of connected suspects and accuse him. The killer is a stranger, so strange to us that we can have no idea who he might be, because it isn't about anger, it's about the lack of it, an absence of any emotional core that might provide a motive. And I don't know how to deal with that.'

'Then you have to find a new way of shuffling the deck, John. You're good at that. You've always been an early adopter. Arthur's too set in his ways to change but this time I think it's down to you.'

Longbright had long been used to assembling information and leaving it before her superiors without comment; she rarely talked to either of the detectives in this manner, but now she sensed May's need for support. He doubted himself. Perhaps he felt he could no longer rely on his partner. Arthur Bryant was venturing further into the arcane than was healthy for the unit; nobody said anything, but it was clear how the rest of them felt.

'You're the only one who keeps us focussed on hard fact, John. Facts are all that Faraday's interested in. We're all relying on you to provide them.' She saw the tension rumpling his forehead. 'What happened on the estate? Why were you there?'

'Luke Tripp was visiting someone. You should have seen him – he knew exactly where he was going. What was so important that he would walk through a no-go area in semi-darkness? Do me a favour, call the residents' liaison officer Arthur met with, and find out who uses the community centre. Get me a list of everyone who's been there this week. Where *is* Arthur?'

Longbright was almost embarrassed to tell him. 'He went to see someone about some rare library books. He said it was to do with the case.'

The page containing May's drunken implication in the Vampire investigation was weighing heavily on Longbright's mind. So far, she'd had no luck tracing the two officers who had co-signed it. One had left the Met, but the other was female and had married someone in the force. It meant she was probably operating under her married name, and would be harder to find.

'Are you free for a moment?' Dan Banbury put his head around the door. 'There's something I think you should be aware of.'

May followed Banbury to his office and looked for a place to sit down, but found only a clear plastic inflatable ball. 'Where's your chair?' he asked.

'That's it. Good for your posture, you soon get used to it. I bought one for Mr Bryant after he complained about his back, but he deliberately and maliciously punctured it.' Banbury rolled the ball towards him and May lowered himself tentatively. 'Take a look at this. I was waiting for the lab results on the boot prints to come back and ran a couple of search engines on the Highwayman.'

'My God, tell me that figure is wrong.' May found himself looking at a projection of over 12,500 separate websites.

'These are sites dedicated to the Highwayman in the UK alone. He has a motion-graphic symbol that's been posted on some kind of shareware and distributed to everyone who's asked for the download. There's souvenir memorabilia up on a couple of auction sites, patently fake but selling for a fortune, and the prices are rocketing. There are several bands, the biggest of which, Stand and Deliver, is clearly being sponsored by some corporation chasing the teen demographic. Plenty of merchandise – boots, decals, T-shirts, sweatshirts, masks, jackets, gloves, heavy-metal songs about vengeance and justice, most of the material originating right here in the Camden area. The speed with which this stuff has appeared is absolutely unprecedented, and it's getting a political spin; it's all good old-fashioned right-wing propaganda about law and order. The Highwayman is no longer just a source of prurient interest. He's on his way to becoming a cult hero.'

'I don't understand. He's killed popular national celebrities; he should be despised. Look at the public outrage over the murder of Jill Dando,' said May, remembering the much-loved TV presenter who had been shot on her own doorstep.

'The Highwayman's achieving fantastic popularity among teenaged girls,' Banbury pointed out. 'Check this.' He opened another site. '"Why I want Highwayman to be the father of my unborn baby." The girl who wrote this is fifteen years old. "Why the Highwayman may be good for us all . . . Rough Justice: *Hard News* is the first national newspaper to openly support the Highwayman." There's much darker stuff turning up on the fan sites, pornographic stories and home-made movies about him. We're going to have imitators on our hands.'

May threw his hands up in disgust. 'What is wrong with these people?'

'I suppose you could cite underdog heroes like Bonnie and Clyde . . .'

'They were grassroots thieves, robbing banks that were universally hated by the disenfranchised for foreclosing land,' said May. 'The Highwayman is just a killer.'

'Think about it, though. The last decade has seen the rise of celebrity culture, personality replacing altruistic ideals. This could be the start of the backlash.'

'So he replaces such ideals with romanticized images of himself?' asked May. 'How does that work?'

'I guess in some twisted way he thinks he can become the anti-celebrity celebrity. And it looks like he's right. He's committing the kind of crimes people love to read about or see at the movies, the sort of murders that hardly ever occur in real life. He's pandering to his public.'

'That's what Arthur said. He wants us to set a trap.' He glanced back at the *Hard News* headline. 'I think we've found someone who can help us.'

33

CRIMINAL LANGUAGE

'Where's Dorothy Huxley?' Bryant demanded of no one in particular, sauntering into the dingy South-East Greenwich library that smelled of fish-glue, lavender polish, fungus and cats, with just a hint of warm tramp.

He glanced at the depleted shelves and stood some books upright, checking their spines – *The Papal Outrages of Boniface VIII; Lost Zoroastrian Architecture: Vol. VI: Iran; A Treatise on Catastrophe Theory Concerning Saturn and the Number Eight; The Cult of Belphegor* and *Biggles and Algy: Homoerotic Subtext in Childhood Literature*. No wonder nobody ever browsed here, he thought. Hardcore readers only.

Jebediah Huxley's literary bequest appeared even more run-down than it had been on his previous visits. Lurking in the grim shade of the rain-sodden flyover, awaiting the wrecking ball of cash-keen councillors, it remained a defiant bastion of the abstruse, the erudite and the esoteric. The crack-spined volumes were flaking with neglect; Dorothy and her gloomy unpaid assistant Frank were unable to save more than a few books a week with their meagre resources. That they continued to do so at all was a miracle.

As Bryant peered into the shadowed shelves, Frank's face

materialized between two volumes of the *Incunabulum* like an unpopular Dickensian ghost.

'You nearly gave me a heart attack,' said Bryant, theatrically palpitating his waistcoat. 'You haven't got the sort of face you should be creeping about with. Kindly don't do it.'

'I was expecting you earlier, Mr Bryant,' Frank said gloomily. 'You missed her.'

'Well, when will Dorothy be back?'

'A good question. It depends on how soon we can arrange for the medium to visit.'

'What on earth are you talking about?' Bryant had little patience with the prematurely aged assistant librarian.

'He can't come round for a few days because he was cat-sitting for a sick aunt, but her Persian swallowed a hairball and coughed itself to death, so he had to find an identical replacement, and the trouble is that the new one has one green eye and one yellow, so he's waiting to hear back from the vet about whether they can put a contact lens in.'

'I'm sorry, Frank, you seem to be speaking some foreign language designed for people who care about your problems. Back to me. Where is Dorothy?'

Frank glumly pointed a long forefinger to the floor. 'She's dead.'

'Dead? I was picking her brains on Etruscan pottery a fortnight ago, how can she be dead?'

'Stroke. We buried her on Tuesday. I tried calling your mobile, but there was no answer.'

'There wouldn't have been. I traded one for a picture of a murderer, and dropped the other in a hole I was digging. This is awful news. Poor old Dorothy, what a terrible shame. I suppose she had a good run, though. Give me the name of her nearest relative and I'll send some pears.'

'She had no relatives left alive, Mr Bryant. I was the closest to her. Er, pears?'

'Golden Delicious. She loved them, and they can plant the pips.' A horrible thought struck the detective. 'What's going to happen to the Huxley collection now?'

'It's in safe hands,' Frank assured him. 'She passed the building over to me on the condition that its purpose as a library remained unaltered.'

'Could she do that? I mean, you're not her next of kin.'

'Actually, I am.' Frank stroked the side of his long nose thoughtfully. 'She adopted me four years ago.'

'Dorothy never told me that.'

'That's because you only ever came to see her when you wanted information.'

Bryant wasn't used to someone answering back, and was momentarily stumped for a reply.

'She did it so that Greenwich Council wouldn't be able to touch the building. They've been sniffing around, sensing a real-estate killing to be made, but we've foiled them.'

'Good for her. She always was a crafty old bird.'

'I've always wanted to ask you – did you go out with her once?' asked Frank. 'I heard she was a bit of a goer in her time.'

'That's none of your business, even if you are her son,' Bryant bridled. 'Really, this prurience is most distasteful. I'm sure she would have wanted us to continue as normal, so I'm here to avail myself of your utilities.'

'You mean you're looking for a book.'

'Precisely so.' He looked around, smacking his lips, uncertain. 'Dorothy always knew where everything was . . .'

'And so do I, Mr Bryant. It's hard to share a room with someone for twenty years without learning everything they know. What are you after?'

'A canting dictionary. You know, an English code of thieves and cut-throats. I understand that highwaymen and outlaws used their own language to leave messages for each other, in much the same way that burglars still mark houses

283

today. I wondered if they had ever committed their code to print.'

'Such a book would, by its very nature, have been illegally published, but I'll see what I can find in our Private Reference section.'

Thunder rolled lazily across the roof of the library, rustling the damp pages of forgotten periodicals and sharpening the air with static. 'I'll need to get a light,' Frank explained. 'The electrics don't work back here.'

Bryant extracted an usherette's long metal torch from the voluminous folds of his overcoat. 'Don't worry, I have my partner's Valiant.'

They made their way between stacks of books, like divers negotiating coral reefs, until they reached a row of rusting cabinets. True to his word, Frank knew exactly where to look. He lifted down a heavy leather volume with mouse-chewed corners and laid it on the table. After consulting the index beneath Bryant's beam, he tapped the page meaningfully. 'Do you know about the thieves' key?'

'Yes, done that, what else is there?' asked Bryant with characteristic rudeness.

'Well, there's the Thieves' Exercise. It goes hand in hand with the key.'

'What is it?'

'Hm.' Frank read in silence for a few minutes. 'Appears to be a series of lessons passed on from lawbreakers to their pupils, full of slang. Listen to this: "Dinging the cull upon the poll" – that is, bashing someone over the head if he offers resistance. "Mill the gig with a Betty" – to open a door with a crowbar; "Faggot and storm" – to break into a house and tie up its residents. "Gammon . . . Bowman . . . Angling-Stick . . . Squeezing chats . . . Pike on the been . . . Main buntings . . . Nubbing chit" – there are hundreds of phrases here.'

'Can I take this away with me?'

'No, but I can make you some photocopies.'

'That will have to do.' Bryant flipped the pages. 'It says that attackers chewed liquorice to make them more long-winded during foot escapes. Sensible advice. There are cases here that go back to Charles II.'

'This might be of use,' said Frank, wiping a thin green layer of mildew from the cover of a small tome. '*The Grammatical Dictionary of Thieves and Murderers.*'

'Show me.' Bryant flicked his fingers at the librarian. On the front of the book was an embossed drawing of a highwayman. In his right hand he held playing cards – a four of clubs, known as the Devil's Bedposts, and two pairs, aces and eights, the so-called Dead Man's Hand.

He read the frontispiece: ' "Being a Collection of Words, Terms, Proverbs, and Phrases Used in the Modern Language of the Thieves, Cut-throats, etc., Useful for All Sorts of People (Especially Travellers) to Secure Their Money and Preserve Their Lives." Oh, this is interesting. *Backt*, meaning dead, deriving from the backing-up of a coffin on to six men's shoulders. *Cloud*, tobacco, as in "to raise a cloud". *Sneaking Budge*, one that robs alone. Jolly good stuff. Not much use to me, though.' He slammed the book shut.

'Why did they need their own language?' asked Frank.

'Because the criminals of London were transported for petty larceny and buying stolen goods, and hanged for everything from shoplifting to murder. They needed to be able to function below the eye-level of the law.'

'Well, you can take your pick here. It's a complete linguistic guide. Substantives but not many verbs, plenty of adverbs, and something referred to as the Copulative. Do you honestly think all this stuff is going to help you with the case?'

'He's leaving me clues,' said Bryant. 'I need to be able to understand them. There's not a society of highwaymen, is there?'

'How do you mean?' asked Frank.

'Oh, you know the sort of thing, people who dress up and

research their favourite characters. I presume the library is listed as a resource for all sorts of clubs and associations.'

'Yes, it is,' Frank agreed. 'I can probably get you a few addresses, but it'll mean making some phone calls.'

'I haven't got much of a budget,' Bryant warned. 'Do it for Dorothy.'

Back outside the library, though, Bryant began to wonder. He was cold and tired, he'd forgotten to take his tablets, and his legs were playing up. He was also halfway across the city poking about in arcane library books when he should have been getting his report ready for Faraday's inspection.

If the time he'd invested in this esoteric trawl through the forgotten world of London's thieves failed to pay off, there would be no way out. How did knowing that the Leicester Square Vampire had modelled himself on Robin Hood help to close the case?

May had insisted on re-attaching himself to the Vampire investigation. Bryant knew that his own erratic methods could drag them both down, as well as stranding some of the country's best minds without hope of employment.

You have to give up this behaviour once and for all, Arthur, he thought as he walked to the corner in the rain and tried to remember where he had parked the car.

As he passed the murky trash-filled alleyway behind the library, the Highwayman was close enough to reach out and touch his scarf-wrapped neck. Instead, the leather-clad wraith shifted back into the darkness, until only the dull gleam of his eyes remained.

34

ELABORATE ACTS

'Let's go Peculiar!'

Dan Banbury raised a hand on either side of him. The rest of the group stood in a ragged circle, joined at their fists. Only Meera Mangeshkar looked sceptical, mainly because she was having to hold Colin Bimsley's hand.

'Come on, you lot, put your backs into it this time,' said Banbury, attempting to sound hearty.

'Let's go, let's go, let's go Peculiar!' echoed the group, lifting their arms high. They stopped in mid-chant and turned towards the door.

Arthur Bryant was watching them with his mouth open. 'What on earth is going on here?' he asked finally. 'What are you all doing in my office?'

'Team-building, Sir,' Banbury began confidently, but his voice broke. 'Stimulates the brain and releases stress-inhibiting hormones. Only way to keep our spirits up.'

'Well, could you kindly not,' snapped Bryant. 'I don't want this place infected with happiness. Nothing will be achieved unless you're all dead miserable.'

'I thought in the light of Mr Kasavian's announcement this morning, it might prove beneficial.'

'Well, you thought – what announcement?'

'About closing down the unit on Monday, Sir.'

Thunderheads rolled into Bryant's eyes. 'Whatever you've heard is wrong, and whoever told you is a lying hound. Besides, if that had been the case, Raymond Land would have been creeping around here by now, visiting his particular form of spiritual ebola on us.'

'Come on, there's no need to cushion us, we all received the memo, old bean,' said Kershaw nonchalantly.

'I'm not cushioning you, you upper-class nincompoop, I have no idea what you're talking about.'

'There's to be an internal investigation of the whole Leicester Square Vampire business. Your comment about him possessing eternal life made the papers this morning.'

'Eternal life?' repeated John May, stepping in from the corridor. 'Tell me you didn't say that, Arthur.'

'I've been misquoted. I said he was an example of an eternal myth,' Bryant barked. 'I was just answering a question posted on the unit website.'

'And you didn't realize it was from a journalist?'

'I stand by my remark. The Leicester Square Vampire's physical appearance is a universal archetype, a perverse spirit of old England, if you will. Take a look at the evidence in engravings and photographs – every few years the same kind of creature appears. Ultimately he eludes capture, because question marks hang over the guilt of the condemned culprit. Look at the mythology surrounding the Vampire – he ran through alleys, launching himself at strangers, drawing symbolic blood before soaring aloft, untouchable and unstoppable, and vanishing through brick walls. He didn't, of course, they were merely illusions caused by our unwillingness to accept more mundane truths. We want to believe in divine retribution, even when it appears to be directed at innocents. We never checked back far enough. All the evidence was there. When the first crime occurred we only studied the recent files. Nobody thought of going back through the centuries.'

'I wonder why,' said May bitterly. 'Arthur, I gave you licence to be unorthodox, but this mental meandering has to stop.'

'Even you noticed the similarities between the Highwayman and the Vampire,' Bryant reminded him. 'The same ideals connect them spiritually and ideologically, if not physically. They share a common root, and it goes right back to Robin Hood. The idea that a murderer can somehow be rehabilitated in the public mind as a hero, a people's champion, has enduring appeal. The Vampire knew it and so does the Highwayman. And the reason why I'm performing this "meandering", as you put it, is to get the Vampire's case closed before Faraday uses it against us.'

'Then you're too late. You should have concentrated on the factual evidence, because that's all the Home Office is prepared to recognize.'

'We still have time to give them the kind of report they're expecting.' He slapped the engravings he had pinned behind his desk. 'There's a split between appearance and meaning. If we only read the surface signs, we'll always get it wrong. Has it ever occurred to you that the time period between fear and acceptance has become radically truncated in the modern age? The Vampire attempted to strike fear into people's hearts, but compared with most modern criminals he seems quaint and rather absurd. Two weeks ago a man was kicked to death by fourteen-year-olds and thrown off Hungerford Bridge "for a laugh". How would the Vampire's antics have struck them? Would they have shown him the respect he craved? The Highwayman is merely the externalization of a centuries-old inadequacy, except that now his actions are accelerated to suit faster, darker times. We have found our motive.'

'What we need is the identity, Arthur. This is about capture and punishment, not apportioning blame to society. Right from the start, this unit should have been dealing in tangibles. You've had your chance and wasted another day. No more poking about in archives or consulting with psychics. Oskar Kasavian is not a man to be trifled with. He's taking us down because we've failed to make connections.'

'The victims have no links, John! Don't you think I've looked? They never appeared on the same TV show or were interviewed in the same article, they never met one another, they shared no mutual mourners, weren't the same age, race or class. The only common factor between any of them is this man Leo Carey, the publicist who was married to White.'

'There's one other,' said May. 'Elliot Mason. The relief teacher once taught Paradine's son.'

'I hate to make matters worse,' Banbury interrupted, 'but I got the results of the footprints back this morning. It seems we have two radically different sizes of the same boot. The first print, taken from the floor of the Burroughs Gallery, is a size eleven. The second, lifted from the roof of the Oasis Baths, is a size eight. We know that from the height of the gallery tank, he would have to be abnormally tall – and extraordinarily strong – to lift White over the edge. However, we should be able to get another height estimate from the picture taken by the girls on the Rolande Plumbe Community Estate.'

'According to Jack Renfield, the picture wasn't taken there at all,' said May.

'Doesn't have an effect on the result,' said Banbury, clicking open the photograph on May's computer. He expanded the background brickwork behind the blurred shot of the Highwayman. 'These are half-bond yellow-brick balustrades, so by factoring in the standard sizes of brickwork we can calculate their distance from the foreground figure and work out his approximate height. Either he's bending his knees, or he's become shorter.'

'Don't be ridiculous. You're telling me our Highwayman is capable of changing size.'

'I think he possibly wears something in his shoes to give him added height on certain occasions.'

'Why would he do that?'

'Perhaps he has something wrong with his legs. I suppose it could be some kind of a brace. The gallery prints are deeper and heavier than the rest, as if he was burdened with extra weight.'

'I hate to say it,' said Bryant, 'but this supports my hypothesis.'

'I didn't know you had one.'

'I'm wondering if the Highwayman doesn't exist.'

He glanced up at the stunned faces of his team.

'I asked myself, was the London Monster a real flesh-and-blood character, or something created for self-publicity? In 1788 he abused, assaulted and cut fifty-nine Mayfair ladies in the buttocks until they started sticking frying pans down their knickers. Epidemic hysteria produces symptoms of so-called "conversion reactions" wherein illogical, aberrant behaviour spreads through the populace. The Monster ceased to operate, and perhaps some other member of the public, taken with the idea, copied the example he had set. He received fan mail from women across the capital. In early twentieth-century Paris, someone pricked women with hat pins. In 1956 in Taipei, there was an epidemic of razor slashings. In Illinois in 1944, a mad gasser sprayed women with paralysing "nerve gas" that proved to be nothing of the sort. The Leicester Square Vampire was also a manufactured monster. With this in mind, the witness statements from the time could be viewed with suspicion.'

'You're suggesting he was someone we interviewed?'

'The complicity of the public in creating the myth suggests so, yes. The originator stays around to help fan the fire of notoriety.'

'But we no longer have the statements, and there's no way of tracing the people we questioned.' May thought for a second. 'You think the same is true of the Highwayman? That it's someone we've placed at the crime scenes?'

'You've been on the estate where this picture was meant to have been taken,' said Bryant. 'You've seen the signs and symbols the Saladins scrawl on the walls like talismans.'

'You think a bunch of disenfranchised kids could bring a killer to life and direct him to murder whomever he pleases?'

'History shows us that the poor have to claim back what they should rightfully be able to share,' said Bryant.

'So they conjure up a supernatural hitman from bones and hair and magic tokens.'

Aware of the silence, May looked around to see that everyone was watching them. He had resolved never to argue with his partner in front of the unit, and had broken his promise. Furious with his lack of self-control, he left the room.

'Well, that was a load of bollocks,' said Mangeshkar finally. 'Anyone care for a mutiny?' The blank looks provoked her. 'You're a bunch of cowards. Maybe Kasavian has the right idea: shut this place down and save the taxpayer some money.' She, too, stormed out. The remaining staff members could hardly blame her.

With dissent and confusion breaking out at the unit, John May took positive action and borrowed the staff car to track down Lorraine Bonner. When he found her, he tried to find out who Luke Tripp was meeting in the estate's community centre.

'We keep a room-hire roster.' Lorraine took him to her office and consulted the bulletin board behind her. 'I heard about your trouble on the staircase. Sorry we couldn't be there, but I did warn your partner. Let's see, we had addiction counselling from two to three, followed by a meeting of the garden committee.'

'This would have been just after four o'clock. Anyone take it out between four and five?'

'That's a session handled by a teacher from St Crispin's,' she explained. 'He's a former crown prosecutor who helps out with some community work on the estates, in collaboration with our anti-gang initiative. Last night was his directional guidance and confidence-building task force, a fancy title for improving low self-esteem among disadvantaged children who join gangs to provide themselves with alternative families. Whenever trouble flares up, the usual things are blamed: hip hop, pop videos, horror films, gaming, violent websites – but the kids around here are always broke, and little of what they see enters their real lives. They don't believe much of what they see.' She gave a wry smile. 'Well, except all those commercials that show the kind of beautiful life you should be having instead of sitting around here smoking dope. They want the things they'll never have in a straight job, so they set out jacking other kids right on the street.'

'There's nothing sadder than the poor stealing from the poor,' May agreed.

'Are you a Christian?' asked Lorraine.

'I share certain fundamental Christian beliefs,' May admitted cautiously.

'Let me tell you what *I* believe, Mr May. The passage from youth to age? It's a staircase we climb throughout our lives, from one step to the next. We learn something new with each step, and keep changing our behaviour. That staircase is as old as the human race itself, but now some part of it has ruptured, so that it's harder for us all to make our way across the gap. We need to repair the passage to responsibility and adulthood. Either we find the next step or stay where we are, endlessly repeating our mistakes.'

'So you set about making your own repairs with community classes.'

'Three years ago we had a problem with methamphetamine-based drugs on the estate that led to several tragic deaths, so the parents got together and paid for a volunteer to come and take a community class.'

'What's his name, the teacher taking this class?'

'Kingsmere, Brilliant Kingsmere.'

'You're telling me his name is Brilliant?'

'It was a very popular name once. Way back in Victorian times. And he's a pretty cool guy. The kids look up to him.'

That was why Luke Tripp had visited the estate. He was in Kingsmere's exclusive extracurricular set. 'Why did the parents pick a teacher from a private school?' asked May.

'There's been bad feeling between the school and the estate – we heard tell that a few of the private boys were beaten up, some stupid argument about right of way to their playing fields. The parents thought it would be a good way to heal the old wounds.'

'Are his groups successful?'

'How can you tell?' Lorraine sighed. 'Kids sense when they're being preached to, no matter how smartly you sweeten the pill.'

'Do you have an attendance list for Kingsmere's meetings?'

'Don't need to, Mr May. They're open to anyone. There's another meeting tonight. Why don't you go along?'

Kingsmere. It was odd how many times the teacher's name had appeared in the investigation. In the absence of any other course of action, May decided it was time to check him out.

35

BRANDALISM

'Your chairs are horribly uncomfortable,' complained
Arthur Bryant. 'I crossed my legs and fell off.'

'They're Philippe Starck,' said Julio Stamos. 'They're intended as a style statement.'

'If you're going to keep people waiting for twenty minutes
you could perhaps try making a comfort statement. Treat
yourself to some cushions, it wouldn't compromise your
ideals too much.' Bryant brushed himself down irritably.

Stamos usually knew what to expect when the police came
calling, but this rumpled old man wrapped in an absurdly
large overcoat and a lint-covered green scarf had thrown
him. There was a peculiar miasma of herbal tobacco in the
air, or perhaps smouldering straw, and he felt sure it was
emanating from his visitor.

'You are from the police?' he asked by way of confirming
that some moulting tramp hadn't simply wandered into the
offices of *GRAF* magazine by mistake.

'You spoke to my sergeant,' Bryant confirmed. 'I require
fifteen minutes of your time, no more.'

Stamos led the way to a graceful white box with free-
floating backlit walls and chocolate leather sofas. 'Perhaps
you'll find this a little more comfortable.' He indicated a

seat partially occupied by Lazarus, his snuffling Vietnamese pot-bellied pig, a retro-eighties pet accoutrement currently favoured by style gurus all over Hoxton.

Bryant eyed the pig warily. 'My sergeant tells me you're the country's leading expert on graffiti.'

'Street art is a movement with its roots in folklore. It protests against the system and creates beauty from dereliction.'

'It's also illegal.' Bryant hefted the glossy fat copy of GRAF, flicking past the slick ads for Land Rover, Nike and Nokia. 'I can't believe this retails at twenty quid a copy.'

Stamos decided he was dealing with an idiot. 'It's bought by art directors, fashion photographers, music-video producers. They're not buying it with their own money.'

'The examples of art in here are very beautiful,' admitted Bryant.

'They fetch high prices, too. Many artists have become highly collectable.'

'But their work is not what I see on the street.'

'No. Ninety per cent of that is admittedly bad. Tagging, piecing and bombing over each other on trains and scratching on windows, that's not the real stuff. Graffiti is about possession and ownership, making a name for yourself.'

'You said this was art from the street, but your magazine shows work in galleries and is full of ads placed by corporations. You're encouraging kids without training to make the environment even more polluted, threatening and ugly.'

'Who's to decide what's ugly?' said Stamos hotly. 'Those see-through posters for underwear that cover the backs of buses? That's just corporate crap. Is graffiti any more of an urban blight than advertising? Public spaces are tightly controlled by capitalist interests. Unless you're rich, access to public walls is blocked, and if you do get into a public space, chances are you have to be selling something. The average London resident is subjected to hundreds of ads every day, and at least 10 per cent of them are illegally sited. Graffiti is social communication from the heart. It creates folklore because every act of tagging has its own dramatic story of why and how it was sprayed.'

'Yes, I saw what kids did to the *Olton Hall*,' said Bryant. Graffiti artists had spray-painted several carriages of the elegant old Scarborough-to-York steam train, wrecking it and earning the outraged hatred of the public.

'Yeah, you can't buy publicity like that.'

'Perhaps not, but your advertisers can discreetly sponsor it in your magazine.'

Stamos sighed. 'No one's denying that the media is complicit. They see it as shorthand for cool. I presume you didn't come here to give me a lecture on morality, Mr Bryant.'

'If I gave you a lecture, it would be on hypocrisy, Mr Stamos. Can you identify particular kinds of graffiti?' Bryant opened his scarred leather briefcase and pulled out the photographs Banbury had taken at the Rolande Plumbe Community Estate. 'I need to understand what these mean.'

'Graffiti means "little scratches", from the Italian *graffiare*, but it's also from the Greek word *graphein*, meaning "to write",' said Stamos, surveying the pictures. 'Examples have been uncovered in Pompeii. Much of it was political, related to specific social events, and usually appeared under authoritarian governments. The state removes such graffiti in order to depoliticize the marginalized. After this, you get personalized graffiti, racial and sexual slurs from men, very little from females. Gang graffiti hit-ups convey identity and territorial supremacy. What you have here is the most common kind of graffiti, tagging, which began at the end of the sixties and is largely associated with hip-hop culture. The idea is to get up in as many places as possible to establish territorial rights. This is from central London, north side of the river, right?' Stamos examined each shot carefully. 'Police try to create links between taggers and organized crime – car-jacking, drug use – but in truth there are rarely any at all. You've got tagging and piecing here.'

'What's the difference?'

'Tagging only takes a few seconds – it's about sticking your signature somewhere. Piecing is rarer and altogether more elaborate. You can trace it back to the artist more easily, and it requires a lot more talent. It started within black subcultures, but has moved out into a white middle-class arena.'

'Can you identify the gentlemen behind these markings?'

'That's harder. Artists frequently change their tags. Not that they're worried about getting caught; it only means a bit of community service – repairing bikes, folding leaflets or power-jetting walls. But there are some tell-tale symbols here. What are you expecting to find?'

'My partner has a suspicion that the boys who created these signs may be involved in a number of serious crimes,' Bryant explained.

'I don't think so. These elaborate arrows here? They indicate territory. These numbers, 187, refer to Californian penal code for murder. The large red-coloured 'K' stands for Killer. Most of this style is just copied from the USA, American gun culture, re-used by European wannabes. These drawings – a slice of bread and what looks like a duck and a chicken – are marks of disrespect against rivals who are trying to use the same area. The drawings of hands represent a personal warning. The arrow points to the initials NJ, which stand for "New Jerusalem", an immaculate Christian city where "nothing unclean may enter".'

'From the Book of Revelations,' said Bryant, intrigued. '21:27, if memory serves.'

'Then there's the K wrapped around by the symbol for a rival gang. Finally these tiny initials, NSED, are a mark of defiance and conviction. They stand for "No Surrender Every Day". So, what you've got here is a reiteration that this is pure, or innocent, territory, with the arrows and initials pointing elsewhere. You could literally read the

298

entire wall as follows: "We are not the ones who should take the blame. We're wrongly suspected but we're clean, and you should be seeking amongst the ranks of our enemy, because they're hiding a killer." However, there's also a confirmation that they will not help you by revealing information.' Stamos thought for a moment. 'There's another reading for the wrapped K – it could be the initial of the person you seek.'

Bryant sensed progress at last. 'You've certainly been more helpful than I expected,' he said, somewhat ungraciously. 'I'll see myself out. Good luck with your magazine. I think it's utterly hideous, but then I'm old and poor.'

The publisher's choice of phrase had been interesting. The message he had translated echoed the words stencilled on a wall in the East End, in Goulston Street, supposedly written by Jack the Ripper on 30 September 1888. 'THE JUWES ARE THE MEN THAT WILL NOT BE BLAMED FOR NOTHING.'

As he stepped from the building, he considered the gang on the Rolande Plumbe Community Estate in a new light. Not only were they aware of the police investigation; they knew the true identity of the Highwayman.

Now he was faced with a new problem: how on earth could he extract the information from them?

36

SKULDUGGERY

'I don't have to do it, John,' said Sergeant Longbright. 'This is not part of my job description.'

'What are you talking about? None of us has an official job description because Arthur deliberately keeps losing the forms.' May was exasperated. He had only asked Janice to attend Brilliant Kingsmere's Friday-night community meeting undercover.

'The last time I did this for Mr Bryant, I ended up in an Egyptian lap-dancing club, remember? I didn't even get to keep my dress. Whenever I attend a meeting in your place, something odd happens. Switch me with Bimsley and stand me in the rain all night, guarding a witness or running surveillance on a suspect, I'd rather do that. You've been to the estate now, you're known there.'

'That's exactly why I can't go, because the kids will behave differently when they see me, and it's important that they respond with their guard down. I've already had one run-in with them.'

'Any evidence I record will be inadmissible, you know that.'

'It doesn't matter. I want to find out what Kingsmere is up to. The Saladins know the truth about the Highwayman.

Arthur thinks that they're trying to point the finger of blame at someone through their graffiti warnings. They could simply be deflecting attention away from themselves, but then why leave any message at all? If any of them, or anyone close to them, attends Kingsmere's sessions, I want to hear what they have to say. I'd send Meera, but she's too blunt with men.'

'All right,' Longbright sighed, 'but this is the last time. How do you want me to play it?'

'Don't ask too many questions. Don't tape or take notes. Just observe and steer the conversation if it's needed, but whatever you do, don't lead anyone on. There must be no coercion. As for image, you might try to tone yourself down a little.' He eyed her spectacular breasts with alarm. 'Be inconspicuous.'

She threw him a hooded look. 'You mean cover up my best feature.'

'Your best feature is your mind, Janice. Don't let anyone tell you differently. Find out something we can use.'

'Guess how many privately managed societies are currently operating in London?' asked Bryant, looking annoyingly pleased with himself.

'You mean with registered memberships?' asked Dan Banbury.

'Registered in the sense that a committee holds member lists with names and contact details, yes. We can't measure them otherwise.'

'Oh, I don't know, three hundred?'

'Seventeen thousand. Upstairs in pubs, in halls and churches and living rooms, everything from the Enrico Caruso Appreciation Society to the National Warlocks Confederacy. Fans of Locked-Room Mysteries meet in the Edgar Wallace pub near the Law Courts. Moroccan cooks get together at the Queen's Head and Artichoke in Fitzrovia. The Metropolitan Police have their own Magic Circle. The

Pagan Federation meets at the Rose and Crown, Egyptian researchers gather at the Museum Tavern. The Vampire Society and the Dracula Society aren't on speaking terms at the moment because they're arguing about Darwinism and an outstanding beer bill. Everybody wants to belong to something. So tonight I'm going to the Grand Order of London Immortals.'

'In heaven's name, why?' Banbury had yet to adjust to Bryant's investigative leapfrogging. He was still cataloguing evidence information, and resented Bryant wandering in to discuss his latest fancies.

The elderly detective raised a badly photocopied sheet in triumph. 'A somewhat unexpected lead from Frank at the Greenwich Library. I asked him to send me a list of London societies. The order's Hall of Fame includes the Leicester Square Vampire.'

Over in the converted Catholic school in Bayham Street that housed the unit's mortuary, Oswald Finch was growing more suspicious by the minute.

He checked the ID sheets against the ziplocked bags, touching the lettering as if expecting to discern some clue in Braille. 'I don't buy it, Mr Kershaw. I saw the email too, you know. I'm not entirely out of touch with modern ways, despite your boss spreading rumours about my impending senility. If this man Kasavian is really determined to shut down the unit, why would the Home Office allow the exhumations to go ahead? What about the permission of the surviving relatives? Who signed this order? I've never heard of permission being granted as quickly as this. It's all highly irregular.'

'It's still in their interest to close the case. And technically, the permission was granted several times before but never acted upon, so I didn't have to return to the relatives. Two of the bodies had been placed in storage at the Central Mortuary in Codrington Street. The third was exhumed last night.'

302

He shrugged. 'All right, let's get it over with.' Finch handed his young colleague a mouth-filter. 'I have no sense of smell, so it won't bother me, but the ventilation unit in here is temperamental, and I don't want you contaminating the site by throwing up.'

'Let's do it.' Kershaw's nervous swallow betrayed his inexperience with cold-case cadavers. The three civilian victims of the Leicester Square Vampire whose reexamination had been granted approval lay before them, awaiting assessment of their DNA. Out of deference to John May, only Elizabeth's body had been left undisturbed.

Finch unzipped the first bag and thrust his head inside with unnerving enthusiasm. 'Good, this one's dry. Nice and easy.' He withdrew two samples from a three-decades-dead black female so withered that only her dyed red hair had survived unravaged. Kershaw pushed a short, razor-tipped needle into her thigh, then took several minutes locating a heart ventricle for a second extraction. 'We're supposed to record this procedure, you know,' he admonished.

'Can't do it, they won't buy me a new camera and old Bryant accidentally dropped the last one off Brighton Pier taking pictures of seagulls.'

Finch rezipped the first bag and gingerly prodded the second. 'Watch out, this one's going to be a leaker.' He opened six inches at the top and shone his pencil torch in. 'Very runny. I had an Italian cheese at a restaurant in Lake Como with this consistency. I'll do it.'

'Do you need a broader gauge syringe?'

'For bodies like this I used to use a soup spoon, but the lab techs don't like you giving them too much. You get students who fill stool sample tubes so full that they can't get the lids on. On very recent exhumations, colon matter is still usually on the move.'

Kershaw's face remained stony, but his cheeks paled a shade. They worked in silence for the next few minutes, until it was time to open the last corpse-bag. The sound of the zip was loud in the former gymnasium.

'Wait a minute, someone's playing silly buggers.' Finch checked the accompanying file again. 'This is not a woman who has been in the ground for thirty years.' He shone his torch down, puzzled. 'Furthermore, this is not a woman. She possesses what those of us in advanced medicine refer to as a willy.' He tapped Kershaw's clipboard. 'Show me Bryant's signature. I hate to say it, but he doesn't normally make mistakes of this kind.' Finch switched to a second pair of spectacles and examined the writing. 'It's a perfect facsimile, but this is too steady to be Arthur's hand.'

'What do you think's happened?' asked Kershaw, puzzled.

'Something rather nasty, I fear. This isn't the kind of mistake that happens any more. As you get older, you become more suspicious. I think our Mr Kasavian is chasing an accusation of negligent procedure, and is tipping the scales in his favour. The trouble is, when men in unassailable positions start taking the law into their own hands, nobody is safe.'

'You mean he deliberately forged an approval slip on the wrong body?' asked Kershaw. 'What can we do?' Nothing in his training had allowed for such a situation, but Finch had seen all kinds of cover-ups after the war, when so many bodies had lain unidentified and unclaimed.

'Give me the file.' Finch tore the exhumation order to pieces and dropped them into his lab coat pocket. 'We have to get the body put back at once. It was never here, you understand? There are a couple of people I trust at University College Hospital. I'll make the call, wait for them and clean everything up here. Time is of the essence. If I was Kasavian, I'd send someone around to check that we took the samples.'

'But your friends, how will they know where to – '

'Stop worrying, Mr Kershaw. As far as you're concerned, all three cadavers came from the same site – I'll reassign the paperwork. Two DNA samples will be enough to bear out Bryant's theory, but I bet we'll need a confirming third in court. I'm sure Kasavian will be counting on something like that.'

'Mr Bryant will really appreciate what you've done for him tonight,' said Kershaw admiringly.

'I'm not doing it for him,' Finch snapped. 'I won't have skulduggery of any kind in my mortuary. A medical examiner builds his entire career on absolute truths, and I will not be derailed from this path in my final moments.' As he drew himself upright, he was filled with the ideals of his youth. For a moment the years dropped away, and Kershaw glimpsed the determined young scientist inside.

37

LONELINESS

It was the first time Detective Sergeant Janice Longbright had gone out in public without make-up since John Lennon was shot. In a world of fleeting fads, she was a benchmark of consistency, wearing her mother's lipstick and the kind of wired undergarments that narrowed her waist and accentuated her bust to the point of altering her uniform into fetishwear. She was used to spending two hours in wardrobe and make-up listening to old Beverly Sisters albums before venturing out. Now, as she approached the grey concrete box of the community hall in cheap sweatpants, a hooded top and trainers, she felt perversely conspicuous. Through the rain-smeared glass of the small, grimly overlit hall she could see nearly twenty people slumped in orange plastic chairs waiting for the meeting to begin.

Nobody noticed as she entered and took her place at the rear of the room. She discreetly examined the audience. Most were kids in their early to mid teens. No adults were present. Longbright wondered how they could have been coerced into attendance.

Brilliant Kingsmere made his appearance with a theatricality that suited his Christian name, appearing onstage apparently from nowhere. Watching him stride confidently towards the only upholstered swivel-chair in the room, Janice knew he would use the kind of Blairite semantics that designated males and females alike as 'guys', couching conversation in such reasonable tones that he could make the Final Solution sound like a fair deal. She hoped there would be no roll call; the last time she had been expected to provide a false identity on the spot, she had dredged up the name Diana Prince without recalling that it was the secret identity of Wonder Woman. *Don't do anything that might arouse his suspicions,* she reminded herself, scraping her chair with a squeal that made everyone turn around.

'I see we have some new faces in tonight, which is good,' Kingsmere began, his eyes lingering on her. Longbright looked down at the dowdy trainers with which she had replaced her heels and willed herself to become invisible.

'Last week we were discussing the unfairness of branding law-breakers as criminals,' said Kingsmere. 'If you remember, we decided that it's quite normal for us to conduct some form of illegal activity as we grow up, and that sometimes it's the only way we can develop certain skills. In particular, we talked about the territorial problems that have arisen lately from fixing the aerial for a pirate radio station on the roof of the estate's central block.

'You know, few people in authority consider the amount of hard work that goes into making a living, even when it's something that's considered illegal. Let me give you some examples. In 1703, a young man named George Psalmanazar made a fortune by translating the catechism into Japanese for the Bishop of London. Actually, he didn't speak any Japanese at all, but was such a highly talented linguist that he fooled everyone. In 1993, currency dealer Nick Leeson, a twenty-six-year-old plasterer's son, destroyed the venerable British institution Barings Bank by losing 850 million pounds of their money. Both men worked hard for superiors who were blinded by ambition. Which raises the question, how much blame should be shouldered by those in positions of power, when they turn a blind eye to the ways in which money is made? If your radio station attracts lots of listeners and enriches their lives, why should you be arrested for running it? And how can you make real money legitimately? Let's start by working out how far each of you would be prepared to go, in order to get the things you want. When does it become a good idea to break the law?'

This is a familiar recruitment technique, Longbright realized. *He's lining them up for something, but what?*

At first she had thought that this lecture on morals was aiming too far above their heads, but the audience quickly responded. She watched and listened as Kingsmere carefully drew experiences from even the surliest attendees. The spirited argument that followed provided the teacher with all the information he needed. At one point he began blatantly making notes on each of the speakers. Longbright knew she was the oldest person in the room, and wondered how long it would be before he picked on her. He was working his way between the rows of chairs, heading her way.

Kingsmere's lecture was interrupted by the arrival of four smart schoolboys in St Crispin's blazers. The teacher looked up in clear discomfort. 'This isn't your class,' he told them.

'No, Sir,' said Billings, who looked smaller and more ratlike than ever. 'We heard you were here and thought you wouldn't mind us sitting in.' The boys quietly arranged themselves in the front row, acting as a barrier between their master and the rest of the room.

They know something, thought the Detective Sergeant. *They're shielding the other boys from Kingsmere's influence, policing him.* She recalled that he was their favourite teacher. The atmosphere in the room subtly changed. Kingsmere seemed distracted and uncertain, his buoyancy now muted, as though he was anxious to finish and leave. He distributed some leaflets offering gardening work and carpentry, then wrapped up the session in ill-disguised haste.

Longbright caught up with the St Crispin's boys as they left the hall. They regarded her with the usual suspicion created by the age gap that stood between them. But Longbright had inherited her mother's ability to hold the attention of any male, whatever the age difference, and used it shamelessly now, questioning the boys about the school and their teacher as she walked back across the rainy quadrangle.

'He's a good guy,' said the pustular Parfitt. 'He doesn't just recite stuff from set texts. He makes you think in a moral dimension. He tells us there are no clear-cut answers, then gets us to make up our own minds.'

'Sounds like he wouldn't be very popular with the school authorities,' said Longbright.

'St Crispin's is a progressive school,' Billings pointed out, 'but he wants his ideas to go wider. That's why he does community work. And he can test out some of the more extreme theories he has about inherited criminal genes, because to look at him, no one would ever know that—'

'We have to go the other way here,' said the alarmingly thin Gosling, shoving an elbow into his fellow pupil's ribs. Longbright watched them leave, wondering how much Billings might have given away if he'd finished his sentence.

Across town, Arthur Bryant was attempting to enjoy a pint of John Smith's bitter in the smoky brown upstairs den of the Plough in Museum Street, while he listened to several members of the Grand Order of London Immortals entering a spirited debate on the Flash Houses of Seven Dials, and why Hogarth used rooftop cats to indicate brothels in his engravings. He was about to add his own opinions when a familiar face bobbed in front of him.

'You said you'd call on me again after our date, Arthur,'

said Jackie Quinten, suddenly elbowing her way to his attention. 'You never came back.'

'Hello, fancy seeing you here,' Bryant stalled, eyeing Kentish Town's diminutive local historian, the only person dressed more haphazardly than himself. 'Er, there was a rather important case to deal with, I was very tied up.' He searched for an escape route, but members were blocking the staircase exit, spitting crisps over each other as their arguments grew more heated.

'I wouldn't mind, but I'd made the most enormous kidney casserole because you said you were a big eater. We seemed to have so much in common when I helped you out on that Water Room business. Did I misread the signs? Am I too old for you? I know I'm not very smartly turned out. It's funny; I don't mind men of my age, but men don't like women of my age, they all want someone younger, and that strikes me as profoundly unfair.'

'I'm sorry, I can't hear you,' replied Bryant, pretending to fiddle with a non-existent earpiece.

Mrs Quinten was on a roll. 'Why is it,' she asked, stabbing the smoky air with a beringed digit, 'that we're expected to put up with old men's ways, all breaking wind and nose-hair and toenail clippings in the bath and not wanting to go anywhere, yet when it comes to the reverse . . .'

'What we men have to do in return,' Bryant interrupted, 'is eat our own body-weight in trifle while you hoover the curtains forty-three times each week. Curtains hang vertically, for heaven's sake, they don't need hoovering.'

'I thought you said you'd never lived with a woman,' said Jackie suspiciously.

'I haven't – I don't think of Alma as a woman, she's my housekeeper and merely happens to be of the female gender, like a ship.'

'So you have someone to take care of all your . . . personal requirements.' Jackie couldn't have extracted more innuendo from the sentence if she had been Kenneth Williams.

'It's not like that at all. Mrs Sorrowbridge is a respectable widow whose duties include washing my clothes whenever they're left without somebody inside them for more than twenty minutes, and the insertion of mothballs into my socks when I least expect it.'

'But every man has other needs,' Jackie pressed on.

'Possibly, but my needs are not every man's. They involve the prompt arrival of my Gold Top and finding a shop that still sells sherbet lemons, although I assume you're presumptuously referring to sex, to which all I can say is Self-Control, Madam.'

'Look, I'm a woman of the world,' Mrs Quinten reasoned.

'Ah, but which world?' asked Bryant. 'What are you doing in this one?' He gestured about the smoky room.

'The Immortals? It's just a fancy name for a bunch of dry-as-dust historians. They'll talk the back wheels off an omnibus, but this is the only society of its kind, which makes it special. They're interested in London's most infamous characters – political brigands, celebrity criminals, unapprehended murderers, anyone who has managed to become immortalized in the city's collective memory by doing something notorious and getting away with it. Jeffrey Archer used to come until they banned him. A step too far, they felt, but he'll probably enter the pantheon after he's dead.'

'Murderers who aim for immortality,' repeated Bryant, absently studying the nicotine-stained portraits around the walls.

'Oh.' The realization hit her. 'You're here about the Highwayman. Do you think someone in the society might be responsible?'

'Not at all,' Bryant revealed. 'I'm here about another case entirely. I imagine these people understand the historical power of manipulation. A killer might well be drawn to such a meeting of like minds. Do you know many people here?'

'I should do. I'm one of the founding members. We don't

311

get much new blood, I'm afraid. These are all very familiar faces. We occasionally attract researchers and lecturers.'

'Anyone new in the last few weeks?'

'A girl planning a documentary for the BBC. And a rather sexy teacher from a nearby school. That's about it.'

'Tell me about the teacher, Jackie.'

'He had a funny name. Something Victorian, like Kingdom.'

'Brilliant Kingsmere?'

'That's it – you know him?'

'Our paths have crossed. Do you remember what he was doing here?'

'He gave us a lecture about the history of Robin Hood. We ended up discussing London murderers, mainly from a political perspective. We mostly attract ineffectual men and bossy women here, not exactly your cup of tea. He made a nice change. Didn't come back, though.'

'You don't think I might learn anything from him?'

'Knowing you, Arthur, you've established the psychology behind the murderer's actions without turning up a clue to his identity.'

Bryant frowned, hating to be found out. 'I've never had less information this far into a murder investigation. All I know is the usual stuff: that he's emotionally frozen, driven by cold ideals. Probably let down by someone in the past, statistically likely to be in his early thirties, guarded, crafty, living a solitary life within a five-mile radius of the deaths.'

He sighed, his eyes straying to the window. 'There is another city inside London, you know, one that can't always be seen, only sensed from sidelong glances, caught in snatches of conversation, spotted from the upper-deck windows of night buses. Do you have any idea how much of the population lives alone? You only have to examine the backs of flats in Earl's Court or Stepney or Hammersmith or Bow from the night bus. You spot tenants pottering around their conversions, the kitchens overlit and narrow as ship galleys, spindly spiderplants neglected on window-ledges.

'Loneliness is such a normal state in this city now that public demonstrations of affection are frowned upon even by lovers. In the 1950s, couples were making love in Hyde Park in the middle of the day. The war had taught people to be glad they were still alive. How quickly we rewrite the past to suit ourselves.' His watery blue eyes seemed focussed far beyond anything in the room. 'But the city is still filled with secret idealists, finding temporary ways to defer pain and solitude. Some are worn down and leave for good, a few grow strong and stay until they die. And there are the others, the odd ones out – who kill to keep the pain of loneliness at bay.'

'You think killing stops him from being lonely?' asked Mrs Quinten. 'Is that any logical reason to commit murder?'

'It's been reason enough for many recent murderers. Besides, logic is all I have to go on,' muttered Bryant. 'Take it away from me, and I would have no way of solving anything. These are crimes without anger or financial gain. Loneliness is the only other motive I can imagine.'

He surveyed the crowd as he turned up his collar. 'You read of detectives who put themselves inside the minds of criminals. I've never been able to do that. I only see ideas and circumstances and secret histories. I can learn nothing more here.'

'At least let me come with you, Arthur. Just for a while.'

From the way he looked at her, they might never have met before. 'No,' he said with finality. 'I'm lost, and I will lose those who follow me. I have to make my way through to the end of this alone.'

She remained watching helplessly as he carefully threaded his way towards the door.

38

HAPHAZARD

It was a long shot, but worth a try. Kasavian and Faraday were closing in fast, and by midnight the unit still had nothing. It was time for John May to talk to one of the Haphazards, and that meant staying up through the night in order to track him down.

The detective was presented with several choices. Each Haphazard had his own skill. Nalin Saxena was a disgruntled former member of the Shadwell Posse, in hiding after a scuffle that had caused a fatality on the track of the Docklands Light Railway. He kept watch on the night streets of South and East London, reporting back to the unit once a fortnight with information about the alliances and turf wars of various street factions.

Rufus Abu was the homeless hacker who had crashed Microsoft's email system with the infamous TooLarge virus, working from the reconfigured computers of an internet café in Stoke Newington, which he had broken into one night. He weblogged May daily, keeping him up to date with the latest technological scams.

Polly Sharrant ran an SM club in Southwark and a number of pirate music companies from a base in Bermondsey. She knew all of the major players in the city's fluctuating club scene, and what they were up to, any time of the day or night.

After careful consideration, May decided that Rufus was the only one who might be able to help.

These were kids who often risked their lives to provide information, not through any misplaced sense of altruism but because the unit provided them with a safety net when vendettas became too dangerous on the street. Bryant referred to them as the Haphazards in homage to the Baker Street Irregulars. They were itinerants, thieves and scammers, the city's eyes and ears, who kept the detectives in touch with the capital's unruly behaviour. They were not to be entirely trusted, nor were they to be ignored. Bad boys like Nalin and Rufus looked like a million other youths, branded by Nike, Adidas and Puma, low-slung jeans, grey cotton hoodies, baseball caps with peaks that had been kept to an exact curve by pushing them into coffee mugs overnight; each teenager an exercise in operational invisibility, working from his own peculiar vantage point within the system.

Now, below him, a thousand people gyrated through shimmering spheres of light, blood red, turquoise and vitreous green. John May carefully picked his way through the knots of teenagers who filled the rear of the upstairs bar. The music was so loud that it had lost any sense of form or content. All that was left was a heavy bass throb that vibrated the material of his jacket as he walked. As he searched each face, May hoped that the boy would remember the favour he had promised to repay.

The detective had not expected to find himself in an Elephant and Castle nightclub at two a.m., but there was no other way of locating Rufus. The thirteen-year-old computer genius spent his life underground, and could only be lured to the surface with a bait of pirated software. May was confident that the package in his pocket would not appear on the hackers' black market for days yet, and would be enough to gain an offer of help.

Meera Mangeshkar had offered to take his place tonight, being nearer to the clubbers' age group, but the young black boy was wary of strangers. Nobody seemed to know where he came from, where he lived or who his parents were, if indeed he had any. He spoke with a terrible New York accent and used a cheesy brand of street slang, but was smart enough to assume this as a disguise.

Rufus had been known to help the police on several occasions in the past, but only if the case suited his sense of the bizarre, and only under conditions of strict anonymity. He had an IQ in excess of 170, but what he saw as attempts at exploitation by adults had led him to a life beyond the law. These days his whereabouts could only be ascertained by following newsgroup rumours and checking recent hacker outrages. His exploits left a luminescent trail through the electronic ether, faintly glowing blips in the virtual darkness.

As if identification wasn't hard enough in the club, ducting pipes now jetted clouds of dry ice across the dance floor, filling the air with a searing crimson haze. The dancers were moving in a grey concrete cave the size of an aircraft hangar which remained nightly filled until the sun rose over the river beyond. May narrowed his eyes and peered into the stifling mist, but could see nothing. It was the third place he had tried tonight and definitely the last, although he had to admit he was starting to enjoy the music. He was about to leave when he felt a tugging at his sleeve.

'Hey, Incoming Blues, is this a raid?' shouted Rufus, glaring up. He turned to a tall blonde girl who stood beside him in a tight black rubber dress, and pressed a stack of notes into her hand. 'Take a cab, baby, I got business to attend to.'

Rufus held out his hand and buzzed the detective with an absurdly complex handshake. He was four feet eight inches tall, and in his baggy sweatshirt and baseball cap appeared even younger than his thirteen summers. May wondered how they ever let him in. Behind them the bouncers were frisking clubbers for weapons and drugs.

'I assume you wanna talk a deal.' The boy jerked his thumb at the door, and they left the main auditorium. Rufus blew on his fingers as a long-legged Chinese girl was being frisked at the door. 'Check it.' He turned to May. 'I think my libido developed same pace as my brain, but who wants to date a smart dwarf? Hey, how's your partner, Bryant? You two still a perfect match?'

'He's fine, and that's a terrible joke, Rufus. If you want to go somewhere quieter, I have a car outside.'

'*Excel.* There's a really bad coffee bar a block from here, bad as in bad but at least it's quiet. How come you always look for me after the good restaurants are closed?'

'I was looking for you hours ago. You're a hard man to track down.'

Rufus hated being referred to as a child. He argued that he had the mind of an adult, although May knew that he found his accelerated brainpower as much of a handicap as a blessing.

They parked and walked to the cheerless plastic all-night snack bar, set back from the main road that led to Waterloo. A few of the other tables were occupied by Covent Garden lorry drivers. Rufus settled away from the window, while May brought a tray of coffee and sugary doughnuts.

'How are you getting along these days?' asked May.

'Same old,' said Rufus. 'As bored as a person can be when he recognizes that his resource access is more finite than his development bandwidth.'

'You haven't been in touch for a while. We were beginning to worry about you.' May knew that the boy could look after himself in spite of his size and age. He had a very wide-ranging set of friends. *Core 'tacts*, Rufus called them.

'I've had the damned welfare people breathing down my neck again,' the boy explained, tearing off a chunk of doughnut and sinking it into his mug. 'They're trying to put me back in care, and you know what happens when they do that.'

'You disappear.'

'I'm gone, outta here, High Beta nonlinear vaporization. I can lose social workers faster than you can scream Satanic Child Abuse. I'm a human flash drive, travel light, plug myself in wherever I'm needed. The system doesn't recognize that anyone living outside the statistic majority could possibly be happy. They're talking about therapy and special schools again. I may even have to upstream from London. The case against has *that much* granularity.'

'You're not thinking of leaving before you help us, I hope.'

'You're talking about the Highwayman. Well, I been wondering about that too. What can you tell me beyond the usual random-scatter output?' He meant, what hasn't made it into the newspapers.

'This,' said May.

He handed over the not-for-press details they had logged to date, together with a classified set of internal reports. If the PCU was to continue functioning according to its original intentions, it had to bend the rules regarding access of information. 'He's following a sequence that conforms to no known pattern.'

'You telling me you have no hardcore suspects?'

'We have a couple of people we're looking at, but nothing concrete,' May admitted. 'The double deaths have thrown us. Once again the murderer was seen but not apprehended.'

Rufus scanned the documents. 'What makes you think the vics aren't chosen at random?'

'The premeditation of the murders suggests someone is aiming for a specific effect, but what it is escapes us.'

'This feels mathematically arranged, John, kind of a murderer's Turing Code.'

May assumed he was referring to Alan Turing's celebrated solution to the wartime Enigma Code. The logician had

318

successfully cracked cryptographic messages created on a typewriter attached to a random print-wheel, and had suggested that computers would only be capable of human thought if a random element, such as a roulette wheel, was introduced. 'Why would anyone go to the trouble of doing that?' he asked.

'Maybe he's scoping victims according to occult significance. Bet you that's what Bryant thinks.' He dunked the rest of his doughnut and dropped it, dripping, into his mouth. 'I agree about the methodology, though. There's logic at work. It's like the victims have been demographically targeted. By what coordinates, though?' May could see ideas spinning through the boy's brain, each examined and discarded in rapid turn.

'Four across a single week. No correspondence to a lunar cycle, no mutilation, no mess and no fuss. He's not getting off on it. The double-header is easy to figure. He's angry because he thought you'd work it out earlier, so he wants you to get closer, where he can confront you. It's probably someone you've met, because this guy really hates you. He knows you, and it's personal. Can I keep these?' Rufus folded up the pages.

'Just so long as you don't show them around.'

'I'm only asking out of politeness. I already memorized them.' He looked over at the bulge in May's jacket pocket. 'You got a little something in there for me?'

'Just some prototype programs I'm taking home with me when I leave,' said May casually. 'You haven't given me any solid leads yet.'

'I told you, he's not doing it for himself. He's doing it to mess with your head. He's more interested in being seen by the public than by his victims. Why? Because the victims can't report back.'

'Rufus, this is serious.'

'Look, first murder.' The boy withdrew a chewed pencil stub from beneath his shirt and drew numbers on a napkin.

'Publicity. Second murder: feed the flame. You get a week on the front pages, no more, so it all has to be done fast. The third and fourth deaths are a catch-up meant to force you guys out – he wants you to do something stupid and risky, crash and burn in front of him.' Rufus thought for a moment. 'OK, here's something. I noticed one corresponder.' He tapped the chart with his finger. 'And you ain't gonna like it because it don't lead nowhere.'

'At this time of the morning it doesn't matter if things don't make sense,' said May with a sigh. 'I'm feeling old and tired, and I'm going to be out of a job on Monday morning. Hit me.'

'Don't ask me how I know this, 'cause it's the kind of crap I just carry around in my head the whole time, OK?'

'OK.' May moved forward, listening carefully. The boy had given him strong leads in the past and deserved a hearing, no matter how strange his ideas seemed.

'The Horse Hospital. It's a bar in the back of Clerkenwell where local artists drink. Saralla White got herself banned for throwing a punch at a photographer in its bar. Apart from White, it was home to another celebrity drinker when it was still an inn called the Queen's Head. It was where Dick Turpin stayed before heading north.'

'Rufus, what on earth am I supposed to do with information like this?' said May, dropping his head into his hands.

'Don't you see? He selected his first victim because he'd already decided to behave like a highwayman. She got picked at random. All of the victims are just losers who've dropped on to the radar by accident. There's no motive at all.'

'Rufus, there has to be a motive. Even serial killers have a motive.'

But the boy had risen and vanished back into the night before May could ask him anything else.

39

ENTRAPMENT

Oskar Kasavian was seething. He slammed through the offices one after the other, searching for a scapegoat or something to hurl, knowing that he could blame no one but himself, but it was early on Saturday morning, and the building was nearly empty. He had not expected the detectives to call his bluff by refusing receipt of the third cadaver, slyly returning the body to its resting place via a couple of taciturn orderlies at University College Hospital. This was going to be trickier than he thought. At least the gloves were off now. His ambition had been made clear, as had their intention to fight back. 'Where the hell are they?' he shouted at his secretary in passing. 'There's no answer from the PCU. They can't all be out on assignment. Don't they realize this is their last weekend in full employment? What the bloody hell is going on?'

'I have to let her do it,' said May. 'We're running out of time.'

'I don't need to remind you what happened before,' Longbright warned. She had returned to find a lead on the remaining constable registered as a witness on May's 'confession', an email from a colleague who remembered the officer's married name. But now there was a new complication.

'We were more foolhardy in those days. Besides, this was Janet Ramsey's idea.'

'What makes her so sure he's going to turn up?'

Before them lay the unfolded Saturday-morning edition of *Hard News*, the last one of the week, headlined HIGHWAY-MAN'S SHOCK SECRET REVEALED.

'The article states that she alone knows the Highwayman's identity, and that she'll give it to the police at six o'clock this evening. She's had the article constructed by some psychologist to include provocative phrases that will find resonance with our man. She's recorded the article, and they'll be excerpting it on radio and television throughout the day. She's also making sure that her whereabouts are known on the internet, just as the others did.'

'I know she's doing it to boost circulation, but she's being very stupid.'

'We can't stop her from doing it, so we'll have to help control the event. Colin and Meera are going to stay with her the whole time. She's due here any minute for a briefing session with us. I was going to ask you to sit in with me. I might miss something; I haven't been to bed yet. Did you speak to the publican at the Horse Hospital?'

'He confirmed the old inn's claim to fame as Dick Turpin's rest-stop, and he remembers the night White was banned. He doesn't recall who else was in that night, but he promised to ask around.'

'Have you seen Arthur?'

'Is he not answering his mobile?'

'I tried calling him at home but Alma hasn't seen him either. Perhaps it's best that he's not around. He doesn't approve of journalistic entrapment techniques.'

Janet Ramsey looked like a housewife from a faded seventies sitcom, bulky and floral, with hair arranged in stiff red peaks, but her voice betrayed the late Thatcherite steel of determination without conscience. She fixed Longbright with a searching eye before accepting the sergeant's offer of a seat and coffee, as though suspecting her of a trick. She also refused to say anything of consequence until a male entered the room, a habit Longbright deplored in other women.

'We think the Highwayman has some kind of link with Clerkenwell, and he certainly knows the area,' May explained. 'The apartment we have for you is inside a converted watchmakers' factory. It's a monitored site with only one main entrance, right between the school and the estate where the Highwayman was sighted. We'll block off the rear exit and roof access, and we can cover the windows front and back. If he turns up, he'll have to use the front hall.'

Ramsey knew that the unit had never supervised such a sting operation before, and that she was forcing them to maintain a police presence at the site. 'You've got me for the whole day,' she told him. 'If he doesn't show, I want to record an exclusive interview with you in the afternoon, for Monday publication.'

By Monday we may not even be here, thought May. 'You know you'll never get a straight answer from a police officer, Janet. We always hedge our answers to cover all eventualities.'

'Then I'll conduct the interview with your partner.' She smiled slyly, knowing that Bryant's inability to lie had exposed the unit's plans on a number of occasions.

'That's up to him,' May countered. 'I'm not striking deals with you. You're doing this with our knowledge, but without our approval.'

'Let's face it, you haven't got very far by yourselves. Besides, I'm helping you to catch the man. I'm performing a public service.'

'Your altruism is touching,' said Longbright.

'I make it a policy never to use words my readers wouldn't understand,' replied Ramsey. 'If you're planning to provide me with protection against this maniac, I'd say you're involved.'

'We have a remit to protect the vulnerable and innocent,' Longbright told her, 'but we also cover journalists.'

'This one's a caution.' Ramsey jerked a thumb back at the sergeant. 'Which old movie did you find her in?'

'We'll want you to wear a radio mike, in case anything unforeseen happens,' said May.

'Don't worry, darling, I've done this sort of thing many times before. I used to specialize in ending MPs' careers by posing as a call girl.'

'That must have been a stretch for you,' said Longbright. May glared at her, but only for the sake of keeping the peace.

'Ah, there you are,' said Bryant, sticking his head around the door. 'John, a word?'

May followed his partner out into the corridor. 'I wanted you in the briefing with Ramsey. She's going into the apartment in an hour's time. Where have you been?' he asked.

'The Leicester Square Vampire,' he explained. 'The DNA samples from the bodies Kershaw and Finch examined need to be matched up against the evidence we archived in the Paddington lock-up. I'll go there myself and sort it out. Heard anything more from Kasavian?'

'He's called several times already this morning, but I've instructed everyone to stay away from the phones when his direct line comes up. I wanted you on the Highwayman case, Arthur. We're out of time. Putting a lid on the Vampire won't do us any good now.'

'There are circumstances where I can imagine it would help,' said Bryant mysteriously. 'If you need me, I'll be poking through our bric-a-brac in Paddington.'

*   *   *

An hour later, the unit moved Janet Ramsey into St John Street. Colin Bimsley took up his position behind a fortress of cylindrical rubbish containers at the rear of the converted warehouse, while Meera Mangeshkar waited with May and Banbury in the unit's unmarked white van. An immense West Indian constable named Liberty DuCaine had agreed to make himself available to the unit for the day. He was positioned on the other side of the building, awaiting instructions.

St Crispin's appeared silent and empty, the front gates closed. The edge of the Roland Plumbe Community Estate was visible through gently falling rain, but also appeared deserted.

'It's a stain gun,' said Banbury, holding up the narrow-barrelled device with some pride. 'Lightweight aluminium, my own design, converted from an animal tranquillizer.' He opened the top-loading chamber and showed May the cartridge inside. 'There's a secondary needle on the front of the dart to keep it in place after striking home. The contents are under pressure and the plastic casing shatters on impact, spraying blue dye over a radius of about a half a metre. It's harmless, but impossible to get out, and takes weeks to wear off.'

'What about clothing?' asked May. 'Our man wears motorcycle leathers. Surely it won't penetrate that?'

'If the needle can get through, the dye will follow. The best way to use it is to fire into an object above the target's head. There's no way he can avoid being covered.'

'Do we have a marksman?' May wondered. The unit had never been authorized to use weapons.

'You have me,' said Banbury. 'I have a licence to use this.'

'So now we wait,' Mangeshkar sighed.

By mid afternoon the clear sky had clouded over and drizzle fell like fading memories, leaching colour from the streets and returning the city to the indistinct texture of box-camera

325

photographs. Banbury and Longbright waited in May's BMW, parked diagonally opposite the front door of the building. Colin Bimsley was numb and soaked, his long legs cramping behind the bins. He text-messaged Meera inside the van, asking if she'd seen anything. She replied with some disparaging remarks – he could tell she was just as bored.

Five minutes later, she sent back a single word: *movement*. He uncoiled his legs, rubbing life back into his thighs, and awaited the call to action. Looking through wet leaves, he could see DuCaine across the alley, ready to make a move.

'He's outside the building right now, just strolled around the corner,' said Mangeshkar. 'Man, he has a lot of nerve. He's just gone inside.'

'You're sure it's him?' asked May.

'No, it's probably some other guy in a highwayman's outfit.' She lowered the glasses. 'Of course I'm sure. Why don't we grab him now?'

'He's in disguise, Meera. For all we know, he could have paid someone to wear the outfit. We need as much incriminating action from him as possible, because we can't afford to leave any loopholes. Notice he only wears the cape for photo-shoots.'

'The rest of the outfit's almost normal for London. Take off the eye-mask and the tricorn, he'd look like any courier in town,' said Mangeshkar.

'Call Ramsey. Warn her he's on his way up, and tell her to keep the door locked. I'm sending in Bimsley and DuCaine.' Banbury made a move to open the door of the van. 'Where do you think you're going?' asked May.

'I need to get closer. I won't get a clear shot in this rain.' Banbury raised the barrel of the stain-gun.

'I'd be happier if you stayed in the van,' said May.

'It's OK, I'm wearing a protective vest.' Banbury hopped out of the van and crossed the road, slipping into the entrance hall.

They waited. Two minutes passed, then three. The crackle of Ramsey's handset made them jump.

'I heard someone on the stairs,' she whispered. 'Wait, I can see him through the spyhole – he's right outside the door. Where the hell are your men?'

'They should be on the staircase below you,' May answered. 'They're waiting for him to make a move.'

'I don't want to be carried out of here in a body bag just because your people were waiting for the right moment,' she snapped back.

The sound of an electric bell filled the van. 'I don't believe it,' said Ramsey. 'He just rang the doorbell. What do you want me to do?'

'Don't let him in,' May warned. 'What can you see now?'

'He's gone – no, wait, he's – '

There was a burst of static, and the line went dead.

40

LOSS AND MEMORY

A different handset came on-line this time. 'I can see him,' whispered Banbury. 'On the floor above me. He's just standing there outside the door. I'm going to try and get a clear shot at him.'

'Where's DuCaine?'

'On the lower landing. He can't get past both of us.'

May chewed a fingernail, listening and waiting. Banbury had left the line open for him. He heard a sudden tumble of movement, buffeting and scuffling against the built-in microphone.

'Are you all right?' called May.

'He winded me,' Banbury checked in. 'Barged past me on the stairs – looks like he was expecting a trap. Yow! He just grabbed the handrail and jumped right over Liberty's head! How did he do that?'

There was a firecracker pop as Banbury fired his stain pellet.

'Tell me what's happening,' demanded May.

'OK, I fired and caught our man on the back of the left wrist. He's wearing gloves but the needle should have gone right through. There's ink everywhere. He'll be out of the front door any second now. There's nowhere else for him to go.'

328

May shoved open the van's tinted side-window and watched. 'Who's in charge of keeping the street clear?' he asked, as he saw the gates of St Crispin's swinging open from the corner of his eye. 'What's going on? I thought Kershaw had both ends of the road sealed off.'

'He does. It's Saturday – there's nobody in the school – ' Pupils were pouring out through the gate, a sea of navy and gold blazers moving quickly through the drizzle, filling the street.

'It's private,' said May, shocked at his own stupidity. 'They hold classes on Saturday as well. We have to get them off the street.'

May saw the door of the warehouse's entrance hall swing open. The Highwayman stepped out into the rain.

'Colin,' called Mangeshkar, 'get around the front. He's on the steps.'

There were children everywhere now. The Highwayman stood head and shoulders above them all.

'Christ, where are our men?' cried May, slamming back the van door and alighting. 'Meera, stay with me.'

Bimsley came sliding around the corner and took a number of schoolboys down like skittles. The black-clad figure was slipping through crests of blue and yellow, moving further away. May tried to keep him in focus, but the blinding rain reduced his vision.

'He can't get out without being seen,' called Mangeshkar. She charged into the crowd, slipping between the children, heading towards her target. Moments later she was looking back with her hands raised, puzzlement and apprehension flooding her features. Bimsley and DuCaine fought their way through the children towards her as Banbury appeared on the steps clutching his arm. Longbright was there too, buffeted by the raucous tide of pupils, searching among them.

'He can't have just vanished,' cried May in exasperation. He looked from the dissipating teenagers to the high brick walls of the converted warehouses, then down at the slowly clearing road. He saw only two other adults, a teacher heading for the school's car park, and a single parent who had managed to slip through the cordon.

'Didn't anyone realize that the school was holding classes?' he asked, exasperated.

'The Highwayman obviously did,' said Mangeshkar.

May knew then that they had lost their quarry.

'Well, he didn't climb a wall, and he didn't drop into the sewers,' Longbright concluded. 'There was nowhere else he could have run, except on to the estate. Both ends of the street were closed.'

'Anything show on the CCTV outside the school gates?' asked May, opening the rear door of the van.

'I've already got an up-link, but I think you need to see it for yourself,' warned Banbury. 'They've a new system that records directly on to a hard-drive. The picture resolution is much clearer. Here we go.' He punched in the code and forwarded to the moment when the school gates opened. 'Watch the background.' The sea of uniformed pupils swirled across the lower half of the screen, but the Highwayman could clearly be seen descending the steps of the building. Banbury slowed down the images and tapped the screen with his pen. 'He stopped here for a moment, as if he was remembering an escape route. Now watch.'

Suddenly, the leather-clad man stepped forward and dropped lower in the picture. For a moment it seemed as though the children were engulfing him. At the point when he reached the bottom of the steps, he continued to descend until he was below the height of the surrounding pupils.

'It looks as if he's going right into the ground,' said May, amazed.

'Not possible,' said Banbury. 'I checked. There's nothing there but tarmac.'

The little group continued staring at the screen in disbelief.

The tide of schoolchildren gradually parted and withdrew, leaving nothing behind but blank pavement.

'That's insane. Where's he gone?' May was mystified. 'Re-run the footage.'

They watched again, stepping through one frame at a time, but the images yielded no further clues. The Highwayman's movement became too fast and blurred to be fully discerned. He lowered his head and folded down in a tumble of passing figures. The collapsing image disturbed May more each time he watched it, but it took him a few minutes to realize why. The Leicester Square Vampire had supposedly vanished in the same manner, over thirty years earlier.

Arthur Bryant trudged doggedly through the downpour, checking each litter-cramped alleyway as he passed. He had forgotten to bring the address of the lock-up with him, and was now no longer convinced he would recognize the turn-off by sight.

Lately, certain sections of his memory had started to retreat. The process was peculiarly selective, so that, while he recalled every detail of the trial of Neville Heath, the whip-wielding wartime RAF sadist who suffocated and mutilated his girlfriends, or the investigation surrounding Gordon Cummins, the brutal 'Blackout Ripper' traced by the serial number on his gas mask just as he was about to strangle his fifth victim, Bryant could not remember where he had parked Victor, or when he had last filled it with petrol (the gauge was not to be trusted).

He felt as though he had been quietly but firmly sidelined from the investigation, given some displacement activity to get on with while the real work was being undertaken by professionals. Nobody trusted Bryant with the contemporary investigation. Instead, somewhat at his own behest, he found himself relegated to rooting about in the detritus of the past. Bryant was a contrary man; in other circumstances this would have been his ideal assignment, but

331

today he felt as if he was missing out on something important. The unit had sailed near the edge of disaster before, but never quite this close.

He raised his rain-spattered spectacles, peering down a cobbled alley with nasturtiums and vines splitting its dripping brown bridges, and knew he had found the right place. Paddington had always been a contrary, broken-backed area, riven by rail lines and fragmented by landlords, but rendered lively by the economic migrants who perched behind the counters of its late-night shops or cooked in takeouts that filled the air with unfamiliar spices. Now, the smart new basin and rows of expensive executive apartments had supposedly regenerated the area, but as far as Bryant could see, the renovation was merely driving out the people who made the neighbourhood so intriguing.

He checked the bunch of keys Longbright had released to him, and stood before the creosoted wooden door cut into one of the last bricked-up arches. The evidence archive was one of four kept by the PCU across London to house items from earlier investigations. The catalogued bags and boxes could not be disposed of until all of their cases were concluded, but court appeals and queried verdicts kept many investigations 'live' far beyond the unit's involvement. DNA profiling had meant that many of the items stored here were now active once more, and Bryant was under strict instructions not to handle or remove anything.

He stepped through the narrow slatted door into the spidery gloom and searched for a light switch, before remembering that the Paddington and King's Cross lock-ups had no electricity. Hefting May's Valiant into his palm, he shone the cinema torch around the arch. Mildew and moisture had taken their toll: many of the heavy clear plastic sacks were now acting as greenhouses for fungus. Bryant found himself looking at the accumulated details of his career. Here was a painted mask worn by Euridice in a scandalous – not to mention murderous – wartime production of *Orpheus in the Underworld*. In another box was one of the seventy-seven clocks that had inadvertently caused mayhem among the members of one of London's oldest families in 1973. Shards of education and experience, past mistakes and private moments, triumphs and failures, now eaten by rust and damp and rodents, crushed and crammed together in buckled boxes like scrapbooks of barely recognized memories.

It took the best part of an hour to locate the box marked LSV1973, and another ten minutes for his cold-slowed hands to cut open the seals.

Bryant needed to remove the instruments of death. The Vampire had thrown his knife into the alley after the last attack. The bloodstained handle had been examined and its group noted at the time, but this had been before the era of DNA testing. At least the result could now be matched against the samples taken from the stored bodies.

As he unwrapped the knife, a wintry draught raised the hairs on his arms. Other hands had gripped this handle, pushing home its blade with terrible force. Two girls and a boy had died, assaulted, stabbed and bitten almost as an afterthought. Some had lost blood before stumbling terrified into the square, desperate for help. Elizabeth had fallen silently in an alley, her life seeping out into the drain beneath her as the officers had desperately combed the corridors behind Leicester Square. Hundreds of witnesses had been interviewed, but only a handful had been called back for further questioning, and they had surrendered blood samples. The files of these few lay rotting in the bottom of the box.

When confronted with the hard evidence of violent death, instinct and emotion took hold of him, forcing rationality into retreat. He tried to remember the panicked night patrols, the anxious faces, but saw only the face of Elizabeth, smiling and waving back to John as she turned to walk the path of her murderer. What had happened in the minutes after the attack? How long had it taken for the shock of the event to make itself felt? He had taken charge of Elizabeth's cooling corpse, careful to shield it from his partner. John was in shock, and someone had poured him brandy. Bryant's interest in the Vampire's identity had died at that point. Who had he been? What did it matter? Nothing could bring back John's daughter, April's mother. She had joined the ranks of those who had died viciously, needlessly, on the streets of the city.

Bryant's knees cracked as he lowered himself down to the wet concrete. Normally he would simply have taken what he needed, but as Faraday had forbidden him to remove anything, he was forced to examine the documents by torchlight. He did not expect to find anything new; what little evidence there was had been studied by everyone except the office juniors. Vaguely remembered faces glinted before him, unfortunates photographed in the aftermath of their loss. Pictures of the killer's victims in happier times – backpacking, squinting into sunlight, gurning happily at flashlit nightclub tables, their halted histories stapled to their faceshots like casting cards for some melancholy documentary.

The old detective's bones protested as he changed positions to spread a sheet of plastic across the floor and lay the files on it. The events of the past had split like thawing pack ice, incidents drifting apart so that it was almost impossible now to see the greater picture. He recognized his own crablike handwriting on the files, adding dense sidebars where none were necessary, noting that the first victim was a member of an occult society, as if that somehow had a bearing on the case. His errors of judgement were augmented before him, mocking and misguided, making him ashamed. He had repeatedly avoided obvious lines of questioning to focus on the obscure and the arcane, sidetracking his uncomfortable subjects, repeatedly twisting the interviews to his own ends. Mystical connections, oddball acquaintances, they had assumed an unnatural level of importance, all because he could not bring himself to accept that the real answers might be mundane, that his job might be grimmer and more prosaic than he was prepared to believe.

And yet there were successful conclusions – how did one account for them? He thumbed through the photographs, wondering what his partner might have seen had he not commandeered the case. Connections – private, public, family, business, social, accidental – that was how May worked. He remained thorough and methodical, endlessly searching and collating. It was how Bryant tried to think now. *Keep to human dimensions*, he told himself. *Make it plain and simple.*

The rain dripped in through the cracks in the bricks, drumming on to corrugated iron above his head. He studied the dead victims' backgrounds once more, adding his own notes on those who had survived their attacks. He noted their birthplaces (New Zealand, Nottingham, South Africa, Norway, Wales, Madrid, Chile – not even in the same hemisphere), their lodging addresses (Earl's Court, Marylebone, King's Cross, Acton, Wandsworth, Wembley, Hackney), their jobs, (student, student, artist, insurance assessor, secretary, builder), their extracurricular activities (pubs, parties, football, tennis, walking, cinema, night classes) and stopped, re-reading his water-stained notes. Comments were scrawled in margins, cramped and indecipherable. Reading by torchlight was hard work; he found himself returning to the typed background files assembled by Longbright, because they strained his eyes less.

With the files laid out on the damp concrete floor, he tried a process May had taught him. *Future stars begin as unknowns in old films,* said his partner. *When you go back to these early titles now, their names jump out. With cold cases, you return to see if any of the participants have since become notorious.*

A single link had been noted at the time: several of the

victims had been taking night classes in the weeks preceding their deaths. The connection had been dismissed, because no two students attended the same college.

One victim had been heading for a class in economic history on the night she died. No specific venue for the course was listed, but in the contents of the second victim's backpack Bryant found a folded copy of the school curriculum. The class was circled in red biro, with the name of the lecturer printed beneath it, and a small photograph.

It would have meant nothing at the time, but now it assumed momentous significance.

Alexander Kingsmere, MA, BSc Oxon.

Brilliant Kingsmere looked so much like his father.

41

PSYCHIC TRAIL

Janet Ramsey turned her key in the lock and admitted herself to her Chelsea apartment. She had been expecting the PCU to prove incompetent – it was what always happened when you placed academics out in the field. Their hopeless mishandling of today's attempt to lure out the Highwayman had achieved the desired effect. She kicked off her shoes and rang Oskar Kasavian's mobile. It made the call traceable, but was better than calling him at a government office.

'You were right, they were even worse than you said they would be,' she told him. 'The Highwayman showed up, just as I expected. He obviously sensed it was a trap and didn't stick around, but he wanted to use the photo opportunity and made sure my man got plenty of shots. God, a blind man would have sensed the police vehicles scattered around the street. I must admit, though, it hadn't occurred to me that the school would be in session on a Saturday. The unit staged the most extrovert undercover operation imaginable, flatfoots thumping up and down the pavement barking into walkie-talkies, huge officers lurking behind tiny garden walls, quite ridiculous.'

'I want a full report detailing their incompetence,' said Kasavian. 'Your end of the deal.'

'Don't worry, you'll get it.'

'What happened to the Highwayman?'

'He waited outside the apartment, then trotted back downstairs and out of the front door, unapprehended. They managed to lose him, despite the fact that the entire street had been sealed off.'

'It doesn't surprise me, but I don't understand how.'

'They hadn't allowed for two hundred kids suddenly pouring into the street. The sudden confusion allowed him to use an escape route.'

'Did you get a good look at him?'

'Not really – the officers had turned off the light in the hall – but he'll show up in the pictures. I'm not in the business of helping to identify him, Oskar. The longer he stays active without running to ground, the better it is for the paper's campaign.'

'You have to get the report typed up tonight,' Kasavian instructed her. 'I need to work on it over the weekend.'

'Let me take a nap first,' said Ramsey. 'I've been on my feet all day.'

'I thought we were going to meet up later.'

'Are you sure you want to risk being seen with me? I thought you were taking your wife to the opera tonight. I could damage your credibility.'

'I hardly think so, Janet. Your newspaper has no credibility, so why should it damage mine?'

'We represent the voice of the people, darling, don't forget that. Sometimes I wonder what I see in you. I'll call you in a couple of hours.' She rang off and made her way to the bathroom, hopping out of her shoes and shucking her dress.

The day had worked out well. She had an exclusive story and plenty of saleable images to work with. What she really needed now was another murder to keep the outrage of the public at its peak.

*　　　*　　　*

May had found Bryant standing at the centre of Waterloo Bridge as usual. By now the sky had become icy and inhospitable, and billowing black sheets of rain were spattering his neck.

'I was on my way back from the Paddington lock-up,' Bryant explained, pulling out a plastic bag containing several slips of water-damaged paper. 'Several of the Vampire's victims were taught in evening classes conducted by Brilliant Kingsmere's father. I think that's how he came to stalk them in the first place. I ran a check on him. He has a charge sheet – disturbing the peace, causing an affray, assaulting a police officer and molestation of a minor, a young woman who failed to press charges. Unfortunately there's not much detail in the reports. There's no answer from his current address, so you'll have to talk to his son.'

'Wait a minute, you're telling me that one of my witnesses in the Highwayman case is actually your suspect? Do you realize what the odds are on the two cases being connected? It's astronomically unlikely. Are you sure you haven't made a mistake and muddled up the documentation or something?'

'My mental faculties may be in decline, but I don't get cases mixed up,' snapped Bryant. 'You're becoming quite unpleasant as you get older. Here, I was saving you some of this.' He pulled a leaky plastic freezer-bag from his pocket and handed it to May. 'Alma made a sherry trifle. I've had it on me all day. It's got a bit squashed.'

'What am I going to do with you, Arthur?' May examined his partner's peace-offering and reluctantly slipped it into his pocket. 'Today's operation was a nightmare. If you'd been there, you'd have realized that something was wrong from the outset. As unlikely as it sounds, I just don't think clearly without you. The whole fiasco has merely given Faraday more ammunition.'

'It wasn't your fault, John. The unit was never designed to carry out such operations.' He stopped abruptly and looked out at the sluggish olive water blossoming beneath the bridge.

'But what? Go on, you were going to say something. You know I messed up. What would you have done differently?'

'It's just that you're looking at it from the wrong perspective. You thought you were luring him, but I think it was the other way around.'

'What do you mean?'

'It wasn't a trap but an opportunity. She and the Highwayman both used you to get publicity.'

'But why would he show up at all? Why risk being captured?'

'Because he knew he wasn't going to be. Such bravado requires the extreme level of calculation he adopts in everything he does. The Vampire's bravery stemmed from the wildness of psychological aberration, but the Highwayman's methods are more sophisticated. It happens over time. A pity, because I was thinking the two killers might be one and the same person.'

May looked at his partner in horror. 'There's nothing else to suggest that the cases are connected other than your scraps of paper, Arthur. You can't just follow some kind of psychic trail in your head that makes links where none exist.'

'If you don't think there's a connection, go and see him. Ask Brilliant Kingsmere about his father.'

'What can he do beyond admit that his old man taught thousands of pupils, some of whom suffered tragedies? Teachers touch so many lives, and we're talking about a very specific London neighbourhood, so it's hardly surprising their paths crossed. But the two cases together? How old would Kingsmere's father be now, and why would he be running around dressed as a highwayman? It just raises more questions than it can answer. Oh, and did I mention that the idea is utterly ridiculous? The Highwayman is an incredibly strong man, tall, athletic, not someone of your age.'

'All right, but he still has a link with the Vampire, whom we were intended to see as Robin Hood, a real-life thief and murderer changed into a mythical champion. Kingsmere's an idealist, a reformer. He must know about the Vampire, because his father was interviewed by police at the time. Suppose it gave him the idea for a warped kind of social experiment? Kingsmere was missing when the first Highwayman murder was committed, apparently at home with food poisoning. Was he missing from school again today?' Bryant was fired with a fresh spark of enthusiasm. 'We need to get him in for questioning immediately.'

'We can't do that without Land's permission, and he's out of town until tomorrow night.'

'Kingsmere must have his own office at the school. We could search it.'

'I doubt there are sufficient grounds for a warrant, Arthur, and we wouldn't get one until Monday at the earliest.'

'Then we'll need to break in. I can get hold of Felix.'

'Oh no, you promised never to use him again. Not after we paid him to break into Sharon Letts' house.' Letts, a notorious London thief known as the Queen of Shoplifters, had stolen a fortune in gems from Harrods' jewellery counter. It was hard to tell how much she had looted, because Felix had stolen back the diamonds for the police, only to hide several of them in a glass of water which he had drunk before anyone could stop him. After the Met boys arrested him, they waited for the stones to pass through Felix's alimentary canal, but the cat burglar had managed to lock them in their own squad car. He was later captured and sent to prison, where he discovered that Letts' family had placed a contract on him. Thinking he would be safer in solitary confinement, he picked a fight with a small ginger Irishman in his wing, only to discover that his victim was a Real IRA terrorist, whose people promptly placed a second contract on the hapless burglar. Since then he had lived in fear of his life, running discreet small-scale operations for anyone who needed his services.

'Lend me your phone. Nobody need ever know we hired him. Besides, he owes me a favour.'

'Give me one good reason why I should agree to this.'

'We're about to lose the unit. What else is there left to lose?' Bryant fumbled about in his overcoat and produced two scraps of paper. 'Look, this is a photocopy of Luke Tripp's Highwayman drawing.' He unfolded the second piece. 'And this I took from the Paddington lock-up. It's the only witness sketch we ever had of the Leicester Square Vampire. Apart from the tricorn hat and the mask, the outfits are almost identical. It looks like Kingsmere stole the idea for some mysterious purpose of his own.'

'This is against my better judgement,' warned May, handing over his mobile. If their superiors discovered that the unit's most senior members had hired a cat burglar to break into a suspect's house, they would prosecute the PCU. However, having failed to make his own plan of action work, May had no choice but to trust his partner's instincts. He had reached a stage where any action was fair if it yielded results.

'Do it,' he told Bryant. 'Get him on the phone, and God help us if we get caught.'

42

DESCRIBING EVIL

Janet Ramsey checked the temperature of her bath and laid out fresh clothes. She rarely questioned the wisdom of her actions, but the events of the last few days had give her pause for thought. She was editing a tabloid with a shrinking readership and a record number of hits lodged against it with the Press Complaints Commission. She was continuing an affair with a married man despite the fact that Oskar Kasavian was never likely to leave his wife. She had a son she had hardly seen since her ex-husband had unexpectedly been granted custody.

And she wasn't getting any younger.

Tugging at the creases around her eyes in the bathroom mirror, she wondered how much longer she could maintain the balancing act. The real problem was that she no longer believed the stories she wrote. Once she had been able to convince herself that the public had a right to know about the mistakes made by those whose lives were lived in public. There were new magazines appearing out there that made hers look positively scrupulous. Everyone had jumped on to the celebrity bandwagon until there was nothing of interest left to report. It was no longer about news but bargaining power, and she doubted they would be able to raise the cash for many more exclusives. But *Hard News* had hitched its reputation to a rising star; the Highwayman could restore their falling circulation.

A movement in the darkness through the glass of the front door caught her eye, and she turned from the mirror. The worst part about living off the Brompton Road was having to place steel trellises across all of the ground-floor windows and a bolt over the main entrance. She had upset plenty of people through the newspaper, but none had ever dared to turn up at her house – the press made too powerful an enemy. She always felt safe here, but it was still like being shut in a cage.

The shadow cut reflections from the glass for a moment, and she realized there was definitely someone outside. *Don't go out to look,* she told herself, walking calmly towards the lounge, *that's how trouble starts.* Buried far beneath her commercial instincts, the small spark that had once fired her desire to investigate, to 'put matters right', was fanned back to flame, and she approached the lounge window, through which the front door could be seen.

He was standing outside with his back towards the house, his hands clasped together. This time he wore a spectacular dress-cape with a triangle of crimson satin lining exposed, as though he had dressed for an audience with her. He was taller than she remembered. He turned and rang the doorbell with the polite apprehension of an internet date.

He's desperate to talk, she thought. *He needs the air of publicity and wants to grant an exclusive interview. If I'm careful, it could be the scoop of the year.* Her hand hovered above the bolt handle.

She thought of calling the police and warning them first. There was a problem with that, though. The local cops hated her after she had approved the publication of an article exposing the sex lives of two female sergeants, both of whom were now being investigated. She thought of calling Toby, her ex-husband, then remembered that he was still in Geneva on business.

The Highwayman rang again. If she let him escape, she would lose the greatest journalistic chance of her career. He had never directly attacked a victim before, so he was likely to be unarmed. And he was waiting for her, trusting her.

She withdrew the bolt and opened the door.

Whenever she had commissioned features on the Highwayman, she had asked her writers to exaggerate his height and sinister presence. Now she saw there was no need to do so. The tip of his tricorn hat almost grazed the top of the doorway. He stepped into the hall, his face lost in shadows, took another pace towards her and froze. There was an unnerving stillness about him, a dead heart of indifference that made him more dangerous than she had ever imagined a human being could be. She knew at once that his masked eyes had seen men die.

She had an idea. Without removing her gaze from him, she slowly reached for her mobile and speed-dialled the number of the Peculiar Crimes Unit. The Highwayman remained motionless, studying her as if watching an alien species.

DS Janice Longbright answered on the third ring, calling her by name; it had come up on her screen.

'He's standing right in front of me,' Ramsey murmured, daring him to move. She had rarely been granted a chance to describe evil at such close quarters, and was determined to make the most of the opportunity. 'He's taller than I expected, around six two, slim and rather sexy. The outfit has been modified from ordinary motorcycle leathers. The buckled knee-boots come from a goth store called Born In Camden. He's not wearing his gloves. The back of his left hand is badly stained with your man's indigo dye. It looks like he's wearing make-up.' She found her old investigative powers returning as she studied him. 'Brown eyes, still and rather dead, pointed chin, straight black hair, the kind of pale skin that suggests Eastern European extraction. Wait, I think the hair's a wig.'

'You must leave while you still can,' said Longbright urgently. 'He's far more dangerous than you realize.'

'I don't imagine he's armed.' She tried to sound braver than she was. 'I think he knows I'd give him a good kicking in a fair fight.'

'Janet, you have to stop this and get out right now. He has every reason to hurt you.' While she spoke Longbright was trying to raise the alarm on her mobile.

'No, he doesn't want to hurt me.' She smiled at him confidently. 'He's hardly moved a muscle since he stepped into the room.' She moved a little closer. 'There's a strong intelligence working behind his eyes. I think we're just going to have a little chat, as equals. Wait a minute.' There was a brief silence. 'Well, I'm damned, he's not a man at all – '

The phone fell to the floor with a clatter. A moment later, the line was cut off.

Bimsley and Mangeshkar took the young Indian DC's Kawasaki and took off, coasting around stalled traffic at Hyde Park Corner, hitting seventy in the deserted backstreets behind the Brompton Road. As they roared into the quiet cherrytree-lined street off King's Road they could see that the communal door to Janet Ramsey's apartment building was still open.

Bimsley had no qualms about kicking in the locked front door on the ground floor, but Meera stopped him. 'She might be behind it,' she warned, calling to Ramsey and getting no response.

'I'll do it gently,' Bimsley promised, but as he leaned on it, the door swung in.

Ramsey was lying at the foot of the stairs, her cracked forehead still wet with a vivid slash of blood. Mangeshkar checked for vital signs as Bimsley reported back.

'She's still breathing,' said Meera. 'He's not here. But he's messed up badly this time.'

43

THE DYNASTY

While the staff of the PCU worked on through the rainy Saturday night, Janet Ramsey reached a stable condition at the Chelsea and Westminster Hospital. Her X-rays revealed a single wound: a skull fracture caused by a sharp blow to the head.

Early on Sunday morning, Banbury enlisted Kershaw to take photographs and conduct further analysis at the editor's apartment.

'High heels, old chap, hardly surprising she couldn't keep her balance.' Kershaw checked the screen of his digital camera, playing back shots. 'She's an old-school journo, hasn't been out of cocktail outfits since her days of attending mayor's banquets for the provincial press.' He looked around disapprovingly at the pastel cushions, ribbons and flowers. 'Janet Ramsey has a secret – despite what she publishes in *Hard News*, she's a born romantic.'

'Good for me. Soft surfaces hold more fibres.' Banbury hated examining hardwood floors because fresh evidence became balled up with older detritus and gathered around the edges of the room. 'Let me see the fissure on the back of her head again.' Banbury's partner turned his camera around to reveal the uploaded photographs taken by the admitting doctor. 'Can you enlarge the contusion area and lighten it a little?'

Kershaw worked the camera controls. Together they examined the damage that had placed Ramsey in a coma. 'Three leaves,' Kershaw muttered.

'What are you saying?'

'You can clearly make out three V-tipped indentations at the hairline of her right temple. She's got a fleur-de-lis pattern stamped into the front of her head.' He began searching around the base of the staircase.

'Over here.' Banbury pointed to the antique ironwork railing that stood a few feet beyond the front door. After Kershaw took shots of the area, Banbury sprayed Luminol on the bannister and lifted impressions from the points of the fleur-de-lis. 'Looks like she fell down head-first and banged her forehead against the railing. The force would have been enough to dent her skull. The brain is probably bruised, and there could well be bone-splinters in it, so I imagine she'll be too whacked out to be interrogated just yet.'

'The Highwayman rings her doorbell – the second time he's done so – and this time she lets him in,' said Kershaw, thinking aloud. 'She calmly fronts him out, but then he makes a move towards her, as if he's going to attack, and she's jumps back – '

'What was he going to hit her with?' asked Banbury. 'She said he wasn't armed.'

'She said she *thought* he wasn't armed. Perhaps he pushes her. Either way, she falls headlong, cracking open her skull. Point is, there's no way of proving whether it was attempted murder.'

'Then we have to find a way,' replied Kershaw. 'This is the kind of street where the residents will tell you they saw nothing.'

'We have one reliable witness, Ramsey herself.' Banbury ran a hand over his cropped head. 'The phone call. She got closer to him than anyone. And on the transcript, she tells Longbright that the Highwayman is not male.'

'That's ridiculous, a woman wouldn't be strong enough.'

'You haven't met my wife,' said Banbury. 'She works in a pub and was still changing the barrels two days before giving birth to our nipper.'

Kershaw crossed the road and began knocking on doors. An elderly neighbour opposite thought she had seen someone being attacked, but didn't call the police because she had 'no desire to interfere in the affairs of others'. Chelsea was home to much of London's old money. Phalanxes of pathologically self-centred venture-capitalists, wine traders and art dealers lived behind its triple-bolted doors.

'Did you at least get a full statement?' asked Banbury when Kershaw returned. The crime-scene manager was in Janet Ramsey's hall, lying on his stomach and sliding sheets of sticky acetate across the carpet.

'I tried to get the witness down to the unit, but she refused to go. Besides, what I got didn't add up.'

'Tell me.'

'The old lady says she looked out of her window and saw Ramsey's front door open. She knows Ramsey to nod to, nothing more, actually referred to her as "that frightful newspaper woman". Ramsey came out on to the steps, then dropped, as though she'd lost her footing on the first step, and fell head first, glancing against the railing. Witness reckons she was alone. When she landed, she didn't get up.'

'And she still did nothing to help?'

'Carried on dead-heading her nasturtiums.'

'As you say, Ramsey was wearing very high heels, so it's possible she just fell. I need to take another look.'

Banbury examined the treads and took a scraping of a single small scuff-mark. 'I'll see if this matches her heel,' he told Kershaw, 'but it looks pretty straightforward. She was trying to get away from him, and didn't check where she was going – or he had already gone and she was simply in a state of disorientation.'

'Or she may have been lying, and he was never there at all,' added Kershaw.

'Then why would she tell Longbright the Highwayman wasn't male? No, he was here all right. We've got the same ridged bootprints in the hall, and this time they're the larger of our two sizes, same as the one in the gallery.' He ran his torch along the carpet, highlighting the indented pile. 'He walked behind her.'

'So he could have pushed her,' Kershaw suggested.

'I don't think so. The carpet prints are all the same depth. He continued walking and went out the way he came in.' Banbury rocked back on his heels, thinking. 'One odd thing, though. Her prints are clearly distinguishable because of the narrow heel. They come up from the lounge, go to the front door and back, then stop altogether. His prints cross hers, so I guess he might have flattened the pile.'

'But we have an eye-witness report that she tripped and fell,' said Kershaw. 'That doesn't fit with what you're reading from the carpet.'

'It's a recurring MO,' Banbury muttered, lying down with his shoulder against the carpet, examining the skirting boards. 'He's always there, but not, if you see what I mean. He's seen at the sites, but we have no evidence that he ever touches the victims. That's a very unusual behavioural pattern, some kind of fundamental disassociation with the victims. Usually I'd expect to find something on the bodies suggesting the identity of an outside party, but there's been nothing on any of them. It's as though his mere presence is enough to kill.'

'Why would he go out of his way not to touch them?'

'Being careful about forensic evidence, or maybe it's part of the image. Nemesis, a figure of dread. Remember Wichita's BTK killer, all those cryptic messages he sent to the police about his crimes thirty years after he had committed them? Same principle here. The desire to inspire fear and be treated as a celebrity monster. Bryant is right, he has the same profile as the Leicester Square Vampire. No wonder he thinks the cases are related.'

'I take it you don't,' Kershaw suggested.

'No, I agree that they are,' said Banbury, 'just not in the way anyone has imagined. What do you think this is?' He raised a pair of tweezers in his torch beam and showed its contents to his partner.

Kershaw peered at the curved white sliver. 'Looks like plaster.'

'There's nothing made of plaster around here. It's not from the ceiling. The shape's too rounded.' It was Bryant who had persuaded Banbury to always carry an old-fashioned magnifying lens. He was glad of it now as he dug it out to examine the splinter. 'Appears to have been broken off from the ironwork. Identical fleur-de-lis shape.' He matched it against the design. 'Except that there's nothing missing here, and it's made of the wrong material.'

'The Highwayman specializes in the impossible. Therefore, if we assume she didn't fall, he must have wanted to make it look as if she did.' Kershaw bagged the chip for removal, and thought for a moment. 'I think I know what this is. He's making mistakes now. I hope you didn't make any arrangements for your day off.'

'Actually I was planning to attend my sister's wedding,' Banbury replied. 'I'll stick a note in with the flowers.'

Loyalty to this unit is going to be the ruin of us all, thought Kershaw sadly.

'Nobody does this kind of thing any more,' said Felix, lifting away the sticky sheet to reveal a neat square hole in the window. Heavy rain darkened the school, shielding it from the road. The professional burglar set down the pane and proudly brushed back the ends of his grey handlebar moustache. 'It's a lost art. Nobody cares about craftsmanship. The refinement is in the detailing.'

'You're breaking and entering, not carving a bentwood chair,' said May tersely.

'You're lucky I'm operating on this side of the law,' said Felix.

'That's only because we haven't caught you working on the other side yet. Mr Al Fayed is still hoping to get his diamonds back, despite where they've been. We shouldn't be seen with you. You're a marked man. I'm surprised you're still alive.'

'Ah, you didn't hear. I faked my own death and shook them off.'

'We still managed to find you easily enough, so watch it.' May looked back at the darkened schoolyard. 'I thought there would be a caretaker.'

'Caretakers cost money. It's cheaper to install an alarm.' Felix slipped his arm through the window and raised the catch. 'All you need to shut this system down is a magnet and a needle. It's pitiful. They go for the cheapest option because only kids break into schools. What would a professional find worth nicking here? They're too busy reading pin numbers over punters' shoulders at cash points. My old man would be turning in his grave.'

'If he wasn't inside,' Bryant pointed out. 'Are we likely to find any more alarms?'

'What are you expecting, laser beams across the floor?' He slid up the window and pulled Bryant inside with some effort. 'Would you mind telling me what we're looking for?'

'Just get us to the back of the first floor and we'll do the rest,' said Bryant.

'It's a liability having you on the job with me,' Felix complained. 'I'm not insured if you break something.'

They climbed the broad oak staircase and made their way past school portraits dating back more than three hundred years. May tried the door to Kingsmere's room and found it locked. He turned to Felix. 'Over to you, Maestro.'

Felix pushed May aside and warmed his fingers. 'A

Hannen cross-flange switch-bolt, a nice little Victorian number, we don't see many of them nowadays. The screw-gauges are different from modern locks.'

'Can you open it?' asked Bryant.

Felix unfolded a set of tiny screwdrivers. 'Victorian equipment requires Victorian tools. Luckily for you I'm a professional.'

Within ten minutes, Felix had removed the entire lock from the door and carefully laid it in pieces on the hall floor. 'It has to go back in the same way it came out,' Felix explained. They crept into the room and shone torches over Kingsmere's elegant glass desk.

'No,' said Bryant, pointing. 'Start in the cupboards over there.'

'You know where to look, don't you?' asked May, amazed. 'What have I missed?'

'The boys told Longbright that he gave them a lesson using artefacts from his family's history. I think we'll find what we're looking for in there.'

Felix stepped forward and pinged open the tiny lock with a disdainful flick of the finger. Bryant opened the cupboard and checked inside to find cricket pads, footballs, broken pieces of science equipment, a master's gown, rugby kit and stacks of schoolbooks. 'Funny how school cupboards all smell the same. Give me a hand,' he instructed.

Together, he and May lifted down a cardboard box and removed the lid. This was May's abiding image of his partner; nosing into some neglected corner of the city to check out its contents. The box had been taped shut, but Bryant happily slit it open with his Swiss Army knife. It was filled with photographs and newspaper clippings.

'Take a look at this,' Bryant suggested. 'Kingsmere's family tree. I knew he would keep his mementoes here. This room is very important to him; it's where he passes on his wisdom. He couldn't resist a little show-and-tell with his favoured pupils. The St Crispin's pupils are at war with the boys on the estate, so the Saladins are always looking for ways to bring them down. And recently, I think they made a discovery about St Crispin's favourite teacher. They were annoyed with Kingsmere because he had the nerve to conduct good-citizen classes at their centre, so they took revenge on him – and by extension, their enemies – by embedding clues about Kingsmere's culpability in their graffiti, for all to see. How typical of teenagers to take such an unnecessarily complicated route.'

'You've lost me, Arthur,' May admitted.

'This is where a little reading of London history books comes in useful, John. Kingsmere's grandfather was a legendary fascist. Nobody is given a forgotten Victorian Christian name like "Brilliant" without a good family reason. The name rang a bell the first time I heard it. There's a famous photograph of Kingsmere's ancestor throwing a Molotov cocktail at a police cordon in 1935. I saw it at Oliver's picture library.'

Bryant raised a fistful of sepia photographs depicting a thin-faced man shouting on a podium at Hyde Park Corner. 'He went to jail for attacking the so-called anarcho-socialists he deemed harmful to the wellbeing of England. Judging from these photographs, he modelled his appearance on a history of earlier protestors. We tend to adopt the look of those we admire; think of the tree-huggers in the nineties, and how they modelled their appearance on Californian hippies. Kingsmere could have buried his ancestry, but instead he chose to celebrate it and explain it to his class. That says a lot about his state of mind.'

May stood back. 'I don't understand. You think some piece of ancient family history makes Kingsmere the High-wayman?'

'I think he's been following in his family's infamous footsteps. This is about their perception of social injustice. Imagine a dynasty of outsiders and anarchists, each genera-tion committing the crimes that it deems necessary to improve society. The grandfather is politically committed and indoctrinates his children, so that eventually Brilliant Kingsmere is encouraged to follow in the family footsteps, and wipe out those he imagines are symptomatic of society's ills.'

'You can't honestly believe that's enough of a motive to turn Kingsmere into some kind of avenging angel,' said May.

'I'd seen the grandfather's picture on the wall of the Newman Street Picture Library, I just didn't register the central connection. It makes perfect sense. The old man's radical background obsesses and poisons his son, and his son's son in turn. *Ergo*, Kingsmere is the Highwayman, continuing his grandfather's work.'

'You've come up with some rubbish theories in your time, but this beats them all.' May shoved the photographs back in their box. 'You think the grandson's motive must also be about upsetting the social order? The targeting of celebrities considered to be champions of the masses is a bit of a perverse way of meting out social justice.'

'I haven't worked out the finer points yet,' Bryant admitted, looking sheepish.

May was unconvinced. 'This is one of your potty dot-joining exercises. I don't see any damning evidence here.'

'You don't?' Bryant was holding something aloft with a smile creeping across his eerily white false teeth. Dipping into the box once more, he withdrew a black leather eyemask. A moment's more rummaging brought forth a padded courier's jerkin, similarly stitched in black leather. 'The mask and tunic of the avenger. We're going to find Kingsmere's prints all over these. He followed his grandfather's aberrant ideologies. We've found our Highwayman. Let's bring him in.'

'I know why you're so out of sorts,' said Alma Sorrowbridge, picking up Bryant's mud-spattered trousers and bundling them for the wash. 'You're working too hard and it's stressing you out, making you forget things. Worry plays merry Henry with the bowels.' His Antiguan landlady tutted and shook her jowls. 'Fancy leaving piles of filthy old toothbrushes all over the hall with germs and ungodly crawlies leaping off them, and forgetting the nice packed lunch I made you.'

'It wasn't nice, it was covered in lard,' Bryant complained.

'You need some fat on your chest with the bad weather coming. And eat some fruit. You're an old man. You got to eat properly and make your peace with God before it's too late,' she warned.

'Thank you very much, that makes me feel a lot better,' said Bryant with heavy sarcasm. 'All this emphasis on youth and fitness is unhealthy. Why, only a few weeks ago I was shut inside a London sewer, and suffered no after-effects.' He searched the mantelpiece for his pipe, but Alma had hidden it again.

'I had to burn your clothes and fumigate the house. You could have brought back the plague. The neighbours came round complaining,' she replied, releasing a burst of lavender polish into the air and grinding it into her sideboard. 'It's Sunday. Why don't you come to church with me?'

'My dear woman, at some point you must realize that you're wasting your breath. I am quite beyond redemption. I'll only come to the church with you if the vicar has been found murdered.'

'I don't care for blasphemy, Mr B. Did you take your pills? You know you mustn't get them muddled up.'

'Just for once I wish everyone would stop mollycoddling me!' Bryant exploded. 'I'm not a six-year-old child, I'm in charge of a major murder investigation!'

He managed to beat her to the phone when it rang. 'Ah, John, any luck with our man?'

'He's out of contact at the moment – walking in the country, according to his girlfriend, and he doesn't have his mobile with him,' May replied. 'He's due back in two hours' time. I don't like the idea of him being on the loose – could we get him picked up?'

'It'll take that long just to bring him into the unit,' said Bryant. 'He's got no reason to run. Let's keep him under close surveillance until the morning, and talk to him the moment he arrives at the school. This needs to be handled with tact and care. I don't want him put on his guard.'

'All right, but I hope you know what you're doing.'

'Don't worry, I've got everything under control,' said Bryant, swigging his pills down with a small tumbler of whisky. He replaced the tablet box in his pocket, failing to notice that he had switched his energizing morning blue pills with his disorienting night-time red ones.

44

LOCKDOWN

'What's the problem?' asked Meera Mangeshkar, drawing alongside and pulling off her motorcycle helmet. It was seven thirty a.m. on Monday 31 October. Unit staff usually arrived early at Mornington Crescent on Mondays for a group meeting that decided the week's schedule, but this morning they were all stranded outside the building.

'The front door's stuck,' said Longbright, fiddling with the key to the PCU's main door. She stepped back and looked up at the unlit windows beneath the crimson tiled arches.

'Let me take a look.' Mangeshkar peered through the keyhole, then tested the latch. 'The lock's been changed. The old one's been drilled out.'

'That's impossible, I was the last to leave yesterday evening.' Longbright threw her considerable shoulder against the door, but it would not budge. She dug out her mobile and snapped it open. 'I'm going to call Faraday. This is his doing.'

'I'm afraid you won't get in by bashing the door down.' Leslie Faraday's tone was regretful when she managed to track him down, apologetic even. 'I fear my hands are tied.'

'But I don't understand,' said Longbright, shielding her mobile from spattering rain. Bimsley and Mangeshkar were huddled in the unit's doorway, waiting for her to finish the call.

'Mr Kasavian,' said Faraday. His speakerphone made him sound as if he was in a public toilet. 'He's terribly exercised about the bungled attempt to catch the Highwayman on Saturday. And yesterday's attack on Mrs Ramsey was the last straw. You should have seen him, utterly distraught – '

'He's not taking the case away from us?' asked Longbright.

'No,' replied Faraday. 'He's closed your unit down for good.'

The Detective Sergeant was outraged. 'He can't do that.'

'I'm afraid it's entirely within his remit to do so. I was hoping to tell you myself, but things are rather hectic here, what with London's tourism-development seminar occupying all my time at the moment. I have a lot of functions to attend, and frankly, the closure of a small unproductive department is all in a day's work.'

Longbright decided it might be for the best not to lose her temper. 'What happens to the investigation now? All our details are inside the unit.'

'Mr Kasavian has handed this case back to the Metropolitan Police,' explained Faraday. 'They'll take charge.'

John May's confession was still lying in Longbright's unlocked desk. She needed access to the building right now.

'Sergeant Renfield is on his way over to remove all your files from the building. I do hope you're not going to be awkward about this, Longbright.'

If Renfield can get in, she thought, *that means we can too.*

April watched the falling rain from the window of her Holloway Road apartment and wondered if it was about to become her prison again.

DS Longbright had called her a few minutes ago with news of the unit's closure, warning her not to come in, but without the offices at Mornington Crescent to visit every morning, she knew she might easily slip back into her old ways and become a recluse once more. How could her grandfather have allowed such a thing to happen? Clearly, the detectives had been so used to getting their own way that they had failed to notice how badly matters had slipped from their control.

She blamed herself for not warning them that Janet Ramsey was conducting an affair with Oskar Kasavian. She had made the connection two days earlier, while compiling internet information about the editor. There had been no direct references to their relationship, but April was adept at reading between the lines, and noticed a matching pattern in the duo's published schedules. Ramsey was divorced, but Kasavian was reported to be happily married. Civil servants were expected to behave with impartiality, and Ramsey's paper, for all its sexual salaciousness, was harshly and actively conservative. Law and order had been a political issue since the time of Dick Turpin, to be used as ammunition by the opposing party, but Kasavian clearly considered himself above such rules.

She knew that he had taken his vendetta to a personal level, and as he was the most senior official in charge of the unit, there was no higher authority to which to appeal. The PCU would remain closed, and its longest-serving detectives would finally be forced into retirement without honour or the satisfaction of finishing the task at hand. It would be the end of Bryant, if not her grandfather. John had hobbies and friends, but Arthur lived for his work.

It was too late to save the unit, but she wondered if there was a way of rescuing the partners from their predicament. Seating herself back at her computer, April followed a line of thought that she suspected might prove beneficial to them. Arthur had taught her always to trust her instincts above the facts, an attitude that irritated her grandfather. Bryant solved the most tangled cases by tracing barely visible psychic paths hidden under the weight of empirical data. For him, it was like following emergency lights through dense fog. This time, though, she was sure that the opposite was needed. The basic elements of logic in the case had been ignored, and it was time to reinstate them. April had a head for connecting simple facts.

She had sent her office notes to her home computer, in order to work at her apartment over the weekend. Now she looked through them, beginning with the first interview of the investigation, and its most fundamental paradox: the testimony of Luke Tripp.

She wanted a cigarette. She wanted to rearrange her desk so that all the pencils were in perfect alignment. Instead, April forced her mind towards the bare facts. *Do it for them,* she told herself.

Luke Tripp had gone on record stating that he had seen the horseman ride into the gallery and raise Saralla White up to the tank. Despite the absurdity of the claim, Banbury had been required to check it out. Where was the summary of his notes? She trawled through the hundreds of pages they had already amassed on the Highwayman and found his conclusion, an obvious point, but one that had been consistently sidelined: that it would have been quite impossible for a horse and rider to enter the building and secrete themselves within it.

Luke had been the first to describe the Highwayman, but that didn't mean he was not lying. His testimony had been accepted for two reasons: the Highwayman logo on the Roland Plumbe Community Estate letterhead matched his description, and the pose in the sketch was similar to earlier reports of the Leicester Square Vampire and even, according to Bryant, Robin Hood. Assuming this latter point was merely coincidental, how to deal with the former? She realized that Tripp would have seen the estate logo when he visited its community hall.

So why would he have insisted he was telling the truth, even surrounded by police officers?

Because failure to do so was a more frightening prospect than admitting the lie to the authorities. He was covering up for someone who threatened him. She found Tripp's mobile number at the foot of the report and called him.

Kershaw and Banbury were able to set up their makeshift work station in the Rio Café, Inverness Street, because its owner had done the catering for Banbury's sister's wedding. He gave them a table beside the window and all the coffee they could drink.

'This is embarrassing, being shut out of our own unit,' Kershaw complained. 'The Met boys must be killing themselves.'

'I'm not stopping now,' Banbury told him. 'We're so close. The plaster chip we found in Ramsey's flat is definitely part of the ironwork pattern at the base of her staircase. I thought perhaps it had been used to fill a crack or replace a missing piece – except there was nothing missing. Yet it matches the indentation in Ramsey's head.'

'I don't understand.'

'Impossible crime,' Banbury explained, without explaining.

'Let me get this right – she was hit with a fleur-de-lis from the staircase to make it look like she fell down the stairs?'

'Exactly. I've thought of a simple way he could have pulled it off. Suppose our man broke into the house earlier and took a mould of the pattern from the ironwork. Then all he would have to do is make a positive cast in plaster, setting it over the head of a hammer. When he hit her, it left behind an impression.'

'Which is why the witness saw her fall straight to the ground. She didn't see the blow from the hammer.'

'But he hadn't reckoned on the plaster cracking and leaving behind a clue.'

Kershaw flicked his hair from his eyes. 'Oh, that's rather good. Who needs the unit anyway? We could work here from now on. The coffee's better. There's still something very bonkers at work here, though. It feels so elaborate, don't you think? I keep asking myself why. What kind of person would go to so much trouble?'

They made a sadly bedraggled little group, huddled together in the rain as Mornington Crescent's morning traffic sloshed past them.

'What do you mean, we've been locked out?' demanded Arthur Bryant, thumping his walking stick on the puddled pavement. Rain sluiced from the brim of his shapeless brown trilby. 'It's coming down stair-rods and I can't afford to get my vest wet at my age. Open this door at once.' He rapped on it with the head of the stick.

'That's the point,' said Bimsley. 'We can't, Sir. They've changed the bloody locks.'

'Sergeant Renfield is coming around to take away all our files,' Longbright added.

Bryant brightened up. 'Wait, that means he has keys.'

'Just what I was thinking.'

'He's your opposite number, Janice. He's always fancied you. This calls for subterfuge. And lipstick. And unbutton the top of your shirt.'

Longbright was appalled. 'I will do no such thing. It's pouring.'

'That's sexism, Mr Bryant,' complained Meera.

'Rubbish, it's using your feminine wiles. I would if I was a woman. I'd have no qualms about being an utter strumpet if the situation called for it.'

'Here he comes now,' warned May. 'I don't think I'll be able to bear his gloating.'

Renfield squeezed his unset bulk from the rear of the squad car and waddled over to them. 'What a miserable bunch,' he said, barely suppressing a smirk. 'I know we haven't always seen eye to eye in the past, but you can't say we didn't warn you. Home Office can only allow things to go wrong so many times before they step in to pick up the pieces.'

'You have no jurisdiction here, Renfield,' said Bryant. 'I've been meaning to ask you: did your mother read Bram Stoker when she was pregnant?'

'What do you mean?' The sergeant fixed him with a glassy eye.

'Renfield was the obsequious fly-eating sidekick to the prince of darkness,' Bryant explained. 'How is Mr Kasavian? I do find there's something of the night about him, don't you?'

'Are you trying to be offensive, Mr Bryant?' Renfield hissed, sounding unpleasantly nocturnal. He pushed between them and brandished a bunch of keys. 'None of you is allowed inside, so don't think you'll get around me.' He spread himself fatly in front of the unit's entrance.

'Don't worry, I couldn't spare the time to circumnavigate you,' said Bryant. 'I'd lose an hour passing the international dateline at the back of your belt.'

Renfield wasn't able to follow the complexity of the insult about his weight, and soldiered on. 'There's no point in standing around out here like a bunch of wet dogs,' he told them. 'You're not coming in.'

'You need an independent monitor with you,' warned Longbright. 'It's in the regulations.'

'Well, you're hardly independent, are you?'

'It can't be one of your own men, Renfield, and there's no one else here. Mr Bryant has no filing system, but I know where everything is. It'll take you hours to collate all the material otherwise. You'll be here all day. Watch me all you want, I won't try to remove anything.'

'All right,' said Renfield reluctantly. 'But I'm not taking my eyes off you.'

Longbright winked back at her bosses as she followed Renfield inside.

'It's up to her now,' said Bryant. 'If she doesn't sabotage

364

him, it's all over for us.' He pulled the Mini Cooper's keys from his raincoat. 'Come on, John, you and I have to get to Kingsmere first. If the Met get their paws on him, we'll never discover what's really happening.' He paused to lean against a wall, furrowing his already wrinkled brow still further.

'Are you all right?' asked May.

'I feel a bit dizzy, that's all. I think I forgot to take my pills.' He dug into his overcoat pocket and slapped two more red night tablets into his mouth. 'Let's get over to Clerkenwell and finish this.'

'But the unit's been shut down. We have no power of jurisdiction.'

'We won't need it,' Bryant replied. 'We're going to get a confession.'

45

ACCUSATION

April felt protected by the overhanging plane trees. She found Luke Tripp seated beneath the dripping bushes of St Paul's churchyard, in the shadow of the great cathedral. Hidden beneath the raised hood of his navy-blue school coat, he looked tiny, pale and miserable. 'What are you doing out here?' she asked.

Luke folded back the corner of his hood and peered at her. 'I needed to make a really big prayer, and I thought it would get there faster if I picked a big church.'

April smiled at the thought of prayers functioning like broadband messages. 'Do your parents know where you are?'

'My father's working in Dubai, my mother's in France with her new boyfriend.'

'So who's looking after you?'

'Gretchen. She's the nanny. Is Mr May really your grand-father?'

'Yes, he is.' She passed him her lidded cup of coffee. 'Do you want some? Be careful, it's hot.'

The boy took a sip and grimaced. 'He's incredibly old. Why hasn't he retired?'

'He'll probably have to now. We're not dealing with your

366

case any more, Luke. We couldn't find your Highwayman, so the investigation is going to the regular cops. They'll want to come and talk to you again, and I'm afraid they'll be tougher to deal with.'

'You're not police-trained, are you?' asked the boy, studying her.

'No. Is it that obvious?'

'You don't say the right things.'

'Maybe that's good. Now that I'm no longer working on the investigation, I feel like I can ask you something, just between the two of us. Last Monday in the gallery? I know you didn't really see a horse. You're a smart boy. You know it would have been completely impossible for someone to ride into the room. I believe you told a lie to protect someone, and perhaps he threatened you, perhaps you're still afraid of him.'

'I saw a horseman,' said Luke carefully.

'That's not the same thing, is it?'

'No. But I'm not afraid of anyone.'

'Then why did you lie?'

'It's more complicated than that. You wouldn't understand.'

'But you did lie. You broke the law and lied to all of us.'

'Now you sound like someone who belongs to the other side.'

'There are no sides, Luke. I just want to get to the truth.'

The boy looked up at her from beneath his hood. 'Why is the truth so important to everyone? It won't help matters. It only ever makes things worse.'

'If we don't understand who criminals are and why they commit terrible crimes, we will never be able to help them.'

'The criminal justice system doesn't have much of a reputation for helping people,' said Luke, sounding older than his years. 'People manage to sort themselves out in spite of it.'

'Then you must think of me as being outside of the

system. I know you know what happened, Luke. There's no real reason why you should tell me, but a secret is hard to keep, and sharing it might make you feel better.'

The boy seemed to consider the idea for a minute, kicking his heels against the struts of the wet green bench, his face once more hidden by the hood.

'What if I did tell you something? You'd have to tell Bryant and May, wouldn't you?'

'How would you feel about that?'

'Let me make a call,' Luke said finally, hopping up and flipping open his mobile. He walked some distance away from her before speaking.

He's calling Kingsmere, she thought. *John and Arthur should be on their way to bring him in. But I could get to the truth right now.* Digging out her own mobile, she hastily punched in a text to the detectives. DON'T CONFRONT KINGSMERE UNTIL YOU HEAR FROM ME. She finished just as Luke Tripp turned and began walking back to her.

'I've arranged a meeting for you,' said Luke. 'It's the last thing I have to do.'

'Don't touch anything,' warned Sergeant Renfield, guiding the detective sergeant away from her bosses' open doorway. 'I know what you lot are like.'

'You act as if we're a threat to you,' Longbright pointed out. 'But we were always working on the same side.'

'I see it differently,' replied Renfield, scratching himself disconsolately. 'We're like doctors, and you're like alternative therapists. Your system is full of mumbo-jumbo, and doesn't work. You got lucky a few times, that's all. We use tried and tested effective methods of policing.'

'And you kill the patient in the process. You could have worked with the unit instead of fighting us for so long.'

'What difference would it have made? We won eventually. Now, would you mind telling me where your case files on the Highwayman are?'

Longbright looked around the chaotic room. 'Only Mr Bryant keeps hard copies. Everything else is stored on the main server. You'll need the access codes. I'll put them in for you.'

'No, just write them down and I'll do it.' Renfield eyed Bryant's Tibetan skull with trepidation.

'I can't do that. Mr Banbury added a security device. The codes have to be logged at different speeds to open the file gates. He taught all senior personnel how to alter their typing technique.' *I can't believe I just made that up,* she marvelled. *It sounded almost authentic.*

'Very well, but I'm watching you,' warned the sergeant, wedging himself in a chair beside her.

As she accessed the documents, she maintained a steady stream of distracting conversation, until the sergeant broke his attention to glance briefly out of the window. It was all the time she needed to add her own private email address to the files.

'I want everything printed out,' the sergeant commanded.

'It will take ages to produce hard copies. We only have a very old printer. I'll queue all the relevant folders, then you can get someone to take it all to the station.'

'No, I'll wait,' said Renfield doggedly, folding his arms.

'As you wish.' Longbright rose and walked towards the door.

'And you're waiting with me.' He pointed to the seat behind her own desk. 'Just sit yourself back down.'

She sat and waited while Renfield cleaned his nails, picked his nose, examined the breakfast stains on his shirt and scratched his bottom. Pulling open the lowest drawer of her desk with the toe of her boot, she leaned forward, making a show of adjusting her hem. She could not allow the sheet of paper containing May's confession to be bagged up and taken with the rest of the unit's contents. Kasavian would be only too happy to misinterpret it. Slowly and silently, she slid the page from its hiding place.

Suddenly, Renfield looked at her. 'I can't trust you for a minute, can I?' he sighed. 'What have you got there?'

Reluctantly, she raised the hand with the page in it, turning the blank side to face the sergeant.

He snapped his fingers at her. 'Bring it over here.'

Longbright rose and walked over, furiously searching for a way out. She held John May's career in her hand.

'Give it to me.'

Renfield snatched the sheet from her, glanced at it, saw that it had nothing to do with the Highwayman, screwed it into a ball and tossed it back at her. 'Go on, get out of here,' he said. 'I've got more important things to do.'

The detective sergeant fled the room, heading for home and her waiting laptop.

As April was sending her text, the detectives were just pulling up before the gates of St Crispin's. May patted his jacket pocket. 'Have you still got your other mobile?' he asked.

'In a manner of speaking,' Bryant replied with a hint of evasion that suggested it might have fallen under a steamroller or been torn apart by wolves.

'Then where is it?'

'Ah, that would be more difficult. I do still have it, in the sense that it hasn't left my possession, but it's full of meat.'

'What are you talking about?'

'I was cooking a spaghetti bolognese for Alma last night and it fell out of my apron pocket into the sauce pot. We dried it in the oven and now it seems to be working intermittently.'

May shot him a murderous look. 'And my battery's dead. Let's go in. God help anyone trying to contact us.'

The corridors of the school were in darkness. Classes had yet to begin. Outside, the rain had given way to a wet autumnal mist. As it rolled in from the Thames it thickened, clinging to the hedges, blanking the windows and deadening sound from the street.

'He doesn't behave like a mature, rational human being,' said Bryant, looking unnaturally pale in the gloom. 'The Highwayman keeps baiting the police, getting us to run after him before dropping out of sight. That's what I didn't appreciate before. It's like a series of dares. Multiple attackers actively court publicity. Does that mean he wants to be caught? Perhaps at some subconscious level. He's anxious to stop just short of capture, but the impulse takes him closer to the edge each time. He has an antipathy towards his fellow creatures. We're nothing to him, just objects to be used as a means to an end.'

'Which is?'

'His eventual deification, of course.'

'I can't imagine why anyone would go to so much trouble to be noticed,' said May, pushing open doors and searching for a light switch. 'All this complex ingenuity, the sheer work involved.'

'First of all, he finds it no trouble at all. Second, this kind of killing is an achievement that ultimately requires some form of acknowledgement. Respect, fear. And finally, approval. Third – ' Bryant stopped to wipe his brow, trying to understand why he felt so strange. He'd forgotten what he was saying.

'There's a light under his door.' May had reached Kingsmere's study first. He leaned forward and twisted the doorknob. 'You know we don't have enough to make a formal charge,' he whispered to Bryant. 'All we can do is take him in for questioning, unless he chooses to incriminate himself. Are you ready?'

'I was expecting you both earlier,' called Kingsmere, anticipating them.

He was seated behind his desk, marking term papers, and barely bothered to look up. When he did so, May noted that he appeared to have aged. He removed a pair of wire-rimmed spectacles and studied them wearily.

'Tell us about your grandfather,' suggested Bryant, unravelling his sepia scarf and gratefully drawing up a seat.

'What's the point?' Kingsmere countered, tossing his glasses on to the desk and massaging his eyes. 'I imagine you already know quite a lot about him. He had very little respect for the forces of law and order. He went to jail for the values in which he believed.'

'He was a fascist, a Mosley supporter.'

'In later life, yes. His ideals became a terrible burden.'

'What about your father?' Bryant asked, trying to concentrate. 'How did he feel?'

'You should know,' replied Kingsmere, making eye contact for the first time. The teacher rose and opened the cupboard behind him, reaching in for the bundle he had left there. 'You're probably looking for these.' He dropped the mask and tunic on the desk.

'Do you want to make a formal statement?' asked May, surprised by Kingsmere's calm attitude.

'If you want,' he replied. 'There's not much to say. I guess you'll want to test these clothes for proof, but I can save you time. My father was the Leicester Square Vampire.'

46

APPEARANCES

It was hardly the confession they had been expecting.

Brilliant Kingsmere stared into the shadowed oaken corners of his study. 'The other masters will be arriving soon,' he said. 'Perhaps there's just time to explain a little.'

He rose and locked his office door before sitting on the edge of the desk in front of them. 'You know, it's strange watching someone slide into an illness brought on by the very things in which he believes,' he said. 'My grandfather was an idealist. He wanted people to be better than they ever could be. When they repeatedly failed him, he grew bitter. We thought he would be content to turn into one of those caricature colonels, firing off angry letters to the press. Instead, he started accosting people in the street. At first his demands were trivial, telling them to pick up litter, warning them about antisocial behaviour. Later my father discovered that he had been following teenagers and threatening them. He could be a very intimidating man.

'Even then, we thought it was harmless enough. My father had started to follow in his footsteps, preaching to classrooms when he should have been watching what was happening in his own family. One day, he was picked up by the police after threatening a young girl who had been attending his class. She didn't press charges and they dropped the case. We never mentioned the matter. Families like ours rarely discussed their problems in those days.'

'Then how did you discover he was carrying out attacks on women?' asked May.

'I only found out the truth about his late-night disappearances when he was dying. The outfit was in a mildewed cardboard box on top of his wardrobe. I didn't know what it was, so I asked him. By this time, my father was eaten away with bowel cancer. It seemed so wrong, me questioning this shrunken yellow man, lying in hospital dosed up with morphine, pestering him about things he had done when I was just a baby. It seemed absurd to imagine him spending his nights dressed up in a cloak, accosting young women. During the war, Leicester Square and the surrounding area had long been used by prostitutes known as Piccadilly Commandos. After the fears of the war faded, some measure of old-fashioned morality returned, but then came the original Summer of Love. My father was horrified. He had become a champion of morality, and the strain of his evangelical zeal took its toll. Look through history, and you'll see a point is reached when rabid Christians decide that killing is better than curing. No one suspected him. The police were searching for someone of a lower station in life. The idea that the murderer might be a middle-class academic was unthinkable to them. The only one who came close to realizing the truth was you, Mr Bryant. You understood why he acted as he did. You even interviewed him once. But instead of following your instincts, you trusted the word of a fellow academic.'

Bryant looked down at the pile of black clothes on the desk. He realized now that the Highwayman's outfit had been modelled on its earlier incarnation. The present-day killer was someone close to Kingsmere.

'I don't understand how you can preach social responsibility to children, knowing what you do about your·father,' said May.

'I would have thought it was obvious. I want to make amends for the things he did. I'm not ashamed of my family history. Nor have I tried to cover up my father's misdeeds. Quite the reverse: I told my extracurricular class about him, and even brought his clothes along as proof. It was our secret, a matter of trust between us.' Kingsmere surveyed the darkened schoolroom. 'Ten years ago, I was idealistic enough to try teaching in a state school in Deptford, but my tenure proved disastrous. I wasn't prepared for what I found there, and things are worse now. You meet eleven-year-olds who can text-message faster than I can write, but who can't read a book because the teachers don't know enough grammar to teach them. Kids who can name a hundred clothing brands but can't tell you why it's wrong to stab someone. The national literacy strategy has left everyone confused about the fundamental basics of teaching. Pupils are encouraged to pick soft subjects because it makes everyone's lives easier. There's no discipline, no interest, no empathy. The few who learned anything in my Deptford class did so against superhuman odds. In the absence of any enforced methodology, children invent their own language, new ways of communicating, and as George Orwell pointed out, once they start to do that, they change the way they think. Remove the language of sustained concentration from their vocabulary and you remove the concept itself. I want to help put a stop to that. It's a reasonable dream.'

'If you knew about the crimes your father had committed, you should have gone to the police,' said May.

Kingsmere appeared not to hear. 'I know teachers who are as stoic as bollards, ploughing on through a wild sea of feral children, never trying to tame and shape their ideas but accepting their new world order with implacability. The intelligence of Western youth is being transformed. You either accept the fact, or fight a losing battle of old ideals. I retreated to the calm haven of a private school, into the world of so-called proper education, where I could find an attentive audience. But I found the same strange dissonance existed here too, albeit in a subtler form. The children are craftier, more knowing; they'll say what you want to hear in the hope that you'll be fooled and will leave them alone.

'Once I saw through that, I petitioned the board of governors to start conducting extra-curricular classes. All you need is a hint of achievement, and you get messianic about such things. You think you can change the world, but the world incrementally changes you. My father had been filled with the same fervour, but he allowed his lack of achievement to wear him down. He would lecture teenagers on the importance of civility, barely noticing the laughter behind his back. He preached old-school socialism to heckling, uninterested Thatcherites at Speakers' Corner, wrote letters, fought councils, demanded answers, to no avail. His desire to challenge the system corrupted him, and he became mad in the process, committing terrible, desperate crimes. Then he died in agony. Tell me, what good would it have done to come forward?'

'At the very least, it would have helped the victims' relatives,' May said flatly. 'The state can't take all the blame for an individual's behaviour. Are you prepared to give us a statement?'

'I suppose it's the least I can do, given the trouble you've been through over the years,' said Kingsmere, pulling his coat from the back of the chair.

'Wait,' said Bryant. 'Mr Kingsmere, I wonder if you would be so good as to roll up the left-hand sleeve of your shirt for me.'

Puzzled, the teacher did as he was asked, revealing pale unmarked flesh. Banbury had specifically mentioned hitting the Highwayman's left wrist with his dart gun.

'You can go ahead, John.' Bryant looked back at the piled

clothes on the desk. 'I'll bag these up as evidence and follow you in a while.'

As the pair left the room, he took over the teacher's chair and bounced back in it, thinking. Something was not right. If Kingsmere had told his favoured pupils about his father, painting a picture of a life spent struggling against the system, why had none of them mentioned it? Was it because they knew the Vampire had inspired another murderer, and were anxious to keep him hidden? The shadow of the Highwayman remained here in the school, in the very bricks and stones of ancient Clerkenwell. The Vampire had mercly provided a template for his successor, the latest in a line of mythical London monsters stretching back into the city's distant past . . .

He carefully folded the Vampire's mask inside the tunic, and was about to remove it as evidence when he noticed something lying under a chair in the corner of the room. Unzipping the fallen backpack, he saw what appeared to be the Highwayman's tricorn hat sticking out of one of the pockets. But when he went to pull it free, the hat came apart.

Bryant found himself looking at two plain black baseball caps, one with its brim curled upwards, the other with its brim twisted down. Placed over each other with the peaks at opposite ends, they formed a perfect tricorn.

He dug deeper into the bag and found a second leather mask. Somewhere, he now realized, there was another tunic. His submerged suspicions began to surface, synapses reconnecting, tumbling logic on its head. The effect of the red pills seemed to be phasing his electrical responses into disturbing new configurations.

The paradoxical impossibility of Saralla White's murder.

The convoluted absurdities of the deaths.

Elliot Mason changing his boots at the gallery because the old pair hurt his feet.

The placing of the Highwayman at the site of Alex

Paradine's death, outside the recording studio; two witnesses had seen the killer, but only one had mentioned his cape.

Janet Ramsey's recorded telephone call, picked up by DS Longbright. Not 'he's not male', as Banbury had reiterated, but 'he's not a man'.

The echo of the Ripper graffiti, conveniently located along the walls of the estate staircase.

Murder committed on a spot connected with the executions, the Knights Templars and the blood of Christ.

Brilliant Kingsmere's lectures about his father. Why this school, these pupils?

The mythical connections between Robin Hood, the Leicester Square Vampire and the Highwayman.

The Saladins.

The desire for celebrity.

Checking from the window, he saw that May had taken the unit staff car. It was too late to call him back now. Bryant climbed woozily to his feet, left the evidence on the desk and walked around the classroom, trying to focus his mind. This was where Kingsmere took his extra-curricular lessons.

He checked the cupboards and desks one by one, but all personal items had been placed in lockers for the weekend. There was nothing more to be found here.

Walking back through the still-darkened assembly hall, he noticed that its ceiling skylights were streaked with rain. He felt drugged.

Ahead was the stage, and the pale oak podium from which he had made his disastrous speech. His first contact with St Crispin's School for Boys. He climbed to it now and balanced behind the lectern, looking down into the empty hall.

There was no speech lying here this time, just a discarded recruitment brochure for the school, aimed at wealthy parents.

He flicked it open, found his spectacles and squinted at the introductory paragraph:

St Crispin's was founded in 1623 by the Right Honourable Sir Thomas Lindsay. For almost four hundred years the institution has prospered, its pupils bestowing honour and glory that reflect the talent and diversity . . .

The usual waffle designed to open wallets, he thought, skimming.

. . . many of its Old Boys have gone on to great achievements in the world of politics, sport and the liberal arts, although one particular former pupil is remembered for a different reason, and has become a part of London's mythological fabric. When the young Richard Turpin first arrived here . . .

The thieves' key. The key was the thief.
Dick Turpin opened the lock to the entire investigation.
But even as he became aware of the truth, he knew that the Highwayman would have the means to escape justice.
The opening bars of Offenbach's *La Belle Hélène* played in his overcoat pocket. Bryant dragged out his mobile, flicked mince from its keypad and managed to access the message before it cut out completely.
' – tried to reach granda– there was no rep– I think his and Jan– mobiles – still locked inside the unit. I know your phone never w– Arthur, but I thought I sh– tell someone where I'm going, ju– be on the safe side. I'm on the Ro– P–'
Bryant slipped out into the rain with his car keys, heading for the Roland Plumbe Community Estate.

47

THE MOON CURSER

April looked at the rainswept green quadrangle with the darkened street running around its edge and felt uncomfortable. The old panicky fear of open spaces settled over her. 'Where are we going?' she asked Luke, but he had already moved on ahead.

'You want to find out the truth, don't you?' he called back. He seemed so thin and vulnerable that she found it hard to imagine he could be involved with anything sinister. If he had lied because he was being threatened, why had he not confided in someone who could help him?

They entered the dim concrete corridor and made their way to its rear staircase. 'The lift's not working,' Luke explained, climbing the steps. April felt safer away from the bare breadth of the estate, but as Luke continued ascending, she realized with horror that they were heading for the great flat roof of the building's central block.

'Luke, I can't go any further,' she warned, stopping outside the fire exit as he pushed it open.

'You don't have to,' the boy promised, coming to a halt.

Ahead, a terrible wide sky beckoned, drawing her forward into the effulgent mist and rain.

She did not see the gloved hands dropping on either side

of her. They held a roll of nylon rope that pinned her arms to her sides before she could make a move. The Highwayman stepped forward, dragging her out on to the gravelled roof. She tried to twist around and study him, but he kept her facing forward.

April felt the scudding grey sky bellowing down above her head in a funnel of wind, until it seemed as though it would pull her out into the moisture-laden air.

As the Highwayman began dragging her towards the far side of the roof, she dug the heels of her boots into the gravel. His grip on her arms tightened. She screamed just once before realizing that it would make no difference up here. Gradually, her fear of the vast open rooftop was replaced by the sinking sensation that no one from the unit knew where she was.

April was in greater danger than she realized, for in her headstrong haste she had duplicated the fate of her mother, unwittingly running into the arms of a killer.

Arthur Bryant dragged on Victor's handbrake, but the rusting Mini Cooper was difficult to bring to a halt, and it continued to judder on after he had removed the keys. The engine had never run smoothly since Maggie Armitage had poured her own blend of sealant into the radiator in an effort to consecrate the vehicle against accidents. Miraculously, his mobile was finally working once more, and he called his partner as he walked towards the estate's central block.

'John, is that you? Have you finished with Kingsmere?'

'I'm just about to take his statement,' came the reply. 'Congratulations, you're using a mobile.'

'Yes, but you won't like what I have to say on it. I need you to leave him and get over here. I know who the Highwayman is, I just don't have a reason why.'

'Where are you?'

'I'm at the estate, heading for the roof where you saw the

graffiti. I'm going to need your help. Banbury was right, the Highwayman isn't a man at all. He was hidden in plain sight right from the start. You encouraged me to be sensible and practical, but I should have followed my instincts.'

'I don't understand what you mean, Arthur. Don't do anything until I get there, all right? Promise me?'

But Bryant had already closed the mobile and set off into the estate. His legs were failing, but his long-distance eyesight was excellent. And he had just spotted the windswept black figure striding across the roof of the central block.

The Highwayman threw April to the ground, where she lay gratefully hugging the gravelled roof. When she finally summoned the nerve to look up, she saw that he was disrobing, splitting the tricorn hat into two black baseball caps and casting them aside before removing his gloves. The tall boots, she noticed, had heavily built-up heels and soles. She could hear the murmur of other voices beneath the rising wind. As the Highwayman turned to face the boy who had led her here, she recognized her captor.

'You brought the wrong one, Luke,' he said tonelessly.

'I thought you said the old man would come to you.' Luke dropped to the floor cross-legged and dug a pack of Marlboros from his blazer, oblivious to the falling rain.

'I guess he's not so smart after all. We can still do seven in seven days and set a new house record. You don't need to know about the back-up plan.' He crouched down beside April and smiled. 'You do see now, don't you? I mean, why there's no such person as the Highwayman. You can't catch a murderer who doesn't exist.'

Arthur Bryant stopped to catch his breath on the staircase. *Trust the lift to be out of action on the one day I need to reach the roof*, he thought. Leaning on his stick, he studied the sprayed graffiti. He should have read it as a series of

382

arrows leading him towards the truth; that was what had been expected of him. What he still didn't understand was why this had happened. If not for revenge, then what? When he looked down, the stairs retreated in a spiral, like an unwinding clock spring.

In the poem by Alfred Noyes, he thought, *the highwayman was saved by his lover's sacrifice, only to die on the road and be resurrected as a ghostly apparition. In this way, he achieved a form of immortality.* Bryant held out his right hand and studied its liver-spotted back. He was shaking, either through anticipation or sheer exertion. He pushed on to the roof, frightened of what he might find but unable to stop himself. Understanding the truth had become more important than anything, even survival into an uncertain future. He and John had enjoyed a good run. Perhaps this had always been destined as their endgame.

He stood on the dark concrete landing behind the roof exit, gathering himself, waiting for the pounding of his heart to subside.

Then he turned the handle and pushed the door wide, flooding light into his vision.

The Highwayman swivelled to face this new arrival. 'You got here after all,' he said, smiling pleasantly as the others surrounded him. 'We're glad you managed to make it – even though you're earlier than expected. Tell me, do you know what a Moon Curser is?'

'No, I don't – ' Bryant was momentarily confused by the group of six people before him.

'It's a term taken from the thieves' key. A Moon Curser is a link boy.'

Bryant fought to think clearly, exhausted by the stairs and the mistimed medication. 'You mean a boy who used to run ahead of his client, leading the way through the night with a torch, in return for a few coppers.'

'That's right. A Moon Curser is a specific kind of link boy. He's one who lights the darkness, only to lead his employer into a gang of thieves and murderers.' He pointed down at the boy seated on the roof. 'Appropriate, eh? We read about that in some boring old book we thought you would find interesting. Luke is our Moon Curser. He brought you here to us. To your death.'

48

SACRED VILLAINY

On the roof of the Roland Plumbe Community Estate, Arthur Bryant faced his imminent demise.

He knew that his career was over, but was not sad at its loss. He could do nothing more now, solve no more crimes, save no more lives, because those who committed cruelties were finally beyond his understanding. He had warned John May that he would retire when logic ceased to be of use in criminal investigations. Nothing could ever fully explain what he faced here. The world had moved on into darkness and left him in its wake.

He was afraid only for April, because she was just learning how to live. She was shivering with cold, kneeling on the gravelled roof before him in torn wet jeans, her arms tied at her sides. She looked at him with pleading eyes.

And he looked back at the Highwayman: not a man, not even a single entity, but a group of boys.

Gosling, pale and blond, dressed in a padded black leather tunic and boots.

Parfitt, spotty, sour-faced, still wearing his soaked school blazer.

Jezzard, bat-eared, red-faced and overweight, disconsolately picking his nails.

Billings, small and feral, dangerous-eyed, waiting for instructions.

The four teenagers who had disrupted his lecture, who had shouted him down and led the rebellion against him. Four ingenious, privileged, bored and heartless children who saw themselves above the law because they were more intelligent, more cruel, more willing to risk everything. Because the time was right, and there was nothing at all they cared about.

'What do you think of our invention now?' asked Gosling. 'Do you get it? Do you see what we did? It was you who gave us the idea, the day of your stupid lecture. You'll be the sixth victim of the Highwayman, and there will be one more tonight. Seven carefully staged deaths in seven days, high-profile murders to create a super-celebrity who can never be brought to justice, because he doesn't exist. The press and the public are willing him into existence. They want to believe in him, and they'll make him live for ever. No one has ever managed such a stunt in this city's two-thousand-year history. Fame doesn't get much bigger than this.'

'What about April?' he asked.

Gosling shrugged. 'She can have an accident. Her death won't count because it's not part of the plan.'

'You don't have to kill her. She's done nothing wrong.'

'It's not open to negotiation,' said Jezzard, hauling April to her feet. 'Don't you want to know how we did it? We want to tell you 'cause it's so totally mint.'

'I think I already have an idea. Luke lied for you at the gallery, while you – all of you – told the truth. You said no one else had come into the room, and you were right. Saralla White was already there, checking on her installation, and you simply surprised her, throwing her into the tank. With four of you to hold and lift her, it must have been easy.'

'I wouldn't say easy,' said Parfitt. 'We chloroformed her

but she still kicked me and bit Billings. But she gasped as she went under, and sank quickly.'

'I found this great website that tells you how to make fast-acting narcotics,' said Billings. 'It's dead simple. Kingsmere lets us have the run of the school in the evenings – he trusts us to use the labs by ourselves.'

'So – how do you make a man immortal?' asked Gosling. 'You give him superhuman abilities. You make him tall, like me, and agile, like Billings here, and strong, like all four of us combined. We take turns being the Highwayman.'

'The different-sized boots, you stored them at the school – that's where you got wood glue on them,' Bryant comprehended. 'A padded jacket, masks and wigs – all it required was the ingenuity of malicious children.'

Gosling ignored the slight. 'I'm taller than everyone else, so I do the big stuff. Parfitt's a good runner. Billings does the climbing and Jezzard did the camera shots for you, which he paid the estate girls to contact you about. It was easy to divide up the Highwayman's outfit into our backpacks, which were small enough not to get checked. We left you plenty of hints, just to make sure you got the picture.'

'The thieves' key,' said Bryant, recalling Banbury's discovery in the gallery. 'Why did you only leave it the first time?'

'We couldn't get back into the metalwork shop to make another one,' Gosling explained, amused. 'We borrowed the logo from the estate symbol, which was in turn based on the area's most famous inhabitant. We wanted to watch you at work, but May showed up instead, so we had to keep leaving you more clues. What else do you know?'

'You came up with the Highwayman as a character because you knew about Kingsmere's father, and how the Robin Hood legend had been subverted. Plus, there was the Dick Turpin connection with your school, in the prospectus.'

'He's on the school weathervane, too,' said Jezzard.

'Seems the governors find notoriety more appealing than good scholarship.' He was standing near the edge of the roof with April.

Bryant tried to buy more time. 'You got Kingsmere out of the way, didn't you? You couldn't afford to have him overseeing your class at the gallery on Monday.'

'Stomach bug. That part was easy. Something we whipped up for him in the chem lab. Keep going, Mr Detective.'

Bryant watched April, trying to keep eye contact with her. 'Martell's electrocution and Paradine's incineration, that was a bit over-elaborate. The sort of thing schoolkids would come up with. I suppose you wired up the gym when the morning cleaners went in.'

'Ever met a kid who couldn't find his way into a building? We had to keep your interest piqued. That's why we did two at the same time. We were showcasing our woodwork and metalwork skills. And we thought you might enjoy the local history of the area we chose. You're a sucker for all the old London mythology; we saw you talking about it in your BBC2 documentary. We planned the week like any good media campaign. Seven deaths in seven days, in time for the national press to run the entire story today, which, in case you hadn't noticed, is Hallowe'en.'

'You're running behind schedule. And you've slipped up – Janet Ramsey isn't dead.'

'We'll make up for that,' Gosling warned. 'I'm interested to know something. We were careful to blame the kids on the estate, but you didn't go after them. Why not?'

'Your little graffiti message, based on the one left at the site of the Ripper murders. It was a bit too clever. And the K for Kingsmere, rather over-emphatic. He thinks you hero-worship him, but you must really hate his guts.'

'Not at all,' said Gosling. 'We don't hate anyone.'

'You should be pleased,' said Jezzard. 'You inspired us to create a living legend. Your history will be forever linked with ours.'

388

'I don't want the kind of fame you think you've bought. You've got it without earning it.'

'How can you say that?' asked Gosling. 'Do you know how much time and effort we put into this? Those poor morons we killed spent years creating their own images, only to lose virtually everything they'd gained. We've bypassed that problem. It takes ten seconds for someone to die. That's a fast track to immortality. Nobody screws with you if they're scared of you.'

Bryant thought of the community officer's comment about building a staircase to adulthood. It was inevitable that someone would try to build a faster one. 'Nobody will remember you in a month's time,' he warned hoarsely.

'They will, though, because the Highwayman is never going to go away. If we don't choose to keep him alive, someone else will. Hyde-Brown, Pond, Whitchurch, Ramsden, Armstrong, Ibbetson, Metcalf, Unsworth – any of our friends could take over from us. They all feel the same way.'

'And how is that?'

Gosling looked blankly at him, as if surprised by the question. 'We feel dead.'

'It was you who gave us the inspiration to do something about it,' said Billings. 'If you hadn't come to the school, we might never have got our act together.'

'I don't understand how you choose who should die,' said Bryant, rubbing his temple. Everything seemed overlit and spatially twisted. Jezzard was moving too close to the edge of the roof. April was silent, immobile. Time itself seemed to have slowed down. Even the rain was falling more slowly, glistening and drifting between them.

'You don't remember what it's like to be young, otherwise you'd know who has to go. The liars, the fakes, the hypocrites, the spreaders of poison, the ones with the *lifestyles*.' Jezzard peered over the low wall, then forced April up on to it.

'I remember what it's like to have someone claim to represent my generation,' Bryant called urgently. 'The politicians of the past sent us to war. Young men had a reason to fight back. They had a political purpose. You're just a group of bored children who are upset that their rich parents ignore them.'

'Think what you like, old man.' Jezzard seized April's arms and twisted her to face out over the quadrangle.

'You've touched her,' Bryant pointed out. 'No matter what happens, you'll be traced this time.'

They all started to laugh. 'Who the hell cares?' said Gosling, the spokesman. 'You still don't get it, do you? It doesn't matter who we kill, it's how we live. Martyrdom is a requirement of immortality.'

Jezzard smiled slowly in agreement and gave April a hard push from the ledge.

49

IMMORTAL

He had not been expecting her to twist around so quickly and kick out at him. April's boot caught Jezzard squarely in the face, snapping the septum in his nose in a gout of blood, sending him sprawling across the gravel. She fell hard on to the wall, but was quickly on top of him, punching and tearing at his face as he screamed for her to stop.

The others moved to separate them, and were still attempting to do so as John May burst on to the roof with a team of armed officers.

April sat in the passenger seat of May's BMW with a blanket wrapped around her wet shoulders. She stared through the smeared windscreen as he started the engine and gently pulled away from the kerb.

'Are you all right?'

She nodded, but remained silently watching, lost in thought.

She did not speak to her grandfather until they were nearing the unit at Mornington Crescent. 'You don't have to explain,' she told him finally. 'About my mother, I mean. I've always known what happened to her.'

'Wait – you knew?' May was astounded.

'Your pal Sergeant Renfield told me about Elizabeth when I was sixteen, but I wasn't sure whether to believe him or not,' she said carefully. 'Remember how I used to hang around Bow Street station waiting for you? He didn't mean to hurt me. The investigation was the talk of the Met. Officers used to go quiet when they walked past me. I never blamed you, Grandad. But I never understood why she did it, until now.'

'What do you mean?'

'I did the same thing. I got myself more involved than I meant to. There were warning signs and I ignored them. I'm my mother's daughter.' She smiled weakly. 'Bad behaviour must run in the family.'

'So this hasn't put you off working at the unit?'

'I'll be fine. It's Uncle Arthur you should worry about. He doesn't understand why a bunch of teenagers would need to create a figure like the Highwayman. He has to be made to realize why this happened.'

'I'm not sure that's possible to explain,' said May. 'Our lives are changing so quickly. Arthur grew up in a time when every crime had an underlying cause. It was a simpler world. Those boys had everything, but still craved something different.' He shook his head in amazement. 'God, when teenagers get together to plan something they're really interested in, they're smarter and more dedicated to their cause than any adult.'

'You sound like you admire them.'

'No, but I think I understand how such a thing could happen. They created a moral code appropriate to the times in which we live.'

'You've still got to find out who they planned to make their seventh victim. Seven in seven days, they said.'

'Surely the question is academic now,' said May.

'Gosling mentioned that others would take their place. It took four boys to be the Highwayman, but how many more are waiting for their shot at immortality? How much of an open secret was it among their friends? And how can you ever hope to stop it? They all want to become part of the legend.'

The rain had blackened the buildings of Camden Town. Mornington Crescent Tube station, with its smartly polished crimson tiles, stood out like a beacon. The lights were on in the crescent windows of the PCU. Renfield was presumably still waiting for files that would never be printed. April opened the car door. 'We borrowed Colin's crowbar for the door. Are you going to come up?' she asked.

'In a minute.' May laid his head back against the seat, exhausted. He had asked Bimsley to take his partner home. Bryant had seemed confused and dislocated by his experience on the roof of the estate. He'd been happier last month, wading through sewers in the search for a killer. The knowledge that he had inspired schoolboys to commit murder had to be weighing heavily on him.

Perhaps it really was time for both of them to retire. He only partly believed the boys' story about seeking fast immortality. It seemed to May that they did it for fun, because the challenge had presented itself, and because they had no moral qualms about following it through.

It seemed that they did it because logic – the kind of practical sense the detectives needed so badly to survive at the unit – was finally dead.

But then May looked up at the windows of the PCU and saw his granddaughter outlined against the desk lamps. So long as there were people who still carried dreams of something better in their heads, he and Arthur had no right to desert them.

Wearily, but a little happier with the thought, he climbed out of the car and headed back into the building.

50

GRAVE TO CRADLE

MEMORANDUM
PRIVATE AND CONFIDENTIAL

Attachment Supplied: 20059PH

TO: Leslie Faraday, Senior Home Office Liaison Officer
FROM: Raymond Land, Acting Head, PCU,
London NW1 3BL
DATE: Tuesday 1 November

Dear Mr Faraday,
Having outlined the recent problems I experienced at
the PCU at your request, I now feel it necessary to make
an addendum to my report in light of succeeding actions
to close down the unit, undertaken by yourself and Mr
Oskar Kasavian.

I would be grateful if you would destroy my notes on
Mr Arthur Bryant and Mr John May (file 3458SD) as I
no longer feel that they provide an accurate reflection of
the matter at hand. Subsequent to my report, the long-
standing investigation of the so-called Leicester Square
Vampire has been brought to a successful conclusion,

and all surviving relatives have been notified of the outcome. There can be closure for them of a kind that was never possible when the case came under the jurisdiction of the Metropolitan Police.

Concerning the disbanding of the Peculiar Crimes Unit: in anticipation that you may find it difficult to abandon a process that has now been placed in motion, I would like to remind you that I am prepared to release a full account of the investigation surrounding the arrests of Nicholas Gosling, Thomas Jezzard, Daniel Parfitt, Marcus Billings and Luke Tripp. Part of this report will, of necessity, need to focus on the relationship between Mr Kasavian and the features editor of *Hard News*, Mrs Janet Ramsey.

I anticipate that you may encounter some resistance from Mr Kasavian to returning the Peculiar Crimes Unit to its former operational status, in which case may I request that you make the focus of my report known to Mr Kasavian, in order that he may decide for himself whether or not he wishes to commit career suicide and face personal discomfort at the sight of his fragrant wife being questioned over her knowledge of his extramarital affair, and the possible security risk it poses to Her Majesty's government. I do this with the full knowledge and cooperation of Mrs Ramsey herself, who no longer wishes to be associated with her former partner, and is fully prepared to explain her side of the story in the above-mentioned periodical if her wishes are not met.

Please also find attached the PCU's official request for increased funding, which I trust will be received favourably in light of the above.

I remain,

Yours sincerely,

Raymond Land

Acting Temporary Head of the Peculiar Crimes Unit (1973 – present day)

They sat on the black iron bridge crossing the converted warehouses on the fourth floor of Shad Thames, peering down at the narrow cobbled street beneath them. The faintest traces of cinnamon and pepper, imports that had given the Spice Wharves their name, still hung in the evening air. The setting sun had turned the river a bilious shade of heliotrope. Tourists wandered between the glowing art stores and neon restaurants, looking lost.

'How could you possibly afford a place like this?' asked Bryant. 'Is there anything left in that bottle?' He gestured at the magnum of champagne standing on the occasional table they had dragged out from the tiny kitchen.

'I'm swapping a huge apartment in St John's Wood for this minuscule flat because I want to be near the Thames again,' May explained. 'When I was a kid, only the poorest of the poor lived here. In a sense, I'm coming home.' May watched the distant golden river pensively. 'I don't need much space. My world is shrinking. Friends are dying, opportunities are disappearing. Soon all I'll have left is my work.'

'Welcome to my world,' said Bryant, dipping a Jaffa Cake in his champagne and sucking it pensively. 'Although if you're really going to be like me, you'll start forgetting where you left your shoes. The main thing is, you have April back. All that time the two of you wasted, when you could have been close.'

'How was I to know Renfield had told her about Elizabeth's death? And I hadn't seen this.' He removed the crumpled page of his confession from his jacket. 'Janice gave it to me. She managed to trace the female officer who acted as my co-witness. Apparently I once recommended her for promotion, back in 1996. She told Janice I'd signed the statement under abnormal circumstances, and that she would never betray my secret.'

'Give it to me.' Bryant held out his hand. He touched a match to a corner of the sheet and watched it blacken and curl in flame.

'Are you OK about the Highwayman case?' asked May. 'My granddaughter is worried about you.'

'I have to accept a new order of criminal,' Bryant replied, sprinkling ash over the balcony. 'I need to try and understand. London has always been a city of sedition and disorder, from the Peasants' Revolt to Bloody Sunday, Broadwater Farm and the Poll Tax riots. Violent dissent is in our blood. It is simply taking a spiteful new form. How can we be surprised when television teaches children that it's normal behaviour to tear each other's characters to shreds in public?'

'Television is dying. It's being replaced by a computer network in which everyone has a right to say what they feel, and about time too. Those schoolboys had the measure of you, didn't they?' May reached over for a biscuit. 'Choosing the home of the Knights Templars to kick your psychogeography fetish into action.'

'Christ's blood is still out there somewhere,' said Bryant. 'I'll go looking for it one day. I've got the surveillance maps. If the bones of St John the Baptist can survive to this day in Istanbul, then why not the blood of the Saviour?'

'I was just thinking about Gosling and his friends. I looked into their eyes and saw nothing at all. No love, no hate, just blankness. All bets are off now. What's to stop any teenager from buying their way into celebrity by committing murder?'

'We have to pray that the spirit of a more benevolent myth hangs over the city to protect it,' said Bryant. 'Something that can counteract the cruelties of murderers and highwaymen – the benign and secret spirit of Mother London.' He refilled their plastic cups. 'The mistake I made was thinking that the victims were worshipped by the young. The young don't feel represented by such people, they feel ignored and invisible. We'll never understand them, and we'll have no way of stopping them next time. It's the kids on the estate who have a staircase to the future. They have to fight or fail. Their victories are small and hard-won. The boys in Brilliant Kingsmere's class are already lost.'

Bryant tore open a fresh packet of biscuits; no mean feat, considering he was wearing woollen mittens. He squinted at the label. '*New advanced recipe*? What does that mean? Advanced beyond the poor-quality recipe they were using before? Everybody lies to you. Especially in this city. London is the ancient personification of corruption.'

'Now you're sounding like the Highwayman,' said May. 'Or even Robin Hood.'

'Perhaps I'm reconnecting with my own past,' said Bryant. 'I certainly remember it more clearly than the present.' He looked over the balcony. 'I say, some traffic wardens are trying to tow my car away.' He removed the pickle fork from his jacket. 'They'll be lucky. I've got the key. Pour some champagne over them.'

'We still have to find out who the week's final victim was supposed to be, you know. None of the boys is talking.'

'I would have thought it was obvious,' said Bryant. 'Brilliant Kingsmere was being saved for last.'

'But why?' May was mystified. 'He's a well-intentioned liberal who's spent a lot of time trying to understand their generation.'

'Exactly,' Bryant replied. 'But it's not his prerogative to do so. Nor is it ours. Perhaps we must be content in our seniority, and stop trying to manipulate the young. We should enjoy being our age and appreciate the benefits of experience. It's like a favoured old jumper, something one can relax in. Besides, Kingsmere was more likely than anyone to discover the truth. He was the connection between the past and the future.'

May gave in. 'I'm not going back to the unit tonight. Let's finish the bottle. I keep thinking of Luke Tripp sitting there, impassively watching while his classmates drowned Saralla White in her own installation. In a way, he was the worst of them all, lying with such wide innocent eyes. What will he be like when he grows up?'

'Gosling, Parfitt, Billings and Jezzard may find themselves confronted with a younger, altogether darker nemesis. Each generation fears the one coming next. But on we go, dancing merrily towards the grave.'

'It's strange,' said May, watching the translucent evening mist curl up against the embankment railings in ghostly tentacles, 'I thought this case would be the end of us, but somehow it feels like a new beginning.'

'If that's so, I'm getting rid of these. They're supposed to improve my balance. Instead, I nearly fell off a roof.' He pulled the boxes of red and blue pills from his pocket and threw them as far as he could from the balcony, which wasn't very far at all, but at least the point was made. A pair of young women were peppered with tablets, and looked up at him in annoyance. 'And now that we've regained respect for the unit, I want a rise. And bigger bookcases. And new hips. And the return of everything we've lost. Kindness, grace, taste, politeness, self-restraint, dress sense, the Wednesday Play, Fry's Five Boys chocolate bars, the BBC Home Service, the Pakamac, *I-Spy* books, pensioners' cinema double bills for 1/6 on Monday afternoons, and at least five more years spent successfully solving horrendous crimes. What do you want?'

May's gentle, melancholic smile was lost in advancing shadows. 'I want, more than anything – ' But he stopped himself from speaking, and allowed himself to be engulfed in the encroaching darkness.

'I know what you want,' said Bryant. 'I was just thinking of the city in the most recent quarter of its life. All the dark and bloody history that's being forgotten so quickly out there. London, the site of the Guy Fawkes plot, home of Newgate and Bedlam. The tarred heads of Jacobites on spikes at Temple Bar, the Cato Street conspiracy, the Sidney Street siege, the Gordon Riots and the Lollards. Thomas Blood and the stolen Crown Jewels, the highway robbers John Cottington, Dick Turpin and Moll Cutpurse, John Sayer stabbed in the Mint, Elizabeth Brownrigg torturing her maids, Jack the Ripper, the Krays, Ruth Ellis, Jonathan Wild, Jack Sheppard, the Fenian outrage of 1867, the Dynamite Plot of 1883, the Battle of Stepney, the death of the bomber Bourdin, Charlie Peace, the Mannings, Franz Muller the Railway Murderer, Crippen, Christie and Nilsen, the Tichborne Claimant, the Smithfield burnings, the crowds at Tyburn Tree, Execution Dock at Wapping, the Ratcliff Highway murders, the Shooter's Hill executions, the scaffolds and gaols at Southwark, Bridewell, Clerkenwell, Wandsworth, Coldbath Fields, Ludgate, Millbank, Brixton, Holloway, Pentonville, Wormwood Scrubs, Fleet, St George's Fields and the floating prison hulks at Woolwich – an overwhelmingly populous timeline of death, desperation and the damned. You want to be here, amongst it all.'

'Until the very day I die,' said May, his smile first shy, but slowly broadening.

'Then we must drink to your continued health,' said Bryant, raising his glass.

'And to yours,' replied May. 'And to the dark lady who always stands between us. To London.'

They drank and watched in contented silence as an iridescent sun sent shivers of golden light across the water of the Thames, lighting the serpentine channel of the radiant river, opening a path to the heart of the city.

THE END